COTTONWOOD

COTTONWOOD

Scott Phillips

BALLANTINE BOOKS | NEW YORK

A Ballantine Book
Published by The Random House Publishing Group

Copyright © 2004 by Scott Phillips

Cottonwood is a work of fiction. Names, places, and incidents either are
a product of the author's imagination or are used fictitiously.

www.ballantinebooks.com

Library of Congress Cataloging-in-Publication Data can be obtained
from the publisher upon request.

ISBN 0-345-46100-2

Manufactured in the United States of America

First Edition: February 2004

1   3   5   7   9   10   8   6   4   2

To Anne and Claire, again,

with all my love

COTTONWOOD

PART ONE

THE GRASS WIDOWS

1872–1873

1

COTTONWOOD, KANSAS
DECEMBER 1872

The Grass Widows

There was no visible sign the day had broken when I poked my head out of the warm, dark pocket of my buffalo robe and into the stinging air of the blacksmith's loft where I made my bed. Up the street, though, I could hear a wagon rolling over the uneven ground, its driver cursing his team, the dry hinges of the big doors of the livery as they swung open, banging as they glided over the occasional chunk of frozen mud, someone idiotically ringing the bell that hung from a post in front of the Cottonwood Hotel. Ordinarily by this hour the blacksmith's boisterous activity would have awakened me, but he appeared to be late in arriving, so I rose shivering from the straw, stretched and pulled on trousers and shirt and then, clutching the robe about me, climbed down from the loft.

I started the smith's fire for him and stood before it for a minute or two, until I felt able to haul on my boots and overcoat and step out the door. Unlatching the padlock I walked one of the big square doors outward and found the day scarcely any brighter than when I'd closed my eyes the night before, the sky like cold ash and threatening snow. I couldn't leave the fire unattended and was about to douse it when the blacksmith showed himself, wheezing and spitting chunks of milky phlegm onto the rock-hard ground.

"Morning, Bill. See you got the fire going."

"You don't sound too good, Otis."

"Nope." His enormous, grizzled mustache and the narrow patch of wavy black beard under his lower lip were encrusted with frozen saliva and worse.

"You ought to be home in bed."

He made a horrible noise in his throat, that of half-solid matter being reluctantly dislodged, and spat into the fire, appearing to take some comfort in watching the stuff spatter and shrink therein. "The hell I ought. I got work to be done." Otis's apprentice, an industrious and formerly reliable young man of eighteen or nineteen by the name of Perkey, had gone off two months earlier to visit his ailing, widowed mother in the town of Lawrence and failed to return, and now it was all poor Otis could do to keep the livery supplied with horseshoes.

"All right, then. Stop in after lunch and get yourself a shot on the house."

He grunted his assent and began fortifying the small blaze I'd started, and I walked off stiff-legged up the street to the hotel, where six other men, laborers sharing a room, sat at the main table of the dining room. There I got a tin cup of coffee like axle grease and horseshit along with a plate of biscuits, and set about eating them as quickly as I could.

"Where've you been sleeping, Bill, to get your hair all afright like that?" The serving girl touched her hand to my hair, which must have been considerably askew. I pushed the hand away without a word or a direct look. "I believe I'll get you a comb for Christmas," she said as she headed out of the tiny dining room with a jaunty wiggle of her hind end, her long, wavy dark red hair shaking to the rhythm of her teasing laugh.

Two or three of the others at the table laughed with her. "Appears Miss Katie's taken a shine to old Bill," Tim Niedel said, his voice slow and high-pitched, his face wrinkled and flushed. This time of year his face was plain white and went bright pink when he laughed or got sore, but in the summertime he burned so brown even with a straw hat on that only his red hair kept him from being taken for an Indian. Tim had helped me build the saloon a year and a half previous, and when he had cash he was a customer there as well; he and the others were currently at work on a new house of such scale and ostentation that it seemed to belong in another town entirely. Its owners were as yet absentees and known only to the foreman of the project; there was speculation that their decision to locate their house in Cottonwood had been prematurely made, that once they actually saw our underdeveloped little settlement they'd dismantle the thing for reassembly in the more civilized climes of Independence or Fort Scott, or even Wichita.

"She takes a shine to anyone's possessed of a cock and balls, Tim," his neighbor answered in a lovely baritone that could be heard bellowing hymns on Sundays at Methodist services in the meeting hall down the street. Though she didn't live in town, the woman under discussion often attended those services herself; as neither man had troubled to lower his tone, she must have heard their remarks.

When she came back in she was still grinning, and she flicked a dishrag at Tim Niedel's head and then at his chum's. The other four seemed not to know anyone was in the room with them, so intent were they on shoveling down their corn mush. I gave Katie her dime and a half and went out, ignoring her efforts to get me properly bundled before I got out the door. It wasn't that I wanted to step out into the punishing morning air with my coat undone; I just didn't want her hands on me, and I couldn't have said exactly why.

On the wall next to the door of the hotel I saw that the proprietors had allowed her to post a fresh copy of her flyer:

PROF. MISS KATIE BENDER

CAN HEAL ALL SORTS OF DISEASES; CAN CURE
BLINDNESS, FITS, DEAFNESS AND ALL SUCH DISEASES,
ALSO DEAF AND DUMBNESS.
RESIDENCE, 14 MILES EAST OF INDEPENDENCE, ON THE
ROAD FROM INDEPENDENCE TO OSAGE MISSION ONE AND
ONE HALF MILES SOUTH EAST OF NORAHEAD STATION.

Katie Bender
June 18, 1872

Beneath the printing she had scrawled APPLY WITHIN. Katie's sporadic attendance at Christian services hadn't affected her primary vocation as a spirit guide and faith healer, which for a while had earned her something of a following in Cottonwood and the surrounding towns. I hadn't heard much about it of late, probably since her clientele hadn't notably prospered or healed or become lucky in love.

There wasn't time to ponder the question, though; even in the midst of winter there were things that needed doing every morning, and that time of year I only kept one hired man. I mounted my rheumatic old nag and rode the three miles out to my claim thinking about the day when the income from the saloon would allow me to hire more and be done with farmwork forever.

Because of my delayed start it was late morning, though the sky was still dark, by the time I got to the saloon, where I found old Alf Cletus and Clark Bingham huddled around the side of the building against the wind and waiting for me to open her up. I lit both oil lamps once I'd closed the door and still it looked like the dead of night in there, just a smidgen of illumination coming in through the window opposite the bar as I fired up the stove and put on my vest and necktie.

When Alf removed his hat the skin at the crown of his head was high pink from the cold; he was ill dressed as usual and still shivering as the stove began warming the place up, complaining bitterly about my irregular hours of operation. His griping ceased when I set a glass in front of him and poured. Clark, quiet as usual, was fresh off of losing the homestead he'd staked eight months earlier, having failed to make the initial improvements necessary to maintain his claim. Despite my repeated arguments that he was better off, he was unable to see the happy side of this; he believed that he had been born to farm that piece of land, drunk or not. They had both downed their first shots of the day when the door opened and a man walked in wearing a fur coat and bowler hat. He had a drummer's sample case in his right hand, and with a cursory greeting to the assembled he shut the door and set the case down on the floor before the bar.

Alf had been just about to buy a bottle to take back to his room, but the drummer offered to stand him and Clark to a round of drinks, doubtless expecting that the gesture would be reciprocated by at least one of the two, an impression I didn't bother to correct.

"I presume you'll be able to change this?" He held out a gold double eagle, yellow as the mustache that curled over his upper lip.

"I can," I said, though I was certain he had smaller. The other two looked longingly at the gold piece; like just about everybody else they paid for their whiskey with whatever small coins and ten-cent shinplasters they managed to get their hands on. It had probably been years since Alf or Clark had held twenty dollars at one time in any form.

"Pleasant little hamlet you fellows have here," the drummer said, having established that Alf and Clark were locals. They both nodded in silent agreement.

"What are you peddling?" I asked, just to keep the conversation going in case he felt like going for another round.

"Pots and pans, the finest available in these United States." He said it with gusto and quite a bit of wind, probably thinking he might make a sale.

"Shit," Alf said, a gob of tobacco spittle flying from beneath his mustache and into the spitoon at his feet, "old Otis down at the forge makes all the pots and pans anybody needs around here."

"Not lately he don't," Clark mumbled, as if to himself.

"These are copper," the drummer said. "I just took a large order from the local hotel."

"Is that the truth?" I said, suspecting it wasn't; there wasn't much call for fine copperware in this part of the world. "Must be interesting work. Meet lots of people."

"Most of my clientele is made up of ladies," he said. He leaned in. "That's got its advantages and disadvantages, naturally. The former outweighing the latter." He winked and leered.

"How's that?" I said, playing innocent. He was thirty or thereabouts, and clearly hoped to cut the figure of a dandy. But if the bowler on his head looked brand-new and expensive, his coat's fur was worn away altogether in patches about the pockets and buttons, and when he opened it up, the suit under it was of medium quality, and threadbare to boot.

"Well, now, some of these ladies, they see a well-spoken, well-barbered, well-dressed man at the door and they can't control themselves. The husband, see, maybe he's off on business. Hell, sometimes he's just out plowing the back forty."

"And you're plowing Madame in the front room."

He snickered. "That's about the long and short of it."

"I just bet you could get you some of that around here," I said.

He nodded and leaned forward, lowering his voice as though

there were others in the room whom he wished to keep in the dark. "Just yesterday afternoon I had the pleasure of screwing a nice big heifer of a dutchwoman, blond upstairs and down. Then she fed me lunch and afterward she had me climb back aboard."

"Oh," I said. "You must've been out at the Schwemm farm, up the road toward Neodesha. Lady of about sixty, got a wandering eye."

Having seen Mrs. Schwemm he was appalled at the suggestion. "By God, not her. I seen she wasn't going to buy and I got out of there quick as I could. Lord, what do you take me for, thinking I'd wet my dick in a crabbed old pot like that?"

"I guessed it was Mrs. Schwemm because the only other big dutchwoman around these parts is Mrs. Ogden, and I couldn't picture a slick fellow like you giving a married lady a poke and then coming into her husband's saloon to boast of it."

I watched him turn that around in his head for a second, and then he laughed. "Oh, that's a good one. I seen her husband, though, out back cutting wood. Enormous fellow with an even bigger head and a shock of black hair like a wild Osage."

He was so sure of himself that my coming around the front of the bar only bothered him a little, and when I got his head down in the crook of my elbow he still seemed to think it was a big joke. That pretty hat fell onto the floor as I bent him downward, and he was still chuckling, albeit uneasily, when my knee cracked his nose.

"That's my hired man that cuts the wood, you flapjawed imbecile," I told him, and he hollered and wept as I gave him the rush to the front door and threw him out into the street in front of the saloon. The lower third of his face was red, his mustache dripping onto the dirt, and he looked up at his hat in my hand as if he expected me to throw it at him.

"This is mine now," I informed him, placing it on my head as I turned away, finding it a comfortable fit. I slammed the door and stepped back behind the bar. "How do I look, fellows?"

"Just fine, Bill," Alf said. "Like a fancy man right out of Chicago."

Clark just shrugged as the drummer walked back in, leaving the door open, pointing a Dragoon straight at me. "All right, you dirty dogfucker," he said, his throat ragged and dry, "you hand that back over."

I took the hat off and looked inside the band. Real silk, probably a twelve-dollar hat. I took my own Colt from beneath the bar and stuck it into the hat's crown, aiming it toward the open door. "Best stand aside," I told him. He failed to comply, and as a result the bullet came whistling very close by his head, and he dove for the floor, his gun clattering to the puncheons beside him.

I fired again, producing a second hole in the crown of the bowler. I was aiming at a plank nailed onto the trunk of a dead tree twenty yards or so across the dirt road from the saloon's front door. The plank splintered pleasingly with each successive impact, and upon emptying the Colt I stepped over to the prostrate drummer, picked up his Dragoon and placed it onto the bar. "I'll take this too." He nodded, dripping blood from his twisted honker as he backed out of the building.

"Bill, you forgot old Mrs. Bender, on the road to Cherryvale," Alf said.

"How's that?"

"She's a big old heifer of a dutchwoman, too."

"That may be true, Alf, but I very much doubt our fancy drummer man there would have fucked her any faster than he would have done old Mrs. Schwemm. No, it was my own dear Ninna entertaining him yesterday afternoon."

"It could be that you ought to go out and have a talk with that wife of yours," Alf said, and I had to admit his point was well-taken. I didn't so much mind Ninna laying with other men, really, but I did object to her indiscreet choice of partners. I walked over to the open door and looked out to see the drummer (whose name,

I would discover, was A. J. Harticourt, though I never learned what A. J. stood for), hurrying up the street, trying to get someone to listen to his sad tale, pointing at the crown of his ruined bowler. The last I saw of him he was going into the hotel. The owner of the feed store across from the hotel glared at me and, turning away, said something I couldn't hear; then I noticed Tiny Rector standing in front of his dry goods store and scowling, and I felt a measure of shame at my lack of restraint.

I sold Alf his bottle and he was gone; poor Clark nearly wept as I ordered him outside, as he'd counted on spending the afternoon there and didn't want to invest in a pint to take along with him. When he was gone I locked the door and remounted for the ride back to the farm for a word with my good wife.

It had finally begun to snow when I got to the farm, and I found the boy outside waiting for it to accumulate enough to play with. As always he appeared neither happy nor unhappy to see me.

"Oughtn't you to be in school today, Clyde?" I didn't recall seeing him around that morning when I was helping Garth with the chores, and it occurred to me that he may have been hiding.

"Mama says long as I got this cough I don't have to." He essayed a none-too-convincing cough.

"If you're well enough to play out in the cold, you're well enough to be in school."

"Mama says I don't have to."

Faced with that irrefutable logic I abandoned the argument. He was years ahead of the other children anyway, even the older ones. "Where is she?"

"In the parlor, at her knitting." He scooted off in the direction of the henhouse, and I stepped onto the porch of the third dwelling I'd erected on that property, a large wooden structure of which I was quite proud. The first had been a rude dugout constructed in

1868 for my own use only, while I commenced setting up the farm and building the second. That was a sod house, small but comfortable, and when I'd finished it I sent to Ohio for Ninna and the boy. They had been living with her mother and father in Columbus during that time, Ninna earning her keep helping out in her father's photographic studio.

We'd been two years in the sod house when I exercised my husbandly prerogative and took some of the money Ninna's old Danish Papa had presented us with on the occasion of our marriage to buy some lumber and hire some workers. I then set about building a proper gable-and-wing house, under whose roof I had not slept since six months after its completion.

I stepped into the house without knocking and found her making a man's thick woolen sweater. Plump and red in the face, her beautiful blond hair done up in elaborate braids draped across her head, she sat placidly near the fire, working her needles and dreaming. She greeted me quietly, with no curiosity as to the reason for my presence in her parlor when I ought to have been tending to the saloon in town, then returned her attention to the work at hand. Above her head was a framed print of the single-spired cathedral at Strasbourg I'd managed to salvage from my parents' effects upon my return from the war.

Without preamble I accused her of allowing the drummer access to her person, which seemed to disturb her not in the least; when I finally asked her to deny or confirm it she nodded and said gently, "Twice, second time nice and slow."

"For God's sake, he said Garth was right outside chopping wood."

She shook her head. "Sawing, not chopping. That big dead oak."

For a moment I was distracted by my lingering satisfaction that the enormous *Quercus alba* was finally down. Its removal was a job I'd delayed far too long; it was already minus all its removable branches—dry wood being at a premium in a land where most people burned the dried excrement of cattle in the winter—and amounted to not much more than a denuded log with roots by the time Garth and I had pulled it out of the ground three days prior. A look of glassy-eyed reverie on her cretinous pan brought me back to the matter at hand. "And you weren't afraid he'd chance to look in?"

She shrugged. "I ain't Garth's wife."

"Just don't be laying down with drummers," I pleaded. "They tell everybody. That's part of their job, telling stories to please people."

"Mm-hm," she nodded.

"I don't suppose the sweater's for me."

"For Garth." Garth was my second full-time hired man since I'd quit running the farm myself. I'd fired the first one and chased him out of town after the boy let slip quite innocently that with all the noise coming from Mama and Juno's room he had trouble sleeping at night.

Had I known that she would take the next hired man into her bed just as quickly as she had Juno I would have let the old boy stay on. When he left he took a ring that had belonged to my father, and I nearly set out after him when I became aware of its loss. His trail was cold by that time, though, and I could find no one who would admit to seeing him since the afternoon of his leaving. Despite the sentimental value of the stolen ring I was inclined to forgive Juno; he was a good and conscientious worker, particularly skilled at construction. He had in fact helped me build the saloon in early '71, when I first decided I'd seen enough of life on the farm; a simple oblong building with a pine bar running two-thirds of its length, and a skylight in its rear to allow for the taking of photographic portraits. The owner of the town's previous saloon, a shack containing a table made of a plank set upon two empty whiskey barrels, had passed out in a snowbank at Christmas, and in his squalid demise I saw my opportunity. The financing required some effort on my part; after I'd spent the first part of it building the house, an expenditure of which she did not approve, Ninna had carefully hidden the remainder of her father's wedding present. After a fruitless day or two's search I found a cast-iron Dutch oven buried next to the dead white oak, full of coins; I brought it inside, cleaned it up and set it, empty, next to the hearth without comment. I took the bulk of the gold to buy the land and put up the building and used the remaining thirty-five dollars, spitefully and with a grateful nod to her father, to order a stereographic camera. As soon as the saloon was bringing in money I was sleeping nights in the loft above the blacksmith's shop, returning to the farm only in the mornings to share in some of the daily work.

As I was the only farmer in the area with a second income I was also the only one who could afford a hired man on any regular basis, and there was some grumbling from my harder-working neighbors, who considered that I was violating the spirit and probably also the letter of the homestead act. There was also grumbling from Ninna, who met my suggestion that we both move to town with a derisive Danish snort. She'd married a farmer, and a farmer's wife she would remain, even if the farmer went off and tended bar and took pictures. In the end I didn't insist that she and the boy accompany me, principally because an attorney-at-law and land agent in Independence advised me that the whole family leaving the farm would likely have resulted in forfeiture, house or no house, improvements or no improvements. We were only two years away from proving up the claim and owning the land outright, so I relented and continued my solitary life in town, far from home and hearth.

Our condition was much improved in the financial sense, as saloonkeeping pays better than farming, but Ninna never hid the fact that she didn't consider it honest work on a par with the killing labor of running a farm. She did consider the photographer's trade an honorable one and couldn't have complained if I'd abandoned the farm for that, but I made so little money taking pictures that it didn't enter the argument.

Her infidelities didn't chafe at me as I would have imagined; I was confident she never had a lover but me before I moved out of our house and into town. By then I was no longer the overgrown apprentice who'd tenderly led her off to bed on our wedding night in Columbus, nor was she still the shy near-virgin with barely a hundred words of English. In those days I imagined that her lack of wit was actually an inability to express herself in my own tongue; as she learned it, though, improving her fluency day by day and month by month, I came slowly and reluctantly to the sad conclusion that I had united myself in matrimony with a dolt. Now she was a large, vapid woman of twenty-six years with a fervid appetite for sexual congress, and though at times I missed her animal enthusiasm, I knew I'd never return to her bed, sullied as it was with the smells and emissions of other men.

I left her to her knitting, hoping I'd made some sort of impression. There was no sign of Garth, and I crossed behind the barn to the sod house to find the latchstring out. I unbarred the door and entered; the front room was colder than the outdoors, and so was the second, where my old rope bed stood piled up with Garth's soiled clothes. He had pasted up an additional layer of the *Optic* on the wall, and my eye was drawn to a yellowed article about the local grange, scarcely legible in the daylight streaming through the front door and the single window. Momentarily the room darkened further, and I looked up to find Garth standing in the doorway, fists clenched and mouth set in a scowl.

"What the hell you figure you're doing in my house with the got-damn door wide open?" He filled the doorframe, having even to stoop a bit as he crossed the threshold. His head was big for his body and looked even bigger since his thick black hair wanted cutting.

"It's my house, Garth," I pointed out helpfully.

"And letting the cold air inside, I'm liable to catch a got-damn chill and die." He shut the door behind him, darkening the room and creating the vivid impression that he intended to do me harm.

"Hell, it's colder inside here than out," I said. "Don't you build a fire at night?"

The hearth was nearly bare, the few ashes therein gray and cold. "Don't get in here until real late, and I'm too tired to start one then."

"Why don't you just sleep in there with her? Hell, you don't think I mind, do you?"

He looked away sheepishly, relaxing his fists, and his shoulders sank as the air escaped from his lungs in something resembling a sob of despair. "It ain't you, Bill, it's her. Mrs. Ogden. She don't, she don't permit it."

"You call her Mrs. Ogden?"

He looked down at the hard dirt floor and nodded.

"At her request?"

He nodded again, and I shook my head and chuckled. At that he gave me a sharp glance, but soon looked down again, then to his left. He picked at the exposed sod next to the doorframe, pouting like a babe.

"There's all kinds of things a man'll do for his sweetheart that he mightn't have thought he would've," he said quietly, and all at once I believed I knew some of the things she'd been making him do, things she'd learned from me. She knew enough not to ask a passing drummer to perform such acts upon her person, but with my besotted employee she didn't hesitate to insist upon them; probably she suspected that he would become shamefully addicted to them, as it appeared he had.

"All right, it's up to you, Garth, but if I were you I'd tell her you're not putting your mouth down there again until she lets you sleep in the room with her."

He nodded but continued to look away as I passed by him in

the doorway, pushing the plank open with my shoulder. I passed by the house on the way to untie my horse and looked in the window, annoyed with Ninna for her lack of charity toward the poor fellow. It was snowing harder now, and little Clyde was attempting to pack some of it into a ball for throwing.

"Who's that for?"

"That's for drummers," he said.

"What you got against drummers?" I asked him, a little concerned about what he might have seen the day before.

"Just don't like 'em," he said, and he threw the snowball at the side of the house. The snow was too dry and powdery, and it disintegrated before it reached its target. Undeterred, he reached down and started collecting some more. He bore an uncanny resemblance to my own father, both physical and temperamental. At seven years of age he had the demeanor of a middle-aged minister, and had accumulated as much learning as most adults; it was my hope to send him east for his schooling when he was twelve or so. As I rode off in the direction of town he seemed perfectly and happily unaware of me.

Shortly after I returned to the bar late in the afternoon, the door opened, letting in a dose of cold dry wind and the stately bulk of Tiny Rector. At six and a half feet his height was as striking as his obesity, though once the novelty of his size had worn off it was his rheumy, pale blue eyes that held your attention. Set against the near-black of his buffalo coat they seemed even lighter in hue, almost as white as the surrounding vitreous.

"Afternoon, Tiny," I said. Winded, he responded with a mere rasping grunt and quickly became distracted by a headline on a newspaper I'd plastered vainly onto the wall for insulation. It had been less effective here than in the old sod house; the papers quickly split along the cracks between the planks of the wall, and the wind blew through in miniature gusts that cooled the room considerably, no matter how hot the stove might be burning. In the blue white light from the window he squinted at the small type of one of his own advertisements with his back to me, and I began to suspect that the visit was official in nature; he was Cottonwood's mayor and de facto constable as well.

It was unusual to see Tiny before closing time for his store, so as his wind returned I broke the silence by pointing this out to him.

He turned toward me, as though just remembering the reason for his visit. "Goddamnit, Bill, what's this I hear about you firing shots across Main Street?"

"You heard those shots yourself, Tiny, I saw you standing on the sidewalk in front of the store a minute later. What's the matter, somebody bellyaching?"

"A whole lot of somebodies, Bill. There's one or two want you arrested as an example. My own wife, among them, and you know how fond she is of you."

"You planning to arrest me, Tiny?"

He held a finger out at me. "By Christ, I sure will if you do any such thing again. Goddamnit, Bill, we're trying to run this like a real town. What the hell was the idea, anyway? I heard you gave that poor clothwit drummer a licking, too."

"That poor drummer laid my wife and bragged about it."

I had him there and he knew it. He propped his forearm onto the bar and leaned in for a different tack. "Let me tell you something, Bill. There's going to be some big changes around Cottonwood and damned soon, too, when the railroad comes through. How old are you, anyway?"

"Twenty-seven."

"There's going to be opportunities for an ambitious young fellow like you, provided you don't wreck things beforehand."

The old opportunity-knocks-but-once oratory was one I'd heard many times, and I was only half listening as I poured him a shot of bourbon, his usual vice. "Uh-huh." I nodded as he droned on about the future growth of Cottonwood and the part I could play in it.

He downed his bourbon and held the glass up for inspection, as though it might hold more if he looked carefully enough. "When I saw him he didn't mention the shots, so maybe they passed unnoticed. I hope that's so, for your sake."

"Who's that?"

He set the glass down and glared at me. "Mr. Leval and his wife."

"Who're they?"

He slammed his palm down onto the bar. "Goddamnit, Bill, you haven't been listening to a damned word I've said! Leval's the fellow that's putting up the mansion. They got into town last night, and that's why you can't be carrying on any more like you did this morning."

"Oh."

"This Leval's got plans I can't tell you about, but believe me, in a year's time you won't know this poor little town. We'll outshine Cherryvale and Independence both."

I filled up his glass again. It didn't seem likely to me; I was used to hearing grand schemes hatched at the bar. He looked sideways down at the bourbon and seemed as if he were about to turn it down, but there it was in his glass, and it would have been a shame to let it go to waste. He knocked it back and wiped his beard with his sleeve.

"Two bourbons and still an hour and a half before I can close the store," he said, shaking his bearded jowls in a mock shudder. "Christ, Lillian better not find out about that." His wife was a pleasant-looking but stern woman, and Tiny's return to the Dry Goods and Grocery with liquor on his breath would be occasion for a haranguing. "I'd better get along, now, Bill, but you mind what I said. There's no room for them kind of monkeyshines in Cottonwood any more."

He waddled to the door and gave the frame a slap with the palm of his hand, then gave me a tiny, perfunctory wave good-bye. After his departure I took advantage of the lull in trade to remove Suetonius from beneath the bar and, pulling a chair up next to one of the lamps, began to read.

I hadn't got far when Ed Feeney stepped through the door. Ed was the editor and publisher of the *Labette County Optic*, and he rubbed his hands together against the cold.

"Jaysus, Bill, why don't you paper over those cracks? Cold as a witch's tit in here."

I looked up at him without offering a verbal response.

"I heard there was gunplay this afternoon. Care to comment?"

"You want a drink, Ed?"

"Give me a shot of rye. I heard Tiny came by to give you hell, too."

I poured him his shot and took his coin. He peered over his spectacles at me, waiting patiently for my answer, but I leaned back and returned to *De Vita Caesarum*, or pretended to.

It was my ambitious father who began my studies in Latin and Greek, at an age when most schoolboys are still learning to figure simple sums and read the simplest of Bible verses. They are all I got from him besides the slant of my jaw and the signet ring, since lost; if all that my education had ended up affording me was a little time of quiet reflection between rounds of serving drinks, I thought, it was probably enough.

There was no business until the late afternoon, at which time Tim Niedel and Michael Cornan walked in, and Tim slapped a quarter down onto the table.

"Whiskey, barkeep."

"Same," Cornan said. He claimed to be a preacher, though he had no church and worked with Tim six days a week when it was to be had. His face resembled an unbaked bread loaf just punched down by the baker's powdered fist; that the distal part of his nose had been eaten away by some ailment, most likely venereal, added to the impression of concavity. He countered it with a thick whisk broom of an unwaxed mustache so large and unruly that it would have been funny if not for the sullen hostility expressed permanently by his gray eyes. Other than those glistening, cunning slits, he resembled nothing so much as a neglected corpse left unburied on the field of battle to puff with methane, just beginning to slowly deflate.

"Looking at the Good Book, are you, Bill?" Tim said.

"History," I corrected him.

"There's plenty of history in the Bible," Cornan said with some menace. Offering no further argument I poured him a shot.

"That Leval got to town last night," Tim said. "Stayed in the second floor suite of the hotel with his wife."

"That's what I hear."

He spit a cheekful into the spitoon at his feet and slammed his whiskey down. "Yep. Wants to keep an eye on the building, is my guess, as it goes up. Though they say he's looking after railroad business. Jobs going to be opening up soon."

"How come you're down here and not at the site?"

"Nothing more to be done. I'm short of lumber. Third time we've run clean out of one thing or another and had to wait while he ordered it up from Kansas City."

"Has he got trouble paying?"

"Not so's I can see. Payroll's always on time whether work's proceeding or not. Say, speaking of the hotel, I'd watch out for that drummer, the one selling the pots and pans. His nose is broke and his new hat wrecked and he says he's gonna get you."

"Well, I got his Dragoon," I said, and I hauled the gun out and laid it on the table.

Tim nodded. "All the same, keep an eye out. Your sweetheart Katie Bender says he's talking pretty big about it."

"She's not my sweetheart, for Christ's sakes."

"Also he's telling everybody and his brother that he fucked your missus."

"Ah, shit. Guess I'd better get back after him." No matter what Tiny said, letting such an affront go unpunished was a considerably bigger mark against my name than the stigma attached to the violent settling of a score.

"I wouldn't worry about it. Nobody believes what a drummer says, bragging the way they do."

"Besides," Cornan said, "the whole town knows about your wife pleasuring that hired man. No offense."

"They do?" I'd been under the impression that Ninna's liaison with Garth was a well-kept secret.

Tim nodded. "Well, sure, old Juno told everybody as he was leaving town. He was pretty sore at you for firing him."

"Can you mind the till for a few minutes? I already lost two hours worth of business this afternoon."

"For two shots of rye I will."

"That's fine. I shouldn't be long."

Tim leaned into the bar and I put my coat back on and walked up the street to the hotel, where the boy at the desk looked up at me without surprise.

"If you're looking for Mr. Harticourt he's already checked out."

"That the drummer with the hole in his bowler?"

"The one that says he's had knowledge of your wife, yes sir."

"When did he leave?"

"An hour or so ago. Left with Katie, heading out for Fort Scott. Probably going to stay at the Bender place overnight."

I couldn't hold back a laugh at that. "That's pretty brazen."

"No sir, they put travelers up for the night somewhat regular, and she thought her old mother might be wanting some pots and pans."

"Bullshit," I said. "He's gonna give her the business just like he did my wife, only Kate'll probably charge him for the privilege."

At that the boy rose from behind the desk and made a fist, his eyes wide and watery. "You take that back, mister."

I laughed again. "All right, you win. Miss Bender's only concern is for the poor drummer making his sales quota for Labette county." I felt some pity for the lad as I left; he was sixteen or seventeen, and his dreams of the lovely and otherworldly Kate were no doubt things of frail, crystalline beauty, liable to shatter at the slightest cynical word.

My first thought was to mount up and ride out to the Bender place, the saloon be damned. Once out there I would thrash the drummer; I might also take his fur coat, and his money, which probably didn't amount to more than the change for the twenty dollar gold piece. That last would of course depend on the presence of the Bender menfolk, who didn't know me particularly, and whether or not they were inclined to come to the man's aid. I didn't think they'd begrudge me at least the beating, though, once I'd explained the circumstances.

As I approached the saloon a party consisting of six or seven men and one woman crossed the road and entered. I hurried in, took Tim's place behind the bar and began serving. All the men but one were in working clothes, and well-known to me, some of them daily customers of the saloon; the last was paying for all the drinks, and he was dressed as a gentleman, with a better hat than the one I'd destroyed that morning and as fine a fur coat as I'd seen since leaving Ohio. The woman was dressed like no woman I had ever seen in any bar, any place, in fur and a fine hat, and dainty shoes peeking out from under the hem of her coat. It wasn't her clothing that captivated, though. It was her face, long and sweet, her eyes large and luminescent, even in the dim lamplight; it wasn't so much the fineness of the features, either, as what she did with them when I served her a glass of port wine from a dusty bottle that had sat untouched on the backbar since the day I opened, and on the backbar of my dead predecessor before that. An expression of merriment at her mouth stopped just shy of being a smirk, one that conveyed at once fondness, amused regret and recognition, as though we had once known each other in some distant, civilized locale. What was more, that look seemed there for my benefit alone, the result of a joke only we two shared, and I was sure it was visible from no one else's vantage point, not even that of the dapper gentleman who was her husband.

They were of course the much-discussed Levals, and the men with them were the ones building their house. Leval took a drink and swept his gaze slowly around the room as though dispassionately appraising it for sale.

"What's a saloon need with a skylight?" he wanted to know.

I was annoyed but I answered him. "It does double duty occasionally as a photographic studio," I said, though at that point I hadn't taken a photograph in six months or more.

"Oh, you'll have to take our picture," his wife said.

I calculated roughly the expense of buying fresh chemicals in my head. "Maybe it would be best to wait until your house is complete, and we could do it there."

"That's a wonderful idea," she said. Her husband didn't respond, lost in thought as he contemplated the primitive skylight Juno and I had installed. For a while now I'd considered it a waste of money, like the stereograph camera, since neither one was being put to regular use. The prospect of photographing this woman, even in the company of her husband, made me think differently.

"All right, Maggie," the husband said. "Best get you back to the hotel before tongues start wagging about me letting my wife frequent saloons." He said this with a broad wink, and as they walked out the front door into the frigid night and down the street to their lodgings she waved at the laughing men in a familiar way.

Leval was back in forty-five minutes or so, and he seemed so much more at ease that I presumed he had taken the time to screw his lovely wife, but that may have just been the way my mind was oriented that evening. He was close to Tiny Rector's age, which is to say fifteen or twenty years older than I was, but with the apparent vitality and energy of a much younger man. His wife couldn't have been many years past thirty; presumably she inspired some of that youthful vigor.

"What's the volume I spy behind you on the bar?"

"Suetonius," I said, handing the volume to him. He opened it to a random page and examined it as though he understood it, going so far as to nod as if in appreciation of its contents; then he smiled wistfully and returned the book to me.

"I did very poorly in Greek and Latin both. I like to think it was for lack of effort rather than denseness on my part."

I put the book back in its niche and smiled politely, none too interested in his schooldays.

"My wife, on the other hand, she reads both like she reads English."

"Is that so?" I asked, at pains not to betray my excitement at the thought of so enticing a creature in possession of a classical education.

"She's mad for it. In a month or so our library will be arriving. You can feel free to borrow anything in it."

I thanked him. My own library's holdings were so meager that I was on what I reckoned to be about my twentieth reading of *De Vita Caesarum*, and I told him so.

He looked askance at me. "How does a saloonkeeper in a remote place like this come to read the classics?"

I took offense and had to temper my response. "May as well ask how a reader of the classics comes to keep a saloon in a remote place like this."

"How, then?"

One thing I particularly valued about the prairie was the reticence of most of those living there, and the lack of interest, or overt interest anyway, in one's neighbor's origins. Though the substance of his questioning grated at me, his tone was one of gentle, amiable curiosity, and I gave in. "My father was a minister, and he instructed me in the classics from an early age. After his death my education was provided by the church, up to a point. After that I taught myself."

"What else besides Latin and Greek?"

"Bits and pieces of various other subjects," I said. My education was spotty enough that I didn't care to shed light on the specific lacunae therein.

"Any other languages?"

"I know French and German. My mother was from a town called Mulhouse, in Alsace, and she spoke both to me."

He leaned over the bar and slapped me on the shoulder. "My Papa was a Frenchman. We're probably cousins, somewhere down the line. Though I suppose Alsace is part of Prussia now." He tugged at his mustache, where it met with his sideburns. "What brought you to Kansas?"

"I had the foolish notion I wanted to be a farmer."

"You abandon a claim?"

"Still working it, with the help of a hired man," I said. I laid out for him the particulars of my situation, leaving out Ninna's slatternly behavior, and he nodded thoughtfully.

"A man with several irons in the fire, then," he said.

"I suppose that's true. I'd be glad of giving up farming, though."

He looked over toward the door for a moment, lifting his chin and scratching it absently, and then he turned back to me.

"You strike me as a man in constant search of a new challenge."

"Maybe so," I said.

"What would you think of taking on a partner here?" he asked quietly, having first assured himself that the other men were engaged in other conversation.

"I'm doing fine on my own," I answered, somewhat taken aback.

"What if I was to tell you that within a year this town is going to grow like a damned weed? You think it might be good to have a bigger saloon, one that won't be overshadowed by any newcomers?"

"Town's been growing nice and steady since it's been here."

"Started with, what, about fifty men, half of them married?"

I hadn't lived in town at the time, but that seemed about right, and I nodded.

"And it's three hundred, three twenty-five now."

Again I nodded. "Not counting the farms outside of town limits."

"Bill—can I call you Bill? You call me Marc. Bill, this is between you and me." He looked about him again, to satisfy himself that the others were still paying no attention. There were perhaps fifteen men in the bar in various degrees of inebriation, singing, laughing, and telling dirty stories. "There's a railroad going to come through here," Leval told me. "The Kansas City, Illinois, and Nebraska."

I shrugged. "Track's just a few dozen miles to the north and east right now. Two, three months it'll pass through here. That's not a secret."

"I was instrumental in putting the bond issue on the ballot that paid for it, and getting the railroad to consider this as a route. You know why?"

"I don't," I allowed.

"Cattle pens are going to go up, Bill. That's the part that not everybody's privy to. Once the railroad comes through so will the cattle trails. Do you follow me?"

"I believe I do."

"And are you familiar with the economic workings of these cattle towns?"

"I know there's money to be made from cowboys and ranchers and railroads."

"Goddamn right there's money to be made. Now keep this to yourself, but Cottonwood's going to be a cattle town to make Wichita look small and tame."

"And that's how come you're building a house here without ever laying eyes on the place?"

"I'd laid eyes on it. I spent a week here at the hotel last year, drawing up plans and maps for the railroad and the cattle companies. Now why don't you come see me tomorrow morning and we'll discuss this. I'm setting up shop down at the bank. I'll show you the maps of the railroad extensions and the new cattle trail."

I nodded, considering this, and after ordering another round he left. As the evening dragged on I thought more and more about money and a new building for the saloon, about being in at the start of a cattle boom; it was past midnight, the revelers all gone home, before I thought of the drummer again, out at the Bender place, and my plan to ride out there and beat the tar out of him. The devil with him, I thought, and I limped, exhausted, down the street in the direction of the blacksmith's loft for a night's sleep.

I'd been so busy I hadn't thought of sending to the hotel dining room for something to eat, and all I'd eaten was a little pemmican I had under the counter, salty and mummified. I wandered over to the hotel to see if any of the staff were awake, and knocking gently on the pane I found the other serving girl, dressed for bed. Hattie Steig was a plain, good-natured girl of about twenty-two or twenty-three, a widow whose husband had left town the year before, heading for a homestead in Russell County, where he was to establish the necessary improvements and then send for her. A month after Hiram Steig's leaving, a body that had been discovered floating a few miles downstream in the Verdigris river shortly after his departure was confirmed as his; the identification had been weeks in coming as the man's head had been crushed as by a hammer, its throat slit, and the body stripped naked. The money he had been carrying, all that he and Hattie had saved, had been stolen. Poor Hattie, unexpectedly alone and impoverished, had gone to work at the hotel, serving lunch and dinner and cleaning the rooms, all the while fending off the crudest of advances from the lodgers and guests.

"Anything left to eat in there?" I whispered when she opened the door.

"It's all been put away until morning," she said. "The Barneses lock the eats up so's we don't raid the larder at midnight. You want to come upstairs? I got the room to myself tonight, Kate's gone for a spell."

It had been a week since I'd last had a crack at Hattie, and the flesh was weak. At the moment there was no one else in town available to me, except for her mad co-worker Kate and my Ninna, neither of them acceptable alternatives. I was tired and hungry, but it was hard in my circumstances to turn down a chance at female companionship. Anyway, I told myself, it would curb my appetite for self-abuse for a day or two, thus staving off blindness or insanity for a while longer. "You sure it's safe?" I asked her.

"I'm sure. The Barneses are at home tonight, and none of the guests is the kind that'd talk," she said. She let me in and shut the door, leading me through the dining room to the stairs, and watching her ample rump swaying at the level of my eyes as she led me up the dark staircase I began to feel the first pleasurable stirrings of arousal.

The serving girls' room was a tiny attic affair, with a single bed barely wide enough to accommodate two, and dark as pitch despite a large window; no moon or stars shone through the clouds. As we quickly disrobed and slid beneath the covers I wished I could stay the night, hating the idea of having to dress again and make my way back to the forge to sleep in the frozen loft. But the owners of the hotel would be there before sunup to get the kitchen ready, and if I were seen it would be Hattie's job.

Fifteen minutes later I was creeping back down the stairs, having served what I suspected was Hattie's real motive, that of warming up the bed; at the moment of ejaculation I had thought of

Maggie Leval's lascivious grin, which image had intensified the sensation considerably, as did the thought that she lay sleeping peaceably with her husband just one floor down in the hotel's only suite.

My stomach growled as I opened the padlock on the forge, but I didn't care. It was time for sleep.

2

COTTONWOOD, KANSAS
DECEMBER 1872–JANUARY 1873

The Copper Pot

Ninna grumbled all the way into town, and the boy said not a word, just sat there in the back of the wagon looking miserable and cold in his thin coat, despite the sweater his mother had just finished knitting him. It matched the one she'd made for Garth; I had not received one.

"Christmas," Ninna said. "Ought to spend it at home. Might be a good idea to go to church, even."

"No Lutheran church around here," I said. "Where would you go?"

She shrugged. "Ought to go to church on Christmas."

Despite my best efforts to keep the day harmonious I opened my mouth. "And why would that be?"

"Jesus's birthday," she said quietly, gazing in her placid, bovine way at an abandoned dugout just outside of town. The land was unoccupied and had been since before I'd arrived, and I'd never heard whose place it had been or why it had been abandoned.

"Nothing to do with Jesus. It's just a way to mark the fact that winter's halfway over. People were lighting fires and having Christmas parties a long time before Jesus came along."

She clucked, looking rather pretty with her cheeks ruddied by the wind. We saw the Rectors on their way to the Methodist services, and Tiny called out to us as we passed them. I waved back and so did the boy, but Ninna made as though she didn't see them.

I tied the horse and wagon to the post in front of the hotel. "Now goddamn it," I said, helping her down out of the wagon, "try and be nice to these people. They're our business partners now."

She stuck out her lower lip. "I don't care if that saloon burns down to the ground." She stepped up onto the wooden sidewalk and entered the hotel without another look in my direction; the boy hopped out of the wagon and we followed her inside.

The Levals' suite had been temporarily appointed with their own furniture, brought over from their home in Chicago, and it was as fine a setting as I'd seen since leaving Ohio. The suite—a somewhat grand description of what was essentially an enlarged version of the hotel's standard room—was crammed to bursting with settees, stuffed chairs, tables of various kinds, two chests of drawers, and a large sofa, all of it finely wrought and expensive. Maggie and Marc steered us over to the sofa, after which Maggie ignored me and fawned over Ninna and Clyde, the latter in particular, feeding him cakes and hard candies imported from the east and generally behaving as if she'd never seen a boy child before. He seemed embarrassed but pleased at the attention, and even Ninna was disarmed in the face of Maggie's onslaught of charm. Marc and I stood off to the side and discussed business, in particular the price for lumber for the new saloon, and we lost interest in the doings of the women and the child. Marc had become dissatisfied with his

Kansas City supplier and wanted to know what I thought about a lumberyard he'd heard of in Bourbon County.

"He thinks he can gouge me when he can't even guarantee delivery on time," he said. "I'm inclined to go with this yard in Fort Scott just to show the complacent son-of-a-bitch."

It was fine with me. I'd bought the lumber for the current building there at what I considered an extortionary rate, but Marc told me it was less than he'd been paying for the materials for his house. I was momentarily distracted by the squealing sound of Clyde's laughter, and on the sofa I saw him doubled over in hysterics as Maggie clutched him from behind, tickling him below the rib cage. Ninna was smiling rather sternly now—she was not a particularly affectionate mother, at least physically—and I believe she was on the verge of intervening when a loud knocking came at the door. Maggie and Clyde, both flushed and breathless, sat upright as Marc opened the door. Cy Patton stood there, hat in hand, and Maggie stiffened. As he often did, Patton looked like a little dog who'd just evacuated his bowels on a rug, wet-eyed in anticipation of a whipping.

"Mr. Leval? Sorry to stop by unannounced on Christmas Day, but I heard you were entertaining and I thought it might be a good piece for the *Free Press*."

"Come on in," Marc said, and if he didn't look in his wife's direction it was surely to avoid the furious shaking of her head and the exasperated rolling of her eyes back into their orbits, but by the time Patton was in the room she had made her expression one of polite welcome. He was quick in his work, taking just a few notes and asking about the Levals' families back east. Their responses were none too specific, if not actually evasive, and after a few questions of the same type to me and Ninna he left. As I shook hands with him at the door I noted that there was a chunk of some sort of food clinging, dried, to the corner of his mustache, and he mistook my smirk for a comradely smile; he shook my hand and wished me a Merry Christmas, and I wished him the same as he disappeared limping down the staircase.

Maggie's spirits had dampened considerably since the knock at the door, and she tried to raise them again with the suggestion that we exchange presents. Our gifts to the Levals were meager: a wooden pipe for Marc (who, I subsequently learned, didn't smoke, but who accepted the gift as graciously as if he did) and an embroidered Christmas stocking for Maggie, handmade by a somewhat resentful Ninna. From our generous hosts Clyde received a new coat—I hadn't mentioned the need for one to the Levals, but having seen him on several occasions they could hardly have failed to notice—and a sled, store-bought. Ninna was given a hat in the current mode, which she sniffed at, uncomprehending. I received a Latin book, its spine stiff and uncracked, its leather still fresh and fragrant; it was the *De Senectute, De Amicitia, Paradoxa,* and *Somnium Scipionis* of Cicero, and in the same volume Cornelius Nepos's *Life of Atticus*, with notes in English by Charles Anthon. My stupefaction and stammered thanks seemed to lift Maggie, who had certainly selected it herself, from the doldrums Cy Patton had inspired, and upon opening the book I was strangely thrilled to see that its inscription was in her own hand, with Marc's added almost as an afterthought:

To Wm. Ogden,
our friend and partner in our newest ventures.
Merry Christmas 1872.

"I don't know if you ever bother to read the commentaries," Maggie said, "but I found Mr. Anthon's notes to be most illuminating."

"I'm sure they're wonderful," I said. On Marc's face I read a fleeting smirk, gone too fast for me to tell whether it was born of fond indulgence or condescension toward his wife's and my pretensions to erudition.

Though Ninna managed to be pleasant she remained suspicious and uncertain as to why these people were treating us as friends, and after we had drunk the eggnog and sung the carols (all of them unfamiliar to her) she rose and said that she'd had a delightful time and was sorry it was time to go.

Maggie had the good sense not to try and talk her out of it, and we went downstairs with their merry voices trailing us from the landing. The streets were deserted, or nearly so, as we headed out, and I couldn't help noting how much happier the boy looked in his new, warm coat, his belly full of sweets and his head full of the ministrations of a pretty woman. He held the sled as if the snow might start any moment, and kept his face skyward.

We arrived back at the farm by four o'clock. Garth sat brazenly in the front parlor, reeking of the corn whiskey I'd given him that morning for the occasion and not troubling himself to hide his resentment at his exclusion from our Christmas celebration.

I returned to town at six o'clock or so that evening and opened the saloon, which we had not yet begun to dismantle. I poured whiskey until well past midnight, feeling hollow at the core for reasons I could not elucidate. To judge by the lugubrious air in the room my melancholy was shared by the majority of the drunkards present that night.

Patton's article, when it appeared that week, didn't amount to much, but I learned from Marc that it had offended Maggie anyway.

YULETIDE AT THE COTTONWOOD HOTEL

Our newest arrivals, Mr. and Mrs. Marc Leval, entertained on Christmas Day Mr. William Ogden, of Cottonwood, and his young family, in their grandly appointed suite at the Cottonwood Hotel. It was a jolly scene, reminiscent of many a winter's holiday back home in Chicago, where the Levals resided before making Kansas their home. Asked if she missed family and friends there, Mrs. Leval pleasantly replied that she was delighted to be in Kansas, and tried only to look forward. Their splendid new house will be finished soon, we hear, and we hope soon to have details of Mr. Leval's plans for the town, said to be as grandiose as the manse itself.

I saw nothing to offend there, but Marc told me that the day it appeared she took to her bed for the remainder of the afternoon. Ninna read the article and sniffed that she hadn't been mentioned by name, but Clyde begged me to cut the article out with my penknife, and once I had he pressed it lovingly inside his copy of *The Pilgrim's Progress*.

A little more than two weeks later I made the trip to the lumberyard in Fort Scott to procure the lumber and fixtures required for the new building. Between the coming of the railroad and the building of the cattle pens, Marc lacked the free time to go, and I was happy for the chance to escape the saloon and the loft for a few days. The day of my departure we had talked into the early afternoon about finances and construction plans, and it wasn't until past four that I got started on the road to Fort Scott. I left a teetotaling farmboy named Horace Gleason in charge of the saloon in my absence; he was willing to ply the devil's trade in return for instruction in the art and craft of photography. He had worked the bar one afternoon before, and afterward I had received so many complaints about the temperance lectures and Bible verses he dispensed alongside the bug juice that this time I had to extract a solemn oath that there would be no proselytizing until my return. I quit town astride a new mount, a chestnut mare purchased as company property by Marc, imaginatively named Red by its former owner.

In retrospect, I should have delayed my departure until morning; it was already dark by the time I was but a few miles north of town, the moon full and shining across the hills, the frozen ground shimmering in its glow and creating an atmosphere that suggested neither day nor night, precisely, but a dreamlike state somewhere between the two. The last snow had been some weeks before, on the day of the Levals' arrival, and only patches of it remained on the sides of the mounds, mostly in places that stayed shady on clear days. When I got to the Big Hill Creek ford the mare's shins cut like boat's prows through a thin crust of ice on its surface, and presently I detected movement in a grove of trees on the other side and a grunt which I interpreted as human in origin.

"Who's that?" I called out.

The noises ceased, and so did the grunting, though I believed I could now detect the sound of clothes rustling.

"Better show yourself," I yelled, drawing my Colt as I did so.

"It's all right," came a male voice from the darkness, "I'm coming out."

A moment later a stout young man appeared, hands clearly visible. "John Bender," he yelled. He was Kate's brother, and unlike her he spoke with a thick German accent. I had heard people claim that they were not brother and sister but husband and wife, offering as proof his awkwardness with the English language in contrast with her eloquence. I had only seen him once or twice before, but it did strike me now that there was no family resemblance between the two of them. He was squat and thick, with a square, flat face and the eyes of an imbecile. His trousers were imperfectly fastened, and it was my impression that, despite the cold, he'd been evacuating his bowels or abusing himself in the quiet solitude of the grove.

"Where you headed?" he asked.

"Fort Scott," I answered. "Off to purchase some lumber."

"You won't make it tonight. Why don't you stop at our house, have dinner and stay the night? Thirty cents, and you can have breakfast, too."

Until then I had supposed I would stay at the hotel in Cherryvale, though it was a short distance out of my way; cold as it was, I had no desire to set up camp for the night, and Leval had entrusted me with cash for my expenses. Now, though, the prospect of turning in early for once appealed, and I considered the offer seriously.

"I was on my way to the Cherryvale Hotel. I don't think it's much further."

He waved his hand in dismissal. "My sis used to work there," he said, which I knew to be true. "Cost you seventy-five cents and you don't get fed. My ma's a real good cook," he said, beckoning me, and he mounted a fine-looking horse and I followed him up the bank to a trail leading to their claim. "My sister's a real beauty, too," he called over his shoulder, and I had the sense that his statement was in the nature of an offer, rather than a mere boast.

After a few minute's ride over the Hieronymous Mounds we arrived at the house, a square frame building with smoke rolling from the chimney and a warm, yellow-orange glow in its two front windows. There was a skeletal orchard a stone's throw from the house, the branches of its thin young trees stretching upward into the moonlight as if in supplication. Bender dismounted and hurried to the door.

"Let me tell Ma and Pa we got us a guest." He pronounced it "kest."

A minute later he came out, followed by a short, scowling bear of a woman and a hugely muscular blackhaired man, his thick neck so bent as to be nearly parallel to the ground, and with a look on his face that made the old hag next to him look positively sweet. The old woman, whom I had seen on a few previous occasions, did not seem to remember me, and she snapped something to the boy in a *Hochdeutsch* patois that sounded remarkably like my mother's Alsatian. The young man indicated that I should dismount, whereupon he led my horse away.

I entered the tiny dwelling and found it divided into two rooms by a large canvas sheet. On a small table against the wall stood a lamp, its luminescence dimmed by its smoke-darkened glass; the only other light came from a fire in the hearth. Something was cooking in a still-shiny copper pot suspended over the flame; the drummer had found a customer in old Ma Bender that night after all. I wondered if he'd screwed Kate or not, and whether he'd reduced the price of the pot accordingly. I decided he probably had on both counts.

By its smell I took what was bubbling in the pot to be corn, but before I had been in the house for half a minute another smell assaulted my nostrils, a very vague one, merely an accent to that of the cooking corn, but it soon overpowered my senses and I began to sicken. It was in fact a number of odors working in concert, ranging from dull to sharp, to produce a unified stench that called at once to mind graveyard detail in the army as well as the summer before I'd joined the army, when I'd worked stunning cattle in a slaughterhouse.

Mrs. Bender, huffing and shuffling painfully, produced a ladle and a large wooden bowl from the other side of the house and approached the pot. She pointed at a large, rough wooden table and indicated that I should sit; when I did so the faint odor that was causing me such unease intensified to such a degree that I was forced to stand. Then I saw that beneath the table was a section of flooring that did not fit the rest, precisely, giving the impression of a trap door. The two men had entered at this point, and they both stared at me with some degree of consternation, apparently because I remained on my feet.

"Sit," the old man said, pointing to the chair I had just vacated, and it was an order rather than a suggestion.

His son was more diplomatic. "Take a seat, Ma will serve you up a bite to eat," he said, but all eyes in the house were on me, defying me to stand any longer when I had been told to sit.

"I've had a change of heart," I said, and I started for the door. "I thank you for your kind offer, but I'd like to make some more time tonight."

The old man stood in the doorway, blocking my exit, and I repeated my statement in German, in case they hadn't understood; my Alsatian accent took them by surprise.

"You won't get far tonight," John Bender said in Alsatian.

"Sit and eat," his father said, still there in the door. "You insult my house."

I pulled aside my coat, which I had not removed, and put my right hand on the grip of the Colt for the second time that evening. The old man's expression grew more venomous, and I began to appreciate what an enormous beast he was; were his neck not bent as it was he would have reached six feet four or five inches in height, and he looked half that wide. He looked at the Colt and then gave me an appraising glance, as though calculating whether I could draw and fire before he reached me. I eased the Colt from my belt, simultaneously pulling the hammer back, and still I didn't sense that the likelihood of old Bender moving aside had increased much. Then from the exterior came a sound that distracted him, that of a horse arriving at a good clip and then stopping. I heard someone dismount not far from the door, and a moment later Kate Bender appeared in the door behind him, shouting in German that I was the saloonkeeper in the town of Cottonwood and well-known locally. Before she got any further the old man shouted at her in a tone that would have curdled milk: *"Er versteht Deutsch!"*

She stuck her head in and moved past her father. "Well, Bill Ogden, isn't this a pleasant surprise," she said cheerily, as though I was the last person she had expected to see upon poking her head in the door. She was breathing hard, and sweat had frozen patches of that long red hair. "Will you be joining us for supper this evening?" Though she looked at the Colt in my hand, noting presumably that it was cocked and ready to fire, she said nothing about it.

"I was just on my way," I said. "Pleasure to see you, as always, Miss Kate." I stepped past her father and crossed to where the horses were tied and retrieved my mount. Next to it was Kate's, wheezing from exertion, and cold sweat shone on its coat. I heard them arguing in the cabin as I rode away in the direction of Cherryvale, the loudest belonging to old Mrs. Bender, and listening to the voices diminish in the distance I remembered my old Alsatian grandfather yelling at my mother and grandmother in German and French, demanding his meals and his pipe and sometimes just yelling because he liked the sound of it.

That night in the dining room of the Cherryvale Hotel where Kate had once worked, I told my host what had happened and we shared a laugh over my unease amongst the Benders. The hotelier proceded to share several anecdotes about Kate's eccentric behavior, and then he called down a tiny old woman from one of the rooms who cradled in her arms a rifle.

"Don't mind the gun, it goes where she does. Mrs. Kearney, tell Mr. Ogden here what happened to you out at the Bender house last year."

She took a good look at me and, having decided I could be trusted with the tale, sat down in a chair. "I just got here to town, and I seen them signs she posted up all over about healing, and when I moved in here and got to know her some she told me she got her healing powers from a dead Indian chief. He told her how to do it, you see? And then she tells me she can talk to the spirits generally, and I says how I'd sure like to talk to my dead sister up in North Dakota."

"I thought it was your mother, Mrs. Kearney," the innkeeper said.

"No, Mother died in Wisconsin and I got nothing more to say to her. So she invited me out to her house, and we rode out together, it was getting to be sundown. We went in, and she told the family we was going to commune with the spirits, and the menfolk started acting peculiar and left the room with the old woman. Then Kate started drawing on the walls with a piece of coal. Drew up a picture of a man, and you knew it was a man because she went ahead and drew his rutting gear sticking out like a thumb. Then the old man, bent over double, walks in with a knife and damned if he didn't stab that drawing of that man right in the heart, and while the knife's still stuck in the wood there old Kate collapses like a rag doll and falls to the floor, crying out and talking in tongues. Right about then's when I edged my seat a little closer to where my rifle was. The old man disappeared into the other room without a word, and I asked Kate if she was communing with the spirits yet and she said 'I sure am, and what they're telling me right now is to kill you *daid*.' Well, I grabbed my rifle and charged out that door over to my horse. Sun was just going down, and I could hear Kate laughing while I rode away. I bet you I could hear her for half a mile or more, carried on the wind. I was scared to death she was following me until I finally got back here."

"And how'd she act after that, in town?" the hotelier prompted her.

"Just like nothing was ever doing. I'd see her in here and she'd say 'Morning, dearie,' like we was still the best of friends."

Mrs. Kearney excused herself and went upstairs and we poured a couple of glasses of whiskey.

"Bear in mind that Mrs. Kearney also believes that the phantom of Andy Jackson comes to her in the night and satisfies her carnally," he said as the door upstairs closed. "But who knows but there's a germ of truth to that business with the Benders?"

I drank my whiskey, trying to remember if I'd seen the outline of a man drawn on the wall at the Bender home, then went upstairs to my own bed, for I had a long ride ahead of me in the morning.

As I lay in bed that night something got me thinking about the ring Juno had stolen from me, a small masonic intaglio which I would have liked to pass on to Clyde, who would never know the grandfather he resembled so strongly in feature and temperament. As a boy of seven I had surreptitiously removed it from my father's finger as he lay in his coffin; knowing he would have wanted me to have it I felt no guilt for its purloining, but even twenty years hence, abed in the Cherryvale Hotel a thousand miles to the southwest, I could still feel the great relief I experienced then when the lid was placed onto Papa's coffin and the evidence of my crime laid into the ground.

I returned from Fort Scott a few days later, on a route that skirted the Bender place by some distance. The winter remained harsh and dark, and once we had begun tearing the old saloon down in anticipation of the lumber I had ordered, I opened up shop in the open air from the back of an old wagon, an arrangement that suited neither me nor my customers. Like me they longed for the warmth of the stove and the shelter of the thin walls, and I sustained myself with the thought of the new saloon and its grand setting, and of the money it would pull in. There would even be a stage, upon which women might dance and sing, and Leval and I had even discussed the purchase of a piano for me to accompany them upon.

In the meantime I had tried to hammer out a deal with the hotel whereby I could have set up shop temporarily in their dining room, but despite almost ruinously generous terms from me they declined; the Barneses were opposed to liquor on general principle. Daily and nightly I stood in the open air, wrapped in the old buffalo robe, dispensing booze and growling at my clientele. Marc offered to pay young Horace Gleason to do it for me, saying that eventually I would have to abandon the tending of the bar to some employee or another, that it ill became the owner of a saloon of the higher grade to be seen working there himself. But I had little else to occupy myself with then, save the demolition of the old saloon; with a crow-bar I had ceremoniously pried away from the structure the first of the planks, and watching the creaking separation of the still-soft wood that Juno and I had nailed together was bittersweet. I loved that kind of physical labor even less than I did farm work, and chose to remain at my post as the wrecking continued.

Late one afternoon in January I stood at the wagon passing the time of day with a man named Paul Lowry. He was about my age, with a bald head and a luxuriant red mustache; he had lived in Cottonwood for more than a year, working at various jobs requiring limited skill, and he claimed to have worked as a copper in Boston before heading west. He hoped I could put a good word in with Tiny or Marc, who were discussing the establishment of an official police force. I wasn't inclined to recommend him, since he was a mean drunk who picked exclusively on smaller men, and slow to pay his tab besides. He also drank on the job; as he stood there downing one shot after another of my lowest mark of rye, he was in Marc's employ as a day laborer on the house. He and another man, a long-bearded Bohemian, had been sent to Cherryvale where a load of lumber had been offloaded from the train, and the other man sat fuming in the loaded wagon, refusing to join him in a drink and anxious to return to work. Unlike myself Paul seemed not at all flustered by the approach of his employer's wife; while I found my pulse racing and my mouth going dry, he merely doffed his hat and smiled, then mounted the wagon alongside his sullen colleague.

Once he was gone Maggie, who carried over her arms what at first appeared to be a perfectly inert black dog, favored me with that off-center smile that seemed to be mine alone. She seemed to flush, though I thought it be the cold air on her face that made her purse her lips in that shy manner, pleased with herself for some reason she was anxious to tell.

"Good day, Bill."

"Maggie." I tipped my hat, embarrassed at its condition. "Cold enough for you?" I asked idiotically, robbed of my wits by an adolescent tightening of my chest and a tingling in my groin.

"That's what I'm doing here," she said, and she held out the thing in her arms. It was a beaver coat, long and finely cut. "That's from me and Marc, it was meant to be a gift at Christmas, but it hadn't arrived."

I took it from her and examined it without daring a guess at its cost. "You already gave me a book," I babbled, for want of something gracious or clever to say.

"A last-minute substitute, so you wouldn't go empty-handed Christmas morning."

"I much enjoyed it in any case," I said. "I'm well into my second reading." I put on the coat and buttoned it up against the wind. "Thank you kindly."

"It's been breaking my heart, watching you out here in the cold every day with just that old buffalo skin to keep you warm."

Again I felt embarrassed that she saw me in such an unflattering light, and all I could think to say was "Thank you" again.

As she took her leave I noticed Hattie watching down the street in front of the hotel. Maggie greeted her as she passed, a greeting Hattie majestically ignored as she walked my way, her arms crossed in front of her and pressed in tight against her bosom.

"She's spoiling you, Bill."

"It's from him, too, Hattie."

"I don't see him bringing it down to you. Bet you fifty cents he don't even know about it."

"And how could that be when he's got to have paid for it?" I asked her. Three nights before Hattie had snuck out of her room and made her way to the forge, knocking quietly and throwing rocks at the side of the loft until I woke and let her in. She stayed up there under the buffalo robe with me until so close to dawn I was afraid she wouldn't get back to the hotel before her employers did; the whole time she kept going on about how wonderful it was to be abed together the whole night, how that was the way man and woman were supposed to be, and further on in that vein. To me, all it meant was that I had swapped a whole night's sleep for a quick screwing, and the more she went on about how cozy and nice it was the more I felt I'd made a bad trade.

Now she leaned forward, her index finger extended toward my face. "Anyway, I got news for you, Bill Ogden. Francis Comden at the hotel asked me to marry him." I rarely saw Hattie in daylight, and now she struck me as homelier than she had before, rounder of face and duller of eye; this may have been the result of having just seen Maggie, whose countenance was the more beautiful for being slightly reddened by the chill. It may also have had to do with the harshness of Hattie's emotion, which had pinched her mouth and eyes smaller than usual.

"Which one's Comden, now?" There were two Francises at the hotel, and I didn't know the family name of either. The first was the boy at the reception who loved Kate, the one whose beard had not yet started growing and whose voice still cracked merrily when he spoke; the other was a long-faced ex-rebel who never quit talking about the war. I liked them both well enough and thought in either case she'd have done well to accept.

"You know exactly who he is! Anyway, the question isn't who asked me, it's what are you going to do about it?"

"Do about it?" I was confused for a moment, and thought perhaps she wanted me to take a poke at him. "Do you mean to say you're insulted he asked?"

"I mean what are you willing to do to keep me from saying yes?" When I made no answer she elaborated, "Are you going to make me a better offer?"

I could think of no reason why I would want her to say no to such a proposal, save the potential loss of the occasional physical release she offered me, and I would hardly let that stand in the way of the happiness of a girl I considered something of a chum. I knew that wouldn't pass muster as an answer, though. "I'm already married, Hattie" was what came out.

"You're indecent," she hissed at me after a moment's pause, then turned on her heel and ran back to the hotel. I might have followed her and tried to straighten it out, but a trio of livery workers was making their way toward me and they looked thirsty. When I'd served the three of them I looked up and saw that Maggie had been watching the whole time. She was across the street about a hundred feet away, staring at me with that odd half-smile, and she gave me a small, shy wave with her hand at her waist, as though she'd been waiting just to catch my eye, and then hurried on her way. I was delighted, or at any rate I was until I saw that she was walking toward Kate Bender, who greeted her enthusiastically. They walked off together in the direction of the Levals' uncompleted house, and my heart dropped from my chest into my belly when I saw that they were arm in arm like the best of friends.

Once the farm's bitter morning demands were met, my time was mostly taken up with operating the booze wagon and overseeing the construction of the saloon. During this same period Marc was occupied with myriad projects, grand and small, from establishing the Cottonwood Livestock Pen Company to annexing an unincorporated plot of land east of Lincoln Street. The annexation effectively doubled the physical size of Cottonwood, though its southern half was empty grassland. Already, though, the population of the town had begun to swell with word of the construction work his various projects offered, and Marc predicted that building would soon commence there as well. "Prosperity and growth are self-perpetuating, given the right sort of men to promote them at the start," he said to me one evening, slightly in his cups. I had taken the evening off and Gleason stood in my stead, manning the wagon. Marc and I sat on a couple of empty wooden crates in the drawing room of his unfinished house with a bottle of brandy between us.

In the light of the lantern the unfinished walls of the house cast strange and ominous shadows, and Maggie had declined an offer to join us there. The wind whistled through the beams, and Marc laughed affectionately at his wife's superstitious nature.

"That'd be the ghost of an Osage chief, there," he said of a low moaning blast of air from the north. I laughed, too, but despite the fur coat's warmth I wished we were back at the hotel. No fire could be safely built in the incomplete fireplace, and my fingers were stiff, their skin cracking as I rubbed them together. Marc was, or affected to be, completely unfazed by the temperature, and I didn't mention my discomfort for fear of disappointing him. He was in an expansive mood, as he often was, and had just offered me a share of the Livestock Pen Company.

"I don't have anything to invest," I told him honestly. My investment in the saloon had been 100 percent of its existing equity, since all my liquid assets had gone into its construction. I had a little cash set aside from its running, and Marc was paying me a small salary now, but it didn't amount to a tenth of what he was proposing to award me in the cattle pens.

"You'll invest the sweat of your brow," he said, and he slapped me on the back, then handed me the bottle. "You're my friend, and in Cottonwood, Kansas, that's enough to guarantee a place of honor." He'd swallowed more than his usual fill that evening, and he was one of those drunks who get full of bonhomie and sentiment; it was true, though, that I was his only friend in Cottonwood. There were other educated persons in the town, but none he'd taken a liking to. Dr. Salisbury, our physician, had a solid enough background in the sciences and the arts, but he was a sot, and in his cups he railed bitterly at the fate that had brought him west, and often as not he dissolved into tears; we had a pharmacist of some learning as well in Archie Collins, but Archie kept to himself and didn't seem interested in companionship or conversation; Tiny Rector's wife Lillian had been educated at a fine girls' school in New England, but she was tetchy and had to be handled gently at the best of times.

He sat back on the crate and turned around so that he could see the town through the frame of the house. "One day there'll be streets named after us," he said.

"Bill Boulevard," I joked, but he didn't laugh; in fact he got more solemn.

"Every town of any importance has great men behind it at its beginnings. We may not have founded the town, Bill, but you and I are the ones who'll make it known to the world." He sounded right then as if he were hollow, and only by being that great man could he fill himself up again.

"I guess that's so, Marc," I said, and he was quiet for a while. I handed him the bottle again and he took a slug.

"What brought you here?" he asked. "I know you staked a claim, but why'd you want to do that?"

"I wanted to make a living, I suppose."

"Not much of a living, farming. You're an educated man."

"I suppose I wanted to be in at the beginning of things. Osage hadn't been gone long, territory was practically empty. I guess I thought there'd be opportunities here to make a dollar."

"Aha," he said, pleased with himself. "And there weren't many of those until lately, were there?"

"There was the saloon."

"Aha," he said again. "A man of vision who saw a need and filled it."

"Well, the old saloon was gone by then. You had to buy whiskey from Tiny or George, and neither one of them'd let a man drink on the premises."

"And so you quit farming."

"Didn't quit, exactly." I, too, had drunk more than I was accustomed to, and the words I wanted weren't forthcoming in precisely the way I wanted them to be. "Tried to quit."

"Why don't you sleep at the farm?" he asked.

I nearly told him it was none of his goddamned business, but the words were slow enough in coming that I was able to hold them off. "Too far to ride," I said.

"You ride there in the morning," he said. "What's the difference from riding there at night? You could save yourself the rent you pay that smith."

What he really wanted to know about was Ninna, I knew. He'd seen us together only once, at Christmas, and seen the way we acted with each other; not like a husband and wife, but like a man and a woman who didn't like each other much playing at it for an afternoon. And of course he'd heard stories. What the hell, I decided; we're comrades and business partners, Marc and I, and we're drunk besides. So I told him about Ninna and the men, and why I wouldn't go back now. He listened and nodded.

"You say she's a Dane?"

"Born in Copenhagen. Her old man got into some sort of a scrape and had to leave, ended up in Columbus, Ohio, operating a photographer's studio. That's where I met her. I was learning the trade from the old man."

"Why'd you marry her in the first place?" he asked.

"I was twenty, the war was over, and she was a big, healthy, pretty gal. Her old pa had a little money, too. Next thing I knew little Clyde was on his way and I was still working as her pa's helper, tending bar after hours, working those kinds of jobs and trying to figure out something more promising."

Marc handed me back the bottle. "Woman's infidelity is so much more treacherous than man's. Why do you suppose that is?"

"I haven't been living the monastic life myself since I left the farm."

"Still, she'd forgive you for it, wouldn't she? But you can't forgive her. It's a different sort of treachery. Different in kind, not degree."

I just nodded. We finished the bottle and left it standing there on the unvarnished parquet next to the crates, from which we then rose. Upright he proved to be drunker than I'd thought, and he nearly crashed to the ground stepping down from the veranda onto the lawn. Theirs was a large property and there was no one about as we crossed it, Marc veering from left to right and holding both arms out for balance, as if he were feeling about for a railing on either side. Abruptly he slowed and then stopped, and I stepped aside, having seen it happen a time or two tending bar. He knelt and spewed, finishing with a noise I first thought to be a whimper of self-pity, but which quickly revealed itself as laughter.

"I trust," he said, "that my regurgitation will remain a confidential matter." He kept laughing, and I helped him to his feet and we ambled over the lawn and crossed Seward and First Streets to the hotel.

There in their rooms Maggie sat waiting for Marc. The rough-hewn sitting room was even more overstuffed than it had been at Christmas, its plain wooden walls completely obscured by furnishings too elegant for it by half; presumably the bedchamber beyond was similarly jammed. It wasn't nearly enough to furnish the house they were building, though, and I had been told that there were three times this much houseware in storage and at least that much on order from back east. It was cramped, but the dry warmth emanating from the stove, specially installed for them, was deeply satisfying to a man who slept in a converted hayloft.

Maggie clucked at our drunken state and we helped Marc to bed, where he immediately began to snore. She stepped outside the door with me when I took my leave and whispered to me in the dark hallway.

"I hope you enjoyed yourself," she said.

"Sorry about this," I said, mistaking her quiet tone for one of reproach. "Didn't realize how soused he was until he tried to walk."

"That's all right. Marc doesn't really take much time for his own pleasure, he can get drunk once a year if he wants to."

She was giving me that look, the one that made me feel certain the man we'd just put into bed wasn't her husband at all; I just nodded, afraid that if I spoke I'd say something foolish. "Good night," I managed to stammer, and I carefully picked my way down the staircase. I didn't hear the latch of their door click shut until after I was out of her sight.

Several days hence I was invited to join the Levals in their suite for an afternoon's entertainment, and I found that young Gleason was again available to stand in my stead at the booze wagon except for a brief period when he would serve as my photographic assistant. Having fetched my good suit of clothes from the farm that morning I reported to the hotel promptly at three o'clock in Gleason's company, carrying between us the stereographic camera, a tripod designed for the other, larger camera, a dark tent, and enough chemical solutions to open a drugstore of our own.

In the suite upstairs I was dismayed to find Katie Bender present, apparently as their guest. Her silken afternoon dress, of a similar cut and quality to Maggie's own, was stiff and new, a gift from our hosts. Hattie was there, too, having brought up a tray of drinks, and she scowled at me with unconcealed disgust; we had not spoken since our exchange on the street, and if I ignored her it was because I was demonstrating to Gleason the setup of the camera, composing and focusing on the *canapé* upon which Marc and Maggie would sit for their portrait, facing the main window. With the windows and door thrown open, the room was barely bright enough for portraiture, but Maggie refused to wait for the completion of their house or that of the new studio next to my unfinished saloon, insisting upon a stereographic commemoration of their months in the suite.

I worked carefully at focusing; indoors, with only the light from the open windows and doors as illumination, my depth of field would be perilously shallow, even with a lengthy exposure. In these situations one often ended up with one's subjects as nebulous blurs before perfectly crisp backgrounds, and I had cut only two glass plates for the occasion. Katie and Maggie seated themselves upon the *canapé*, staring upside down at my focusing glass, and as I ratcheted the lensboard forward and backward it was Maggie's face I watched, trying to forget Katie's was there next to it.

"Have you heard Hattie's good news, Bill?" Katie asked me with a smile of such pure ingenuousness it had to be false. I didn't know whether or not Hattie had accepted Comden's proposal, nor whether an announcement had been made, so I said no.

Katie looked over at her chambermate and winked. "She's engaged to marry Francis Comden in the spring."

"Francis from downstairs? Really?" Maggie seemed genuinely surprised. "He's just a boy."

"He's twenty," Hattie snapped with greater venom than she evidently intended; she immediately forced herself to smile. "We're going to go to Topeka to live."

I pulled my head from the black shadecloth and noted that Gleason had finished setting up the dark tent in a corner of the room. In a moment I was gratefully inside it, preparing the first of the glass plates. When it had been coated I slipped it into a tray of silver nitrate and Gleason began preparing a second.

"Isn't that wonderful?" Katie said. "Young Francis has decided to study the law."

Marc curled his lower lip in distaste. "Well, I suppose there's always call for lawyering. The money doesn't add up to much, though, unless you get into politics."

"Will there be anything else, ma'am?" Hattie asked with exaggerated formality.

"No, Hattie dear. You may go. Congratulations on your engagement," Maggie answered sweetly, without condescension and with a smile of such genuine benevolence that the hateful glare Hattie shot back at her shocked me. Maggie paid it no mind, or perhaps she didn't notice. Marc was looking elsewhere, bored out of his wits, and Katie looked at me, her right eyebrow raised in a self-satisfied manner that made me want to strike her.

Hattie stopped for a moment in the doorway and met my eyes, her features softening dolefully until she seemed no longer homely but very nearly beautiful, and though she appeared on the brink of saying something to me she simply closed the door and hurried down the stairs. I thought I heard a sob through the door but I wasn't sure, and I came close to following her. There was nothing to be done, though, and in a moment Maggie's presence and the task at hand chased all thoughts of Hattie from my mind.

In five minutes the first plate was ready, and I mounted the plate holder and made my exposure of Marc and Maggie sitting side by side. They were stiff and glum, the result of my injunction to remain very still, and I knew in advance the picture would have none of their personalities in it. When Gleason brought out the second plate holder, Katie insisted on playing a part in the composition, a suggestion which Maggie enthusiastically seconded. The three of them were at least livelier than the Levals by themselves, though it was difficult to make Katie understand the necessity of keeping her head still for the exposure.

When it was done, I retreated to the dark tent for the final treatment of the plates. Once they were finished I examined them and found their densities were acceptable and their images sharp. I then demonstrated to Gleason the proper technique of varnishing, after which I sent him on his way to open the saloon wagon; I would return the equipment to the forge's loft later with Marc's help.

"Can we see them?" Maggie asked.

"These are negatives," I said, delaying their disappointment by a day. "I'll print them out tomorrow."

"Well, isn't this cozy?" she said. She parked her silken bustle on one of four chairs surrounding a table, and after closing the door to the hallway and drawing the curtains Katie sat in its opposite.

"Wait until you hear about the entertainment they've got in store for us, Bill." Marc looked to me like he'd rather go have his front teeth pulled.

"We're going to speak with the other world," Katie piped up enthusiastically. Maggie looked slightly embarrassed, but I sensed it was directed at her husband's skepticism rather than at the ludicrous nature of the activity itself.

I was directed to sit between Katie and Maggie. At that close range I detected a whiff of eau de rose rising from Katie's considerable bosom, a scent which mingled uneasily with the musky odor that emanated from her normally and which I might have found uncomfortably arousing were I not sitting across from a woman who made Katie look like a hairy-knuckled muleskinner. I surmised that the eau de rose was Maggie's gift to her as well.

Marc spoke up as he took his seat opposite me. "You think we might get to talk to Abe Lincoln?" Maggie gave him a sharp look, and he raised his hands before him in a protestation of innocence. "I'm not making light."

"You'd be well advised not to, Marc," Kate said, her eyes wide and serious. "The spirits despise mockery, and skepticism, too." She sounded like a bad actress playing a part on a stage, her voice deep and sepulchral like that of an old dowager rather than a young woman of twenty-three or twenty-four. Her accent had something vaguely English about it; she reminded me a little of a ham actor I'd seen once in Philadelphia playing the ghost in *Hamlet*, all quavering moans and groans and upraised, waving arms.

I noted that on the center table a single candle awaited lighting. Kate ordered us to lay our hands on the table as she lit it.

"Now, we must be silent for a moment and join hands as I attempt to make the crossing," Kate said. She closed her eyes, and we sat there in silence, holding hands and gazing at the candle's flame in the center of the table. I became aware, as Kate began to moan to my left, of the gentle rubbing of my palm by Maggie's thumb on my right.

"Yes, I hear you, spirit. Make me your earthly lips, tongue, and teeth, I pray," Kate said, her groaning even huskier than before, her head swaying left and right, forward and backward until she snapped upright, perfectly still.

"I'm here among you now," she said in a flat, masculine voice that was quite convincing.

"Identify yourself, spirit, and tell us why you have returned," she said in her own persona, or at any rate the one she was using for the séance. To my right Maggie's hand tightened its grip on my own.

"Nigh on to six weeks now I lay unclaimed on the prairie. I come forth to accuse," the purported spirit said, and despite my absolute disbelief in the present nonsense I felt a cold shudder move upward from the base of my spine like a wave to my scalp, for the voice sounded eerily familiar.

"Who do you accuse, spirit?" Kate said, and at that moment I believe all three of us had to restrain a simultaneous urge to correct her use of the pronoun.

"I accuse a man I wronged of wronging me in return," said the masculine voice, and I was ever more certain that I knew it.

"How did you wrong this man, spirit?" Kate said.

"Upon arriving at his farm in his absence I took advantage of his addled wife's loneliness and allowed her to take me into her bed." With that confession I finally recognized the flat monotone of the drummer who'd screwed Ninna, and I supposed that this was a confidence he had exchanged with Katie in the process of seducing her, or in its aftermath. "He thereafter took my pistol and he shot out the crown of my hat." Katie's imitation of the drummer's cadences and delivery and of his nasal drone were impeccable, based on my recollection of our sole, brief encounter.

"Surely, spirit, these are no great wrongs compared to your befouling the man's marriage bed," Kate said, the very soul of reason.

"Ah, would that that were all he had done, Kate," the ghost lamented.

Kate shuddered. "Spirit, how is it that you know my name?"

"Kate, Kate. It's I, A. J. Harticourt, who spent his last night of life in the hospitable shelter of your family home."

"Mr. Harticourt? But word hadn't reached us that you'd died."

"I was followed, Kate, and when I set out the next morning the blackguard snuck behind me and crushed my skull with a hammer. He then robbed my body of what wealth I possessed, and even took my sample pots and pans."

Maggie gasped and once again tightened her grip.

At this point Kate opened her eyes for the first time in several minutes and looked square into mine, resembling nothing so much as a rabid wolfhound, teeth bared in hateful anger. "*You*. Saloon-keeper. You slew me for revenge and for gain." The drummer's low, dull mumble had metamorphosed into a raucous shriek, and Kate rose slightly from her chair without letting go of my hand or Marc's.

Marc's mouth had drawn itself tighter than usual, his contempt for the proceedings transparent.

I didn't mind Katie's game so much, though I will admit to being mildly unnerved by her performance. Maggie, though, clearly took it seriously, shifting her eyes uneasily between Katie's altered face and my own resolutely calm expression, and I wanted badly to disabuse her of the notion that I had killed the drummer. "Drummer," I said to Katie. "Tell me, if you're really him, what make of pistol I took off of you."

She didn't hesitate. "It was a Derringer, double barrel, given to me by my own brother."

"It was a Dragoon. And what was the hat made of? The one I shot the hell out of?"

"The hat was wool felt, and brand-new, too."

"It was silk, and if anyone wants proof of that it's sitting in my booze wagon at this moment." I looked at Katie as I said it, and her eyes shut again.

"Are you a deceitful spirit, then?" Katie cried out, and no reply in the other voice followed.

"I didn't know such a thing existed as a lie from the other world," Marc said with a low chuckle, and that earned him a glare from his wife.

Kate then began moaning once again, and I had the impression we were to be visited by another spirit, presumably one with a story less prone to contradiction. Maggie was quite excited now, leaning forward and peering at Kate's head, which had recommenced its rhythmic back-and-forth motions.

With Katie murmuring quietly, Maggie started rubbing my

palm again with her thumb, and to my absolute and total shock the dainty, pointed toe of her shoe slid its way under the cuff of my trouserleg and up my shin, which it rubbed very delicately.

That slight friction had what I presumed was its desired effect upon me physically. Moments later when we first heard shots fired into the air and the bell began ringing I found it somewhat inconvenient to have to stand and open the door. Now the sounds were joined by shouting in the street, but Kate seemed not to notice, as she was babbling away with her eyes still closed, and Maggie sat there looking confused and culpable. The prick-stand she'd inspired had softened somewhat by the time I got to the bottom of the stairs, Marc at my heels, and when I got outside and saw what the commotion was about it melted away completely: the forge, my second home for all the long months since I'd opened my saloon, was burning.

To be more precise, the loft was what was burning. White smoke poured out the back of the building, filling the sky to the south; men were running into and out of the lower portion, and orange flames danced obscenely through the blackening boards of the upper part of the structure. Marc and I took our places and ran buckets of water back and forth with the others from the well at the end of Main Street in an attempt to douse the flames, but by the time the fire was discovered the loft was already well ablaze, and before long it was all we could do to keep the fire from spreading to the adjacent buildings.

We were lucky that day in that there was no wind to speak of, and we managed to control the blaze until it had burned the forge down to a smoldering, blackened frame surrounding the anvil itself and the chimney. We continued to splash the charred wood with water well into the early part of the evening, and it was decided that we would watch the ruins through the night in shifts. It was then that I first spoke to Otis, beside whom I had been fighting the fire for several hours.

"For a change I got a little ahead of myself and I thought by God I'll for once go home for lunch like the wife wants me to. Ten minutes after that I heard the bell ringing." He shook his big head and looked like he wanted to cry.

We stepped into the smoky shell, and for the first time it came to me that I had nowhere to lay my head that night. Otis examined the forge itself in an effort to determine whether it or his tools were salvageable, and beneath the spot where the loft had hung I found the remains of my larger camera. Its brass lens barrel was warped by the heat and its glass elements had bubbled and were now clouded to the milky white of a cataracted eye. Its case and lensboard and bellows had been consumed by the heat down to a blackish gray ash, festooned with useless and misshapen metal fittings.

"Loft went up first, Otis," Tim Niedel said, standing behind us. "Seems odd, don't it?"

"It does," I said, and Otis nodded, though he didn't look as though he was giving it much thought. Something made me turn, though, at that very moment, and behind us I spied Hattie, her eyes brimming with tears, staring at me defiantly. Once she'd gotten my attention she lifted her skirts and ran up the street toward the hotel, and in the confusion I didn't think of her again that night. I relieved Gleason at the back of the wagon and announced a round of free drinks for all the firefighting volunteers.

The next morning I rose early, awakened by the cold beneath a thin comforter in a second floor room at the hotel and sorely missing my buffalo robe and fur coat. Around eleven, after my work at the farm was done and before opening up the booze wagon, I prepared to print the stereo views I had taken the day before. I secured the paper and plates within a pair of printing frames and set them out on the roof of the hotel to print out. Even in the negative state I could see that my instincts regarding the first pose had been correct, and this was borne out when the prints were done; the dull Maggie and Marc who peered out from that *canapé* looked mesmerized. On the second they were indeed more like themselves, bright-eyed and wry, but Katie, as I'd anticipated, was recorded only as an oval blur above a dress; I had no stereoscope handy, but was practiced enough in the art of free-viewing that I was able to coax from it a three-dimensional image with my naked eyes. Marc and Maggie stood out in perfect relief against a soft *canapé* with Katie Bender between them, her head a hazy, silvery apparition in which could just be made out several faint impressions of disembodied eyes and teeth. My instinct was to chemically clean the plate for re-use, but something stopped me and I placed it in its padded berth in my negative case.

The talk of the town that day was primarily of the fire, and the work that would be involved in rebuilding Otis's shop. Marc offered to divert the materials from the construction on his house, which would cease until the forge was completed and more lumber had arrived, and to facilitate a bank loan for him. The other item that occupied the idle tongues and brains of Cottonwood was the elopement the night before of the widow Hattie Steig and young Francis Comden, who had slipped out of town under cover of night; I don't believe it occurred to anyone but me that Hattie was the author of the blaze.

3

COTTONWOOD, KANSAS
MARCH 1873

The Occasion of Sin

It had been scarcely three months since Marc Leval's arrival in Cottonwood, followed shortly by that of the railroad and then the cattle town rumors, and already the town bore little resemblance to its once quiet and modest self. Marc now controlled the Citizens' National Bank of Cottonwood at the end of Main Street and had evicted its president, Stanley Eaton, from his office in its rear; the office was full of supplicants of one kind or another from sunup to sundown, looking for funds to start up this new business or that, and often Marc didn't even go home for lunch. Stanley now sat at a forlorn desk behind the teller cage, scornfully refusing to acknowledge any greetings through the bars, and at least once he flew into a rage when an impatient newcomer innocently asked Bernard Stanton, the skeletal teller, when they were going to put in a second cage for the other teller.

I would be hard-pressed to estimate the population of the town at that time, but it certainly approached a thousand people at its height, more than three quarters of them male. Men arrived every day on horseback and on foot and by wagon, and few left. One of the rare locals who didn't stay was Katie Bender; she had been asked by her family to return to the farm and help out at the inn, which had apparently prospered with the increased traffic across the prairie. I was glad to see her go; to my surprise so was Maggie, who, according to Marc, had come to the depressing conclusion that her friend was a charlatan.

The men who came seeking employment generally found it. There was so much anticipatory building going on, and so much money being attracted from elsewhere and spent, that the casual observer would have thought the cattle pens were in place already, but in fact the profits were all in the future. When the railroad tracks had finally reached town a boxcar was taken off the track and set up for use as a depot, pending completion of a more permanent facility a few feet to the west. Every train that arrived brought lumber with it, and it wasn't ever enough. Construction of a proper Methodist church was now under way, financed by a subscription hinging on the faith that new congregants would soon be flocking to Cottonwood alongside the day laborers and speculators who had materialized in Leval's wake. Plans were afoot for its Baptist and Congregationalist equivalents, for which building societies had already been organized. The site of the Methodist church was across Main Street from the former general meeting house in which its services had once been held, demolished now to make way for the expansions of the saloon and the forge. Through Marc's intercession Otis had managed a generous bank loan for the reconstruction of the latter, now complete and operational and doing boom business; he had been able to take on not one but two apprentices to replace the errant Perkey. New houses, not dissimilar in style or size to the one I'd built on the farm, were going up along newly laid out streets, and some were already occupied; our town's only attorney and land agent was, like Marc, overburdened and frenzied from the moment he opened his doors in the morning until he closed them at night. He occupied a brand-new two-story wooden building, completed at the end of February; until then he had done business in a canvas tent at the corner of First and Seward Streets, nearly directly across from the Leval mansion. All the previously existing houses in the vicinity of Seward and Main were bought up and knocked down to make room for new commercial buildings, and both sides of First Street were now lined with new houses finished and unfinished. At the northeast corner of Seward and Main a competing saloon had gone up, as Marc had predicted, and to show that we were good sports and unafraid of their sort of competition we sold them the remaining fixtures from my old saloon. To the south of it a restaurant and a second barber shop had opened, the former offering meals at a variety of prices at all hours, and the latter handling the overflow from Lem Gibson's parlor on Main.

The town had also become a haven for all the sorts of vice that follow any influx of men into such a place without the civilizing influence of women. A gambling hall opened at the corner of Main and Lincoln, and a second followed on its heels at First and Lincoln, each offering poker, faro, monte, roulette, and chucker-luck. Having stopped into both establishments I can report that none of the aforementioned games appeared to me to be honestly run; this naturally had no effect on the crowds lining up to play them, and as long as a down-on-his-luck player was allowed to win a respectable sum once in a while there were no complaints.

On the south side of town a French-style house began going up that rivaled in ornateness though not in square footage the Leval home, and the word about town was that it was to be the city's first brothel. At that moment a number of prostitutes operated from a handful of modest private homes not far from the growing mansion, and a greater number did so outside the town limits in a small, insalubrious tent city. These women were obviously not of the upper ranks of their profession; such a trade would apparently have to wait for the completion of the brothel building. In the meantime the Barneses had just expelled two apparently wholesome and bourgeoise women who had taken a room together at the hotel, after the discovery that they were entertaining gentlemen in their rooms after hours for compensation. This was no surprise to me, since their room was just down the hall from the one I'd taken after the smithy fire, and they were indiscreet about noises. Their confederate was a new employee of the hotel, a young woman who had replaced Kate Bender in the dining room and who supplemented her waitressing income with a percentage of the receipts from the two ladies, plus the occasional direct commission when the overflow of clients called for reinforcements. Though their prices were high enough to restrict their clientele to the more refined sort—the building contractors and some of the local burghers—it was impossible to keep such an enterprise secret for long, and complaints from other guests soon alerted the Barneses to the illicit activity under their roof.

In my leisure hours, which were not many, I took to photographing the town's growth, and Marc agreed to buy prints of all the stereo views I made for the city of Cottonwood. I had an idea that when the town reached its full size and grandeur there would be a national market for such views. I found, too, that I was enjoying the work, particularly now that I had in the person of Gleason an assistant to help in preparing my plates; my speed increased considerably and so did my output, and if I may say so the quality of the images improved as well. The work was mainly restricted to midday, before opening the saloon, but that was the perfect time to capture a view of a rising building, skeletal against an empty field behind it, or a group of laborers upon a scaffolding, or a prostitute before her canvas tent.

The new saloon was a monument to grandeur, with a front and backbar of solid oak manufactured in Pennsylvania and shipped to

Cottonwood in pieces, and a footrail of real brass, with spittoons to match, and a stove twice as large as its predecessor that kept the whole building warm and comfortable. Young Gleason, whose biblical opposition to insobriety had evaporated with the realization that bartending paid better than farm work, labored alongside me every night, and showed himself to be skilled at handling crowds and accomplishing several unrelated tasks more or less at once, which made him a better bartender than I. He was tall, with a long face, jug ears, and a garrulousness that made up for my occasional bouts of unsociability. Soon, however, it became evident that a third man would be necessary at least part-time to handle the crowds, particularly on Saturday night.

Marc and I were making money faster than I had ever thought we would, and yet all the money the men were spending in the saloon was money Marc, or in some cases his Eastern associates, had paid them. For all the economic activity afoot in Cottonwood at that time, the flow of cash was almost completely outward, and would remain so until the cattle began arriving; some found it troubling that they had not arrived yet. Late one cold Thursday evening in March, Alf Cletus drunkenly questioned Marc Leval's motives before a crowd of men who were earning a good living working for him.

Alf had been drinking since five in the afternoon, and it was now approaching nine o'clock. "Bond issue. Sure, we'll do that, we all got gold eagles flying before our eyes, we don't mind voting for the railroad coming. I just want to know one thing: where them two come from in the first place, and where'd they get that money they been tossing around here like birdseed?"

I was working fast, dispensing shots and making change for the constantly shifting, bustling mass of men at the bar. "That's two things, Alf," I said, trying to lighten things, but next to him at the bar was Herbert Braunschweig, a one-eyed carpenter who was working for Marc, and he tugged at Alf's sleeve. They were fast friends, but Herbert had been drinking nearly as long as Alf had.

"Listen, you skin-pated piece of cowshit, you're talking about a man's putting this whole town to work and on the map."

"I ain't saying anything different. All's I'm saying is: where'd all that dough come from?"

"He's from Paris, France, is what I understand, Al," a very inebriated, very loud stonemason said.

"He's from around Chicago," I said, though I wasn't at all certain where I had got that impression. I knew he wasn't French by birth, though, having heard him pronounce the names of the wines from Bordeaux and Champagne that he wanted me to stock alongside the corn and rye whiskies, bourbon, and gin that were my mainstays as they had been in the old place.

"I don't give hind tit where he's from," said one-eyed Herbert. "He's paying a good wage and turning this little town into a city, and I don't like to hear him spoke about that way."

Alf let out a long sigh and closed his eyes for a few moments, gathering what remained of his intellectual forces. When he spoke his tempo was slow and his tone pedantic. "Look, friend, I'm not saying anything bad about our friend Marc, who's done us all the service of constructing this magnificent booze palace. I'm just curious, is all. If he wants to come and put Tiny Rector out of his job as mayor, that's okay, too.

"All's I'm saying," Alf went on, "is why here?"

"Railroad's here now," the other man said.

"Railroad's come through lots of other places."

"And the new cattle trail, up from Oklahoma."

Alf cleared his throat loudly and unloaded into the spittoon with a dramatic, wet gob that echoed superbly upon contact. "I seen no evidence of any trail coming up this way, nor can I think of any reason another trail would be needed this far east."

"A shorter rail trip to Chicago," I offered.

"Maybe. Though the length of the rail trip means less than the length of the driving trail."

"You're talking through your hat, you son of a bitch." Herbert squinted his one eye and drew back as if to slug Alf, and I put my hand on the sap behind the bar just in case I needed to put him down; Alf, oblivious to the violent hostility he was arousing in his companion, once again shut his eyes to gather his wits.

"Let me start again," he said with an exaggerated show of patience, and I was sure that whatever he said next would provoke a blow; at that moment, however, the door opened and in from the cold walked the subject at hand.

Alf looked up at Marc in the guilty manner of a schoolboy and ceased speaking. The rest of the saloon cried out to him as one, however, and swarmed about him as he made his way to the bar and took his place with almost clairvoyant precision between Herbert and Alf.

"Evening, Bill," he said, extending his hand to me. "Looks as though business is booming."

And it was; making the new saloon the first order of business upon his arrival had been a shrewd move on his part, for my old one couldn't have accommodated the influx of laborers his construction projects had drawn. He spoke for a few minutes with Herbert about some construction materials for the pens, and latter's sullen distemper evaporated; he seemed to have completely forgotten Alf's existence.

Within twenty minutes, though, Alf started up again. He talked so loud that Marc could scarcely ignore him, and finally he turned to say hello.

"Say, there, Alf, didn't mean to ignore you that way," he said, shaking his hand. Alf hadn't held it out and was too drunk to effectively pull it away before it had been well and truly shaken, but he scowled just the same.

"I'd just like you to tell me one thing straight. Where the hell'd you come from, and what the hell you doing here really?"

"That's two things, Alf," I said again.

"I'm from Chicago," Marc said.

"I been to Chicago once," said Herbert, his eye blinking rapidly.

He began to raise his voice. "As for what I'm doing here, I'm taking a little town and turning it into a city. I'm giving a whole bunch of men jobs where there were none before. I'm bringing the advantages of civilization to the prairie." By the end his voice was ringing in the rafters like a Chatauqua speech, and then he brought it down low and put a friendly hand on Alf's shoulder. "That's what I'm doing here, Alf."

"I thought you was French, Marc," said the man who'd offered the same opinion earlier. "You talk a little of it, don't you?"

"My father was. I scarcely knew him."

The man from Independence pointed at Alf. "This jackass here's been talking about you all night. Wonders what brought you here, trying to make it sound like it's something not right."

Marc reached out his hands and clasped the shoulder of each of his neighbors, as though entreating them to make peace. He took in a deep breath, preparing to speechify; he had at these times a way of sounding as though he were on the stump, projecting to the very back of the room and pausing for dramatic emphasis as he met briefly the eyes of each listener in his turn.

"That's a natural question, I suppose. I was tiring of the slaughterhouses and thinking I wanted a change, and my Maggie never did cotton to city life too well. The highborn of Chicago never did take us up socially, and I found that I had a yearning for the open spaces of my youth. When I learned from an associate that the Kansas City, Illinois, and Nebraska railroad was planning to make this a cattle depot, I saw my opportunity before me. I sold my packing interests and began making preparations to move my household here."

The exaggerated formality of his enunciation didn't sound quite natural in his mouth, but it struck just the right chord with the crowd. "You see," Herbert hissed at Alf, "innocent as a babe."

Alf shrugged, unconvinced but unwilling to press his point in the company of the man himself. Though Marc was not a large man—five foot five or six, I'd guess, without his boots on—he had a more impressive presence than many a six-footer I'd known, and just standing there managed to intimidate him in a way large, angry Herbert had not.

Later in the evening when things had slowed somewhat Marc and I stepped out behind the building, ostensibly to discuss the trip he and Maggie were planning back to Chicago to attract more capital for the town, with time spent in Kansas City to meet with railroad officials. I was startled, then, when he grabbed me by the lapels and gave me a little shove.

"Listen to me. When you hear talk like that starting up, I expect you to shut it down and do it quick, you understand me?"

Resisting the temptation to remove his hands from my jacket, I responded as calmly as I could. "Man's got a right to speak his mind, Marc."

"Not when he's talking about me. Or my town. And not when he's in my saloon. Is that clear?"

"Mister Leval, I'll ask you only once to remove your hands from my person."

He let go and even in the dim light out back I could see him pouting. "I picked you, out of all the citizens of Cottonwood, to be my friend and right hand. You're poised to make yourself a fortune in the coming years, and you ought to remember that when you speak to me."

Feeling a little better I adopted a friendly air, not too obsequious. "You wanted to talk to me about your trip to Chicago?"

"I did," he said brightly, apparently relieved that I hadn't taken offense. "There are things you'll need to occupy yourself with while I'm gone. I can't trust Tiny Rector with anything."

He stopped speaking when the front door opened and someone came stumbling out. He walked right past us in the dark, muttering to himself, and we both recognized Alf's voice.

"Cletus," Marc shouted.

"Huh?" Alf peered in our direction and saw nothing.

"It's Marc. Bill's here, too. Come around back."

Alf seemed to hesitate, then I saw his shadow making its way carefully in our direction.

"What is it?" Alf asked, sounding none too friendly.

Marc clasped his shoulder. "I just wanted to say Cottonwood needs men like you, who aren't afraid to speak up and say what's on their minds. No hard feelings."

"Oh . . . that's good, I suppose," Alf said, full of whiskey and mistrust as he turned and wandered off into the night.

"Better put a muzzle on that cur next time he opens his maw." He smacked me on the arm and sauntered off into the night. "I'd go back in for another shot, but drink hinders what Milady awaits." For a minute or two I stood there in the dark, looking up at the sky and hating my best friend in the world; then I forgave him and went back in.

By the first of April I had engaged the third bartender, a dutchman named Hans who claimed to have tended bar in Westport. Since three men were only required on Saturday, I began to take Tuesday and Thursday nights off. Before the arrival of the Levals I wouldn't have sought a free evening away from the saloon or known what to do with one. Now I dined with them on those nights at their newly finished home, the undeniable centerpiece of our little town and the new standard against which all future buildings would be measured. A mansion of red brick with a mansard roof in the Parisian style, it stood at the end of First Street a block off of Main, its chimneys and its widow's walk visible from almost any vantage point in Cottonwood. Off the master bedroom and the two guest bedrooms were canopied balconies, and two columnated verandas ran along the outside, a large one in front and a smaller one before a separate entrance to the drawing room. Nearly every sort of filigree within the bounds of architectural good taste found itself incorporated into its design, and upon first stepping inside after its completion I had to suppress a laugh, thinking as I involuntarily did of my first crude dugout house, the one I'd built awaiting the arrival of Ninna and the boy. Here was a house with velvet wallcoverings, marble statuary, and classical molding not three miles from that pathetic troglodyte structure, and scarcely more than three years hence.

Elaborate, multi-course meals were prepared on these nights by a tall and buxom Frenchwoman of forty-five or so known as Madame Renée, thin of lip but otherwise not unattractive except for a distractingly dead right eye. Her English had the charming lilt of the Bretons, as Celtic as it was Gallic, and one afternoon she deigned to speak with me while she prepared a duck liver terrine for that evening.

She had been thrice married and widowed, she told me; the first husband was gored by a bull when she was a girl of twenty and pregnant with her first and only child, a son who was now a functionary in Nantes. I tried to imagine her minus twenty-five hard years, in wooden sabots and *costume folklorique*, weeping over the broken farmboy whose baby she carried. Her second husband, a watchmaker, had died more prosaically on board the ship that was taking them to America and rested now in Davy Jones's locker. Soon after her arrival in America she settled in Boston with a Beacon Hill family; she was an experienced domestic cook, having plied that trade in France between her marriages, and a French cook was a fashionable extravagance at that time. Seven years into her service there, without her employers' permission or foreknowledge, she married the head butler, with whom she had been dallying for nearly that entire period.

The head of the family reacted to this news by summarily dismissing them both. Madame Renée's reaction was angry but philosophical; she had held no fewer than eight such jobs in the twelve years between the death of the Breton farmer and her marriage to the watchmaker. Her new husband, however, had been in the family's employ in one position or another since arriving from Liverpool more than twenty years earlier, and his first instinct was to abandon his new bride and beg for his position back; upon being refused he drowned himself in Boston Harbor. She shook her head as she described her trip to the morgue and the haranguing she'd given her waterlogged bridegroom, for she'd already found work with a family that was in need of a butler. That was the end of marriage for her but not, she said with a wink of her good eye, the end of love. I was not unmoved in her presence—her speech alone brought pleasantly to mind another youngish French widow of my early acquaintance, and a murmured *"prends-moi"* would have been enough to rouse me to the task—but she was employed in the household of the woman I loved, and I resisted the temptation to respond to her coquetry. When she asked me, then, why my wife never accompanied me to dinner I thought it best to change the subject; I complimented her effusively on the elaborate meal I had shared with the Levals two nights previous, and she replied with justifiable pride that her employers ate that well and elegantly always, whether in the presence of guests or not.

But guests there were, that night and nearly every other: primarily bankers and railroad men anxious to court Marc's favor, though the prominent citizens of Cottonwood also joined them at table with some frequency. With my own exception, though, I don't believe the Levals counted any of Cottonwood's own as friends. Katie had not been replaced in Maggie's affections by any of the local women, though by and large these women seemed to think kindly of her, particularly those who had been her dinner guests.

After the meal had been served we would retire to the parlor where Maggie would play the violin and I the piano, together and separately. I was an indifferent accompanist at best. When first invited to play I had not laid my fingers upon a keyboard in five years

or more; my former facility might have returned to me with an hour
or so's daily practice, but pending the arrival of the piano we'd ordered for the saloon this was impossible, and so I served her mostly
as timekeeper for sentimental Irish tunes and bits of Italian opera.
On one occasion we were joined by an officer of the KCI&N, who
sang an adaptation of Bach for solo baritone with great skill and
sensitivity. Afterward he explained gleefully over Leval's brandy
how the railroad was going to chisel a bunch of farmers out of
some land for its right-of-way to our west.

When we played Marc sat back and beamed at his wife with
great pride, and it was plain how much he adored her; even at
those times, though, I felt no shame regarding my powerful yearning for Maggie, which claimed much of my attention during those
months. It was in fact at those times that I desired her the most ar-
dently, listening to her crystalline tone over my leaden hammering,
seeing her bosom rise and fall to the beat that my left hand clumsily
beat out of the keyboard, watching her face flush over certain difficult passages. Often as not I remained seated at the piano after finishing so as to avoid embarrassment upon standing. I suspected
that she received a similarly erotic excitement from our duets,
though the only evidence I could have offered then was the fact that
she steadfastly refused to meet my gaze while I played for her, and
for several minutes thereafter, as though such an exchange would
reveal more than she dared.

A crowd the like of which the town had not yet seen gathered in the
rain to see Marc off to Chicago. A private railcar had been assigned
to him, aboard which he carried a bottle of French wine and a basket of cold foods prepared by Madame Renée. She could be seen in
the throng flirting with Herbert Braunschweig, about whom she
had asked me the previous week before dinner; her left eye was bad
and his right was gone, and the fact that their good eyes met when

they faced each other made things seem preordained, at least to Madame Renée.

Maggie managed to develop what appeared to be a bad head cold two days before the trip was to begin. The more forcefully her husband argued that she should come along anyway, the worse her symptoms became, and by the time of his departure she was too ill even to come to the depot, and he grudgingly left her behind in the care of Madame Renée and Rose, the new housemaid. She was an Irish girl of sixteen or so who blushed in Marc's presence and seemed to wish his wife didn't exist. Waving to the cheering crowd outside as he stepped aboard, he took me into the private car with him, ostensibly to give me a few last-minute instructions but actually, I think, to show it off. There he put me in charge of his various and sundry construction projects, which in practice meant only that their foremen were to report to me any difficulties that might arise. Stanley Eaton would take over his role at the bank, and Tiny Rector still officially held the mayoralty. Any grave problems were to be reported to him at his hotel in Chicago via telegraph.

I was taken aback several days later to receive at the hotel an envelope with my name on it in Maggie's elegantly swooping hand. Inside was an invitation card, again in her hand:

Mrs. Marc Leval requests the honor of your presence for dinner Tuesday evening at six P.M.

I was delighted to receive it, as I had nowhere but the saloon to go that evening, and I didn't want to risk losing my new barman by cutting two of his three working shifts pending Marc's return. The thought of three weeks passing without Maggie's company had been weighing upon my mind as well, and it was with a light heart that I bounded onto the front veranda of the Leval residence that evening at six. I was met at the door by young Rose, who looked indifferently at me and directed me to the drawing room, where Tiny and Mrs. Rector sat waiting. His face was covered with tiny beads of sweat, which he mopped with a handkerchief upon my taking a seat across from him. Mrs. Rector, whose first name of Lillian I never presumed to use, greeted me in a friendly manner but was scarcely able to tear her attention from the room's furnishings.

"Bill, do you suppose that's silk there?"

"What, the curtains? Sure," I said, having no idea what else they might be.

"It's a hell of a place, all right," Tiny said, and his wife was so enraptured she didn't scold him for cursing. It was a measure of Marc's cocksureness that the mayor's office ought rightfully to be his own that he had never bothered to include the incumbent and his wife among the fair number of other local notables who had dined in his home.

"How many rooms you figure there are, Bill?" Tiny asked in a near whisper.

"I believe there are four bedrooms upstairs. There's a parlor and a dining room, kitchen downstairs."

"And all furnished like this?" Mrs. Rector asked me, a look of utter astonishment on her face. She had a squarish, sharp-angled head, softened by large, heavy-lidded green eyes, and looking at you in just the right way she was nearly a beauty.

"I haven't seen them all," I said.

Maggie chose that moment to make her appearance, and having welcomed us, led us out of the drawing room and into the dining room. There at the long table a fifth place had mysteriously been set. In the candlelight Tiny's squinting face looked like a dried-up apple as we sat. Rose poured us each a glass of red wine from a crystal decanter.

"Bill, I'm so sorry Ninna couldn't be with us after all," Maggie said as we took our places, as though it were something she and I had previously discussed. I was interested to note no sign that she had recently been ill. "Rose, will you remove Mrs. Ogden's place setting please?"

I looked over at the Rectors as Rose complied. Tiny was still overwhelmed by the place, but Maggie's pretense was so transparent that it elicited a little involuntary mou of disapproval from Mrs. Rector, who was normally happy to overlook my marital irregularities. I could understand her discomfort, because there was no avoiding the fact that this felt for all the world like one married couple dining with another.

The first course was vichyssoise, and Maggie presumed to explain that it was intentionally served cold.

"Just because I live on the prairie doesn't make me an idiot," Mrs. Rector snapped. "I went to one of the finest girls' schools in all of New England, I speak French perfectly and I know all about vichyssoise." She pronounced it "vichyswah," and I thought it best not to correct her.

"I do wish I spoke French, Lillian," Maggie said, placing her own hand appeasingly upon Mrs. Rector's. "Having a French name would be so much more splendid if I could pronounce it properly."

Tiny was lapping up his own soup contentedly, to all appearances blind to the discord between his wife and Maggie. "Oh, boy, now, that's a good bowl of soup," he said, wiping a goodly portion of it from his beard with his linen napkin. The second course consisted of terrine of duck's liver in aspic, which Maggie had the good grace not to explain. I spread a bit of mine on a chunk of Madame Renée's bread and elicited a curl of Mrs. Rector's lip; she cut hers daintily with knife and fork and ate it as though it were a cutlet, and her husband and Maggie did the same. It was a lovely concoction regardless of how it was eaten, and I offered the opinion that Madame Renée might do well to open a restaurant.

"She sure would, Bill," Tiny said, his beard below his lip now smeared with duck's liver. "That new one on Seward's sure no good. Took my lunch there yesterday and it was godawful. Meat was tough as pine bark and gamy, too. Don't know where they got it."

"Not easy to get supplies in a place like this," I said.

"This was meat, Bill. So much damned meat around these parts you'd really have to make an effort to find a bad cut." He leaned back in his chair and patted his stomach. "Anyway, in a month or so you'll be able to get anything you want, via the railroad, and a good thing, too. My inventory's had to double of late. It's all moving, too, right out the door."

"Don't talk business at the table."

"I'm not talking business," he said. "This is politics. I was by the land office this afternoon and that Sullivan told me the best thing I ever did as mayor was laying out the town in a grid with regular rectangular parcels, 'cause he's doing thirty transactions a day sometimes and it sure makes it simpler. 'Course when I did that I never thought we'd get so big so fast. Almost makes your head swim."

"Well, it's not all good," Mrs. Rector sniffed. "Some of those changes a town could do without. The fallen women, for example."

"All those men need to be entertained," I said.

"Entertainment needn't entail debasement."

"Indeed it needn't," Maggie agreed. "I believe that a theatre or an opera house is what we'll be needing next."

Again Mrs. Rector sniffed. "Just as bad as the brothels."

"I beg your pardon?" Maggie asked.

"Show people," she said.

Maggie's face flushed, but her response was pre-empted by the return of Rose, who refilled my and Tiny's glasses, took up the plates and scuttled quickly out of the room.

Tiny leaned back again, taking the front legs of his chair off the ground. "Well, it sure makes all those men easier to control." Upon receiving a sharp look from his wife he felt it necessary to clarify. "All's I'm saying is, when you get a whole lot of single men together in one place, you get problems. When they can go get themselves a little . . ." He stopped himself and backtracked. "When they can do a little courting, they comport themselves in a more civilized manner."

"That's enough, Henry."

"All's I'm saying . . ."

"That's enough."

He started to open his mouth, but the door opened and Rose brought in the main course, a pair of *canards à l'orange*, and he set his chair back firmly on the floor in preparation for it.

We were mostly silent during the consumption of the ducks, but Tiny was thinking still; once, his mouth half-full, he said, "Whores ain't all bad for a town, anyway." I honestly don't think he knew he'd spoken it aloud, so wounded and innocent was the expression on his face following the jab he received from his wife's elbow.

After dinner we retired as per usual to the parlor for music, but tonight's recital was briefer than most. The Rectors both lacked musical training, and so in place of Marc's blatant adoration we had Tiny looking on in sweaty consternation at my attempt at a mazurka by Louis Gottschalk, and Mrs. Rector next to him, her contemptuous scowl growing thinner and thinner with each measure I played. Upon finishing I stood regretfully to offer my thanks to the hostess, since the Rectors were plainly anxious to leave, and I suspected that for propriety's sake Mrs. Rector would delay their leavetaking until I took my own.

And so, bundled properly against the chill of the night and after some chatter between the women, the Rectors and I made our way out into the evening.

"Say, Bill, why don't we drop Lillian off and you and I'll go get a drink. I got a couple of things I wanted to discuss with you. City business."

That suited me fine, as I already had the intention of stopping in at the saloon for a quick drink and some jawboning before bed. Mrs. Rector said nothing until we got to the dry goods store, at the back of which sat their apartment. Tiny unlocked the front door and we marched single file through the darkened aisles, past the display cases full of leather gloves and corsets, the shelves laden with bolts of cloth and finished goods, the pickle barrels and their briny odor. The store was now twice its original width, Tiny having evicted the clothing merchant who had until recently shared the eastern half of the retail floor, and still, in the dark anyway, it appeared well-stocked. When we reached the rear apartment Mrs. Rector opened the door and hastened inside to light the lamp. In its dim light, she addressed me directly and sadly, and with her hard shell softened by emotion one saw the remnants of the beauty she must have been when Tiny married her.

"Why don't you boys talk in here? Surely this is nicer than going out in that cold again."

"It's not as cold as all that," Tiny said. "And we're wanting a drink."

To my astonishment Mrs. Rector opened a cabinet and extracted from it a familiar, flat green bottle. "There's whiskey here, Hank." I'd never heard anyone call him that before, though I knew Henry was his proper name.

"We got city business to discuss, Lil, I already told you that. Now you just get on to bed and don't worry about where we are."

Silently she retreated into the other room and closed the door behind her; through it a moment later I heard her say, "Good night, Bill, it was pleasant seeing you." Her voice was dull and resigned, and Tiny jerked his thumb at the door.

"Let's get," he mouthed silently, and we did.

They would be moving out of the apartment soon; as he locked the front door of the dry goods store Tiny described to me the large house they were building a block away. Their grown daughter had married a dentist in Independence, and the Rectors were trying to convince them to relocate to Cottonwood, using the promise of a rent-free place in the new house and the opportunity to be the first dentist in a growing town where nearly every night occasioned a tooth-loosening brawl.

Stepping into the street I thought I spied Katie Bender in the distance, carrying a parcel. I wondered why she was in town so late and where she was staying; I knew she hadn't alerted Maggie to her presence, because she'd remarked that very evening on the fact that she hadn't seen Katie since the latter had returned to the family farm. She disappeared around the corner of Main and Lincoln before I could be certain it was she.

"Don't even feel like the same town, does it?" Tiny asked as we walked slowly down the middle of Main Street in the direction of the saloon. As leisurely as our pace was, Tiny still breathed like a racehorse, his open mouth unfairly lending him the aspect of an idiot. There were sounds from all directions—a loud, angry discussion about borrowed money, hoofbeats down the newly-constructed wooden sidewalk (upon which horses, in principle, were forbidden), the whinnying of another horse in the opposite direction; a drunkard's careless laughter, his companion ordering him to shut the hole in his face, the delighted whooping and rebel-yelling of a small crowd of onlookers as the discussion erupted predictably into fisticuffs.

"Sounds like someone's making work for your son-in-law already, Tiny," I said as cheers rose into the night following a loud, bony cracking. The fight sounded as if it was happening on First Street, a block away, and I was tempted to go and watch.

"Two, three months ago this town would have been quiet as the tomb this time of night."

"That's so," I said. "I believe I like this better."

"Me, too. 'Course it changes everything. Shit, you know what it costs to hire a goddamn police force? A lot."

I knew that, because half the newly hired force spent half their pay as well as a goodly portion of the workday at the saloon, which meant I was getting a large chunk of that new municipal funding.

Tiny shook his head in wonder. "Goddamn, I'll be relieved when that friend of yours takes the mayor's job."

"That's good to hear. He's afraid you're offended he wants it."

"Nah. It's not a part-time job any more, and I got enough to worry about just keeping the town supplied with boots and water pitchers."

We crossed paths at that point with Paul Lowry, who despite my frank misgivings had been hired for the new police brigade. He was shoving a prisoner ahead of him in a jocular way, the man's hands secured behind him via an iron cuff. The prisoner was short and slight, naturally, but he met my stare with sullen and fearless hostility.

"Evening, Mr. Mayor. Bill."

"Evening, Lowry. Who've you got here?"

"Won't tell me his name, but he tried to rob a harlot and her client."

"That's a damnable lie and you know it," the prisoner spat, turning to face Lowry, who quickly went for a baton looped in his belt. At the brandishment of the stick the man cringed, and Lowry snickered. As they got nearer I saw that there was blood dripping down the prisoner's forehead. All the menace had evaporated from his mien.

"Is that so? Well, lock him up and we'll see about him in the morning. Maybe a few smacks from that stick would help jog his memory. Good night, Paul," Tiny said, and they proceeded to the jailhouse.

"Shit. Too many damned people to keep track of. I had a man show up this afternoon, wanted to know how he could find his cousin. I said how should I know where your cousin is? He says he was supposed to get here and immediately write back home with an address. Came down from Topeka, heard there was work. Well, he never wrote home, though his father was sick and maybe dying, so the cousin came looking. And there he is acting as though it's my responsibility to keep track of every damned drifter who wanders down here or doesn't. Shit."

"Won't be your responsibility much longer," I said.

"No, it'll be Leval's, and he's welcome to it." For a moment he appeared to lapse into a reverie. When we arrived at the saloon I turned toward the door and started to go in, but Tiny stopped me with a hand to the shoulder. "Regarding Leval, Bill, I'd be remiss if I didn't tell you to watch yourself."

"How's that?"

"You're bird-dogging that Maggie of his and not making much of a secret of it, and I don't figure he's the kind to let that pass."

"I'm not bird-dogging anybody. I was invited to dinner, just like you were."

He waved his hand as though swatting a horsefly in the air before his face. "I'm not the only one's remarked on it. Just about everyone's been there for dinner when you were there's said the same thing. Now maybe Marc hasn't noticed, or maybe he thinks there's no danger his wife might fancy you. But on the basis of what I saw going on between you two tonight I'd say that's wrong."

"Nothing was going on," I protested, but it rang false even to my own ear.

"Just don't give him a reason to want to do you harm. You have a big future in this town, if you don't get your pecker doing all your arithmetic."

"All right," I said, chastened; I had been certain my desires were well hidden, and the fact that they weren't seemed to call for reappraisal of all my plans. I pushed the door open and started inside, expecting Tiny to follow.

"Well, good night, Bill," Tiny said, continuing off to the south.

"You're not coming in with me?" I asked.

He stopped. "Nah, I'm headed down to the whores' camp."

"Watch yourself," I told him.

"Oh, they're all right down there. It's a shame that goddamn Barnes had to throw that pair of ladies out of the hotel, though. They were class, those two. Shit, you'd hardly know they were whores if they didn't ask for payment up front."

"Maybe they'll come back to town when the whorehouse gets finished."

"Nah, those two were strictly independents, not parlor house whores. We won't see them again," he said sadly, then continued on his way. "See, Bill?" he called to me over his shoulder. "We did talk some city business." He laughed and went huffing into the dark, noisy murk beyond, and I walked up the plank steps into the saloon. Inside was no one I wanted to talk to, though the room was jammed with friends and acquaintances; I drank a single whiskey at the bar and indulged in melancholy thoughts about my illicit desire for my friend's wife and, sensing that more whiskey would plunge me into a morass of self-pity, decided to retire for the night.

There was no one in the lobby except for Ingemarr the night man, who was avid as always for a conversation; for the last month or so the hotel had been keeping a man at the desk all night, and Ingemarr had replaced the job's first holder, who had been implicated in the prostitution scheme. I had no more capacity for social intercourse, though, and went immediately upstairs to my room.

Sticking my key in the lock I sensed that something was amiss; turning it clockwise I felt no tumbling and heard no click, but my mind was on other things as I entered the room and undressed in the near total darkness. I slipped under the bedclothes, thinking regretfully of my old buffalo robe, and tired though I was I found myself thinking of Maggie and of a particularly languorous gaze she'd favored me with earlier. I began allowing my hand to creep downwards, thinking to relieve myself as I had almost nightly since

Hattie's elopement; before it reached its destination, though, I was interrupted by a minute rustling, as of someone moving very slowly and deliberately to avoid making a sound. I opened one eye a fraction of an inch and saw nothing, but shortly thereafter I heard another faint friction near the door. I prepared to throw myself from the bed at whomever it was, feigning as I did so a light snore, thinking to lull my visitor into carelessness.

This had the desired effect, and he moved somewhat more quickly now, sufficiently so that I saw his shadow moving along the wall toward the door. I leapt up, sprung from the bed in his direction and landed upon his back with a cry of rage that was easily outdone by his own terrible, high-pitched shriek of terror and surprise. Yanking him to his feet, I smashed my fist into his nose, and as he fell to the floor I heard the stirrings of my neighbors. I picked him up by the collar and punched him again, this time in the teeth.

"Help," my opponent cried out, "murder," failing to anticipate that the other guests would assume that it was the room's legal occupant under siege and not its burglar; he continued to cry out when I opened the door to permit the entry of Ingemarr, who had come running up the stairs at the commotion. The other occupants of the floor soon joined us, and we rousted the intruder to his feet. I dressed in a trice and removed my Colt from the nightstand, grateful he hadn't got that far in his prowl, and stuck it into his ribs.

"Downstairs, quick," I said.

We descended to the lobby along with Ingemarr and several of the other residents. The malefactor was a boy of about eighteen, skinny and pimpled. Some of his pimples were white with pus, and several of those had broken open when I slugged his face. Though he was trying to play the part of the snarling tough his shoulders shook and his eyes watered, and the visible effort of not weeping appeared overwhelming. In his coat we found watches, cash, and jewelry, some of it assignable to guests present in the lobby. Ingemarr went upstairs and began rousing the other guests, room by room, so that the rest of the stolen property could be redistributed.

"What's your name?" I asked.

"Wallace," he answered.

"Wallace what?"

"That's my last name. First name's Clay."

"You from around here, Clay?"

"Nuh-uh. Dubuque, Iowa."

"What are you doing robbing hotel rooms?"

He didn't answer, and he got a little colder looking. Paul Lowry walked in the front door a minute later with one of the guests.

"So, what have we here, a sneak thief? What's your name?"

The boy wasn't talking now, so Ingemarr spoke up.

"Clay Wallace, that's his name," he said, and the boy scowled.

I told Lowry how I'd found the boy in my room, and we showed him that part of the booty which hadn't been returned. I could smell whiskey on Lowry's breath as we talked, and his eyes were red with it, too. When I finished, he looked down at the boy, who was considerably better composed than before.

"Well, Clay, you got anything to say for yourself?"

The lad looked as though he'd like to spit at Lowry. He said nothing.

"All right, then. How'd you like to spend the night in the cala-boose?" Lowry laughed and hit the back of Wallace's chair with his baton. "Get up." The boy rose as ordered and the two of them moved to the door. "Now don't try and bolt or I'll have to give you a walloping." Leering in my direction and still brandishing the ba-ton, he pantomimed a swing at the base of the boy's skull. Seeing this I felt compelled to accompany them to the jailhouse; I was un-likely to get to sleep that night anyway, and so I followed them into the crowd that still milled through the streets.

Our jail was a tiny structure containing a thin accessway be-tween two cells, each large enough for two men, and until a few months previous all either one generally ever contained were bois-terous drunks. Now the drunks were sent home, sometimes after a beating to quiet them down, and brawlers got the same treatment.

It took a real crime to get a place in the Cottonwood jail any more, and most nights it was full of four or five miscreants. Tonight, however, found only Lowry's other anonymous prisoner in the hole, and when Lowry and Wallace entered the structure and the keys jingled I heard the man stir and mumble, as though waking up and trying to place himself.

"Hey, killer," Lowry called. "I brought you some company."

After a moment's silence a dry croak came from the cell. "You go to hell."

"You'll see it before me," Lowry said with a chuckle as he unlocked the cell opposite.

"If that's so," came the voice from inside, "I'll give your ma a good kiss right on the cunt when I get there, for old times' sake."

In an instant Lowry was at the opposite door, apoplectic and cursing. He choked and sputtered as he worked to open the recalcitrant cell door, treating the prisoner to a string of epithets and counteraccusations of low and illegal birth, adding thereafter threats of violence so grotesque I began to fear for the safety of the man in the cell. The tongue-lashing's intensity increased with Lowry's frustration at his inability to open the cell door, and young Master Wallace of Iowa had the presence of mind to take advantage of Lowry's distraction; he rushed out the door and past me while inside the foul barrage continued. It did not stop until Wallace was well into the street, with me in pursuit, when Lowry came out after him, keenly aware of his blunder.

"Stop that man!" he shouted at the passersby. "He's a killer!"

That may have been untrue, but he was a devil of a sprinter; he evaded me easily, making his way east toward Lincoln. A few men turned to watch his flight but none made a move to apprehend him, though I yelled at them to do so. He was near the saloon, with me a good five yards behind, when a shot rang out and I felt the wind of a bullet to my immediate left. It hit the side of the building, though where I could not say in the darkness that surrounded us.

I stopped and yelled at Lowry to stop it but he fired again, and though he came no closer to the fleeing Wallace he managed to hit one of the crowd that had filed out of my saloon at the sound of the first shot hitting the outside wall. Some swarmed around the fallen man and a few witnesses, mostly in their cups, staggered toward Lowry.

The escaped prisoner was gone and forgotten, and Lowry dropped the revolver to his side as the mob advanced and the injured man's companions carried him toward the hotel, calling out for a doctor. Behind Lowry I saw that another mob was exiting the Silver Slipper, one that seemed as drunk and angry as the first.

"Bill!" someone called to me, and I looked over to see my new bartender Hans moving toward me. "They've shot Alf Cletus!"

As the door to the hotel opened I saw that the limp, open-mouthed figure being carried inside was indeed Alf, his shirt black with gore. I turned back to Paul Lowry, who was facing down the man's angry drinking companions. Herbert was taking the lead. As usual he hadn't bothered to cover his empty left eyesocket, and when he came in very close to Lowry and poked him in the chest with his finger the lawman flinched. "Who the hell you think you are, firing your pistol into a crowd like that?"

"I'm a fully deputized peace officer of the city of Cottonwood, that's who."

"I don't give a good goddamn about that. You shot Alf."

Lowry was out of breath, and he looked scared. "That son of a bitch sneak thief got away, thanks to you!"

"That ain't any concern of mine." He poked Lowry again, and Lowry made the mistake of raising his pistol at Herbert's face. The latter grabbed the pistol away from Lowry, turned it around and whacked the barrel good and hard against the lawman's face. Then he cocked it and stuck it into Lowry's gut.

Someone came out of the hotel. "Has anybody gone to get the doctor?"

No one had. Though reluctant to leave the spectacle before me, I headed over to First Street, where E. J. Salisbury's home and medical practice were located. As I rounded the corner and walked down the dark street to the house I found Tim Niedel already on the stoop, knocking and yelling in a voice like a yodel.

"He don't answer, Bill," Tim said.

I went around to the back of the cottage and rapped on the window, hollering for the doctor to come out. Finally I heard a stirring therein, and shortly thereafter the doctor came to his front door. He was fully dressed, and his clothes looked slept in.

He muttered something unintelligible, which from its inflection and context Tim took to be in the nature of a question regarding our purpose in waking him in the middle of the night.

"Alf Cletus just got gutshot. He's down at the hotel."

The doctor nodded his head. His lower lip stuck out in grim contemplation and stepped back into the house for his bag. A moment later he was back on the porch holding his satchel; my assumption was that he had also taken the opportunity to cleanse his tongue and palate with a jolt of the cheap bug juice he favored. That was fine with me since we had no alternative to him, and it was better he didn't operate with the shakes. "Lead on," he said clearly.

On the way to the hotel I consoled myself with the thought that Salisbury wasn't much of a doctor sober, either. When we rounded the corner onto Main we were greeted by the spectacle of the anonymous prisoner, sprung from his cell and held at gunpoint by Paul Lowry, whose revolver Herbert had kindly returned.

"Shit, look at that," Tim said.

"You want to know whose fault this is, here's the man you want," Lowry was saying, and the prisoner looked like he'd had the shit scared right out of him. "Tried to kill one of the fancy ladies for the money she carried and her customer, too, could have been any one of you fellows." I saw Tiny Rector standing at the edge of the crowd, which had enlarged considerably; all the influx was from the direction of Lincoln, and it consisted of men and women alike, the former outnumbering the latter by maybe four to one.

"Looks like you brought that whole whore camp into town with you," I said to Tiny.

"Some kid came running through, saying there was shooting going on and a jailbreak. I bet there's not ten people left down there right now."

"At least the lines are shorter," someone next to him said, sneering at Tiny.

Tiny laughed at that. "Maybe my successor can do something about recruiting more fallen women and relieving the burden on those we have now." He elbowed me and leaned over to whisper, jerking his thumb at his neighbor. "He's sore 'cause I took advantage of my prerogative as mayor and stepped to the head of the line. This whole commotion started before he got his turn."

"Tiny, don't you think as mayor you maybe ought to take charge about now and stop Lowry before things get all the way out of hand?"

"Don't get yourself bothered over a common thief, Bill. Lowry'll have his fun and put him back in his cell, and maybe tomorrow he'll be a little more inclined to cooperate. Anyway, what kind of mayor would I be if I stopped a hell of a good show like this?"

I left him and marched into the hotel to see about Alf. He had been put into a room on the first floor, where he had proceeded to bleed all over the bed. Several of his companions from the saloon stood witness, and they nodded to me as I stepped into the small room. Doctor Salisbury had his face in close proximity to the wound, just below the ribcage, and he was looking nearly as gray as poor Alf. The noise of the crowd outside was terrible, and a cheering erupted that chilled my bones as much as the sight of Alf lying there, making a horrid wet sound with every labored intake of breath.

"I don't know what all it hit, but he's not improving any."

"Can you dig it out?"

He looked appalled at the prospect, but he nodded. "We can try." But as he turned to open his satchel Alf gurgled and ceased to breathe; the doctor looked up at me with a mixture of sorrow and relief, and the man nearest the door slipped out. I followed him, unable to bear the sight of my friend's sightless, bloodshot eyes, and I thought I might try and defuse things with a round of drinks for all at the saloon in Alf's memory.

Outside, though, I discovered that things had taken a dire turn. A noose had been strung from the rafter of Tiny Rector's Dry Goods and Grocery Store, and the prisoner stood on the roof, sniffling and protesting his innocence. Next to him stood a smug Paul Lowry, and several others. A number of lamps had been brought outside from various dwellings and someone had begun distributing puncheons coated in burning pitch; between the lamps and these torches the night was as bright as in gaslit Chicago. I spied Katie Bender again, without the parcel she'd carried earlier, her expression as vapid as if she were watching a patent medicine salesman hawking his wares. I looked in vain for Tiny among the throng, and finally caught sight of him on the rooftop, laughing. It was a noisy crowd, and like the rest of it I didn't immediately hear the words of the man I'd accompanied out of the hotel, but eventually the phrase he was repeating caused a hush to fall over the assembly, and I hoped the gravity of it would bring the mob to its senses.

"Alf Cletus is dead," he kept saying, and by the time he stopped the crowd was silent.

For a few seconds all that could be heard was the choked sobbing of the prisoner, his hands tied behind him. Then Herbert, standing at the front of the mob, shouted "Hang Lowry, too!" It was quickly enough taken up as a chant, and atop a barrel in front of the store a man began tying a second noose, the work of about thirty seconds. I couldn't hear what was happening on the roof of the store, but I saw Tiny yelling at Lowry, Lowry yelling back and looking unhappy, and then Tiny going down on top of him.

I retreated to the back of Tiny's store and climbed the wooden steps to the rooftop, where I pushed my way through the crowd of perhaps twenty men to where four other members of the police brigade were on top of Lowry, tying his hands behind him.

"Let him go," I said, and I found myself ignored. They pulled Lowry to his feet, blubbering. The other prisoner seemed to take no ironic satisfaction in this, and presently the nooses were handed up from below to the men on the roof.

"Tiny," I said. "Put a stop to this."

He looked over at me and appeared to be chewing over the idea for a second. "Like hell," he said.

"You hear me? I speak for the town company and Marc Leval, and I say there's going to be no hanging tonight."

The four who had turned on Lowry now faced me and I began wondering what it would take for the mob to start howling for my blood, too.

"Mr. Leval ain't here tonight, Bill," one of them said, and I began backing toward the stairs.

"That's right, Bill, he ain't," Tiny said. "I'm still mayor and tonight what I say goes, you understand?"

"Pretty well," I said, and I hurried down to the laughter of some of the witnesses. I rounded the building through the alley and crossed the street to the saloon, where Gleason and the new man stood idly behind the bar. Barely a half dozen of the most dedicated or jaded stewbums remained drinking, and they didn't seem to register my entrance.

"Gleason. I need my Colt."

He handed it to me and I verified that it was loaded.

"What's going on outside? How's old Alf?"

"Dead." I put a fatherly hand on his shoulder. "If I'm killed, half of my half of the bar is yours on condition you run it for my son until he's old enough to pull his weight on the remaining quarter. Is that a deal?"

"Yes, sir, Mr. Ogden," he said, and I strode back out into the night with my blood boiling. Tiny Rector was my friend but by God I'd shoot him dead if he didn't put a stop to this. It never got to that pass, though; before I got halfway to the store Lowry decided to put up a fight, and the result was that he went first, shoved over the ledge. The prisoner followed momentarily, and they both dangled there, struggling awfully, until out of pity Herbert and three other strong men from the crowd each took a kicking, shit-smeared leg and pulled. The nooses hadn't been properly tied, and there was still no snapping of the necks; I yelled for the four good samaritans to get out of the way. When they saw I had the Colt in my hand, cocked and ready, they did so. I put a bullet into Lowry's head from beneath his chin, and when his eyes went dead I did the same for the poor anonymous thief, if thief he truly was. The crowd quieted considerably now.

My gaze chanced to light upon Miss Katie Bender again, whom I expected to find grinning in malicious delight at the horrible scene, or at the very least actively suppressing such a look; in fact, her face was contorted in revulsion and fear. When she saw me looking she managed an inappropriate, sickly smile in my direction and a friendly little wave.

I looked up at Tiny, who sat winded on the edge of his rooftop, his own long fat legs dangling to the right of the ropes as they scraped against the shingles in an ever-slowing rhythm. Idly I wondered if we'd ever find out who the prisoner was, or if we'd ever catch the fugitive burglar. Tiny saw me looking, and his face told me nothing except that he was physically exhausted. As the crowd dispersed in morose silence I noticed Mrs. Rector in the window of the store, her face distorted by the moving lamplight and the flaws of the panes, but looking for all the world as if she were enjoying herself. I don't suppose the whole thing took five minutes after the announcement was made; when I thought to look again for Katie she was nowhere to be seen.

Wandering away, I supposed that the thing to do was to shut down the saloon, but a goodly proportion of the masses in the street was headed in its direction and I had no desire to make myself an enemy of this particular mob. On a whim I wandered back in the direction of the Leval Mansion to inform its inhabitants of the night's events.

Rose came to the door, wide-eyed, in her nightclothes, carrying a candle.

"What was all that noise about?" she asked.

"A hanging," I said.

"How's that? At night?"

I nodded and was on the verge of elaborating when I saw a pale figure holding another candle descend the staircase behind her. It was Maggie, in her nightclothes, and she stole up behind Rose so quietly the poor girl let out a yelp, her free hand darting to her mouth.

"Come inside, Bill."

I did so and Rose shut the door. "It's a hanging, missus. At night."

"Thank you, Rose. You may go back to bed."

Rose looked at her, and then at me. She hesitated; she wanted to hear more, and clearly had no desire to leave her married, night-clad mistress alone with a man, but she went obediently on her way.

"Was it awful, Bill?" she asked. That look of weary amusement she wore most of the time was gone, and in the light of her candle I believed I saw tears in her eyes.

"Yes, it was," I said, though I wasn't thinking any more of the night's violence. She moved in closer to me.

"Does it occur to you that there's something wrong with you

coming to my door in the middle of the night with Marc away? Or maybe you really are as innocent as you seem to be."

Though her tone was gentle I was suddenly filled with shame. "I thought you might be fearful from the noise outside. I'll go, then," I said, feeling pitiful and low-down, but she took my hand before I had the chance to turn away. She pulled me to the staircase, and we ascended without a word or a backward glance from her.

4

COTTONWOOD, KANSAS, MAY 1873

Atrocity

The morning after the hanging it was on the verge of raining, and I slipped out of the Leval mansion before sunrise and crossed the lawn, still wet with dew, fighting guilty thoughts of what I'd done with methodical ones about what I had yet to do. I first ascertained that the two men were still hanging in front of Tiny's store; all night long I had been tormented by the thought that they might be cut down before I got there. The dark street was already busy with early risers at work or heading to it, but the town was quieter right then than I'd heard it in months, and I crossed the street to the saloon, just as the first pale signs of the rising sun became evident over the tent city. Above me the sky was clear, and the stars were still visible and even bright, but to the west were thunderheads, and rain and cloud cover would ruin my chances. I devoutly hoped Gleason had stayed the night before after closing too late to return to his parents' home, and when I opened the saloon door he lay there on the parquet, covered with a blanket I wouldn't have used on my horse. I shook him with the toe of my boot and he stirred, shivering.

"Next time you sleep here, leave the stove on. I'd hate to come in and find you'd croaked in the night."

He nodded, squinting. "What time is it?" he asked.

"Time to go to work. Come on, I need a hand."

In my room at the hotel we set up the dark tent and prepared four glass plates; he was good at it and already quicker than I was. Perhaps twenty minutes later we descended as quietly as we could with the stereographic camera, its tripod and the plates in their holders. The sky to the west was black, and to the east perfectly fair, and the light that shone on Lowry and his arrestee was a delicate rosy orange. The rain was already falling in the distance, though how far off I couldn't say, and again I impressed upon Gleason the need for expedition. Eager to keep his mind off the cadavers before us he began asking questions about the amount of light available. The odd atmospheric situation made for a dramatic effect of soft, direct light bathing the dead from one side, creating shadows as black as if the night still lay on the earth.

"Now see if you can't impress upon our subjects the importance of remaining motionless."

He shuddered; somewhere in him were the remnants of a choirboy, appalled and astonished to find himself working in a den of sin. "You really think people want to look at pictures of this?" he asked, wrinkling his nose.

"You'd be surprised at what they'll look at," I said, and I let him focus the lenses himself, instructing him to use as a marker the faces of the dead men. Watching their useless eyes moving in and out of focus on the ground glass would teach him not to take these things personally, I thought, and he performed his task quickly and well. We made four exposures from slightly differing angles and distances, and before I'd sent Gleason back up to the dark tent with the plates a crowd started forming to see what I was up to, and a breeze blew up from the west, strong enough to sway the hanged men's bootless feet by the time I had the camera packed in its case. As I crossed the street to the hotel the first drops of rain hit my face, and after I'd put the camera safely inside the lobby I stood outside for a long time and got good and wet under the black sky, with a sharp clear light shining skygodlin down on me from the east. Then it was time to head out through the mud to the farm.

The next morning the sun came out for an hour or so, and I hurried to the hotel roof with the plates in printing frames and made prints of all four views of the hanging. All the plates were of acceptable quality, and one of them was nearly perfect, with a nice sense of depth between the dangling corpses and the store behind them, and a pleasing range of tones from the highlights on Lowry's shiny face to the inky vitrine of Tiny's store. The thief in death wore a resigned expression, as if hanging at the hands of a mob was pretty much what he'd expected out of life on the prairie, whereas Paul Lowry's eyes, though half-shut and focused on slightly divergent points in the indeterminate distance, still registered surprise and disbelief.

Except for that hour's respite, the rain continued for two solid days after the hanging, turning the streets of town into a thick soup of mud and horseshit. The tent city had things even worse, having no wooden sidewalks, and by the time the rain had quit a quarter of its population had taken sick. The rain was of course welcomed by the farmers, but its only other benefit was to soften the ground for digging graves.

Before the town had a name, even before the decision was made to incorporate, a small patch of ground had of necessity been laid out for the burial of the dead, and the location of this patch now posed a twofold problem. Firstly, the town had outgrown it in a sudden and dramatic fashion; in the preceding half decade barely twenty souls had been put to rest there, whereas a quarter that number had died in or near Cottonwood by misadventure or disease just since the tent city had gone up. In a short time the graveyard would have to annex an adjoining property or two, and with land within the newly expanded city limits worth at least five times its previous valuation this was an absurd proposition. Secondly, its location at the south end of Seward placed it squarely in the center of the cattle pens, half of which were already in place; the question at hand, then, was not whether to move the dead but where to and how.

Tiny and I decided to establish a new town cemetery on a mound to the northeast, and Tiny authorized the disbursal of city funds to hire a handful of denizens of the tent city to dig up the old boneyard and rebury the bodies in the new one. The process of dis- and re-interrment was soon to be the cause of some hard feelings on the part of a few longtime residents of Cottonwood; they objected to the disturbance of their loved ones' bones, particularly since we failed to give anyone notice that the move was to take place. The first anyone knew about it was when a wagon containing a pair of rotten pine boxes side by side in its flatbed careened through the sloppy streets of town at a trot with a quartet of drunken, dirty gravediggers seated laughing and yelling atop their flimsy, rotten lids.

Upon hearing a number of complaints regarding the gravediggers' boisterousness, Tiny and I rode up to the new cemetery late on the first afternoon of the work. It was a beautiful afternoon, the sky blue and clear and the air still smelling of the rain, which had stopped only that morning. At the mound, which offered a splendid view of the town to the southwest and a squalid one of the tent city to the southeast, we found no workers and no new graves dug; the only recently turned earth covered the graves of Lowry, Alf Cletus, and the anonymous thief. A row of four coffins sat on the wet grass in varying states of decay, unaccompanied by the markers that had identified their occupants in the old cemetery. Tiny's mood deteriorated, and he was in a full sulk as we surveyed the mound, not even speaking as we tried to decide where to mark the boundaries. In short order the men showed up with another pair of caskets, and upon disembarking from the wagon hauled the boxes off the flatbed and lowered them roughly onto the wet grass next to the others.

"Howdy, Mayor," the foreman grinned at Tiny as he hopped off the wagon onto the ground. He had no front teeth, top or bottom.

"Now just a goddamn minute," Tiny wheezed, the first words out of his mouth in half an hour.

The men had already climbed back aboard and were on the verge of returning to town, and the foreman cocked an ear in Tiny's direction with a busy man's air of distracted impatience. "You unhappy with something, Mayor? To my way of thinking, if we hurry we can get two more dug up by sundown."

Tiny's eyes looked even bigger and rounder than usual, as if his anger was pushing them out of their orbits from behind. "And when, exactly, were you planning to dig the eight new graves? Were you planning to do it by lamplight?"

The foreman thought hard, trying to provide the right answer. "No . . . When we got all the old ones filled in . . ."

"And your plan is to leave these above ground all night?"

"I don't see any other way to . . ."

"I'll tell you the way to. You dig up two boxes at a time, you bring them up here and you bury them before you go back for more. You understand?"

"You didn't say to do that." The foreman was thin of frame and bald on top, and the fringe of red hair circumnavigating his head had grown to a considerable length; he resembled a mangy, emaciated circus lion.

"I shouldn't have to. Anybody with the smallest lick of sense would know to do it that way. And you didn't keep the caskets and the markers together. Now how the hell are you going to know what marker goes with what casket?"

"Can't hardly read 'em anyway. Probably need to carve new ones."

"All right," Tiny said. "When I carve the new ones, how do I know which goes on which grave?"

The foreman lifted his thick, tangled brows and gave a slight moue of consideration. "I suppose I'll just try real hard to remember which one was which."

Tiny's breath was coming in shorter and shorter bursts, and his face was red and shiny with sweat, making me afraid he might end up a resident of the mound sooner than anticipated. "You'll try? Is that what you said?"

"Yes, sir," the foreman said. "I guess from here on out I'll mark the boxes with a piece of charcoal, huh?"

"And what about these, then?"

"Look, mister, I don't see as how it matters much if Smith's buried in Jones's plot, long as they's both buried Christian." He looked hopefully at Tiny, whose fists were tight at his sides, as if controlling them required a great effort.

"You get down there and start opening them boxes up," Tiny said quietly, like he was choking.

The foreman blanched and shook his head, and the other men on the wagon looked at one another with drawn faces, silently debating whether the opening of the caskets fell inside or outside the job's worth to them.

"You hear me, you drunken son of a bitch? You get down here right now and start opening them boxes up or I'll by Jesus put you in one of your own."

The foreman shook his head again without speaking, and Tiny sprung forward and with one hand around his throat picked the foreman up off the flatbed, lifted him into the air and dropped him onto the ground. Then he was on top of the man, his face redder than before, his big watery eyes even redder, his thumb pressing on the foreman's trachea. That red hair splayed out, and his head pressed down into the mud with the pressure of Tiny's weight on him.

"Jesus, Tiny, let him up. You're going to kill him."

"You son of a bitch!" His voice was louder and clearer now.

I got my arm around his throat and pulled up, to little or no effect; though he was obese he was also strong as a dray horse. "You're a married man and a grandfather. You're still the Mayor, for God's sake."

Finally he let go and stood up, inhaling and exhaling like a bellows for a blast furnace. The foreman lay on the ground with his eyes closed, choking, but after a while he wincingly sat up, his head leaving an indentation in the wet ground; then he pulled a crow-bar off of the wagon and started opening the coffins.

"Lawrence Billings," Tiny said wearily. I chose not to look, as did the men on the wagon, but with each name Tiny called out the foreman ran and fetched the appropriate marker, then shut the box again. When they got around to the fifth box Tiny let out a sob, and I saw him topple down onto his seat like a shot elephant and bury his face in his hands, snuffling and snorting like a whipped schoolboy. The rest of us regarded him cautiously, and the foreman broke our silence.

"Who is it, Your Honor?"

My curiosity overcame my sense of decorum, and I glanced at the open coffin. Inside were a yellow, broken skull and some bones, considerably jumbled at the foot of the casket from the ride between cemeteries. The remains of a black dress were affixed to the bottom of the coffin, and to the skull still clung a few strands of blond hair. I answered the foreman's question. "That's Minnie Lansdown."

"Minnie, my Minnie," Tiny simpered, as if to explain his violent outburst. Minnie had died of a toxic dose of laudanum shortly after my arrival in Cottonwood, so I never knew her well, but I remembered her beauty and vivaciousness, and her husband's misery and confusion at her death. Newt Lansdown gave up his homestead and headed west with the stated intention of hunting buffalo, and no one in Cottonwood had heard from him since. I knew of no sentimental connection between Minnie and Tiny, and

I remembered Lillian Rector's display of sorrow at the burial; still, she meant more to Tiny than a neighbor's wife.

The foreman placed the marker at the foot of the coffin and tenderly replaced the lid, and then opened the next one. Inside he found another skull and bones, an unarticulated mess of a skeleton like Minnie's. Also visible were part of a belt and a more or less intact pair of boots. I shouldered Tiny, who was still in tears, shaking his head.

"Come on now, Tiny, there's work to be done. Who's that in there?"

Sniffling and hiccoughing, he stumbled onto all fours and then rose to his full height, regaining a good portion of his lost dignity in the process. "That's Hiram Bussler. I sold his widow those boots after he died. You know, I believe he was the first one we buried there."

Once all six boxes and markers had been marked, I went into town for torches and two more shovels, and the seven of us dug into the soft earth well past sundown; when the dead were finally at rest once again I took the crew and Tiny down to the saloon for a quick drink, caked with several layers of rapidly drying mud. Before I left them there with a single drink under my belt, Tiny had downed three and was well on the way to drunken parity with the gravediggers.

I stopped at the hotel and ordered a bath to be brought to my room and filled, then selected some fresh articles of clothing; after scrubbing all the dirt off, and giving myself a good over-all washing, I donned my clean suit of clothes and stopped in at the dining room downstairs, where I ate a beefsteak the size of my fist, accompanied by a large baked potato. Then I strolled out the door and east, toward Lincoln, whereupon I turned left and began walking to the north. I passed by First Street and casually examined some of the home construction going on there, wondering what percentage of the carpenter's trade of the states of Kansas and Missouri was currently operating in Cottonwood. After First Street there was no sidewalk, and my fresh boots were considerably muddied by the time I reached the recently dedicated Second Street and turned west. I sauntered casually to Seward and rather than turning south I continued on where the road ended, walking up onto the grass until to my immediate south was the rear entrance to the Leval home. I spun slowly around to determine whether I could spy anyone watching me; I saw no one, and moved through the blackness to the back door. Rose met me as she had the previous three nights, making a mute show of her disdain, but she accepted the half dollar I pressed into her hand and absented herself, leaving me free to roam the house.

Maggie awaited me in her room, reclining upon her chaise longue in her nightgown, which she had drawn up over her thighs, affording me a view of her legs as they met her hips. Her hand was busy at work between them, and her eyes were closed. They did not open when I closed the door, though I deliberately made the latch click loudly to announce myself. I approached her, removing my coat, and as I drew near she smiled, still without opening her eyes.

"Mm," she said, her voice low in her throat, inhaling audibly. "You've had a bath, Bill."

I dropped to my knees at her side and put my mouth to the soft inside of her left thigh, and putting her hands to the sides of my head she slowly drew it down to where she wanted it, and for the fourth night in a row I wondered if I wasn't dreaming.

Accounts and dispatches purporting to be the work of eyewitnesses to the hangings, exaggerated and distorted to the level of travesty, began appearing in the region's newspapers within the week of the event, and not long thereafter spread eastward in ever less reliable form; by the time it reached Marc's eyes one Chicago daily claimed we had hanged not one but seven members of our police brigade, alongside the mayor and town council, and gutshot them as they kicked the air.

The morning after his return Marc called me into his office at the bank. He had collected several eyewitness accounts, all of which ended with me shooting the dying men as they hung there and none of which, apparently, attributed my actions to pity or altruism. I explained myself to him, and though his disposition didn't get any sunnier I did think he understood my part in the evening's events.

"We ought to have Tiny Rector up on charges," he said.

"That wouldn't be a popular move on the part of a man seeking his office."

He gave me a look of disgust but didn't comment; he knew it was true. "Was Maggie terribly upset? I'm told you came by to check on her the night of the riot."

"Somewhat upset. It was well over by the time I stopped by."

He held his eye on mine for an uncomfortable moment, then looked away, toward the room's only window. "I should have insisted she come with me to Chicago. Better yet, I shouldn't have left at all."

You think you could have stopped what happened, I almost asked, but I knew he did think so. He'd hardly ever failed at anything, and such a thing was hard for him to imagine.

"Michael Cornan's down in the tent city, recruiting some new men for the police brigade."

This took me aback, since Cornan had no experience in policing that I knew of; I'd thought he was trying to get a subscription up for a new church, of a denomination he was still in the midst of founding. "What's he doing that for?"

Marc ignored the question. "Why don't you go find him and give him a hand, since you know some of the men yourself?"

"You coming along?"

"Too much to do here." He nodded at the door, outside which a dozen men had already stood waiting when I arrived. I got up and left, happy to leave his reproachful tone and superior air.

"You're invited for dinner tonight, by the way, you and Cornan both."

I smiled as true a smile as I could muster. "Delighted."

Though we all still called it the tent city, it had begun to take on the character of a shanty-town. Its numerous wooden structures were mostly constructed from the less desirable scrap lumber left over from some of Cottonwood's buildings recently knocked down to make room for the new. Since a large number of the workers quartered there were carpenters, some of the work was quite sturdy; the crib of a quartet of harlots was a particular marvel, solid-looking and with makeshift bits of wooden gingerbread nailed about the door and windows for decoration. Tarpaper, doubtless stolen from one of the construction sites, covered the roof and protected the interior from another dousing like the one the whole tent city had received a few weeks before. Gleason and I had photographed it extensively early on three afternoons the previous week, and already its crudely picturesque aspect had changed enough that another session might have been warranted.

I found Cornan near that very structure, striding through the tent city in cavalry boots. This being the middle of the day, the neighborhood was mostly deserted, its inhabitants engaged in constructing the metropolis-to-be. The distinct odors of two or three varieties of shit could still be detected in the spring air, and somewhere to the south one woman could be heard screeching abuse at another, who returned it with enthusiasm, adding some anatomical vulgarity for good measure. The mud had long since dried, but it had done so in such a churned-up state that it was quite uneven and difficult to negotiate, with large crusty ridges sticking out like waves. Before I could call out Cornan's name he tripped and, catching himself with an extended hand, saw me approaching from behind. Though I made no sign of amusement, nor even of having noticed, he acted as if I had laughed, scowling at me as he righted himself.

"Let's see you navigate these rotten gullies for a couple of hours without tripping up once or twice."

"Marc sent me down to give you a hand," I said in the friendliest tone I knew.

"I don't need any help finding police officers. Not from you or anyone else. Good day, Bill."

He turned away and nearly collided with a couple of men who hadn't found work that day, on their way to the whores' crib.

"Sorry about that, mister," one of them offered, though it had been Cornan's offense and not their own.

Cornan surprised them by pulling his revolver and waving it at them. "Them days are over here," he said as they backed away. Then he turned back toward me. "You hear? Over."

They backed into the crib, and a minute later one of its occupants leaned out the front door wearing nothing but a chemise. Her name was Lottie, and I knew her a little from the bar. She came in to drink and didn't conduct any business transactions on the premises, though that would have been fine with me. "Well, hello, gentlemen. Got a few minutes at liberty, have we?"

Cornan was flustered, and he put the gun back in its holster, a fancy one of tooled leather. "Not for the likes of you, you dirty harlot," he said, though I suspected it was no coincidence that I'd found him here.

"No need to be unkind, Mike," Lottie said. "I thought to relieve some of your burden, is all."

"My burden won't be relieved through sins of the flesh," he yelled, and he hurried away from us.

"How about you, bartender? You feel like keeping me company for a few minutes?" Fact is I did feel like it; Lottie was a good-looking woman, despite small eyes and a mean little mouth. I was sore at Maggie, too, since I knew she'd lain with her husband the night before, and probably that morning, too. I had money in my pocket and more on the way, and some free time as well, since Cornan had rejected my help in seeking new coppers, so I stepped inside. There were four rough doors on leather hinges in a short hallway, each leading to an individual crib; three of the doors were shut, with noises coming from inside. As I stepped into Lottie's room one of them opened, and out of it stepped one of the men I had just seen entering. He was buttoning the top of his trousers, looking dazed and happy; I estimated that not three minutes had passed since he'd gone in.

Lottie's crib contained a narrow iron bed with a thin, lumpy mattress, wide enough for two occupants only if they were stacked vertically, a washing basin and a small trunk. She sat upon the bed, opened my trousers and extracted my prick, which she examined with an air of clinical detachment. I saw then a bottle of carbolic acid next to her washbasin, and that got me thinking about all the men who'd passed through that room in the past month or so. That in turn led to memories of wartime camp followers and the ravages their diseases had wrought upon some of my fellow soldiers, and I began to question the hygienic wisdom of inserting into Lottie the part of me she was in the process of examining.

"Looks clean to me," she pronounced. Outside I could hear some of the other girls, finished now with their clients, soliciting passersby. "What's your pleasure?"

"Maybe just a little bit of oral stimulation today, Lottie."

"A little bit of what?" she asked, squinting, head tilted to her left.

"The French way," I explained, and she nodded, brightening.

"A cocksucking. That's easy enough, I don't even have to wash up after."

I slipped it into her mouth, and she worked at it with such skill that I was finished as quickly as the fellow down the hall had done. Having swallowed, Lottie wiped her lips with her long chemise, which she raised to show me her sex, tufted with hair as blond as that on her head. "You'll have to stick around for some of this next time," she said. I gave her two dollars and got ready to go.

"How come you're friends with that son-of-a-bitch, anyway?"

For a second I thought she meant Marc. "Which son-of-a-bitch is that?"

"Mike Cornan. He's got balls, calling me a harlot and stomping off like that just 'cause you was with him."

I laughed at the notion of Cornan being my pal. "He's no friend of mine."

"He just wants you to think he never comes around here. Well, he does, half the time preaching hellfire and damnation, the rest of the time earning it."

"I think he's going to be the new chief of police."

She nodded. "The kind who'll want a free piece of ass every day, plus a cut of everybody's take. One good thing about this town so far is the only one we have to fuck for free is old Tiny Rector."

That didn't sound so great to me, but I didn't say it. She hustled me out onto the street ahead of her and called out to a group of laborers across the street. As a couple of them approached looking eager for fleshly contact I bid Lottie good-day and headed for the saloon.

If Cornan had shown fear at the sight of Lottie that afternoon, he betrayed absolute terror in the face of Maggie Leval. Dressed in a stiff brown suit in a style predating the war and stinking of mold, he stammered and choked when addressed by her, and when he spoke to me or Marc it was in a stentorian bark like a sergeant's, as if no woman was present. Maggie concentrated on the impossible task of putting him at his ease; in doing so she was able to fairly ignore me, and so our interactions had little of the guilty or furtive about them. At one point Marc and Cornan retired to the library to discuss some sort of constabulary business, and upon leaving us alone Marc looked over his shoulder with a particularly sour set to his mouth. "We'll be just a few minutes, so enjoy yourselves."

As soon as the library door was shut I hastened to Maggie's side. "He knows," I hissed.

"How would he? Anyway, he gets himself into spells where he acts like that. It's all about business, not about you and me. Now go and sit down before he finds you whispering in my ear."

As the soup was served Marc was reading aloud a particularly unflattering account from an eastern newspaper of the riot, a declamation full of theatrical bombast; I was uncertain how to react to it, because his dramatic reading combined with the absurd claims made by the columnist, supposedly an eyewitness to the hangings, suggested a certain bleak comedy:

" 'Our Prairie Correspondent reports that in the town of Cottonwood, in Kansas, a crowd of drunken ruffians spilled out of the town saloon'—that's nice, Bill—'in a murderous mood, the cause of which no one seems sure.' " He paused and looked around as we began lapping up the soup. " 'Having hanged one innocent passerby from one of the trees that gave the village its name, the bloodthirsty mob then forced its way into the offices of the City Hall, where it found Police Chief Paul Doughty'—that's d-o-u-g-h-t-y, couldn't even be bothered to get the man's right name—'standing guard. Upon his order to break up the assembly, the leaders thereof disarmed him forcibly and compelled him to disrobe.' " Having bellowed this last word for emphasis, Marc again looked up at us before resuming his reading. " 'At this point the mayor of Cottonwood exited his own chambers and demanded to know what was meant by the disruption to the business of the city. He and the remainder of the city's police force were then similarly ordered to remove their clothing, and the mob, which by this time had grown to include fifty or sixty men, marched the lot of them outside to the same tree from which their luckless fellow citizen swung. From its branches and those of several others in its immediate vicinity the mayor and the town's entire police force were strung, to the applause and raucous laughter of perhaps the lowest group of villains this part of the country has seen. With officers of the peace no longer an impediment, the lawless element has taken over the town completely and chaos reigns.' "

I couldn't help myself; I laughed.

"You find that amusing, Bill?"

"Just picturing Tiny in the raw," I said, and I saw Maggie's hand race to her mouth to suppress a smile.

"That's our town being described there, for anyone to read that cares to. You don't think that's to the detriment of our reputation? Of the future of Cottonwood?"

"There's hardly a grain of truth to it."

"That doesn't matter to some easterner who might otherwise be tempted to come here, or to invest money in the town."

"Seems like we have all the investment we need for the time being."

"We never have enough, Bill. We're going to need more, and if we get the reputation of a Sodom on the plains we won't get it."

"If we're going to get the drivers up here, there's going to be some wildness."

"Wildness is one thing. Debauchery's another. Listen to this: 'The town's fancy ladies, estimated at a hundred and fifty or more in number, now conduct their business openly in the out-of-doors, and think nothing of importuning strolling citizens even when accompanied by wives and babes.' "

Cornan leaned forward and hollered, "Begging your pardon, Mister Leval, but that last is just about the case."

"Prostitutes in the streets? Not downtown, surely?" Maggie asked, her eyes wide and credulous, leaning over her soup.

Cornan reddened at her addressing him directly, and responded without meeting her eyes. "Not in the decent part of town, not yet anyway. In the shanty-town, though, they're whoring openly without regard for decency or the laws of God or man. And we have to face the fact that the shanty-town is a part of this city."

He leaned forward and stared at Marc, who nodded. "I've been thinking about that. Maybe something should be done."

"It's a terrible idea," I said. "Get rid of the whores and you'll have a town full of men with one thing on their minds, and the lack of it will make them as wild as the mob in that newspaper article."

Cornan didn't appreciate being contradicted. "I suppose I shouldn't be surprised at your attitude regarding the town whores, Mr. Ogden, after what I witnessed today south of Lincoln."

Marc and Maggie raised their eyebrows as one and turned to Cornan, riveted.

"You didn't see anything, Cornan."

"I saw you talking to a painted lady that stuck her half-naked body out into the street to see if you could be lured in. By the looks of things as I was hurrying off you were negotiating a price with her."

Before I could respond, Maggie turned sideways and buried her face in her hands, retching. She waved us off with her right hand as Marc and I each rose to her aid, and when she could get a word out she whispered, "Something went down wrong." Her eyes were wet and rimmed with red, and she didn't address me directly for the rest of the evening.

The next morning I rode out to the farm as usual, where Garth and the new hired man were hard at work with the plowing. I pitched in for a while, which left me determined to hire a third man immediately, and when it came time to leave for town I stopped into the house if just to get out of the cold for a moment.

"You been having your way with that woman," Ninna said without accusation or anger, a simple statement of fact.

"What makes you say that?" I asked, considerably surprised.

"Heard he was gone to Chicago for two, three weeks, and I seen the way you looked at her Christmastime."

" 'Saw,' not 'seen.' " It was a constant irritant to me that her English, as it grew over the years, became more and more colloquial and incorrect, but that was what I got for abandoning her to the field hands. "Anyway, that doesn't mean anything."

"Seen how she was looking at you, too, when she thought her man and me wasn't looking."

"But you haven't heard any talk?"

She laid down her knitting for a second and looked straight at me with her big, pale blue eyes. "How would I hear talk? I don't see nobody but Garth and that damned hunky you hired, and Clyde. Once a month I see the neighbors and they know less than me. They're real farmers, do all the work themselves. No time to go to town and gossip." She took up the needles again, and I went out. I hadn't seen Clyde that morning, though I knew he was home, and I wanted to say hello.

I found the boy up in the barn, nestled in the straw for warmth and trying to read Herodotus. "Making any progress?" I asked, and he looked up and shrugged slightly.

"Some." Then he looked back down at the page and scowled, much the way I used to when I was at that stage of puzzling out the Greek letters one by one, constructing them into words, and then reassembling the words to form sentences. I remembered the pride and pleasure I took from that experience, and I hoped that it was the same for him, and would soon become for him as it had for me so long ago, an escape from the day's drudgery into the world of the ancients. I sensed that further interruption from me would break the spell and so crept out quietly, remounted the chestnut mare and rode back to town, calculating as I rode the amount of ill-will to be generated with Garth when Ninna took the new man to bed.

* * *

The day was humid and cold without being foggy, exactly. I stopped in at the bank before I opened the saloon and found Marc in conference with a prosperous-looking fellow, beefy in the face and with a striking roll of fat around his neck like a pink collar. His hair was black, going gray in spots, and his muttonchop whiskers had gone white altogether. His little eyes bulged like a salamander's, and his mouth remained open the entire time I was in his presence. Marc introduced the man as Silas Henniston of Kansas City.

"Mr. Henniston's gone and lost his business partner somewhere around here, Bill," he said. He was in no sunnier a mood than he'd been since his return, and he didn't bother to disguise his slightly contemptuous smile. "He thought perhaps we could help him out."

Henniston, oblivious, leaned forward. "He was traveling between Topeka and Independence, and his presence can be established at Osage Mission as of the middle of March." His quavering hand plucked from his vest pocket a handkerchief that badly needed cleaning and pressed it to his brow, replacing it wet into the pocket.

"What makes you think he's been here?" I asked.

"He had no plan I know of to venture here, but as he never arrived in Independence I thought he might have. I've established that he didn't stay at your local hotel."

"Lots of people pass through this part of the state and don't end up where they're supposed to be," I said, looking over to Marc for confirmation.

"Mr. Henniston, here, is an officer of the Second National Bank of Kansas City," Marc added, and though I knew nothing of the bank I assumed it was one with which the town did business, or intended to. "And his brother Hiram is a member of the state legislature."

"What's this banker's name?"

Mr. Henniston cleared his throat. "Sheale. He's not a banker. We're partners in a lumber shipping venture separately from the bank. Mr. Sheale was traveling with a sum of gold on his person. It was his intention to purchase some land there for a warehouse, but the man he was supposed to buy it from never heard from him, nor did the builder."

The thought immediately crossed my mind that this fellow might have absconded with the cash. It must have shown on my face because Marc quickly discredited it. "He's a rich man, so we're not much concerned with the loss of the money on him as with his safety."

Mr. Henniston cleared his throat again and described the errant Sheale. "Tall, thin, forty-nine years of age, with a long mustache and a short beard beneath his lip."

"No, can't say he sounds familiar to me," I said, though I might have seen a dozen men answering to that description over the past several months.

"Mr. Henniston hasn't been to Cherryvale or Independence yet. I thought perhaps you might take him there."

"I'm tending bar this afternoon."

"Get the new man to cover for you."

"It'd make more sense to have the new man take him," I said.

"You're going, and you're going now. Go to the saloon and have the new man sent for. Good day, Mr. Henniston."

Henniston seemed relieved to be dismissed, and he got up to leave.

"You'll report back to me at the end of the day, Bill," Marc said, his eyes down on a piece of paper on the desk. He peered up at the door when I didn't respond, and I wanted to pick him up by the ears and pull him over the desk and thrash him until that supercilious look vanished from his pan. As if he sensed that, his lips curled slowly into a smile of the surliest disdain, whether for me or for Mr. Henniston I didn't know.

* * *

We got a horse for Mr. Henniston at the livery and set off. The way he sat upon the horse, shifting his great hams from side to side and favoring first one and then the other, his nostrils flaring at the discomfort of it, made me ask if he'd prefer I hired a wagon. He forced a jovial grin and assured me that he would be fine, though every step that horse took brought from him a wince and a short, shallow intake of breath.

Cherryvale was on our way to Independence, and a mile or so out of Cottonwood I asked Mr. Henniston if he wanted to stop there on the return trip or on the way there. He had no preference, and when it loomed to our left we continued on our way past it. By then Henniston had settled into the saddle and nearly looked comfortable as he bounced, content to watch the green grass and wildflowers of the rolling mounds as we rode past them, seemingly forgetful of the matter at hand. Occasionally, though, he would grimace and squirm, clenching the left buttock and then relaxing it and doing the same with the right. Never once did he lift himself out of the saddle by putting his weight onto his stirruped feet, and I wondered if the condition of his knees prevented it. After one such painful readjustment of his ample rump I said it was a shame there was no rail service between the towns.

"Ah, well. Train travel's scarcely any more comfortable."

"Quicker, though. Your timing was lucky."

"How's that?" he said, grunting painfully as the horse stepped into a slight depression in the path.

"If this had happened last year you wouldn't have had the train to bring you down from Kansas City."

His nostrils flared, though whether in pain or in distaste for the railroad I couldn't say. "Stupid thing, that rail line."

"How's that?"

"Think. What's it for? Transport people and goods. Now. What kind of goods is it going to be transporting?"

"Mainly livestock out of Texas," I said, and he startled me with a loud and openly derisive snort.

"Christ almighty. He tried to get money out of us for those cattle pens. He's still trying, which is the only reason I got you out here, watching me wheeze on the back of this scurvy nag."

"What have you got against cattle pens?"

"I have nothing against cattle pens. I just don't believe in 'em this far east. Those Texans don't want to drive their cattle any further than absolutely necessary."

"Marc says the trail that's going to lead up here is faster than the ones out west."

He held out his palm. "The new trail will be faster and cheaper by virtue of access to water, et cetera, et cetera, et cetera. He's tried to sell us all on this and failed. I don't know of any cattle people he's managed to convert either. By the looks of the town there's money coming in, though, so maybe I'm wrong. I hope I am. But if I were you, and I wanted to invest in a cattle depot, I'd be looking a lot further west."

We didn't talk much after that until we got to Independence. There we met the land agent who was to have brokered the sale of the warehouse space; he had seen no trace of Sheale, and after questioning the local hoteliers and rooming houses we concluded that we were too far south for any trace of the man, and we headed back northward. Henniston haltingly suggested that we stay longer, as he might still have conducted some of the business Mr. Sheale was meant to come down for, but I wasn't anxious to wait around for him and I told him no. I was annoyed with him for his lack of faith in Cottonwood's future, for his shortsightedness, and for the slow pace his girth had forced us to set for the day's ride.

By mid-afternoon we passed Cherryvale again, this time turning into town. The first man we saw was a farmer headed for the feed store. He was a big man in a straw hat, and he had just stepped down from his wagon. He got a look at Henniston, leaning over to his right, with some curiosity. Then Henniston straightened up and leaned over to his left. This was another trick to assuage the pain of being in the saddle, one he had started doing in Independence; he hadn't wanted to dismount there for fear he'd be unable to get himself back onto the horse. The farmer began to laugh, and Henniston was quick to take offense. By the time he calmed down we established that the farmer hadn't seen or heard of anything that might explain Mr. Sheale's disappearance, and we proceeded to the hotel.

I dismounted and brought the innkeeper outside. He listened carefully to Henniston's story and reported that no one answering to Sheale's description had stayed there. He thought it might be worth Henniston's while to travel to Parsons or Oswego, but added as I had that a substantial number of men had started crossing the old Osage territory over the last few years without finishing it, vanishing as if the prairie had opened itself up and swallowed them up to feed that rich black soil beneath its grasses.

"My God," Henniston said. "You're just like this one. You talk as if that's a normal state of affairs."

The innkeeper and I traded looks and shrugged. "This isn't Kansas City, Mr. Henniston," I said. "This is the frontier."

Henniston spat. "Don't tell me about the goddamned frontier, Mr. Ogden. I made my money in California, in forty-nine, and I know a damned sight more than you ever will about the hazards of the wilderness." His face was scarlet by then and he was breathing harder than when we'd stopped. I thought the innkeeper was going to say something in rebuttal, but his attention was claimed by something up the street.

"Well, if I'm not mistaken there's an old friend of yours," he said with a wink, and I turned to see the younger of the two John Benders coming toward us in a weatherbeaten platform spring wagon.

I called to Bender and bade him stop. He turned slowly, with a simpleton's smile on his lips, his eyebrows raised in curiosity, and looking me straight in the eyes betrayed no sign that he knew me. He nonetheless slowed to a stop.

"Howdy. On my way to the feed store," he said with a jaunty bouncing rhythm, his accent stronger than I remembered. He had a large scab on the tip of his nose, cracked and yellowing at the borders.

"Mr. Bender. Remember me? I came out to your house one evening. Bill Ogden out of Cottonwood. Your sister Katie knows me."

Sitting there at the reins he nodded dumbly and looked Mr. Henniston up and down as though cataloguing his clothing and accessories; in particular he had his eye on a sturdy gold chain hanging from Henniston's vest pocket.

"This is Mr. Henniston," I said. "He's an officer of the Second National Bank of Kansas City, Missouri."

"Oh," Bender said, transfixed by the gold chain. "Say, mister, do you know what's the hour?"

Henniston took out an enormous gold timepiece at the end of the chain and opened its casing. It filled most of his big palm and looked as heavy as a chunk of marble, and he held it to his ear and shook it. "I'm sorry, I forgot to wind it, I'm afraid. As I often do."

Bender looked like a cat watching birds through a metal screen, and something like horror flashed in his eyes as they saw the object of desire slip back into Henniston's vest pocket.

"We're looking for a man who might have been traveling this way from the Osage Mission."

"I didn't see nobody," he said quickly.

"Wait a minute, I don't mean today. Anyway I haven't given you the particulars. He's about fifty, a tall fellow with a mustache and a beard. Thin."

Bender looked paler than he had a moment before, and the scab stood out harshly against the lightness of his face. "Ain't seen him."

"Would have been about March, I'd think."

"I told you I ain't seen him," he said, and he turned the little wagon around and started back in the direction he'd come. "Ain't hardly seen anyone lately."

"Where are you going?" I said.

"Home, I got chores to do."

"Weren't you headed for the feed store?"

Bender glanced at the store, wide-eyed. "Got all the feed I want," he said, and he hurried off.

"That's a peculiar kind of a dutchman," Henniston said.

We stayed another half an hour, and we didn't find anybody who'd seen Sheale. By the time we got back to Cottonwood it was getting dark, and I discovered that Mr. Henniston liked to take a drink. At the bar he knocked four or five back before Marc came looking for him.

"Come along, Mr. Henniston, we've got dinner coming before too long."

"Can I invite my new friend Bill along?" Henniston asked. Our friendship was a development I hadn't been aware of until that moment.

"Afraid not. Now come along, we don't want the soup to get cold."

After an effusive leave-taking Mr. Henniston left with Marc, who had not deigned to address me, and just for a moment I missed the town the way it had been, with a dismal, cramped saloon, no railroad and no bright future ahead as a cattle town.

The next day at eleven in the morning I arrived at the saloon, where a small crowd of men including Silas Henniston already awaited my appearance, and I unlocked the building and let them in. My mind was turning several thoughts around at once, thoughts of opening the saloon at an earlier hour and hiring another hand for the farm and obtaining some books from the Levals' library for Clyde, possibly even spending a little time tutoring the boy, and I promptly forgot to ask the men at the bar about the wayward Mr. Sheale. So did Mr. Henniston, who immediately ordered a whiskey. When he tried to pay for it I gave Gleason the high sign.

"Sorry, mister, I can't take your money," he said, though it chagrined him not to.

"Thank you, son," Henniston said, and he turned to me with a grin and hoisted the drink. After two of them it occurred to him to bring up the matter at hand. No one had seen Mr. Sheale, and Henniston grew silent.

I was surprised to see Herbert Braunschweig step through the door a few minutes later. He never drank until the end of the working day, yet here he was at a quarter past eleven in the morning, bellying up and slapping his fist to the bar.

"Whiskey, bartender." Gleason poured him one and he drained it and held out his glass for another.

"What brings you here this early, Herbert?"

He scowled. "Henry Flank says I can't work in the scaffolding any more. Wants me to work at framing, on the ground, and I ain't gonna do it."

"How come?"

"Working on the scaffolds, which I been doing since I was fourteen years old, calls for throwing and catching, and Flank says I can't judge distances with one eye. It's bullshit is what it is."

"When'd you lose that eye, anyway?"

"Army, in '63."

"Is that so?"

"Yeah, I got into a scrap with a corporal who made a remark about my sister. Little cocksucker gouged it out."

Herbert was a big man, and I'd have hated to see the man that could do that to him. "Jesus."

"Well, I was choking the shit out of the little bastard, and I probably would have finished him off, otherwise. I spent some time in the stockade for it, but I was a good soldier." He slapped the bar again. "And I was a damned good shot, too, even with my shooting eye gone. Goddamn Flank anyway."

Henniston had taken a couple more drinks by now, and he took an interest in Herbert's troubles. "Maybe my friend Marc could intercede on your behalf," he said, and Herbert laughed.

"He's everybody's friend, that's the trouble. He's Flank's friend, too."

"As a matter of fact, I'm a guest in his home at the moment," Henniston said. He explained his situation to Herbert, who didn't think he'd seen Sheale.

"I'll keep my eye and ears open though. You think of asking down in Parsons?"

"That's what the man at the hotel in Cherryvale suggested," Henniston said, and that got me thinking about John Bender, and from there I got to thinking about the night I'd stopped at his house.

"Mr. Henniston, you recall that dutchman we spoke to in Cherryvale?"

He nodded. "He was a queer sort. Awful skittish, now that I reflect on it."

I told them my story, not forgetting the smell emanating from the floorboards, and Henniston became more and more excited as I went on. Herbert, at a loss for how to spend his afternoon, suggested we ride out to the farm and strong-arm the Benders and see what they really knew. With the promise of a free drink I sent one of the men to find Hans to take my place for the day. Under the bar I kept two loaded guns, my own Colt and the Dragoon I had taken off the drummer on the day of the Levals' arrival in town; I stuck them both into my belt, and we left as soon as Hans arrived, happy for the chance at a second day's extra shift in a row.

We headed to the livery stable where we rented the same horse Henniston had ridden the day before and a second for Herbert, and for fifteen minutes we struggled to get Henniston aboard his mount, a considerably more difficult job than it had been the day before, since in addition to being morbidly obese he was also two-thirds drunk. We made even worse time as a result of it; he rode in humiliated silence, concentrating all his efforts on not falling off the tame old mare. A low fog now lay over the entire area, making matters worse for the fact that the horses couldn't see their feet meeting the ground.

When we got to the Big Hill Creek ford we ran into a farmer on horseback, another German, and I asked him in his native tongue if he'd seen Henniston's partner. He replied that he hadn't, but when I told him we were heading for the Bender place to ask them about the matter he reported that he'd been hearing their animals since morning.

The first sight that greeted us as we approached the claim was a mule that had been staked out in the middle of the mound, thirty feet or so from the house. It brayed frantically at the sight of us and tugged pitifully on its tether. It was a fleabitten animal, with patches of fur missing and a sizeable chunk missing from its left ear.

From the stable to our left flowed the sounds of a cow and a calf frantically crying out to one another. There stood a month-old calf in one pen, and two stalls down was its mother, her udder swollen painfully; she had gashes on her side where she had tried to knock the sides of her pen down to reach the hungry calf. She had nearly succeeded, too, since the whole stable was rudely constructed of scrap wood. I dismounted and reunited the two, relieved to have that part of the barnyard chorus quieted.

Herbert dismounted in his turn and he and I drew our weapons.

"John Bender," I yelled. "Need to have a word with you."

There was no answer, and I leaned over to Herbert. "I'll go to the door, you stand behind me with weapon in hand."

A goat as thin as a two-by-four slowly and arthritically limped toward me as I neared the door. I rapped with my knuckles and again yelled, "John Bender," again with no response. I pulled the latchstring, opened the door and stepped into that dark house and found the front part unoccupied. The roughhewn furnishings remained, and I noted that the copper pot was gone. I stepped behind the canvas sheet dividing the structure into two rooms, calling out as I did so.

"I'm armed and I'll fire without a thought," I said, but there was no one there to hear it. I relaxed and noted the same smell I'd detected months earlier, seemingly stronger now despite the cold, wet air, and I called out to my comrades to join me inside.

"Jesus, Mary, and Joseph," Henniston said upon entering, and after inhaling a single lungful he stumbled back outside, nearly knocking Herbert to the ground as he passed, hurriedly placing a handkerchief to his mouth. As Henniston vomited, leaning against the side of the house, Herbert stepped across the threshold and took a deep breath, his mouth pinched tight.

"Calls to mind a battlefield," he said.

I nodded and pointed at the trapdoor. "See that? I noted that on my last visit." We moved the table and chairs outside, I pulled the curtain down from the window, and then we knelt on the floor. Herbert pulled a jackknife from his vest and inserted it into the space between the trap and the surrounding puncheons. Prying the door loose we lifted the thing up and were nearly overcome by the foulness of the air wafting upwards, to the degree that we tossed the trap door to the side and both exited in a hurry, taking in deep, grateful draughts of the fresh air outside.

"A day as dark as this one we'll be needing a lantern to see what's down there," I said.

Herbert took a deep breath and stepped back inside, and I followed. The house was dark, but there was enough light coming through the door and the window to give a vague idea of what was in the pit.

"Looks to me like there's nothing down there but stink," Herbert said. It appeared to be dirt, soaked at bottom with a quantity of blood and gore, which in itself proved nothing sinister. Old Bender might have used it to kill goats, for all we knew.

We stepped outside again for a break from the noxious gases. "I suppose we ought to head back to town with word of this."

Herbert nodded. "Why don't we take a quick look about the place first," he said, "see what we can find before we go." He nodded discreetly over at Henniston, who still sat on his ass next to the ramshackle structure the Bender men had built, looking dazed. "Shame we can't send your banker back to town in our stead, but he'd never get there." He chuckled, slapped me on the shoulder and set off in the direction of the stable.

I circled the house and could see nothing unusual, hampered as my vision was by the mist, then tried the small orchard to the north. The first thing that struck me was the beauty of the budding fruit trees. The Benders might not have been much to crow about as farmers, but they had a mighty healthy looking bunch of apple and peach trees, and planted just two or three years earlier. The second thing I might not have noticed had I not served on occasion as a battlefield gravedigger, and recently as a municipal one; the low fog gave an enhanced sensation of relief at ground level, laying thick and milky upon a number of rectangular depressions in the soil. These stood out in ethereal, vaporous white against the dark gray-brown of the orchard's tilled soil, varying in width from about three feet to about four, and all were six or seven feet long.

I yelled at Herbert. He came running, and stopped short at the sight of the concave earth.

"I spied a shovel in the stable," he said, and he hurried to get it.

When he returned I eagerly grabbed the shovel from his outstretched hand and began digging at the first mound I had spotted. It was good dirt for digging, neither too viscous from the recent rains nor too claylike, and before I had gotten five feet down my blade struck something solid. I began digging more carefully by hand, excavating around the object, and soon enough I had uncovered most of a man's upper torso. I then reached down and gingerly picked the clumps of earth away from the face. It was dark, loamy dirt and came away easily enough, and before long I saw through the vapor the yellow hairs of a blond mustache; a bit more hand-digging revealed the whole head of Mister A. J. Harticourt, the drummer who'd fucked my Ninna some six months earlier, his eyes sunken into their sockets and his nose gone but otherwise remarkably well preserved for a man half a year in the ground. His throat had been slit open, and even fixed in its matrix of cold earth it was plain that the back of his skull had been caved in by something heavy. Further digging revealed him to be unclothed apart from a pair of long underwear; they had even taken his ruined bowler from him. I felt a little sorry for our disagreement the day he rode away with Kate Bender, and with the dirt of his grave still packed under my fingernails I muttered, sotto voce, that I wouldn't let it go.

"Come along," Herbert said with a hand on my arm. "Let's head back for some men and some shovels."

We determined that I would head to Cherryvale and Herbert would return to Cottonwood. Henniston would have slowed either one of us down, and we insisted that he stay. He sputtered and choked but agreed to stay behind, and Herbert and I went our separate ways, leaving him alone there with the animals and the dead in their graves for company.

5

MONTGOMERY COUNTY, KANSAS
MAY 1873

Gun Play

It was late in the day by the time I returned to the Bender claim, followed by two dozen men and equipped with lanterns, shovels, guns, and provisions for a ride of several days' duration. Word had spread quickly in Cherryvale, and by now it would have reached Independence, and Parsons would get it by nightfall as well; I suspected that by morning the Bender farm would be swarming with the curious and the vengeful.

Linder, the German farmer I had encountered earlier, had run into Herbert on his way to Cottonwood and had hastened to the farm; he was waiting when I returned with the men from Cherryvale. I asked him in German if the Benders typically traveled by wagon or on horseback. He replied that the men usually traveled in the worn-out old platform spring wagon we'd seen young John driving in Cherryvale, with the women occasionally in the back. There was no such wagon on the property currently, and we quickly determined that the two horses Linder knew the Benders to possess were gone as well.

Poor Henniston had retreated to the stables and the company of the cow and her calf, and was barely coherent when I found him there. Soon after that Herbert arrived Marc, followed by a small army of men and equipment. Several of the men had entered the house with lanterns lit and proceeded to remove all the furniture in the house, placing it next to the table and chairs we had removed earlier. I called out to Dr. Salisbury among a crowd that surrounded Marc, and we descended into the pit together with a lantern. The walls were solid enough, but the ground was horribly soft, and our boots sank an inch or more with each step.

"In my opinion, it's earth mixed with a quantity of human blood," he told me, "though I couldn't prove it right here and now."

He climbed out of the pit with my assistance and I followed; then we went outside to the orchard to examine the bodies as they were brought up. The digging was going quickly, as there were many men working the shovels, and most of the graves were no deeper than four feet. Michael Cornan, looking no more disturbed than a man digging for nightcrawlers, and Tim Niedel, looking like a man who wanted to call out for his mother, had just lifted a corpse from the dirt. Despite the damage done to his face by his killers and its subsequent decomposition there was a general agreement that these were the remains of Otis's apprentice Mr. Perkey, and I stood above him wondering about his dying mother, and whether he'd been killed on the way to or from her sickbed in Lawrence. Before Perkey's departure the loft above the forge had been his bed, and if he'd returned as planned I would have had to bunk elsewhere, maybe even back at the farm.

"Say, Bill," Tiny Rector called out to me from above another grave, one row over, "isn't this Juno, your hired man?"

I stepped through the trees and peered down into the hole. It was still overcast and nearly dark now, and I had to descend into the grave with the lantern to see the face clearly. The body was further deteriorated than the drummer's or Perkey's and mostly without flesh, but it was Juno, without question; his high forehead and thick jaw gave him away. What desiccated tissue remained about his throat had been hacked through to the vertebrae, and the back of his skull had been fractured by a heavy blow, as the drummer's had. I began digging around his hands and was sorry to find his soft fingers ringless, though I would have been shocked had the Benders failed to steal the ring he had stolen from me, and which I in turn had stolen from my father's corpse; all seven bodies we had found thus far were naked of jewelry and clothes, except for one or two who still wore the threadbare remnants of their undergarments. As I had for the drummer, I regretted my differences with Juno, who had been my friend once, and climbing out of his grave I wished I'd let him stay on at the farm.

"Looks like they slit his throat, don't it? Wonder how come they cracked his head, too."

A hardware dealer from Cherryvale came over. "We found three hammers in there, in the second room behind the canvas curtain. There's blood on that, too, right about where a head'd be if a man was seated on that bench. My guess is they're all going to have their heads bashed in like that from behind."

"How come they cut their throats, then?" Tim said.

The hardware man looked sick. "You suppose they bled the bodies dry down in that rootcellar before they buried them out here?"

"But what for?" Tim asked.

No one answered him. Another body had just been removed from the freshest-looking of the graves, corresponding roughly to the description of Henniston's partner Mr. Sheale. I went over to the stable to speak to Henniston and found that Herbert had brought him back a bottle from the saloon, which had made him considerably more collected than before. I walked him to the orchard, and he looked down at his friend disappointedly. The feeble sun was nearly down, and by the flickering light of all the lanterns the orchard began to resemble an eerie garden party. I held my own lamp next to the corpse's ghastly face, and Henniston readily identified it despite the mottled gray skin of the face, as wrinkled and fragile as that of an overripened peach. His throat, too, had been cut, and the rear portion of his skull was entirely caved in.

"That's him, all right. What shall we do to get him back to Kansas City?"

"I don't know," I said.

Tim Niedel was standing next to me. "Easy, we'll haul him to Cottonwood in a wagon with the rest of these poor souls and we'll load him onto the train. You paying for it?"

Henniston nodded, then took another consoling nip from the bottle.

"Main question is, shouldn't we be setting out after them sons of bitches already?" Tim waved an arm in the direction of the orchard graveyard, where men still toiled to bring the dead aboveground.

I hadn't thought about it until then, but I called Marc over. "You think we ought to start organizing the men into search parties before the Benders get too far?"

I knew Marc was calculating in his head the amount of damage this was going to do the town's reputation in the nation's press, but I was nonetheless surprised at his response. "Useless. They've a day's head start on us or better." It was the first time he'd spoken to me since he'd arrived.

"All the more reason to set out now, rather than wait for tomorrow. And we can make up some of that time while they sleep."

Several of the men were listening, and unaccustomed as he was to being contradicted he knew better than to allow his anger to show in their presence.

Tim spoke up, loud as he always was and not at all cowed by Marc. "There's seven men dead over there at least, and surely more still in the ground, and who knows how many they kilt and throwed in the river like they did poor Hiram Steig, and we owe it to them to get the dirty bastards."

Another man I didn't know pushed his way over. I saw one-eyed Herbert coming our way.

"We don't even know in which direction they fled," Marc said.

"You think they might have passed through town?" I asked Tim.

"They'd be taking an awful chance. If they thought they was about to be found out, or maybe already had been, town's the last place they'd want to be found passing through."

"Could have gone south."

"Could have," Herbert said. The light from a torch was shining on him at such an angle that his eyesocket looked especially deep and round. "Open prairie down there, though. Nowhere to hide if anyone was to spot 'em, and you can see for miles to the south from these mounds. Me, I wouldn't have gone south."

"North," I said, "along the Verdigris."

Tim nodded. "There's trees alongside the riverbank for miles and miles. That's cover in the daytime, and you could travel at night. They could catch a train at Toronto or Eureka, and then they're gone forever."

I remembered finding young John Bender that night hiding in the trees alongside Big Hill Creek, and it made sense to me. "That's for me, then. Time we started breaking the men down into search parties."

Marc saw that the posses would organize themselves and get under way under his command or not; choosing the former, he raised his voice and made as though it had been his idea all along. "Gather round, men, we're going to split up into companies and head out in search of the assassins."

In the end there were six groups of four men each; each was assigned a particular trail that seemed a more or less likely escape route. My party consisted of Herbert Braunschweig, Tim Niedel, Marc, and myself, and we were assigned the northern track, along the Verdigris river, which all seemed to consider the most likely route for the Benders' escape. There was some grumbling among the other groups, but no one questioned Marc's right to assign himself the best chance for capturing the Benders.

At the outset there were eight of us; we would split up when the river forked into two, up by Neodesha. We reached it after a couple of hours, with the Fall running westward to Eureka and the Verdigris eastward to the town of Toronto, and then we were four. The fog had begun to clear by that time, and from behind a gauzy cloud cover the moon bathed the land before us with enough silvered light to ride without much difficulty. The ground beside the river was soft without being too muddy, and when the last of the fog had lifted we learned that we had unknowingly been following a set of tracks, those of a wagon whose front wheels were narrower than the rear pair, pulled by a single horse with another walking beside it. The hoofprints of both beasts were narrowly spaced, suggesting a slow pace and a heavy burden; whether this was the Benders' own wagon or not we had no way to know, but we took it for a good sign.

At Guilford, whose town limits bordered the river, we spotted a shanty near the trail and awakened its sole occupant. Standing outside, we described to the drowsy farmer the horrors that had brought us there, and the family we sought. Half-sleeping, shrouded in an atmosphere of whiskey fumes, he reported that he had spotted a wagon carrying a man and two women, and another man with them on horseback, sometime late in the day; he had no clock of any kind and couldn't be any more precise.

"Was one of the men bent over at the neck?" I asked.

"Couldn't say," he said. "Too occupied looking at the younger of the women." He sounded like a southerner, maybe out of Tennessee.

"Redhead?"

"She was, too, and she smiled at me." He cleared his throat and spat at the ground. "I was right in the midst of putting up that chicken coop there." He indicated with his thumb a jumble of sticks nailed together with some twisted wire to form the core of a structure considerably cruder even than his shack. "I waved a hello to 'em, and they waved back. They was asking how far it was to Toronto or Middletown, and I told 'em how far, but I knew a better way to Middletown than along the river, and as I told it they kept on a-going, and so I walked along with 'em a ways. Probably a mile and a half. I was awful interested in that redhead, and I asked her 'Are you married to him, there?' and she said no, she was his sister. I damned near proposed marriage then and there." He laughed at the absurdity of it, showing widely and irregularly spaced teeth, two of the upper incisors angled crazily outward. "They said they was going to perform in a show, a traveling thing, and they wondered if I'd like to come along." He looked over at the river in the direction they'd gone, the very picture of wistful regret, apparently having forgotten what we'd told him three minutes earlier about who the Benders were and what they'd done. "I got a claim to work, though, and I'm damned if I'll wreck one more thing in my life."

We bade him goodnight; he nodded and shuffled back into his shack and we continued northward. "You think we ought to have asked him about that shortcut to Middletown?" Herbert asked.

"There's no train in Middletown. They'd be going out of their way," I said.

"They'd have killed him if he'd come along."

"A poor man like that?" Herbert said. "What for?"

"For the amusement of it," Tim said.

Herbert took hold of a metal rod he'd stuck into his saddle bag. He slapped it into the hand holding the reins so hard just the hearing of it smarted.

"Where'd you get that thing?" I asked.

"Bender's hearth. Reckon they used it for a poker. I was thinking I might beat 'em to death rather than just shoot 'em." He grinned and laughed, and so did I, but Marc and Tim acted as if they hadn't heard him.

Two hours later or thereabouts the wagon tracks ended at a broken-down platform spring wagon, abandoned with a split axle. They would presumably now be riding two to a horse, and heavily loaded down. On the wagon were various items of value too heavy to carry on horseback for any distance: two finely tooled saddles, an ornately framed painting of a sharp-nosed woman in a cap and high-waisted dress of the kind fashionable thirty or forty years previous, and an assortment of copper pots and pans.

"That's theirs, all right," I said, indicating the only pot in the bunch that showed signs of having been used to cook. "I saw that hanging over their hearth in January."

"Maybe one of us should go back and tell the others to come this way," Tim said.

"No," Marc said with a dismissive wave. "We'll have found them and dealt with them by the time anyone could reach us."

Herbert spat onto the ground, vaguely in the direction of Marc's left boot. "Gonna hang the women just like the men, if I have anything to say in the matter. You got any objection to that, Mr. Leval?"

"None whatsoever," Marc said, though I didn't expect he intended to be placing the ropes around their necks himself.

"If we don't bring 'em back to town we'll never know exactly what they done or who they was in cahoots with," Tim said.

"I know goddamn well what they done," Herbert said. "I was up to my goddamn knees in it."

Tim shook his head and spat. "Horrible, just thinking about it. Them coming to town and socializing like regular people, and all the while they was slaughtering travelers. You figure they was doing that all along?"

"They showed up in '70, the men first," Herbert said. "April or May, the women a month or so later. That house went up pretty damn quick, as I recall, quicker than the stable. I reckon they was planning all along to lure in travelers."

"Was it '70 or '71?" I asked. "Seems like '71 was when we

started hearing about men setting out for Osage Mission and not getting there."

"What gives me the fantods is that damned cellar underneath the house," Herbert said. "Looks like they were all bled there."

"Well, their throats was cut," Tim said, "they had to bleed someplace, and that way the blood wouldn't be spotted if they had a visitor they didn't manage to do in, like old Bill here."

I had been going over this in my head since we'd left. "But the backs of their skulls were already bashed in. Why cut the throats of dead men?"

"Some kind of sorcery, you think?" Tim asked in a nervous whisper.

Then I told them the story of Mrs. Kearney of Cherryvale, of the rifle, the abortive séance and the priapic figure of the man on the wall.

"I always knowed there was something not right about that Katie Bender," Tim said. "Her and her haints and her curing deaf and dumbness and blindness, I always knowed there was something unchristian about all that business. And you know she used to come to the Methodist meetings on Sundays."

"The hell with that," Herbert said. "A bunch of common thieves, that's all they were. All that spirit business, that's pure bunkum."

"Question is, did Katie Bender think it was bunkum?" Tim said.

"I think she did," I said, thinking of the faked séance at the hotel.

Tim was growing frustrated at our inability to grasp what seemed to him obvious. "Then how do you explain them bleeding them dead men into the soil under their house when they could have just buried them?"

I didn't have an answer for that, and for the most part we remained silent for the next couple of hours. We followed the tracks as thoughtlessly as the horses we rode, with the hoofbeats beneath us and the nearly inaudible trickling of the river to our left the only constant sounds to distract us from our private reveries.

When I was fifteen years old, and circumstances had led me to abandon my formal education in favor of gainful employment, I found work at a big dairy farm nearby owned by a man named Rudolph Harding. Rudolph wasn't a bad man, and not a bad boss, either; for the most part he was fair and even-tempered, but I didn't like him much. Partially it was the fact that he was very religiously inclined, and since I was the son of a minister he tried to draw me into theological conversations as we worked, or ate dinner, or on a few occasions when he drove me to my mother's house in town in his wagon for that express purpose. As he came to recognize that I had fallen away from the church after my father's passing, he decided that it was his Christian mission on earth to bring me back into the bosom of the Methodist faith. I listened politely, since he was my boss, but I found these conversations all but unbearable for the simple reason that I was regularly having my way with Mary Harding, his wife. She was his second wife, and fifteen years or so his junior. Every time Harding and I ended our workday getting down on our knees together and praying (or pretending to, in my case) I was tormented by the thought of Mary's pretty face contorted in ecstasy, or worse, of her mouth wrapped around my prick, and after a year I quit to take a job in town as an attorney's office boy. Harding was wounded when I left, not least because my new position paid less than the farm job, but I had reached the point where I was sure I couldn't stand another of those damned prayer sessions without bursting out with the news that I'd been laying his wife and so frequently that the only excitement left in it was the increasingly likely possibility that we'd be found out. We had to take whatever furtive opportunities arose for our intimacies, and Mary had become progressively more fearless, even brazen, in her certainty that Rudolph was too trusting and witless to ever catch us. By the time I left I disliked Harding because he had treated me kindly and fairly, thereby failing to give me a reason to justify the wrong I had done him.

This memory came to me unbidden and unwelcome as we rode along the river in single file, with my good friend and business partner Marc in the lead. Occasionally the tracks of the horses faded when the ground got hard or when for some reason they took them onto higher and drier land, but always they started up again, the prints closely spaced.

We did not precisely follow the serpentine path of the river as the Benders had but kept to a beeline adjacent to it; twenty miles or so to the south of Toronto we heard a commotion in the bushes ahead of us. It might have been anything, but John Bender's furtiveness in the bushes a few months ago came again to my mind, and I stopped and dismounted, signaling as I did so to the others to continue on.

I walked my chestnut mare alongside the others, handed the reins to Herbert, and then outflanked the shrubbery and drew the Colt, halfway hoping the movement was that of a beaver or a bobcat.

I crept on the ground to the bush and passed behind it; between it and the riverbank I found a grizzled character of indeterminable age, somewhere between thirty and seventy and none too hale looking even at the high end of that scale, seated upon the grass with his back leaning against a tree, oblivious to our presence. His trousers were about his ankles, and he pulled at his swollen organ, moaning dementedly. I cocked the Dragoon, and only then did he stop the rhythmic stroking of his prick. His gun sat just out of reach, atop a hat, and I told him to sit still. I grabbed the gun and pulled back.

The others approached, and I told him to step out slow. He did so, arms upraised and beaming at us like we were his long-lost cousins. His pants remained at his feet and he shuffled forward as though that were his usual way of dressing and getting around. His cock did not deflate; it swung back and forth with each step he took, and I thought Tim Niedel might shoot him just to make that boner go away.

"Any of you looking to acquire some jewelry?" he asked in a croak like that of a man who's just been throttled. At that Herbert took the poker from his saddle bag and once again started smacking it into his palm, and the stranger looked still less certain of himself. That he might be a legitimate dealer in jewels seemed unlikely; open sores ate at his face, and he wore no shirt under his faded union army jacket.

Finally Tim could stand no more, and he faced the fellow square on. "You goddamned dirty pervert, you get that prick of yours back down limp and get your drawers back up or I'll by God shoot it off, you hear me?"

The man covered his cock with his hands but was unable to calm the thing down. He did pull his trousers up, and that soothed Tim somewhat.

"Let's see 'em," Marc said, and the man scampered back into the brush from which, after a moment's rustling, he emerged holding a burning lantern and a finely-wrought ebony jewel box. He opened it and held it up for Marc to see, and then moved it to where Herbert and Tim and I could each in turn have a look.

"How's about that signet, there?" I asked.

"Which one's that?" he asked.

"That one," I said, leaning down and pointing to the ring Juno had died wearing.

The wretch plucked it from the box and handed it to me. "One dollar," he said.

"And why should I pay you a dollar for something that's already mine?" I asked, and the bedraggled jewel dealer looked confused and frightened; he suspected he was about to be robbed. I ignored him and addressed Marc. "This is a ring my hired hand stole when he left, the one we pulled out of the orchard."

"Where'd you get that ring?" Marc asked, drawing his revolver and pointing it straight at the man's forehead.

"Found it. Found some other things, too, next to a dead horse. It was still warm when I come acrost it, if you're wanting something to fill your bellies. I can't eat the whole thing by myself."

"Where'd you find it and when?"

"Around nightfall. Only et a little piece of the haunch."

"Where, I said?"

He pointed upriver, anxious to please. "Little bit up that way. We could build us a bonfire and roast us a whole hindquarter."

Marc holstered his gun, dismounted and took the jewel box. "There are some fine pieces in here."

"They must have a hell of a lot of cash, then, if they're down to dumping gold."

"There was more things," the man said. "In the saddle bags. Hell of a nice saddle, too, nice as that one there." He indicated Marc's saddle.

"If they're down to one horse, we still have a shot at stopping them before they get to Toronto," Tim said.

"That's if we get going now," I said to Marc, who was standing there looking thoughtfully at the man.

Marc handed me the jewel box and climbed back onto the saddle. "All right, let's get a move on, then."

"Hold on," the man on the ground said, his eyes full of hurt and injustice. "You got to pay for them rings and things, they're mine fair and square."

Marc reached into his vest with perfect calm, looking for all the world as if he were going to withdraw a sheaf of bills and pay the man for his trouble. Instead he drew again, and in what seemed like a single, deft motion brought the weapon up, pulled back the hammer and blew a hole in the man's forehead, sending back a spray of gore onto the soft grass. Above it the poor devil collapsed, bitter for a second about his fate but dead before his knees gave up their burden. The three of us looked at Marc, who replaced his pistol and stared back at us, daring us to find fault with his action.

Herbert spoke up first. "That weren't strictly necessary, Mr. Leval."

"He was their confederate," Marc said. "Let's ride."

"Confederate, hell," Tim yelled. "That was just a poor river rat scrounging for food, thought he'd gotten lucky for once in his sorry-assed life."

"Think about it, Mr. Niedel. They killed at least, what? Fourteen men we know of. Then there are those that were found earlier downstream in the Verdigris, and then there are all those unaccounted for. How many of those have there been in the last two or three years? Thirty? Fifty?"

"That don't make this dead man lying here their helper."

"Goddamn it, think. Where are the horses the dead men rode? Their saddles? Where did the Benders sell all those stolen goods? Those men in the orchard had been stripped right down to their skins. Multipy them by five or ten and you've got a lot to dispose of in a place as desolate as this."

Tim thought about it for a minute. "Maybe that's so, maybe they did have confederates, but that don't make him one of them."

"The hell with you, then," Marc said, kicking his horse's flank. "He was carrying stolen goods, and to my mind that makes him one of them. They're five minutes closer to Toronto and the railroad right now."

He started along the bank, and after a moment's hesitation Herbert and Tim went, too. I waited a moment longer and slipped the signet ring onto the little finger of my left hand and followed.

A mile upriver we found the horse, its saddlebags picked clean by the man Marc had killed, and possibly by others. The cause of the beast's death was immediately apparent: the haunch from which the jeweler had sliced a chunk of meat stank, and shortly below the fresh cut an old and festering wound still glistened in the light of the moon, hours after its putrescent fluids had ceased to flow.

"Bet you two dollars that's Mr. Sheale's mount," Tim said as the stink receded at our backs, and that was the last thing that was said for a long time.

After that it was hard to judge the passage of time. We spread out, riding twenty feet abreast and approached every bush and shade tree as if it might contain a nest of vipers. We were all testy from the ride and the lack of sleep, and we debated whether to take the Benders back with us. Herbert still intended to hang them all on the spot, and Marc indicated again that he would make no move to stop it, though without indicating whether he'd sully his own hands in the process. Tim insisted we take them back to stand trial; how, though, if they only possessed one horse and no wagon, were we to return all four of them? In the meantime the tracks of that remaining horse had disappeared again, and I suggested to Tim that Katie might have summoned the powers of darkness to make the horse levitate. He didn't think that was funny.

We had quieted down again, hunkering down in our saddles, wrapped in blankets and all of us wishing we'd brought warmer clothes. I particularly missed the fine fur coat Marc and Maggie had presented me with for Christmas and my old buffalo robe. A few miles south of Middletown we came to a fork in the river, one of many we had encountered since we began heading north, and Marc stopped to point out a spot on the riverbank just short of the fork. There were hoofprints in the mud, but only those closest to the waterline remained muddy.

"Those look like hoofprints to you?"

"Sure, but old ones, and they're leading in from the north."

"They may have backtracked," Marc said.

"And there's three, maybe four horses there."

"They stole some horses, then. Herbert, you and Tim follow this fork. Bill and I'll go on up to Toronto."

Herbert scowled. "What the hell for?"

I imagined some variation of the phrase "because I said so" about to form on Marc's lips, but he remained civil. "If they're headed west they'll catch the train at Neal, not Toronto."

"I still don't think that's any kind of tracks from them. I say we stick together." I looked at the three of them as I said it, but it was Tim and Herbert I was trying to win over. I was sure Marc was wrong, but I'd never convince him of it.

Tim and Herbert shifted their gazes from each other to me and finally to Marc. "I say we split up like Mr. Leval says," Herbert said, and Tim nodded.

"You want to catch up to the whole four of them when it's just the two of you?" I asked.

"We got guns, and two of 'em's women. They killed all those men from behind, unawares. Face to face I ain't scared." Herbert looked over at Tim. "You?"

"Nope."

"Let's get moving, then," Marc said, and Tim and Herbert forded the river there. It was a good spot for crossing, and they managed to get the horses to the other side without much drama. They hurried up the narrow tributary's banks at a trot, and we followed suit along the east bank of the Verdigris.

We hadn't spoken for at least half an hour when the wind began to pick up and slow down and pick up again like the movements of a symphony; when it blew hard it was loud, whistling through the trees along the riverbank and inspiring the animals and birds to call back to it in a cacaphony from which it was possible to distinguish among others the cries of the loon, the bobcat, the whip-poor-will and the coyote.

Amidst all these sounds came, without warning, the sound of a gunshot at close range. It came so close to my shoulder that I felt the breeze as it went by, and I turned my mount around and drew my weapon. Since we were being fired upon by an unknown assailant I couldn't understand why Marc hadn't turned to face them.

Only when he lowered his revolver and fired at me did I understand that he'd fired the first shot, but as this one hit my nag in the throat I hadn't the leisure to contemplate it. The horse shrieked and reared, and while she was still aloft I dismounted to her right, landing hard on my shoulder. Had I done so on the customary left flank I'd likely have been crushed, because she went down with the sound of bone breaking, and let loose another horrifying whinny; after that the loudest sound was the painful, rhythmic wheezing of her failing respiration.

Hiding behind the horse's prone body I called out to him. "What the hell, Marc," I said, though I knew perfectly well what the hell.

Another slug hit the nag, and she shuddered and the sound of her breathing ceased, and though I didn't want to fire I thought I'd better, in case his aim or his luck improved. I got off but one shot from my old Colt; it hit him square in the chest and knocked him right off his mount. He hit the grass beside the trail, and I came up slow, hammer pulled back. His eyes were shut but he was breathing, and the revolver was still in his hand, his fingers limp. Then his breath got ragged, until a minute or so later I couldn't make it out any more at all.

Nausea overcame me then, and I leaned over against a tree and vomited. I had no way to get back to Cottonwood without giving Marc's horse a good long rest, and I didn't know where to find another.

To the northwest I heard more gunfire, maybe a dozen shots in total. I wondered if Tim and Herbert hadn't encountered the Benders after all, and I was about to mount Marc's horse when I heard a voice calling me from the east.

"You hold on right there, you hear me?" The voice was raucous and full of phlegm, and I turned to face a man on horseback holding what looked to me like a single-shot Springfield rifle. He was squinting as if he couldn't quite make me out in the dark. He was fifty or so, with a drooping moustache that along with that squint made his exact expression hard to read. He was fully dressed, with a broad-brimmed white hat, and seemed wide awake despite the absurdly late—or early—hour. The barrel of his rifle was pointed at my head.

"Is that fellow lying there dead?"

"He took a shot at me," I said.

"I don't give a goddamn who shot at you. Now put that iron down and raise your hands where I can see 'em." His voice was hoarser with every word, and he swallowed painfully. "You just made the mistake of killing a man on the property of a deputy sheriff." He moved his head from side to side like a cat judging the distance to a mouse, and I deduced that his night vision was poor. "Unheel yourself or I'll fire."

I took off running to the south, and then turned and ran north. He fired and missed by a good ten feet, and then I charged him. "All right, mister. Don't try and reload. Now you get down off of that beast."

He got down off of it and I tied his wrists behind him with a length of wire to a hickory tree. He didn't say anything until the sound of two more gunshots came from the northwest.

"You part of a posse after them killers?" he said.

"Never you mind," I said, without thinking to ask him how he'd heard about that. "What county is this, anyway?"

"Wilson," he said. He was oddly docile and seemed, I thought, almost pleased at this turn of events. Wishing I could go to Tim and Herbert's aid I hurried instead to my dead horse, took what I could from the saddlebags, climbed aboard the deputy's fresh horse and kicked its flank. Looking back I could see him for a long ways, thanks to that big white hat.

Discretion should have dictated that I stay clear of the Bender farm on my way back to Cottonwood; in fact a man in full possession of his senses would have bypassed Cottonwood entirely, followed the

Benders' lead and fled northward. Instead I rode directly to the murder site. Stopping a distance from the mound I dismounted and approached the house on foot. The crowd that had gathered there was noisy enough to be heard at a distance of a quarter mile, and the atmosphere was that of a carnival. People must have come from all directions to gawk; I would have estimated their number at well over a thousand, a far larger group than I'd ever seen assembled in Kansas. At first I saw no one I recognized, and then I spotted young Gleason setting up the camera next to one of the opened and presumably now empty graves. He glanced up as though he sensed he was being watched and he nodded at me and returned to his work. I watched him at it for a moment and then, curiously pleased by his competence, moved on. I counted seventeen coffins on the ground, all brand new, and wondered whether the cabinetmaker in Cherryvale had been holding so many ready-made in stock or whether he had worked all night to cover the deficit. Standing over one of the coffins was Mr. Henniston, and I nearly approached him to say hello when it struck me that I shouldn't let myself be seen. I didn't think Gleason would betray me, and no one else had shown any sign of recognition, so I turned and walked back to the tree where I'd tied the deputy's horse, and started riding back to town.

Within five minutes I met a party of men and women, denizens of the tent city, in a buggy on their way to the farm. They greeted me with drunken good cheer, though I didn't know any of them, and I knew then that if I continued in daylight I would be recognized. I couldn't appear in town until nightfall anyway, so I rode off the trail and over the mounds and made camp along Big Hill Creek. I was asleep the minute my head hit the ground, warm and safe under the deputy's blankets, and I slept without dreams, at least any that I could remember upon waking.

By that time the sun was low, and I felt perfectly refreshed. After the sun was well down I remounted and found my way back to the trail. I met no one going the other direction, though I could hear another raucously noisy party behind me. I rode fast enough that the sound of them receded into the distance by the time I arrived at the outskirts of Cottonwood, and I took the horse off the trail there, riding to the north until I was directly behind the Leval estate. I crossed it on foot and was shortly at the rear entrance, where I hitched the horse. I was still calculating the time I'd lost by not heading straight for the Osage Territory alone, and the risk involved in asking Maggie to come along, seeing as I'd just shot her husband down. I knocked on the door, convinced the gamble was a good one.

Rose opened the door and was clearly disappointed to see me and not her employer. "Where's Missus?" I asked her, as if the missus in question were my own.

PART TWO

GHOSTS OF THE OSAGE

1890

1

SAN FRANCISCO, CALIFORNIA, JANUARY, 1890

Slumgullion

Once, wandering northward early in the summer of 1864, I came upon a ruined one-and-a-half story farmhouse by the banks of a stream. The house itself, burnt out and long since emptied of all valuables, was practically roofless, and so full of holes as to be useless as shelter against the elements, but behind it stood a greenhouse whose remaining glass shingles glittered gray-brown in the sunlight like river mud.

Inside it I found only faded red pots, most broken, a few still containing a rich, stinking black soil into which all vegetable matter in the structure had long ago disintegrated; two thirds of the panes had fallen from the roof and walls, and lay on the floor in jumbled shards that crunched beneath my boots with each shifting of my weight. A scratching and clicking like those of a squirrel's claws against glass made me glance upward at the ceiling, through which I saw gazing placidly down at me the lovely, spectral face of a woman.

Badly startled, I slipped and fell backwards against a potting table, which saved my hands being cut by the slivered glass on the floor. Leaning on it with my elbows I looked timorously back up to find the transparent lady still staring at me, her wistful smile as faint and pretty as condensed breath on the pane, tendering grace and unearned absolution.

It was a moment before I took note of her neighbor to the left, a seated man in a top hat, or the elderly couple to her right; as my brain digested this new information the lady transformed before my eyes from ectoplasm to ambrotype, her fading emulsion struck by the sun's rays at the precise acute angle required to create the illusion of a positive image. The sheet was about ten by twelve inches in size, and unusual in that the photographer had made a very close composition of the lady's head, his depth of focus so shallow that only her eyes and lips were sharp, her nose, ears, throat and collar all softened into an indistinct haze.

All the other shingles still in place proved to be discarded, backless ambrotypes also, and carefully picking up from the ground a sliver of a broken one as curved and sharp as a scimitar I was able to distinguish a sloppily knotted cravat and the lapels of a coat cut in a no longer fashionable manner. I had no particular knowledge of photography then, but I knew the stories of battlefield photographers cutting windowpanes from their frames in abandoned houses for use as plates. This was, I supposed, the civilian householder's revenge on the vandalizing photographers, letting the sun slowly bake their hard work back into clear, unadorned glass sheets. I had earlier entertained the notion of sleeping in the dilapidated house, but despite the lady's beauty and benevolent aspect, the idea of spending the night in a place that produced phantoms in daylight made me uneasy, and I continued on down the road.

It was a lovely morning, the clouds wispy and slow-moving across the San Francisco sky, and stepping out of my studio with unpleas-

ant business ahead of me I decided a walk would do me good. Instead of boarding a cable car, then, I walked to Kearney and followed it southward; at Clay Street I turned right and descended it until I arrived at a narrow building with no sign on its facade but the word WINE crudely painted above its door. The ramshackle building was in considerably worse condition than when I'd won it in a card game from a cousin of my own landlady's, so drunk he bet the deed on two pair, eights and fives; his losses for the evening would have supported a family of four for a year. That the property was most likely worth less than the cash value of the bet he was trying to cover didn't bother me much at the time, because I thought I'd make some money renting it. I never got around to throwing the current tenant out the door, though, or to making the improvements I'd planned, and in the end the place seemed destined to cost me rather than earn me money.

The reek from inside was almost enough to keep me from my task, but I crossed the threshold and waited a moment for my eyes to adjust to the light. The building had once housed a proper saloon, for there was a blond patch on the floorboards in the shape of a bar, and another four feet behind that against the wall where a backbar had once stood. Stretching into the impenetrable blackness of the rear of the establishment were four long tables crowded with the most dissipated kind of drunk, most of whom looked close to unconsciousness. Most didn't look up at my arrival, but those who did were engaged in nothing more neurologically taxing than tracking a moving object with their eyes, most of those red of vitreous, black of lid and dead in appearance.

At the rear of the building sat a thickset man stirring a cauldron on a low stove, its flame casting an orange glow on his right side. A boy who looked all of eleven or twelve years old scurried between the tables collecting empty vessels with alacrity, darting like a barn-swallow from cup to stein to can, often as not to a wino's urgent but unintelligible protests. Once, arms laden with four containers of different sizes and materials, he neatly avoided a haymaker so wildly thrown that the lad giggled as he ducked it; the man that threw it fell forward over the rude pine bench and hit his head on the next bench over. When the souse got up and looked around he seemed not to remember how he'd ended up on the floor, and the blood that ran down his forehead and past his cracked lips to his filthy shirt collar was a source of mystery to him.

The man at the back of the room squinted at me as I strolled past his degenerate clientele. Once I got to the back it didn't seem quite so dark, and the man lost his demonic aspect. "Stew's a nickel a plate, wine's a nickel a cup. Bring your own cup it's still a nickel." Behind him I distinguished in the firelight a shabby trio of old men, sleeping against the wall.

"You wall-eyed son of a bitch, it's me, come to collect your arrears."

"You can go and fuck yourself, 'cause I ain't got it," Morley said with a throatful of phlegm, which I was relieved to see him disgorge next to the stewpot and not into it. His old gray shirt had no collar attached, and it was open halfway down his chest, which was remarkably hairy except where it was scarred. He was unshaven, and where it still grew the hair on his head was long and hung in dull black oleaginous strings down to his shoulders. His eyes were partly obscured beneath thick orbital ridges adorned with the hairiest brows I'd ever seen, and after a moment he turned his attention, unconcerned, back to his potage.

"Pay up or get out," I said. He continued to stir the pot, slowly, and then leaned in and took a long sniff, which produced a look of great satisfaction, accompanied by a heavy, happy sigh. The smell back there, oddly enough, wasn't as putrid as it was in the front, where the winos sat; still, I wouldn't on a bet have eaten a plate of that stew, upon whose surface sat a slick of yellow grease, its sheen broken occasionally by a bubble rising from the bottom with a gurgle. He actually looked up at me and offered up what looked like a genuine, proud smile.

"Now how'd you like a nickelsworth of the best stew on the Pacific coast, on the house for the landlord?"

"Thanks anyway."

He looked offended, but he was shortly distracted by the arrival of a silhouette at the front door at which he squinted again, painfully, with his jaw hanging open.

A small man in a wretched suit of gray made his way shakily down the aisle, shuffling past the long tables lined with his besotted peers into the darkness of the back end of the narrow building. In his upraised hands he carried an object approximately the size of a paving brick, sloppily wrapped in butcher's paper, and when he got within four feet of us Morley's look got harder.

"What you think you're doing here, Hamner? I told you to clear out."

Trembling, the little man pulled back the paper to reveal a repellent slab of raw gray meat, releasing at the same time a stench so powerful it actually roused one of the men sleeping on the floor behind us. This old man sat up and leaned against the wall, scowling at the odor, and I saw that he wasn't particularly old after all, perhaps no more than thirty, and as skeletally thin as an escapee from Andersonville.

Hamner was a little healthier looking than that, with some degree of sagging flesh on his bent and fragile-looking bones. "I think it's mutton," he said. "I had to do a terrible thing to get it."

Morley took the package from the little fellow and hefted it. "Two jars," he said, then slapped it down onto a cutting barrel next to the cauldron.

"I was sure hoping for four."

Morley made as if to rise. "Are you sassing me back, boy?"

"No, sir, I just sure was hoping I could get four for this here. Like I said, I had to do something awful to get the meatcutter to part with it."

"Three, then." Morley pulled a big tin cup down from one of

the hooks and filled it. Hamner took it over to a table in the corner and took a long swig, holding the cup reverently with both hands.

Morley took as good a look at the meat as the light permitted, and he growled as he started hacking at the meat with a dirty jack-knife. It was an exceptionally gristly hunk of meat, and he had to saw at it almost from the start. "Hamner, you son of a bitch, that's the only cup you'll be gettin' for this lump of maggots and gristle."

Poor Hamner looked up like a boy who'd just lost his dog.

As Morley plucked the maggots from the meat he tossed them onto the floor, which amounted to a kindness, since there was suffi-cient filth there to support their metamorphoses into big, healthy *muscae domesticae*. "Cocksucker!" he yelled at Hamner. "I by Christ oughtta take away the jar I already gave ya, you thieving cur. Mag-gots! Jaysus."

Now Hamner looked like they'd found his dog rabid, and were cocking their hammers back to put it down. His lip quivered, and he pulled the cup close to his chest; Morley made no move to take it, though. Maggots disposed of, he resumed cutting the meat, which hung over the lip of the cutting barrel and dangled over the stew, into which it fell morsel by morsel as he hacked away at it. Jackknife in his big paw, he was sawing with considerable difficulty through a tendon, shifting his weight to get a better angle for cut-ting when that thin man sitting against the wall stood abruptly and began swatting at himself, screaming in terror.

"Maggots? Maggots! Jesus, Jesus, Jesus! They're all over me!" he hollered, letting out tiny, high-pitched yelps at each imagined bite, his bulbous eyes fairly leaping out of the sockets.

"Sit down and shut your fucking hole, Dearborn, all the mag-gots is on the floor and none's on your sorry carcass."

"Jesus, Jesus, sweet baby Jesus," he yelled, his voice rising in pitch. He stuck his hand down his pants and the screaming got louder. "Oh, God, they're eating my balls, get 'em off me, get 'em off me."

The poor wretched bastard was shaking like a dervish and his voice was growing rawer with each outburst, and as Morley chuckled at his torment Dearborn began to spin frantically about, careening as he did so toward the cauldron.

To prevent the burning liquid overturning I moved in between the two of them and shouldered the bag of bones away before he collided with the pot; deflected but still hysterical, he ran smack into me before falling into a cowering heap on the floor. I was knocked back into Morley, whose knife arm slipped.

He looked mildly surprised as he felt the blade give, finally cutting through the tendon and then into something infinitely more tender than the softest part of that mutton. He was looking at me, though, and didn't see the knife slice clean through the pinkie of his left hand at the first knuckle, didn't appear to be aware of its falling from his hand along with the meat, to land with a searing sound on the stew's bubbly surface before sinking with a hiss. It was no doubt the freshest, though not the cleanest, piece of meat the pot had ever contained.

But my wounded tenant's eyes were still focused on me, and brandishing the knife he leapt. "You son of a bitch, you just about made me cut myself."

"You did cut yourself," I said. "Look."

Morley looked down at his left hand with a look of dawning comprehension and horror; from the pinkie's stump blood pumped in appalling quantity. "Where'd it go?" But even as he said it he was turning in horror toward the stew.

He stumbled over to the cauldron and, howling like a coyote, stuck both hands into the roiling, fetid liquid. In a half second or so the source of his keening changed from indignation and sorrow to plain and simple pain, and he withdrew from the pot his forearms and hands but only nine of his fingers. He looked back at me with his arms held before him, dripping with scalding, viscous stew.

"Looky there," he said brightly. "Stopped bleedin'." Then his knees gave way beneath him and he collapsed onto the planks, smearing their decades' worth of ground-in dust and grime into grainy rivulets of mud.

Half the rummies in the dump had roused themselves to see what the noise was about. The boy appeared catatonic, his eyes on me like I was Satan himself, bat wings spread and ready to descend back into Hades.

"Lad," I shouted at him. When he didn't respond I snapped my fingers and shouted louder. "You. Boy. Run fetch a sawbones and make it quick, or your boss is dead."

He kept standing there, silent, and I slammed my open palm upon the head of the cutting barrel. The sound made him jump, but he didn't respond in any more useful way. "Goddamnit, boy, if you don't go fetch a doctor right now I'll make you sorry for it."

Wordlessly he pointed to an old man seated by the front door.

"Him?" I said.

"You're a doc, ain'tcha?" he said to the man, who didn't appear to have heard.

"He's a goddamn rummy. Go find a real doctor."

At that the old man stood, legs shaking. "It's true," he said, "I'm a man of medicine. Where's the patient?"

"To hell with you. You're skunk-drunk."

"That's got nothing to do with it," he said. "You find another doctor within five blocks of here who's not in an advanced state of inebriation and I'll show you a doctor who wouldn't set foot in this shit-hole for a twenty-dollar honorarium."

"There's your patient," I said, indicating Morley, who lay face-down, his breath ragged. His arms, where the flesh could be seen, were blistered, and the vomitous stew clung to his sleeves, coagulating as it dried.

"Morley?" the doctor said. "Ought to let the son of a bitch croak."

"That's a fine attitude for a physician to have," I said.

He gave me a sour look and, mispronouncing the Greek, misquoted Hippocrates. He was displeased when I corrected him, but he knelt to examine Morley's injuries. He grunted and sniffed, and started peeling back the sleeves of Morley's raggedy shirt. "He's in shock," he said. "Best get a wagon to take him home."

I shook the arm of a relatively alert looking specimen and handed him a silver dollar. "Go hire us a cart. Do as I say and you'll drink free until you drop. If you're not back in five minutes I'll come find you and you'll be goddamned sorry for it."

He took the dollar and hightailed out the door. I turned to the boy. "You got any idea where Morley lives, anyway?"

"Sure," the boy said. "He's my pa, ain't he?" He returned to his portering duties. I studied the doctor, who had his ear to Morley's chest. He was as dirty as anyone in the place, yet still bore the remnants of some former dignity.

"So what's a doctor doing in a wine dump in the middle of the afternoon?"

"Getting pickled," he answered without deigning to look in my direction. He pulled his head upright and rose to his knees. "I don't suppose I'd be wise to expect any kind of fee, but I'm expecting some wine out of this transaction."

I grabbed a metal cup off a hook on the wall and filled it from the barrel. At a distance of fully two feet from my nose its aroma proclaimed its vile character, and when I turned to hand the doctor his bug juice I found every conscious eye in the place on me with heartrending supplication.

"Boy! The house is buying a round." His baffled expression told me it was a phrase that had never been spoken there before. "Everyone gets a free drink," I explained, but as one they had all already arisen and had begun advancing toward the barrel.

"Sit down, all of you, or there'll be none. I'll dump the goddamned barrel dry if you don't."

Aghast at the thought of all that wasted snake venom they took their seats, and I had the boy fill every cup. "Make sure they understand it's the only one," I said. "The sawbones and the fellow I sent for the wagon can keep drinking for free."

He nodded and began running back and forth with the wine, serving it as fast as I could fill the containers. When all present had been served the doctor looked up from his jar, somewhat the better for the dose, and watched the boy going about the cleaning of the place.

"Funny how he listened to you like you were his boss, instead of some character just wandered in off the street. Some people are just born to be bossed around."

"I guess so," I said.

He cocked his head at me. "So what do you give a good goddamn for if that son of a bitch loses a half a barrel of wine?"

"I used to run a saloon myself, once. And I'm his landlord. How am I to be paid if you souses are robbing him blind?" I was sorry as soon as I'd said it, and I apologized.

His eyes grew wide with mock innocence. "And why would I be offended at such a characterization? I'm years past the capacity for shame." He knelt and checked Morley's neck for a pulse. Satisfied that he hadn't yet died, he took his seat again. "How'd his finger come off?"

"Carelessness in his meatcutting," I said.

"A good object lesson for him, then. Where was this saloon of yours? Perhaps I knew it."

"Kansas," I said, ready to lie if he asked the town. "I moved on years ago."

"I lived for a time in Wichita. Do you know a part of it called Delano?"

"Passed through it once, on my way out of the state."

"I used to have a job certifying the girls in the cathouses there were clean." He sighed heavily, and his eyes crinkled wistfully with the pleasure of memory. "Municipal pussy inspector. If that wasn't the best part of doctoring in Wichita I don't know what was."

* * *

Soon enough the fellow came back with the wagon. Its driver was a big Irishman who helped me carry Morley outside. His spiteful clientele watched his inert form passing by with a mixture of contempt, hatred, and fear, and there was more than one meager gob of spittle on that floor before we got him to the front. When the driver and I heaved him into the wagon's bed Morley's skin was yellow-white as tallow and beaded with droplets of sweat, and the doctor checked once again to make sure his heart still throbbed.

"It's beating," he said. The boy gave the driver the address, and I left in ignominious defeat. The day was still bright and clear, though, and I decided again to make the trip afoot. Though I'd spent no more than an hour in the wine dump I had the sensation of having spent the night in a hopeless dungeon, and a corresponding one of having been released from it into an entirely new day.

I was anxious to see my landlady, even though at that hour of the day our business was strictly limited to the legitimate interactions of a monied landlady and her respectfully subservient tenant. At the moment she was my only source of erotic distraction, and she'd just returned from a two week stay at the Calistoga baths; I hoped that our brief separation might lead to a relaxation of the house rules. I was therefore disappointed upon knocking at the back door to learn from her maidservant that she was out with one of her legitimate suitors, Mr. Arthur Cruikshank, and wouldn't be returning home until after the dinner hour. I left my calling card and made a note to pass by later in the evening rather than the next morning; after an evening spent earnestly teasing her society beaux her fires often as not required quenching.

I spent the day printing up pictures on the rooftop, since the sun was out for most of the afternoon; no customers demanded any of my time or energies. After dinner I retired to the studio with the day's edition of the *Morning Call* and the orations of Cicero. On the front page of the *Call* I had a considerable surprise, under the rubric IN BRIEF: LATEST ITEMS BY TELEGRAPH IN CONDENSED FORM:

ARE THEY THE BENDERS?

Niles, Mich., Jan. 15—from Our Correspondent—Two Michigan women believed to be the feminine half of the deadly Bender gang, responsible for a notorious wave of savage killings near here sixteen years previous, have been extradited to Kansas, pending a hearing to establish their identities. Once it has been determined that they are the Benders, trial is expected to be held, and there is little question in these parts as to their culpability. The fate of the male members of the family is uncertain, although rumors circulate that they are dead, likely fallen victim to their own depraved womenfolk.

I almost laughed; whatever the fate of the Bender clan, it had never become public knowledge, and fanciful reports of their wanderings and doings continued to appear in the press for several years afterward, sometimes including accounts of arrests made. One such report had the quartet in custody in Paris, France, to which they had escaped by hot air balloon, and over the next year or two any number of solitary old vagabonds were arrested in Dallas or Omaha or St. Louis as the infamous Old Man Bender. Certainly these women would be released, just like all those old vagrants had been, as soon as they were paraded before the citizenry. The only chance to get the Benders had been that night on the Verdigris, and we'd scotched it. Still, it would have been good to see them in the docket, or better still on the scaffold waiting for the trap to drop them into hell.

The hour was only five, and the sun still high enough for me to read by the skylight; it wasn't until after six that the waning light, warmed to a rosy orange, dimmed sufficiently to warrant burning a lamp, and by that time I was restless. Between the mention of the Benders in the *Call* and my reading of Cicero my thoughts kept returning to my errant Maggie. For some odd reason there came to my mind a particular evening in the winter of 1873, shortly after our establishment in Greeley, Colorado, when the snow had drifted up to our parlor window. We'd taken turns that night reading Homer aloud by the light of our single oil lamp, wrapped in a buffalo robe next to the fire. What struck me in retrospect was how fleeting and unimportant our penury seemed then; by the following summer it would be a different story altogether, with me off to Denver in search of steady work while Maggie tried to make a go of our business unassisted. She lacked the technical skills necessary to operate a photographic studio on her own, though, and my periodic returns to Greeley—I was making enough money by then to afford the train fare—became more contentious and less frequent. The last time I saw her we disputed so furiously the neighbors offered to put her up for the night; instead it was I who stormed off into the night and slept in a barn, and took the train back to Denver in the morning without a good-bye. I thereafter refused to answer or even open her letters until they stopped coming, at which time I attempted, too late, a reconciliation.

As usual during these sorts of reflections my mingled longing and worry over her fate turned quickly to resentment and reading soon became impossible; I changed my clothes and shaved again and headed out the door with the idea of a visit to Adelle's.

It wasn't until I reached Polk Street that I felt my spirits begin to lift in anticipation of my landlady's ministrations. This time when I knocked, her maidservant told me that I was expected upstairs. I tapped at the door and, upon her command to enter, found the room awash in candlelight, though there were no fewer than three oil lamps therein. She was seated on the *canapé*, smiling in her prim way.

"My dinner was awful, Bill," she said. "I was so pleased to get back and see you'd called." She patted the silken upholstery next to her thigh. "Come sit and I'll tell you about Calistoga." I set the cash box down on the seat of a wooden chair at the door and complied.

Before she had got past the list of attendees, I had already stopped listening and begun concentrating on the smell of her, and the whispery rustling of silk as she moved.

Fifteen minutes later we were in her bed, the oddly pleasing, citric flavor of her twat lingering on my tongue as it plied the inside of her ear. Afterward, having lain there for a while in silence, she raised herself up on one elbow and spoke as if she could read my mind like a newspaper.

"If you've come to ask for another brief extension on the rent, that's fine."

"Oh," I said, at once pleased at the essence of the offer and nonplussed that she'd guessed my motive so effortlessly. "I thank you."

"But I'm afraid those days are coming to an end soon. Arthur Cruikshank's asked me to marry him, and I'm going to tell him yes."

"Oh," I said again in an attempt to impress her with my quick wit. Such an arrangement implied myriad changes in my life, none of them to the better. "I suppose you'll do what you have to," I said.

"I don't have to do anything, Bill. I've got more money than Arthur Cruikshank." She extended her right leg and raised it in the air perpendicular to her body, then grabbed her calf and pulled the marvelously supple leg down toward her head until it was parallel to her torso, something not many women a quarter-century her junior could do as gracefully. "But he has a certain social position I'd like to attain. I'm tired of being known in society as a vulgar miner's widow."

"You're hardly vulgar," I offered.

"But poor Sandstrom was. I taught him to read myself, at the age of twenty-eight. He ate peas off of his knife at Delmonico's more than once. Anyway, I'm decided."

"Your children hate Cruikshank. You told me so."

"They do as I tell them, and if I tell them to call him 'Papa dear' then that's what they'll do."

I doubted that. One evening her second-eldest son had stopped by for a surprise visit with his wife and twin babes, and she'd tried to explain away my presence in her upstairs with a story about an alteration I wanted to make to the studio, a different sort of land-lady/tenant transaction than that which had actually just taken place. The son, a jug-eared and excitable young man named Stanley, didn't believe a word of it, and he clearly wanted to take a poke at me. His lovely and timid wife couldn't tear her eyes from Adelle's hastily arranged coiffure or her rumpled dress, and after mumbling my excuses I left them to their tense interlude.

"The wedding will take place in the spring, but Arthur will be handling all my business dealings as soon as it's announced."

"What about Mr. Malthus?" He was her business manager, and the man to whom I actually paid the rent.

"He won't be responsible for the tenants any more, I shouldn't think."

She said it casually, as though innocent of the disastrous nature of what she was announcing to me. I could find another suitable female companion without much difficulty, and one with whom I might dally on a more frequent schedule at that; my problem was the imminent loss of my sympathetic and forgiving landlady.

"Arthur knows who you are, because Mr. Malthus mentioned you as an example of a tenant who sometimes lets things slide a bit."

"And did Mr. Malthus tell him I'd obtained on occasion an intercession on your part?" To judge by the overt disdain Mr. Malthus generally demonstrated toward me, he must have guessed at the nature of her indulgences.

"He did, and Arthur told me that was the sort of thing that was going to stop."

I was finished, then. If Cruikshank suspected the truth—which he must have—he'd evict me at the first opportunity, which meant I might as well go straight home and prepare to pack up or liquidate.

"Don't look so gloomy, darling, you can still come and see me. We'll have to be even more discreet, of course. And I won't let Arthur upstairs, not until after the wedding. If then." She snickered and rolled over on top of me, pressing her substantial breasts against my chest, and she grabbed my wrists, pretending to pin me by force. "And now, my friend, you'll have to go. I have engagements in the morning."

Despite the sorry news I'd just been handed I felt my prick begin to stiffen again, and I rolled her over onto her back. "Not so fast, madame," I said, and we had another quick one before I clothed myself again and left, as always, via the tradesmen's entrance.

I walked the rest of the way home, though it wasn't yet eleven and the cars were still running. When I returned home I lit a lamp in the studio and took another look at the *Morning Call*. An article therein on the Cody Wild West Show got me thinking about an old photograph I'd taken shortly after my departure from Cottonwood, and I searched through the various boxes of views until I found the case containing it. Inside were a dozen copies of the view, the only one I'd ever had much commercial success with.

Scenes of the West Series. Copyright 1874 by Wm. O. Sadlaw,
Golden, Colo.
No. 11. A Buffalo Hunter Killed, Scalped, and Left on the Prairie.

It was a stereoscopic view of a dead buffalo hunter, flat on his back and attended by two kneeling soldiers, one of them unable to suppress a shit-eating grin at the prospect of being photographed, even as an element in so grisly a spectacle. Maggie and I had spotted the soldiers to our northeast late one June morning, just a few hours outside of Dodge City; one stroke of ill luck after another had reduced us to crossing the plains aboard a creaking, decrepit photographer's wagon, but when I saw the dead hunter's skinless, bloody skull glistening in the midday sun I knew that our fortunes had changed. Having spent the last of my meager bankroll and the contents of Maggie's jewel box during a brief, unhappy stay in Wichita for that rotting wagon, its meager contents, and a stereographic camera considerably inferior to the one I'd left at the Cottonwood Hotel, I set about committing the pathetic vista to glass, with Maggie's enthusiastic but inexperienced assistance. The work did not go quickly, but the soldiers were models of coöperation, taking more interest in the making of the picture than in the disposition of the hunter's remains, and before the plate was developed I knew I had something I could sell.

Idly I now examined a copy in the light of the studio lamp; despite the primitive conditions under which it was made, it was as fine a view as I'd ever done, with the soldiers, the cadaver, and the background each occupying a distinct plane, as crisp and rounded as the moment the lens projected their image onto the wet glass.

The others in the series were competently made, including a similar composition made low to the ground of a field of dead buffalo, the thick brown fur of the nearest two or three animals like dark cotton, so luxuriant that you wanted to stick your hand through the viewer into it. But none had the attraction of the dead hunter, whose post-mortem image had been seen by more people than he likely ever met in his life; with Dodge City already behind us that day I'd had no way of learning his name.

I replaced the view and started going through the boxes with the idea of throwing out all but my own views. Soon I'd be moving, out of the studio if not out of town entirely, and I might as well travel light. Even among the views I'd made there were precious few I cared to keep, and in the end I saved only the buffalo hunter and the dead buffalo; the rest I took outside to the alley for the ash-man's children, thoughtfully leaving an old Holmes viewer atop the views for their use as well. Then I mounted the stairs and crawled into my lonely bed.

Weary as I was from the day's exertions I thought I'd fall quickly to sleep, as was usually the case, but the memory of that day outside Dodge, of Maggie's endearing desire to be helpful and of her exaggerated grief at the realization that she wasn't, got me thinking about her again, and I was a long time staring at the ceiling.

I spent most of the next day making plans for the liquidation of the studio, and going from photographer to photographer trying to interest a buyer. My spirits were reasonably high; the last few years had been lean ones anyway, and San Francisco's considerable charms had exhausted themselves on me. The prospect of leaving almost pleased me, in fact, except for the galling fact that the leaving had been imposed by others.

Early in the afternoon I stepped out of one none-too-savory studio on Mission Street and strolled past women standing in doorways, revealing as much of themselves as the law and the winter temperatures would allow. I was importuned a dozen times as I walked up the street, with no intention whatsoever of partaking in the wares offered.

"Come on upstairs," one fallen angel said at the corner of Twenty-First Street, "see what a real California Gal can do when she sets her mind to it." She grinned, revealing a mouthful of yellow and gray stumps. Half a block farther another informed me that I hadn't ever seen tits like hers, and her neighbor one door down wondered when I'd last enjoyed the company of two women at once. At Twenty-Second a short, round woman tugged at my sleeve, hissing urgently.

"How'd you like to slide your prick into the very same pussy as Booth and Lincoln both did?"

That one stopped me in my tracks. "You pleasured Lincoln *and* Booth?"

She slipped her arm into the crook of mine with a serenely proprietary smile. At close range she appeared old enough to have serviced the Continental Congress, with dyed black hair showing snowy at the roots and a wizened face that hinted at a beauty whose loss had apparently robbed her of her reason. "All the Booths. Especially Junius Brutus, he would have made me his bride. General Lee, President Davis, U.S. Grant, too. President Cleveland himself could give you a testimonial on my behalf. He likes to work his way up the backstairs with a little spittle." To illustrate, she spat into her left hand and rubbed it into the palm of her right. "That young bride of his can't hardly walk a straight line since they wed. Now he's out of office it's buggery morning, noon, and nighttime, poor thing."

I closed my eyes and tried to picture a rainbow, or a moonrise over the Adirondacks. "Sounds like you get around a little bit."

She nodded, her paint-slathered face assuming a contemplative pout. "I'm very much in demand." She smiled, sweetly, and curtsied, her hand still on my arm. "I used to be Laura Keene, the tragedienne."

I had seen Miss Keene onstage once, in a production of *A Midsummer Night's Dream*, and my natural inclination was to laugh at this shriveled harpy's appropriation of her identity, but to her it was no joke, so I merely doffed my hat and apologized. "Afraid I'm in a hurry, Miss Keene, though it's been a pleasure jawing with you."

Her shoulders were so round her shrug was nearly imperceptible. "You'll regret it tonight when you awake all alone dreaming of this sweet sweet pussy," she said, and so confident was she of her allure that I lingered for a moment to hear more.

"So you knew old Honest Abe?"

"Abe Lincoln could do it five times nightly. Had to, in fact, that was what made Mrs. Lincoln into a madwoman. And when he died and she had suddenly to do without it, why that made her even madder. It's that which finally killed her, in fact."

She still clung to my arm as if we were about to take a stroll somewhere, though we stood rooted to the spot. I tipped my hat to her and told her I'd be on my way.

"Goddamnit," she said, and she finally took her hand away, lifting her skirt to reveal a dark, hairy patch amidst much adipose whiteness, "how can you resist this? How can any man? This is the thing that brought Sherman through Atlanta. Thousands died in the most abject manner so he could shove himself into it quicker."

Several of the street's other denizens were watching us with unconcealed amusement, and I was beginning to get embarrassed. I handed her half a dollar in memory of my fallen Commander-in-Chief and took my leave, promising to visit her again soon.

Over the next few days I canceled what few sittings I had on my schedule and spent the days cataloguing my equipment and fixtures for sale; though I planned to continue as a photographer in some new locale, I had no desire to transport the 11-by-12-inch camera, or the various pieces of furniture and darkroom gear that I had accumulated over the last six or seven years. I hoped to be out of the building and of San Francisco entirely before Adelle's sweet Arthur had a chance to bring the axe down on my head.

Several days hence I was awakened before dawn by an extraordinarily vivid auditory hallucination; I was conscious of the fact that I was in my bed in San Francisco before I knew that the voice wasn't real.

"Sun's up, Bill," it said. "Time to be heading home." The voice was Cordelia Fenn's, and I thought it strange how precise and accurate my memory of its tone and timbre seemed, at more than a quarter century's distance, and without my having given her more than passing thought in all that time.

By the time I'd made it home to my small Ohio town in '65 the Great War had ended, though the massive wave of returning soldiers had not yet crested there. In my absence my mother had passed on to whatever her reward amounted to, and my uncles and aunts were all either elsewhere or dead themselves; I had no interest in my school-day chums and owned no property there, real or otherwise. I had no particular sentimental attachment to the place, and no plans to spend my life there, or any part thereof beyond the succeeding week or two. I visited the town partly for the sake of seeing my parents' gravesites for the last time—and the first, in my mother's case—but most especially in hopes of leaving it with Miss Cordelia Fenn hanging on my arm as my wife.

She'd been my first sweetheart after I'd left the employ of the Harding farm, and scrupulously denied me certain liberties Mary Harding had delighted in granting. These, she said, would be enjoyed by her future husband only; she allowed, however, as how she hoped that would be me, and consequently permitted certain mild pleasures to be had. She was also willing to relieve me manually and on special occasions orally, and I found many opportunities to slip us unnoticed away from church socials and dances and the like, skills I had honed during my shameful liaison with Mrs. Harding. If Cordelia lacked Mary's beauty and some of her charm as well, she had the attractive qualities of being unmarried and my own age and therefore a suitable girl to court; what's more, her father was one of the few men in our town who'd allow me near his daughter.

Samuel Fenn, a deacon in my father's church, had been one of only a handful of parishioners to side with him in his time of trouble, and Sam let it be known to one and all that he would have been proud to have me as his son-in-law, not despite my father's character but because of it.

I had carried Cordelia's picture with me, an artless oval albumen print in a brass locket, throughout the war. After a year her letters became irregular, even by the standards of military mail, and they grew briefer, too, though she still wrote of a future we would face together upon my return. By the end of the second year the letters ceased entirely, and I stopped writing, too, sensing that to put myself in the position of a supplicant would only engender her contempt. I vowed that when I returned I would win her back with all the charm and persuasion at my disposal.

On the sight of what had been my father's church my mood darkened. My anger, directed as much at the parish and its scolds as at the old man himself, had gone cool as the years passed, until I had almost forgotten it was there. The sight of the steeple restored it to full burning life, and the fact that it had been recently painted seemed, absurdly, a deliberate insult to his memory. There was a light within, but I'd sworn long ago never to set foot inside the place again, and I swung open the iron gate that led to the boneyard without stopping in to inquire as to the identity of the current pastor.

It was late in the afternoon, overcast and warm, and I wandered to where my father and mother lay side by side, their differences crumbled to dust. I greeted my father in Greek and my mother in Alsatian and stood there for a moment without much else to say to them in either tongue. I was pondering where to get a room and considering my strategy for approaching Cordelia's family when I was startled by someone calling my name.

I turned to see Cordelia's older brother Peter, fatter than ever, his black hair thinned, huffing toward me from the cemetery gate.

"Good to see you, boy," he said. "Back to stay?" He clapped me on the back and nearly knocked me over.

"Back to see my parents," I said, nodding at the ground. "And back to see Cordelia, too."

"Ah. Didn't know if you would," he said, looking down, and he bade me follow. I thought he meant to lead me into town, to Cordelia's father's house, where he would announce my return. I liked the idea of appearing in his company, as if the initiative were his own, and felt quite optimistic about the whole affair until we stopped at a single columnal marker.

It was inscribed with the name WARREN HEALEY; Warren had been a friend of mine, and I was sorry to see he'd passed on. My attention was then drawn to the name below it, one which puzzled me momentarily: CORDELIA HEALEY, BELOVED WIFE AND MOTHER.

"The baby's in there with her. Wouldn't have lived anyway, the doctor said. Poor Warren shot the back of his mouth out the next morning." I pulled out the locket, hidden as always in easy reach, and clenched it in my hand until I thought I'd crumple it. Despite that small, slightly melodramatic act I truthfully felt very little; surprise, certainly, the kind one feels when a set of truths is upended and revealed as illusion, and disappointment that my plans would have to change. Toward the girl I'd been hoping to wed, though, I felt nothing. I noted that the date of her death was in November of 1863; I had received the last of her letters in September. She had written me the sweetest of her billets-doux, then, with Warren Healey's band of gold on her finger and his child curled in her belly, unaccountably still promising herself to me.

"I know Father would like to see you," Peter said.

Of course I had figured on seeing Sam Fenn that evening for the purposes of asking Cordelia's hand. "I expect I'd better be moving along. Give him my best," I said.

I was on my way that very night. My next stop was Columbus, and upon arriving there I took a job assisting a Danish photographer, whose son-in-law I became in short order. I had only rarely looked back or thought of Cordelia since, and never with much emotion beyond a mild nostalgia, certainly never experiencing the powerful emotions I ought to have felt upon learning simultaneously of her marriage and death; the feeling that enveloped me on that cold morning in California handily outdid any I'd experienced at the time, and I was over it by the time my breakfast was done.

* * *

That day's *Morning Call,* in addition to accounts of the travails of the Brazilians, and news of a dead Empress in Europe, carried another article on the Benders, one which altered my plans:

BENDERS ARRIVE IN KANSAS

Cottonwood, Kans., Jan. 19th, 1890—From our local Correspondent— Mrs. Almira Griffith and her daughter, Mrs. Eliza Davis, extradited from Michigan and accused of being Mrs. John Bender, Sr., and Katie Bender, the notorious assassins, have arrived at the Cottonwood, Kansas, train depot, where an angry throng awaited their presence. A preliminary hearing is scheduled for the second week of January, and once the pair are proven to be the Benders they will stand trial for the murders of more than a dozen men found buried in an orchard behind their house, as well as the shooting of Mr. Marc Leval, a leading citizen of the town of Cottonwood. Mrs. Leval herself was heard at the train station remarking that it was a great relief after so long a delay to have the killers in custody. Be that as it may, Gareth Lassiter, the attorney engaged to represent the women, assures us that they will be freed as soon as he has proven that they are not the Benders.

I re-read the article twice, trying to tease out its meaning—was I to understand that Maggie was in Cottonwood? I had pictured her in a hundred places around the world, imagined her rich again and poor again, wondered even whether she still lived, but never once did it occur to me that she might have returned to Cottonwood and the possibility of hanging for her husband's murder. It took me several further readings to satisfy myself that I had understood correctly, that the two women charged with being the Benders would be charged with the killing of Marc Leval. That such a charge could be filed in the face of what everyone in Cottonwood knew about who'd killed Leval didn't necessarily mean I was free to travel there, but it made the prospect worth considering; on that basis I began pondering a return, the first time I'd entertained the notion seriously since the morning she and I had ridden south into Indian Territory. Whether Maggie would consent to speak to me when I got there was another matter.

That morning I received, as expected, a message from Arthur Cruikshank, ordering me to vacate the premises at 4175 24th Street within fourteen days. When the notice came I was concentrating on the cash sale of a pair of cameras to an ambitious young photographer named Quackerell, prosperous and eager to expand. I had just about convinced him to take the whole inventory for a slightly reduced rate when another messenger arrived, this time with an envelope from Adelle. I opened it in the presence of the buyer:

> *Dear Bill,*
>
> *I am most awfully sorry for what Arthur has done, and hope and trust that you will forgive me.*
>
> *This will, I trust, help you out in your transition.*
>
> *Love,*
> *Your own Adelle*
>
> *P.S. Please destroy this letter. I will send word as to when we can next safely meet.*

Accompanying the letter were three hundred dollars in bills, far more than what I owed her. I must have been gaping in the most stupefied way at the money, because Quackerell improved his offer immediately, based upon the perfectly reasonable assumption that

I'd received a better one. I accepted it gladly, signed his receipt and took his money. In an hour he returned with a wagon for the 11-by-12-inch camera, and I gave him an extra key to the front door so that he could return at his leisure for the furniture over the next day or two.

Having disposed of my studio and inventory, I hoped I'd also be able to quickly rid myself of the Clay Street building. If I could negotiate its sale to Morley for a cut rate I'd be happy; I'd be rid of it, and by selling it to him below market value I'd be doing the poor fellow a favor as well.

When I arrived at the wine dump, though, I was nonplussed to find its entrance decorated in black crepe, with a wreath hanging upon the door, a ribbon marked CONDOLÉANCES draped across it. Inside were all the rummies and the boy porter, looking like they hadn't left since I'd seen them last, and next to the boy stood the most miserable looking woman I'd seen in some years. She wore a black organdy dress, her veil pulled upward and attached to her hat with a pin.

"Mrs. Morley? I'm the landlord." I was about to ask the obvious question, but before I had a chance I caught sight of Morley lying defunct upon a low table. His hands were folded upon his chest, with the left one on top to reveal its horribly infected stump of a pinkie, black and gray and a little green; to judge from the smell he'd been gone from this world for a couple of days at least.

"I hope you come for the wake and not to badger him any more about that rent," she said. Her teeth were half gone, and her right hand was missing its thumb; these were the things I noted in the cellar light of the wine dump; God knows what daylight would have revealed.

"I really came to talk to him about something else," I said, nodding at the lump of meat on the table. My head felt heavy, and as I gazed on Morley's swollen face I began to feel a need to regurgitate.

"Talk away," Mrs. Morley said. "I doubt he'll talk back."

The deed to the wine dump was in my interior coat pocket.

"Mrs. Morley, this is the deed to the building. I'm leaving San Francisco, and my intent in coming here was to turn the building's title over to your husband."

She squinted at me. "At what cost? 'Cause he didn't have any scratch to throw around, and I got less."

"No cost," I said with some difficulty. "A gift to you."

She turned her attention to the document, and after a minute's scrutiny she said, "Let's go find a notary and make it official." In that gap-toothed grin I thought I saw a blessing, permission to return home to Kansas.

2

LABETTE COUNTY, KANSAS
FEBRUARY, 1890

Inter Mortuos Liber

My traveling companion on the train trip East was a treasure: a copy of Procopius's *Anecdota* (or *The Secret History* in English), purchased at an antiquarian bookshop shortly before leaving San Francisco; two hundred years old, it had come into stock just that day, and though its price was high, I had my recent windfall from Adelle in pocket and I indulged myself. It was the first copy I'd ever seen of it, but I'd wanted to read it since learning of its existence in my adolescence via my father's scabrous journals. Procopius didn't disappoint; the book was as full of scandal and ribaldry as those journals were, and my father's affection for it was easily understood.

The diaries had been written in code and in classical Greek, and the hours I spent worriedly deciphering them (worriedly because I feared my mother might find and destroy the lot) contributed greatly to my fluency in that dead tongue; in them he recorded everything from his theological perspective (surprisingly heretical) to his bowel movements (frequent and enjoyable) to his sexual conquests (more so and more so). Before leaving this world he entrusted them to a lady parishioner who, though mentioned often therein, was unable to read them, with instructions to turn them over to me on the occasion of my sixteenth birthday. They were in my mother's house when I went off to war, and I don't know what happened to them after that; perhaps some randy, virginal schoolmaster in Parma, Ohio, bought them at auction for masturbatory fodder.

Before my first change of trains (there were three changes altogether, the last of these heading south and east from Kansas City) it occurred to me that I might be walking into a legal trap of some sort, but the risk seemed acceptable to me if it meant a chance to step off the train into what, strangely enough, I still thought of as my home, though I'd lived longer in Denver and San Francisco, and nearly as long in Tucson. Nothing else I might do, nothing I had planned in Texas or Philadelphia or Bucharest, seemed as compelling to me as a chance to glimpse, however briefly and at whatever risk to my liberty, my son, grown to manhood, or the widow Leval, or even the disappointed town itself, jilted by the cattle trade and me both. The tantalizing possibility of seeing Katie and Ma Bender at the end of a noose, however unlikely that was, beckoned as well.

I had looked the town up on maps a hundred times or more in sixteen years, and noted with satisfaction its continued presence on railroad timetables, but I'd had no specific word about Cottonwood or any of its inhabitants until the recent articles on the Benders began appearing. When the train approached the outer rings of the town the sky was overcast and thick with the promise of snow. To the east of the city limits stood a complex of low, circular, chimneyed structures, each expelling gray smoke into the cold, late afternoon air, arrayed around a central, two-story building with BRAUNSCHWEIG PRESSED BRICK CO. painted on its side; slightly further west was a massive, incomplete brick edifice which a sign out front identified as the future home of the Cottonwood Flour Mill. Where the tent city had stood years before were now houses with fenced-in yards, and in the distance I could see rows of buildings two and three stories tall, including one with RECTOR'S DEPT. STORE painted on its westerly side.

The train slowed to a stop without my having distinguished a single familiar landmark, and I stepped onto the platform in a perplexed state. I stared about me in the cold, watching the breath steam out of my nose and almost wondering whether I'd gotten off at the wrong town. It didn't smell, not the way I remembered it doing, and not the way San Francisco smelled, either; maybe it was the cold.

A porter offered to help me with my trunk, and I told him to send it ahead to the Cottonwood Hotel. "Sure you don't want the Rialto?"

"The Cottonwood's fine," I told him, and gave him a quarter for his trouble and fifty cents to hire the dray. I then wandered east on Main, away from the Leval mansion, to see what the town had become.

My first reaction was a dull disappointment, born of high expectations. I stood on a street that only faintly resembled the one I'd lived on a decade and a half previous, and the warm feeling of a homecoming, even an anonymous and furtive one, eluded me. I'd always held in mild contempt those San Franciscans who couldn't stop talking about how grand the place was ten years previously, or twenty; now I understood perfectly their position. The Cottonwood in my mind's eye was forever fixed in 1873, and anything that didn't fit that picture of it seemed vaguely wrong, as if the Mona Lisa were wearing a flowered bonnet, or Michelangelo's David a starched collar. Where Rector's Dry Goods had stood was now a hardware store of brick and mortar, the original wooden building long gone, and the feed store next to Rector's had been replaced by the Second National Bank of Cottonwood. The hotel had been rebuilt on a larger scale but at least inhabited the same lot as it once had, and I stepped into the lobby, where a small, well-starched young man with an extravagantly pointed mustache greeted me cheerfully.

In comparison to its predecessor the lobby was luxurious almost to the point of comedy, with velvet on its walls, overstuffed furniture for lounging and a multitude of planters overflowing with such exotic botanical items as ferns and small trees. I asked the price of the room directly above the office, and the young man informed me that it was already occupied. "If it's heat you're worried about, we been renovated and all the rooms got steam heat now." I told him I'd take a room on the third floor and told him my trunk would be arriving shortly. He proferred the register and I signed it "W. Sadlaw, San Francisco, Cal." I nearly stopped myself and wrote "Ogden" instead, but discretion seemed called for under the present circumstances, at least to begin with.

Down the street I stepped into a restaurant that stood where Otis's forge had burned and been reborn, only to cede its place to this unexceptional building. It was a brick one like most I'd seen downtown, with a sign painted on its front identifying it as the White Horse Restaurant; inside it sported a shiny tin ceiling and a recently varnished floor. At that hour there were no customers, but a short, thin man stood up from a booth at which he sat in conference with a plump, white-haired woman and asked if I'd like something to eat. He had black hair and white chinwhiskers and seemed not at all unhappy to be interrupted.

There was a circular counter in the center, and booths around the walls, and tables scattered throughout. A skylight provided the only daytime illumination besides the front window, and on a bright day it would have been a cheery place. Today, though, it was gloomy as a sepulchre, and I took a seat at the counter and nodded at the lady, who despite some difficulty in rising to her feet greeted me with a warm smile. Seeing her walk I realized she was more than plump; she had some sort of arthritic trouble, as well. As she came over to take my order her husband, or so I took him to be, tied an apron on and went into the kitchen.

"How about a hamsteak and some mashed potatoes?" I said, reading off the printed menu.

"Yes, sir. Coffee?"

"That'll do fine," I said, and she yelled back at her husband to start a pot.

"You just in off the train?"

"How'd you know?"

"Time of day. Nothing to eat on that train, and nothing good at any of the stops, and most don't know to bring something. Lots of times we get whole families come in starving, kids all cranky from hunger."

She waddled back to the kitchen and yelled the rest of the order at him. I saw an abandoned newspaper on one of the booths, and I went over and rescued it from oblivion. It was the *Optic*, apparently a daily now. The lead story was the Bender hearing:

DOUBTS ABOUT THE "BENDERS"

PROSECUTION SILENT ABOUT WHY THESE TWO ARE THOUGHT TO BE THE KILLERS. THEIR ATTORNEY CLAIMS FALSE IMPRISONMENT

Mrs. Eliza Davis and Mrs. Almira Griffith are still enjoying the hospitality of the county at the charming home of Deputy George Naylor and his wife Rebecca. Many longtime residents of Labette County who knew the Benders are wondering just how these two came to be identified as the murderous pair. If Mrs. Davis is in fact the notorious Katie Bender, then she has changed so considerably as to make a certain identification of her impossible. The editor of the *Optic* knew her well when she lived here and sees no sign that the lady in custody is she.

I had read only half of the article when the woman returned with a cup of coffee.

"Who's the mayor these days?"

"New one as of last month, name of Hutchens."

I nodded. "Never heard of him."

"You spent time here before?"

"Some," I allowed. "It's been a while, though. In fact I used to sleep in a blacksmith's forge on this very lot."

"It's changed quite a bit since we been here," she said, sitting down on a chair behind the counter, which didn't seem wise, given the trouble she had lowering and raising herself up. "That's seven, eight years, and it's grown up like a weed."

"It's a lot bigger than when I last saw it. But there was a time when we thought it'd outgrow Kansas City and St. Louis."

"Well, it still might. There's going to be a college here, you know. And we got the brick plant, they're going to build that up even bigger. And the flour mill."

"Cattle never came through, though."

She clucked. "There's cattle all over around here," she said.

"There's some cattle raised around here, sure, but this was going to be the end of a cattle trail."

Now she looked at me in pure consternation. "Cattle trail? There's no cattle trail."

"No, there's not."

"Anyway, we lived in Dodge a few years back, and I can tell you the cattle trails don't last forever."

At that point her husband shook a tiny bell from the kitchen, and she wincingly pulled herself out of the chair. "Lordy me, I shouldn'ta sat down and I knew it, too."

A minute later she returned with my hamsteak, which I finished quickly and with great pleasure. I left the paper on the counter and proceeded on to my next stop, the county courthouse. On my way there I passed my old saloon, now known as the Palace, and saw someone go in who looked like an older incarnation of young

Gleason, jowly already in his mid-thirties and with earlobes hanging down to his collar, almost. He wore a heavy coat and had his hands shoved into the pockets as if he'd forgotten his gloves, which I had known him to do in the old days.

The central business district had expanded considerably and now spanned as far north as Sixth Street, and sidewalks of limestone slab had been set into place throughout. The courthouse, a massive three-story structure constructed of that same cut limestone, was located at the corner of Lincoln and Second. Upon entering the dim lobby I had the odd and fleeting sensation that I was turning myself in; still odder was the accompanying sense of relief. When I shook my head to clear it I drew a curious glance from a lady crossing the lobby, all bosom and florid hat, so full of figure and narrow of waist that I scarcely noted her face at first, though when I did it was rather pretty. She was bundled up against the cold and preparing to leave for the day, which made me wonder if I'd come too late in the day to find the County Attorney.

"You seem to be lost," she said.

"I'm looking for the County Attorney."

"He's on this floor, over that way," she said, pointing to her left and smiling with such charm I nearly asked her if she was free for dinner. This wasn't libertine San Francisco, however, so I merely tipped my hat and thanked her.

I heard speech from within the office, and I entered without knocking. The room was darker even than the building's lobby, and it took a moment's adjustment to focus on the two figures therein. A narrow-shouldered man of thirty sat at a desk covered with papers and law books, and next to him was a prim young woman at a much neater secretary's table. Her lamp burned brighter than his, for she was engaged in some sort of dictation, and he seemed to have been extemporizing when I interrupted them. Even in the yellow lamplight he looked very flushed, and from the way he asked me my business it sounded as if he had very little time to spare for the likes of me, whoever I might happen to be.

"I'm Sadlaw," I said. "Once known as Ogden."

"I'm Cal Wembly, County Attorney. Hang your hat and coat." He gestured to the single seat available, a straight-backed wooden chair across from his desk, which I took without removing the coat, hat in hand.

He turned to the young woman. "Miss Wynan, you may stop work for the day and go home."

She got up and, reluctantly, I thought, put on her wrap and extinguished the lamp on her desk. Once she'd shut the door the room was considerably blacker, with only Wembly's feeble lamp and what little light came in through the transom for illumination. He made no move to adjust the lamp, which cast a sickly glow onto his face from beneath.

"What's your business, Mr. Ogden?"

"I hear you're prosecuting the Bender women. I was part of the posse that chased them down in '73."

"I know who you are," he said, his arms crossed over his chest.

"I hear they're charged with shooting Marc Leval."

"That's true."

"Am I to understand that I'm not to be charged with that same crime?"

"No warrant was ever issued for you, Mr. Ogden."

That surprised me, and it must have shown on my face. By now I was accustomed to the light, and I could make out a motto, tacked to the wall next to me:

YOU CAN'T

"EXPECT-TO-RATE"

IF YOU

EXPECTORATE

I noted that there was no spittoon in the office, which since I didn't chew was no loss to me, but which must have caused the occasional awkward moment. I thought I could see, nestled in the corner nearest my chair, a darkened spot where some miscreants had flouted the ban.

I stood to shake hands with Wembly, who took mine and then returned to his work as though I'd already left the room. The courthouse lobby was dark by now, and I had the impression he was the last man working that night, and probably was most nights, too. The Bloody Benders would have been a coup for any prosecutor, and for an out-of-towner like him it would have made his career, maybe even set him on his way to the governorship someday. No wonder he's willing to let me get away with shooting Marc Leval, I thought, and then I wondered how many other people in town would be so quick to forgive.

Night had fallen when I made my way to Second Street again and headed back toward Main. I stopped at the Palace saloon and pushed my way through the door. A frosted glass partition now separated a cigar counter from the bar itself, and I stepped through the interior door and found myself among a throng that rivaled any from the boomtown days. The bar was gaslit now, and the crowd jostled and jockeyed for position just like in any high-class saloon in San Francisco or Denver. The place still looked fancy and new, sixteen years into its existence, and I felt a surge of pride that made up for the gloom I'd felt since stepping off the train. The front and backbars had been replaced with even fancier ones than we'd started off with, and the backbar was now backed with fancifully patterned wallpaper, with framed foxhunting lithographs hanging on either side of its central mirror. There were three very busy bartenders, one of whom was Gleason, and I pushed my way to him. He tended to the customer next to me, and when I caught his eye there was no sign of recognition in it.

"Beer," I shouted, and he turned to get it for me. When he put it down on the bar I handed him a nickel and said "Thank you, Mr. Gleason," and at that he gave me an odd look.

"Mr. Ogden?"

I gave him my hand and we shook. "Almost didn't know you with that mustache, there."

"I see the bar's still paying for itself."

"Uh-huh," he said, tugging at his shirtfront. "You seen Clyde?"

"Not yet."

"I don't think he harbors any ill-will for you, if that's what's got you hesitating. Old Ninna, now, she might." He poured a shot of bourbon for a grizzled rummy and took payment for it without a word being spoken between them. "Ninna's married again."

"Good for her," I said, and I meant it, too.

He excused himself to go down to the other end of the bar to serve a couple of shy ones who couldn't break through at the center where the bartenders were. I felt then a sudden and unexpected tenderness for Ninna; I had, I supposed, treated her rather cavalierly, and she'd committed no worse sin than expecting the farmer she'd married to tend to his farm and stay on it.

Gleason returned and asked me where I'd been. As evasively I could I answered him; then I drew on my reserves of courage and asked the question I'd traveled half the continent to ask. "So Maggie's living in town, is she?"

"Um, yes sir, she is."

Before I could ask anything further there was another flurry of activity behind the bar. He asked me if I wanted another beer, on the house, but I didn't care for any. "Maybe I'll come and talk to you tomorrow, when it's not quite so busy."

He nodded. "Isn't very busy before noon, it's just the real bad drunks then."

"It's good to know there are a few constants." I shook his hand and departed, and though tempted to visit one or all of my loved ones, I didn't dare, and so I wandered around the east side of town, eventually ending up at the cemetery Tiny Rector and I had founded in '73. Now it extended all the way down the hillside and was encircled by the town, from which it was cut off by a four-foot-high stone fence. I leaned on the fence and peered into it, but the night was dark and I couldn't see much more than the stones nearest me, vaguely illuminated by the streetlamp on the corner of Lincoln and Sixth, the latter a street that hadn't even been laid out when I last saw Cottonwood. The name on the stone was Gerard Lafferty, dead the previous April, and I'd never heard of him. I'd known most of the first residents of this particular boneyard, if slightly or briefly in some cases, and I felt strangely offended at the notion that it was now filled with strangers to me.

I wanted to see the west side, but headed back to Main Street for dinner, afraid that the restaurants might shut down before I had the chance to eat. The little place where I'd eaten the hamsteak was full of customers and its proprietress looked overburdened, so I stopped into the hotel restaurant where I ordered steak and scalloped potatoes. I'd purloined a battered copy of the *Optic* from the lobby and was leafing quietly through it when a woman I took at first to be my waitress put her hand on my shoulder in a familiar way.

"Bill Ogden."

At my side was a considerably older and plumper Lillian Rector looking nonetheless healthier and happier than I'd ever seen her. She was dressed as elegantly as any woman I'd ever seen in Cottonwood, with a fur collar and jewels that looked as real as any I'd seen Adelle wear, and her white hair was painstakingly coiffed beneath a milliner's confection of satin and feathers that would have turned heads on Nob Hill. Though the room felt overheated to me, her cheeks were so pink as to seem flushed from the cold. Perhaps that was the excitement of seeing an old friend.

"Mrs. Rector," I said, rising to my feet.

"Lillian," she insisted, though "Mrs. Rector" had always been fine before.

"Where's Tiny?" I said.

"Henry's gone to his reward, I'm afraid. I'm dining with my daughter and son-in-law, Dr. Kenneshaw."

I looked behind me to a table where a man and a woman of about my own age sat, sawing away at their dinners, as elegantly equipped as Lillian and completely uninterested in her long-lost friend.

"I want you to know, Bill, that no one who matters here ever took seriously any of the things that were said against you, and you'll always be welcome in my home. Will you come see me tomorrow?"

I suggested nine-thirty in the morning.

"Delightful. I live in what was once known as the Leval home," she said. "I believe you know where it's located." Then she tiptoed with the grace of a tall, plump egret back to the table through the maze of tables and waitresses. Her daughter and son-in-law looked up at me when she took her seat, the latter with such sudden and considerable interest that I waved hello. I wondered if she hadn't just pointed me out as the man who'd murdered the town's leading citizen, just before the depression of '73 stripped it of whatever hope remained of becoming a great Prairie Metropolis.

When I awoke in the morning I was the first guest in the dining room, and I had my coffee and eggs with a nearly fond memory of the gruesome breakfasts Katie Bender used to serve me in the old dining room there, and of the way she used to flirt with me as I forced them down. My breakfast done, I put on my overcoat and hat and stepped into the lobby.

"Is there a city directory I could consult?"

The young fellow behind the desk took out the thin volume. "Any address in particular you want?"

"Mrs. Marguerite Leval."

"Oh, Mrs. Leval. She's right up Lincoln and Third, hold on . . . 254 Lincoln Street."

I thanked him and went outside. The sky's dull cast made the wind seem even colder, and the men, women, and children who hurried past me on the street all seemed bent by it, no matter how warmly bundled. The sensation of freezing on Main Street at the gate of my booze wagon in the winter of '73 came back to me very vividly, and I began to feel the new city merge in my mind's eye with the old prairie town. Despite all the new buildings, and the lack of familiar faces, last night's sensation of being a visitor with no sentimental link to the town was slowly metamorphosing into one of routine, almost as if I were walking up Main for the six thousandth time, as if I'd been there to see the town grow up into a small city and been part of the transition, and not just a small part of a story mothers told to frighten their boys and girls into obedience.

And a city it was, if not one on the scale of San Francisco or Denver. Passersby were dressed for office work, the limestone sidewalks stretched out neat and new, the carriage traffic was slow and courteous; nothing in the picture suggested that all this had been wrested from the hands of the Osage just twenty years before. On the other side of Main I noted the presence of a strange-looking man with long white hair and a beard that jutted a foot down from his chin. He was heading toward me and looking straight into my eyes, and my first instinct was to hurry on. There was something familiar about him, though, and as he drew nearer, limping in an exaggerated manner, I recognized the face of Michael Cornan, still looking like someone had flattened his face with a shovel. Now his eyes appeared even smaller, and his look of concentrated anger had intensified. To my surprise he stuck out his hand, and I shook it.

"Mr. Ogden. You're back."

"I am," I said. He kept clasping my hand, his expression deadly serious. "Are you still with the police department?"

He shook his head. "No, sir." He swatted at his bad leg with his hat. "Not since I shot off my foot. These days I direct the hardware department at Rector's store."

"I saw it, coming into town. Looks like a big operation now."

"Oh, it is. Biggest in this part of the state."

"I'm just on my way to see old Mrs. Rector now."

He nodded his approval. "You tell her I said not to worry about hardwares." He walked away from me toward his place of work; other passersby nodded and greeted him in a friendly way, and I wondered how he'd become so well liked over the years.

The mansion looked in good repair from the outside, and Marc's saplings had grown tall and wide enough to offer some shade in the summer. Some of the land had been sold off, since there were large houses on either side of the mansion on what had formerly been Marc's property, and the one to its north was its equal in splendor.

"Rector residence?" I said to the young woman who came to the door.

"Who's calling?" she asked.

"Bill Ogden," I told her, and she beckoned me to follow her. I stood waiting in the foyer while she ran to find someone, and after hanging my hat and coat on the rack by the door I idly examined a painting on the wall of the entryway. Its gilt frame must have cost more than Tiny used to gross in a good week; I took it for a copy, if a good one, of a bucolic scene of the Petit Trianon, its ill-starred mistress and her entourage playing at being rough-hewn country girls.

Though still impressive, the mansion was as nothing compared to Adelle's, which was in turn as nothing to those of certain of her peers. That part of the house visible from where I stood contained mostly the same furniture as it had in Maggie's day, but there was a greater distribution of knickknacks and gewgaws than she ever would have tolerated. I wondered if she came by often, or ever.

Once again Lillian startled me with a touch, this time the palm of her hand on the small of my back; I didn't ever recall her touching me in the old days, or smiling much either, which she did now so broadly I could see where her son-in-law had planted gold in her molars. "Bill, how delightful you've come. I'll have Hilda fetch us some cocoa."

We sat in what had been Marc's study, now converted into a very feminine drawing room. The wall was papered in a faint, minty green, with every square inch of available counterspace covered in bric-à-brac and silk flowers. Hilda, a thick young woman with blond hair, served us our chocolate and spoke with a German accent. She seemed to have some difficulty understanding Lillian, who snapped at her when she erred, and I imagined the turnover in parlor maids was brisk at the Rector home.

She told me about Tiny's death five years before, and those of several other friends and acquaintances. After giving her a brief and necessarily incomplete account of my wanderings to the west I gingerly asked her about Maggie.

She drew in a deep breath and closed her eyes for a minute. "Bill, you know, I think, that I consider you a person of quality. There are simply people in the world with whom such as you and I cannot allow ourselves to associate."

I started to raise a polite objection, but she cut me off and asked how I found the weather in Kansas. There'd be no news of Maggie through Lillian Rector, and I'd be calling on the woman myself soon enough, so I allowed the subject to change. The seasons in San Francisco were so mild as to seem nearly interchangeable, I told her, and I'd spent so much time there after the extremes of Denver, Tuscon, and Cheyenne that I'd almost forgotten what real heat and cold were like.

"Do you plan to stay here?" she asked me, and I answered quite honestly that I had no idea yet.

I left before long with an insincere promise to attend one of Lillian's dinner parties and headed east with some trepidation. I was a good distance down Main Street when I started fishing uselessly about in my coat pockets for my gloves; most likely they'd fallen out of my coat at the Rectors'. I shoved my hands into the pockets for warmth and checked my watch; it was nearly ten-thirty, certainly late enough for an unannounced visit.

Her house stood at the corner of Lincoln and Third Streets, a handsome, two-and-a-half-story brick affair in the Queen Anne style with stone columns on the porch and an expansive balcony on the second floor. It was an imposing dwelling, if not on the scale of the Leval-Rector manse. I knocked at the door and was greeted by an Irish woman of sixty, who responded with a snort to my announcement that I was an old friend of the family's passing through. The part of the house I could see was dark, and even standing on the front porch in the cold I could smell its closed mustiness. Letting go the front door she turned on her heel and marched up the stairs, bellowing. "Someone to see you, never seen him before," I heard her say before it slowly clicked shut.

She came back down half a minute later and motioned me upstairs after her. "Come on, visiting's upstairs this morning."

It struck me as unusual that I'd be received upstairs without having revealed my identity. Perhaps she was ill, I thought; or perhaps she'd heard of my arrival the night before. I followed the huffing Irishwoman up the stairs and was led to the master bedroom.

"Here he is," the woman said, and she hurriedly departed. The shades were drawn, and the room so dim I could barely make out an invitingly large bed, one I thought I remembered from the Levals' former house. I couldn't make out Maggie, though, and I stepped forward into the room, inhaling a more potent version of that musty smell I'd noted downstairs. I could hear rattling, clogged breaths being taken laboriously into desiccated lungs—surely not Maggie's?— but I couldn't quite place the sound in relation to my position in the room.

"Maggie?" I said.

Something flew past my head at that moment and shattered against the wall behind me, and a wretched, wet cry accompanied the hurling of it; glancing at the floor I saw that the projectile was a glass paperweight, the prismatic glistening of its shards the only element of color in the room. The person who'd thrown it was seated in a rocking chair near the window, and as my eyes grew accustomed to the low light of the room I saw a tormented face grimacing, trying to form words as a gnarled hand groped for something else to throw. Finally, the voice managed something intelligible: "Get out," the voice said, choking with phlegm. I took in an involuntary rush of air as I divined in an instant of horrible clarity the identity of my invalid attacker, whom I took, for a delirious instant, for a ghost.

"Marc," I said, for it was he seated in the rocking chair. He had managed to get hold of a second piece of heavy glass.

"Of. My. Town." He heaved it, and I had to duck to avoid injury; whatever the extent of his incapacity, it hadn't affected his throwing arm.

"You're alive?" I said, none too sure that this was the case.

"Out," he repeated, and as he laboriously attempted to rise from the rocking chair I backed from the room, hitting my shoulder on the doorframe. In silhouette against the window shade he looked even more spectral than he had a moment before. Never a burly man, he'd shed twenty-five or thirty pounds since his prime, and his face had grown haggard beyond his sixty or so years, his eyes rheumy and sunken into their sockets. As I disappeared around the corner into the hallway I thought I detected a trace of sadness amidst his rage, that same bitter disappointment in my character that had led him to fire at my back in May of '73.

Downstairs, more than slightly rattled, I bade the housekeeper good day, and asked her not to mention my visit to the lady of the house. She merely snuffled, and I didn't know if this was in the way of a response or if her sinuses simply needed clearing. She shook her way to the shadowy recesses of the parlor, and she was completely hidden from me when a terrible shriek came from the upstairs, accompanied by a pounding like that of a cane on an oak floor. She came back into view and headed up the stairs.

"Always so nice when a caller brings a little ray of sunshine into a wintry house," she said as she brushed past me on her way to answer Marc's call. I walked out the front door with the unexpected sensation of freedom, for the first time in seventeen years, from the mark of Cain.

Stepping onto the sidewalk, though, I caught sight of a man staring at me like he wanted me dead. He was wearing a fur coat that probably cost six months' pay for the average citizen of Cottonwood, and a pair of snakeskin boots whose price didn't bear thinking about either; he was long and rough in the face, with a long, aquiline nose. Tall, if not very robust, he looked as though he were having trouble staying upright in the northerly breeze, and after baring his teeth at me he hurried away.

Shortly thereafter, at the door of my erstwhile saloon, a trio of early morning alcoholics awaited Gleason's arrival. My first impulse was to wait elsewhere, lest I be mistaken for one of their number, but curiosity trumped pride, and I approached the door with a friendly wave.

"What time's he open up?" I asked.

The three of them held a silent consultation amongst themselves, and finally one of them answered. "Eleven, I believe, sir," he said. He was young, but his face showed signs of a long dedication to booze: sallow complexion, bulbous red nose, and gin blossoms speckling his cheekbones.

"Is that right?" We stood there for half a minute in nervous silence before I spoke again. "You know, I used to run this very saloon, a few years back, and there were always a few waiting for me to open every morning, just the way you are."

Again they seemed to consult one another, as though wordlessly electing their next spokesman. The same one spoke again. "That so?"

"In fact I built this saloon. The one that stood here before it, too."

There was no response to this at first, but one of them cocked his head to the side, as if trying to place me. They were all three young, less than thirty, though this wasn't plain on first seeing them. The one who thought he knew me spoke up after a minute's cogitation.

"You Clyde's old man?" he asked. He spoke with a pronounced lisp, having only half a dozen or so teeth in his jaws.

"That's me," I said.

"I used to play with him when we was little. Went to school with him, too, up to the sixth grade."

I knew the face, but it was that of a child grown into middle-age without ever having passed through its youth, and I couldn't quite say who among Clyde's coevals he used to be. "What's your name, son?" I asked.

"Lester Pelletier," he answered, and then his face merged comfortably with one in my mind from long ago, that of a small boy of limited intelligence but infinitely good humor who followed Clyde around at school and once or twice came out to the farm, unaccompanied by parents. Too dull-witted to have truly been friends with Clyde, they'd associated with each other by default, since there weren't many other boys their age. Though he'd had a shorter distance to fall than many another rummy it still pained me to recognize him in such a degraded state, and I asked after his parents, of whom I had no memory at all, just for something to say.

"Pa's dead, he fell off a horse drunk and cracked his head clean open on a rock, just like a goddamn melon. That was back in '83, and then Ma said good riddance to him"—here the other two snickered—"and married Mr. Garfield from the mill."

I remembered Garfield, a dour fat pink-faced fellow whose energies had been mainly devoted to the Methodist Building Association. "He's a good man," I said, though I'd never had any use for Garfield, who'd been opposed to my building the saloon in the first place.

"He kicked me out of the house; Pa wasn't even dead six months. I was seventeen."

"What'd he do that for?"

"Got some drink in me and passed out in the parlor. Busted a porcelain jug his mama brought over on a boat from England."

The others laughed again, and Lester offered up a dim-witted smile, a puerile mixture of shame and pride. Then he lifted his arm in excitement and pointed across the street. I looked up to see my second ghost of the morning, for it seemed to me that the man sauntering toward us with an enigmatic half smile on his face was my own father, restored to life after nearly forty years under the earth.

"Father," Clyde said, extending his hand politely, only slightly more obviously pleased or surprised to see me than he would have been at the age of seven or eight.

I took the hand, feeling a bit dazed, and clapped him on the back. "Clyde, boy."

He unlocked the door to the saloon and let us in, and I followed the young souses inside. Clyde busied himself setting up the drinks for his former playmate and the latter's companions and, once he'd done that, set up a second round in anticipation of its demand. Only then did he turn his attention to me.

"You know I'm married," he said.

"That's what Gleason told me."

"She's Mickelwhite's daughter Eva, you remember her."

I didn't particularly, but I nodded as if I did. Mickelwhite had worked a plot not far from ours, and he hadn't bothered to hide his contempt for me when I moved to town and let others do my farming for me. "When'd you tie the knot, anyway?"

"Fall of last year. We have a baby on the way," he added contentedly but without undue enthusiasm. "You can come see us if you like. I'm guessing you're here for the Benders, that right?"

"Partly. How's your Ma?" I asked.

"She's all right. She and Gordon opened 'em up a dress shop."

"That's her husband?"

"Gordon Canterwell. Came to town a year or so after you left. Used to own a shoe store, but Ma was earning our living making dresses, and he thought they could do that together."

"You have a sister now?"

"That's right. Fourteen years old, name of Maria."

I asked him his address and left, though not without young Lester and his friends pestering me for a round. I wasn't drinking myself, but I slapped a half dollar onto the bar and told Clyde to keep the change.

The early morning cloud cover had dissipated, transforming the morning into one of those very cold, very bright ones when the sun seems to have lost its will to warm the earth. I was headed east on Main, my hands jammed deep in my coat pockets and my mind elsewhere, when I nearly collided with a lady exiting Rector's Department Store. I apologized to the lady before I'd seen her face, and when she turned it to me to say it was all right we both stopped breathing for a moment, and both began backing away from each other until we were at a safer distance.

The woman facing me down was Maggie Leval. Strands of white ran through the hair piled atop her head, her bust and hips were fuller and rounder than I remembered, and the sharpness of her facial features had grown softer, outlined now with a fine latticework of wrinkles and underlaid with a little fat. She was even more beautiful than when I'd seen her last, and I stammered when I finally thought to speak, out of a mix of outrage and adolescent terror.

"Good day, Madame," I said.

By this time she had fully regained her sangfroid, and was able to regard me with the insouciance of a lady of quality forced by circumstance and the rules of civility to address a moderately repulsive stranger. "Good day, Sir."

Out of the store behind her came the tall stranger who'd scowled at me earlier, and at the sight of me his face reddened and his fists clenched. Those hands looked as though they'd been broken a time or two, and as he advanced Maggie held him back with an upraised kid glove.

Choosing not to prolong my agony, I turned on my heel and headed west, conscious of the stiffness of my gait and trying to keep it dignified and graceful on account of my sense that she was watching me go. When I finally allowed myself a backward glance she was gone, and so was the giant.

Still flustered, I took a walk north up Lincoln Street toward the cemetery, with the intention of seeking Juno's grave, or that first section where we'd buried Alf Cletus and Paul Lowry and the rest. Trees had been planted throughout, and though they were now in the skeletal habit of winter, they'd plainly thrived there. At the top of the rise was a grouping of cottonwoods taller than the rest, and that was where I found that group of mortuary pioneers.

The first grave I identified was Alf's. It now bore a small, plain stone marker, inscribed simply A. CLETUS, 1873. The handful of other graves that had been there in that year had similarly been marked with simple headstones, with the sole exception of Minnie Lansdown, who now lay beneath a granite monument worthy of a senator's wife. Only her name and dates of birth and death were inscribed thereupon, with no indicator of her relation to the memorialist; the customary "Beloved Wife" wouldn't, in this case, have been appropriate.

A few feet away was Juno's grave, with a mummified nosegay wedged into the juncture of stone and brittle yellow grass. To the west of it was that of the drummer A. J. Harticourt, and flanking them were two stones marked KNOWN BUT TO GOD, presumably the only two bodies from the orchard cemetery not to have been claimed and buried elsewhere. I wondered how it was that Harticourt, whose identity was known, hadn't been shipped back to wherever his people were, but then I remembered my sole encounter with him in life and surmised that no one had thought highly enough of him to pay the cost of shipping his moldering carcass.

I was at first puzzled by Tiny Rector's absence from this particular quarter of the necropolis, but I quickly caught sight of another grandiose marker in the near distance, separated from the rest of the dead by a small wrought-iron fence. No other resident of the cemetery had dared move in next to it, and my first impression of it was that it looked a bit lonely. At the top of the stone was a large cross, below which the stone was inscribed RECTOR in suitably bold capitals. Beneath that, in turn, was a space polished smooth for the inscription:

HENRY P. RECTOR	LILLIAN J. RECTOR
BELOVED HUSBAND	BELOVED WIFE
AND FATHER	AND MOTHER
1822–1887	1825–

I wondered what had taken him off; Lillian had been coy about the circumstances of his demise, and it was easy enough to imagine that his love for sporting girls had hastened his end. Gleason or Clyde could enlighten me, I was sure, and while they were at it they might be able to explain to me the circumstances of Marc Leval's return to town, and his wife's to him. I'd have preferred to hear it from Maggie herself, and perhaps I would someday; more likely I'd never get the chance to speak civilly to her.

Any refusal on her part to deal with me was entirely my own doing. Toward the end of her time in Greeley she was writing me at my studio in Golden, Colorado, thrice weekly, letters which I burned, unopened. Toward the end of that time the envelopes began arriving with the words "urgent!" and "please read!" scrawled across their backs. These I consigned to the interior of the stove just as quickly as the others, reasoning that if she sought to reconcile, she had but to sell the house and join me in Golden; but after two weeks, then three, and then a month went by with no letter I was seized with a sudden panic. Without my ever opening one of them they'd had their desired effect upon me.

One September morning, then, I canceled the day's sittings and set off for Greeley by rail, a journey I hadn't thought I'd ever make again. The trip took most of a day; the little houses stood in rows, whitewashed all and gleaming in the late afternoon sun like jewels, and the trees had grown in to a degree that some of them actually offered shade. It was remarkably verdant, the vegetation in general was lush, and the general impression was of the best-ordered little town imaginable. Seeing the place and how pretty it was made it easy to forget how unhappy I'd been there, how unpleasant life could get for any resident who wasn't a follower of its utopian aims, even if he was married to one who was.

Walking up the street to my former studio I passed the Hendricks, a couple Maggie and I had known slightly, and I doffed my hat and bid them good afternoon. Mr. Hendrick did not reciprocate; he looked at me as though I had ruined the digestion of his supper, and Mrs. Hendrick affected not to see me at all.

"The devil take you, then, you thick-witted bastard," I said with a charming smile and a bow, and I put the hat back on.

"What's that you said?" He'd stopped, and now he faced me; his wife still made out as though her husband addressed a ghost, invisible and inaudible to her.

"I said 'the devil take you,' and I hope you'll excuse me, I only dared say it as you appeared to be hard of hearing."

She yanked at his sleeve, and I went back on my way, surprised at the strength of my urge to knock his hat onto the dirt, and him right after it.

In the twilight our street looked much the same as ever. Two children I didn't know played with an iron hoop in the yard of the house next to ours, however, making me think that the widow Dufferin had died since my leaving. Since she was one of the few neighbors who treated me as such in my last days in the Colony I was sorry for her passing; contemplating her house I noticed the Ash sisters, dyspeptic and indistinguishable one from the other, watching me from their front porch across the street with grand operatic disdain, spindly arms folded across their dry, titless chests. They were true believers in the Colony and had pegged me, correctly, as a troublemaker from the day I arrived, though they always held Maggie in exaggeratedly high esteem. I wished I could cross the street and tell them that she and I had never really been married, that in fact she'd been living in a state of grievous sin with her real husband's killer (as I then imagined myself to be).

With no small trepidation I crossed the grass to my own front door and knocked loudly. I had scarcely any idea of what I'd say to her, but I was determined to keep things as calm as possible, despite the strong feelings involved, with only the minimum of shouting or begging necessary to win her to my way of thinking. Nonetheless when the door opened to reveal a bearded man in his shirtsleeves with a napkin tucked into his collar and a mouthful of food wadded in his cheek, jaw working steady and slow like a guernsey's, I felt as though I'd been gutshot, and my next action was the result of raw emotion and not clear thinking.

"Well, you dirty son-of-a-bitch," were the words that came out of my mouth, even as I balled up my fist and slammed it straight into his breadbasket. He went down in surprise, jaw still churning, and partially chewed chunks of corn fell from his open mouth as he hit the floor, scrambling to get back to his feet. I had already begun to regret the rashness of the act when I saw the boy coming at me, napkin tucked into his collar, and heard the scream of the unfamiliar woman at the dinner table across the dining room. The adolescent coming toward me with his fist upraised was sixteen or seventeen, and six feet in height at least, and with their mother at the table sat four smaller children. The lady of the house was not, of course, Maggie, and my failure to block the boy's fist as it closed in on my jaw was at least partly due to the confusion this caused. I began apologizing on my way backward onto what was apparently no longer Maggie's and my porch. The back of my skull made a solid contact with the wood, and to his credit the man I'd slugged held his son back while I regained my bearings.

After a brief explanation the man introduced himself politely as Hiram Wells, the new owner of the house, and explained that they'd bought it from a woman who had subsequently packed up and moved away, pointedly declining to leave a forwarding address. Hiram walked me off the porch while his wife and children stared after me, the oldest boy looking like he'd like to finish what he'd begun. I returned to Golden the next day and moved my studio shortly thereafter to Denver, and fourteen years passed without another scrap of news about her. I stood a better chance of having a conversation with the man in the grave before me about my past sins than I did with Maggie, if her reaction on the street had been any indication.

The day was getting colder, I thought, and I didn't like the melancholy turn my thoughts were taking. There was a westerly egress from the boneyard, and I headed that way slowly, stopping at this stone and that to see if anybody else I knew had been laid low there. Two friendly old acquaintances lay near the gate, a teamster by the name of Bellows who'd passed away in '77, and H. P. Gavin, a stonemason, who'd managed to hang on until ten years after that. Both of them had spent time and money in my saloon; dead, they were more a part of the town than I was.

I had thought that a look at the Bender trial might lift my spirits, but after lunchtime the courtroom was jammed, and I managed only to insinuate myself into the rear of the room, standing against the wall. The courthouse was still so new that everything in the courtroom seemed to creak: chairs, doors, the gate separating the bar from the gallery. I could only see the faces of those in the rear-most rows of seats, and most of these were unfamiliar to me. At the witness table sat two stout women, short in stature, with their ample backs to me, whom I took to be the defendants. Nothing about them seemed familiar, but I was looking from a distance, and after the passage of nearly seventeen years. Mr. Wembly stood before them, examining a witness regarding the business that had brought Mr. Sheale out to the Bender farm. Squinting, I recognized the witness as Mr. Henniston, Sheale's associate, as fat as ever and pinker than before, his sparse hair gone goose white. Involuntarily I summoned to mind the image of his late partner, freshly exhumed and lying naked and corrupt on the soft green grass of the Benders' orchard, even his clothing stolen by his hosts. I wondered if anything stood there now, if anyone now presumed to farm that patch of blood-soaked land.

Henniston was explaining Mr. Sheale's motivations for travel-ing with such a large amount of cash on his person, and though the gallery was properly silent, Henniston's voice was papery and hoarse, and in the end I couldn't hear him well enough for my interest to hold. Before Mr. Henniston's testimony had ended I ex-ited the courtroom, vowing to return another day, early enough to have a seat nearer the bar. Passing through the main lobby I saw a rotund figure tottering in my direction. He was dressed in ex-pensive but threadbare clothing, and his long sideburns were trimmed unevenly; it took me a moment to put a name to the familiar face, and he was already upon me when I called out a friendly greeting.

"Cy Patton," I called out, extending my hand for a shake. He recoiled momentarily, and then he spat a feeble gob of thick saliva into my palm before hurrying past me to the court.

I was more amused than insulted, and since I couldn't imagine what I'd ever done to poor Cy to merit such impertinence, I laughed it off and stepped out into the gelid afternoon air.

That afternoon I rode a hired roan mare out to my old farm. It hadn't changed much, except that the house had been added to on its west side. I dismounted and tied the nag to the old post I'd planted myself and headed out behind the house. On the spot once occupied by the ramshackle barn I'd built now stood a solid new one, bigger than mine, too. Inside it a Negro of middle years was taking apart a bale of hay with a pitchfork and feeding it to some milk cows in a neatly constructed row of pens. When I called out to him from the door, he didn't hear me over the wind; when I repeated myself his backward glance was wary.

"Sorry to trouble you," I said. "I used to live here. I built that house out there, in fact."

He squinted. "You Ogden, then?"

"That's me," I said. He was older than I'd first taken him for, maybe fifty or fifty-five.

"My name's Haxley. And since you mention it, that roof you built was leaking the day I bought it. Had to replace it right then or it would have ruined the furniture, had to replace all the puncheons on the second floor, too. Just been the hired man living there before that, reckon he didn't care if he got rained on. Not at all a properly built roof, Mr. Ogden."

I had never been taken to task by a Negro before, but Haxley had me dead to rights. I'd done that roof myself, and even while I was hammering the shingles down I knew I'd have to do it again before too many years passed. "Sorry about that."

"Your wife's a real nice lady, though."

"Bought it from her, did you?"

"Came up from Louisiana five years ago, she was living in town by then and eager to sell. She led me to understand you were gone for good and she represented that she had the right to sell without you. If you got a problem you'll have to take it up with your wife. Your former wife."

"Well, I have no problem. Just wanted to see the place is all. You've done some work on it, I see."

"Knocked down that old sod house out back and built a shed. Put up this new barn, too. Old one was falling to pieces time I got to it. Might have blown over in a good stiff gale."

Though I was mostly mad at myself for leaving Ninna with a rickety old barn, I suddenly felt equally angry at Garth for failing to restore it for her. "What happened to Garth?"

"Garth. Well, Garth was working the farm all by himself for Mrs. Canterwell, and he wanted to stay on, but he didn't want to work for a colored man. Before he'd stay on he wanted me to agree to call him Mr. Doyle. So I let him go."

"You know if he's still around?"

"Killed by a train two, three years ago. Drunk on the tracks. When they found him he had a forty-five caliber Colt revolver in his hands, and the sheriff was of the opinion he might have got it into his head that he'd rob the train. Engineer said he thought there was two or three men running away, probably Garth's drunken chums."

"Mind if I ride around back?"

"Go right ahead."

I took the mare around the side of the house and Mr. Haxley resumed his hammering. Even in the midst of winter it was clearly a more successful farm than when I'd run it. The furrows were straight and regular, the buildings neat and well maintained. I'd never looked back with any regret at my life as a farmer, and for the first time I felt a little ashamed that I hadn't worked harder at it. I rode back to the front of the house and thanked Haxley for the look.

I rode back into town slowly; I hadn't seen Ninna yet, and I wondered if this wouldn't be the day to go in and make my apologies to her.

The ride into town was considerably shorter than it had been, the town limits having moved so much further out, and by the time I got to where her dress shop was the sun was low and she'd lit her lamps.

"Hello, Bill," she said when I came through the door, with as little emotion as if I'd been gone no more than a couple of hours. She was tacking cloth to a dummy, and she held a half-dozen pins between her teeth when she smiled.

"Ninna." She looked better than she ever had when we were young; still corpulent by any reasonable standard, she now carried it with considerable grace and charm. The once unformed quality in her face had been refined by the years into a look of good-natured tolerance, a quality sorely lacking during our years together.

"Heard you were back in town."

"I am. Went out to the farm today."

"I sold it a while back. Didn't make sense to keep paying a hired man to do what was really the owner's work." There was a teasing quality to her tone, but no real malice that I could detect. Her accent had almost disappeared, and her mastery of colloquial English had improved also, with no sign of the vulgarisms she once favored; I attributed this to the company of a more attentive husband, and to an active life in town.

"I know. Looks like he's done a good job on the place."

She nodded. "Clyde got married."

"I saw him this morning."

"You see Maggie, too?"

"Briefly. She wasn't glad to see me."

Ninna's lip protruded thoughtfully. "You been gone a long time, Bill."

"You look lovely," I said, with some genuine surprise at the regret I felt just then for having treated Ninna so poorly.

"Pish," she said with a wave of her hand, but her face reddened a little further.

As she began tacking another piece of cloth to the dummy, a lady in black opened the door to the shop and strode majestically in, followed by a bucktoothed young woman who meekly looked at the floor and looked as if she expected to be backhanded across the face at any moment.

"Good afternoon, Mrs. Canterwell," she called out to Ninna. "This would be a convenient moment for you to fit me for the organdy."

Ninna sighed so slightly that if I hadn't been married to her once I wouldn't have detected it; though the timing was plainly inconvenient for her, when she moved to greet the woman it was with an enthusiastic flourish and effusive "hello." She turned to me with a nod that managed to be curt and friendly at once. "Good afternoon to you, sir. A pleasure to see you again."

Outside on the sidewalk I heard behind me the words "Son of a bitch!" and then a powerful blow to my back, right between the scapulae, nearly felled me. I turned, ready to fight, and found myself staring into the scarred, friendly face of Herbert Braunschweig.

"Well I'll be dipped in shit," he yelled, drawing sidelong glances from passersby. "I heard you were back, but I didn't believe it."

"You're looking prosperous, Herbert."

He straightened up and grabbed hold of the collars of his overcoat like a caricature of a big business man. "Goddamned right."

He had a glass eye now, which fixed on me more intently than the real one did.

"You have time for a drink?"

"Naw, I'm in a hurry, but listen, me and Renée got married a while back. You come on over for dinner tomorrow. You remember that big old cathouse Hank Jeffries built?"

I didn't know the name but I assumed he meant the fancifully designed mansion that had been going up when I last saw the town. "The one with all the gables?"

"That's it. Come on over about five or so and we'll feed you. Renée still does her own cooking, you know. You're fixing to stay, aren't you?"

"Haven't decided yet," I said.

"You better. Things are happening in this town again. Good place to be for a man like you." He slapped me on the back again and strode away down the sidewalk like a man with places to go, the opposite of my own condition. I hadn't had my hair cut since a couple of weeks before leaving San Francisco, so I walked back to the northwest corner of Seward and Second, where I'd earlier noted a barber shop. There were two barbers, both of them tall, lanky fellows who may have been brothers. The one nearest the door was free, and I sat in his red leather chair and started listening. He was sure he'd never barbered me before, and wanted to know if I was new to town. The easier answer to that was yes, so that's what I told him, and that got him started on the subject of Cottonwood. He was a real tub-thumper for it, having arrived there from Indiana in '76, and he considered it the best town since the Garden of Eden disincorporated.

"Fastest growing city in the region. More churches per head than any other town in the state, and you can look that up in the 1880 census if you don't believe me. No reason to think that'll change with this year's count, either."

"Is that so?"

"You bet. You heard of the Cottonwood Mills?"

"That the big building east of town?"

"That's the new one. The old one, out northwest of town, that's the biggest mill in this part of the state, makes close to three thousand sacks of flour a day. New one out east next to the brick works is going to be bigger."

I wished he'd shut up, but at least he didn't expect me to keep up my end of the conversation. Before he'd gotten very far along the front door opened and Ed Feeney walked in.

"Howdy, Ed," the chatty barber called out, and Ed waved and sat in one of the chairs against the wall. The other barber was just finishing up a cut on a mustachioed fellow who looked like a banker; neither of them had spoken a word since I'd walked in.

"Howdy, Mort, Hal, Mr. Gintley." He looked at me and raised an eyebrow. "How's by you, Bill?"

"Just fine, Ed."

"I heard you were in town, haven't had a chance to come by and talk. Just walking past I saw you in the chair, thought I might get an interview for the *Optic*."

"That's fine with me. You mind doing it while this fellow lowers my ears?"

"That's all right." He pulled out a small notebook and a pencil. "Now how's about telling my readers where you've been all this time?"

"Points west."

He scribbled and, getting no further answer, forged on. "And what exactly kept you from staying last time, Bill?"

"Wanderlust," I said.

"Aha. And it wasn't a belief that charges would imminently be filed against you for the attempted killing of Marc Leval, prominent citizen of our town and husband of a woman you were known to visit in his absence?"

"Not at all," I answered. The barber's scissors had quit snipping, and he spun me around to face him.

"You aren't Bill Ogden?"

"I am," I replied.

He tore the sheet right off of me. "I'll be goddamned if I'll cut another hair of yours. Everybody knows it was you crippled Mr. Leval, not those Benders."

The other barber spoke for the first time. "Calm down, Mort. You can't leave it half-finished."

"Not to mention what you did to his poor wife."

"Now hold on a minute. What am I supposed to have done to Maggie?"

"I won't cut another follicle. Out," he said, holding the sheet and pointing to the door. He called to mind a Spanish toreador attracting a bull, and I stood, fixing the cruelest scowl I could muster to my face.

"Listen here, friend, I mean to get my hair cut before I leave."

I was taller than he, but his mind was made up. The banker was getting down from the other chair, though, and the other barber waved me over. "Come on, mister, I'll finish it for him."

"I thank you kindly," I said, and sat down. Mort went over to a chair in the back corner of the room and sulked, refusing to look at me or Ed or his colleague.

Ed hadn't stopped taking notes. "So in your opinion are the two women in custody in fact Ma and Katie Bender?"

"Haven't seen them."

"Herbert Braunschweig seems to be convinced it's them, and he knew 'em pretty well. He was fucking Katie for a while, is what I hear."

"I didn't know that. Not surprised, though."

"Hell, I fucked her a time or two myself," Ed said, and the barber behind me was laughing.

"Is that so?" he said. Mort, still sulking in his corner, was looking very superior to the likes of us fornicators and murderers.

Ed probably wished he hadn't said it. "Hell, half the men in town did, just about. You didn't though, did you, Bill? I seem to remember you didn't like her. Anyhow, it doesn't matter. Those women aren't the Benders."

"How do you know that?"

"You know how they found them? This crazy woman up in Michigan claims her laundress was telling her fortune, giving her all kinds of advice on her life, told her secrets from her past, all that sort of thing."

"That sounds like Katie."

"Sure, but they stopped getting along, and Mrs. McCann says that Mrs. Davis started trying to strong-arm some money out of her."

"That sounds like Katie, too."

"Sure does, but Jesus, Bill, you ought to meet this Mrs. McCann. Bats in the belfry, no shit. Talks to the spirits and they talk back. So trying to intimidate her, the laundress said 'you'd better do as I say, my mother's Ma Bender.' "

"That was enough to extradite?"

"Didn't take much more than that. First Mrs. McCann wrote the county commission here and said, 'look here, the lady does my laundry is Katie Bender and her mother is Ma Bender.' So Herbert Braunschweig went up there. He came back and said yep, it's them; they're in the county jail, and if we can put together the funds to extradite and prosecute we can hang the bitches. He said that to a meeting of the county commission. I was watching the stenographer, she'd never heard such a word pronounced in court before."

The barber was done cutting and he started the shave. "Want me to wax that mustache?" he asked, and I told him no.

Ed and I left together, and heading across Seward I stopped cold at the sight of the tall, angry fellow I'd seen with Maggie, looking smart in his fur coat and a silk top hat. Again the look he gave me was full of frank hatred. He turned from me and hurried around the corner to Main Street, and Ed laughed at the look on my own face as I watched him go.

"Who the hell was that?" I asked.

Cackling, Ed headed up Seward, calling over his shoulder, "That's George Smight, he's Leval's factotum. I'd say he's taken a dislike to you."

3

LABETTE COUNTY, KANSAS
FEBRUARY, 1890

Two Gentlewomen

The Braunschweigs' house was bigger than the Leval-Rector mansion, and though staffed with several maids there was, as Herbert had boasted, no cook, and the lady of the house did make all of the meals. Long since converted from its original design, it still retained traces of its origins as a bordello, in particular a large number of small bedrooms upstairs, each of which Herbert felt obliged to show me while Madame Renée finished dinner.

"Now look at this here, Bill," he said, pulling down a framed lithograph of Abe Lincoln from a wall of one of the bedrooms. It hung at a peculiar height, seven feet or so off the ground, and behind it was a small hole, angled downward, through the bedroom wall. Standing on a chair I looked through it and had quite a nice view of the bed in the room next door.

"There's three of these that I've found. This must have been one hell of a whorehouse. I was already with Renée by the time it opened, and she's got the second sight, so if I'd've tried anything like that she'd have killed me." He shook his head sadly at the waste of it all. "You know, you ought to be staying in one of these rooms instead of the hotel."

"That's all right, Herbert," I said, a little put off by the peep-hole in the wall; still, I wasn't making any money for the moment and if I spent too much of my cash reserves I'd have nothing with which to establish another studio.

"Hell, you stay here. I'll tell Renée and she'll by God make you."

"All right, I'll bring my things by tomorrow morning."

"There you go."

He slapped my back for the fourth time that evening and we headed downstairs for a glass of whiskey before dinnertime. We took our seats in the parlor and he leaned forward. Outside it had begun finally to snow, and big chunky flakes drifted down outside the window. The door was closed, and he kept his voice low. "Listen, I don't know what happened with you and Leval, but he told everybody it was the Benders what shot him."

I nodded. "It wasn't, though. He shot at me first."

"We heard it, me and Tim. We'd rode out as far as we thought we could and we was about to turn around when all of a sudden someone fired on us from a thicket down by the water, hit Tim in the thigh. He kept fighting, though, and we held 'em off for a while until they rode away."

"It was them?"

"Sure as hell was. I saw the old man plain as day when they mounted. If Tim hadn't been hurt I woulda rode after 'em."

"How's old Tim, anyway?"

"Shot to death in '84."

"How'd it happen?"

"He'd married him a gal from Fort Scott, opened up a lumber-yard up there. Payroll robbery. They hanged one of his men for it, looked like old Tim'd recognized him even with the masks they had on. He never did admit he'd done it, pissed himself before they even got the noose over his head."

"Sorry to hear that. Tim was a good man."

" 'Course you know I got a brickworks myself and part of a flour mill. We're building another mill, too. And I'll tell you something else about what's happening here right now, all this is real. Not like Leval's cattle trail." He took an angry puff of his cigar, getting freshly worked up over it. "I've been in business with old Marc for a while now, and he's all right. But if I'd known about business then what I know now I'd have seen right through that son of a bitch."

"Probably would."

"Anyway, why don't you come down one of these days to the brick plant and I'll show you around. You ought to think about staying, and I've got a job for you if you do."

"What kind of job?" I asked, picturing myself stoking a giant kiln for ten hours, ending up sunburnt in January with my hair dry and brittle as wheat straw.

"Hell, I don't know. Something good. Something pays better than taking pictures."

I was about to protest that I'd made a good living at it over the years when a servant girl knocked at the door and stuck her head in. "Madame's got dinner ready to serve."

The main course was blanquette de veau, and it was as good as anything I'd had in a restaurant anywhere in the west. Madame Renée was pleased to hear me say it, and she patted my hand. Like Herbert, she'd been fitted with a glass eye since I'd seen her last, and its effect was more disconcerting than the dead, frosted one had been. She told me about her son, who worked for the department of wells and quarries for the city of Paris. He had provided her with six grandchildren, none of whom she had ever seen.

"Your boy didn't waste any time knocking that gal of his up," Herbert said.

"Baby's due in May, I think."

"Dites-donc," Madame Renée said. *"Vous avez déjà vu Maggie ou pas?"*

"Goddamnit," Herbert roared, and he pounded his fist down on the table so hard some of the blanquette splashed over the rims of our plates. "Talk English!"

There followed an argument of such intensity and volume that I was tempted to excuse myself. When I rose, though, they both froze and looked at me.

"Where you going?" Herbert said.

"I thought I'd leave you in privacy," I said, and they both looked at me like I was crazy. The storm had passed for both of them, though, and they regarded me with the same pleasant, mild curiosity as before, and Renée repeated her question in English.

"I saw her on the street yesterday and she looked at me like I was covered in flies and cowshit."

Herbert was soaking a crust of bread with the sauce of the blanquette. "You know, Bill, when she came back the *Optic* printed a whole pack of goddamned lies about you and Maggie both. The *Free Press* tried to defend her but that just made it worse for you."

I shrugged. "There's not much the papers can say anymore to help or hinder my reputation locally," I said, and we let it drop. I made a mental note to go and see Ed tomorrow, though, and have a word about it.

In the morning it was still snowing, and it had drifted to such a degree that carriage traffic was slow and walking difficult. I hired a dray and had my effects moved from the hotel to the Braunschweig mansion, into a bedroom I was relatively certain was free of spyholes. After luncheon I set off for the offices of the *Optic*, where I found Ed setting type himself. He assured me that he'd be at it for only a few minutes more, and I sat down at his writing desk to wait.

"You ought to hire a typesetter after all these years," I said.

"Had one until a couple weeks ago, but the disloyal son of a bitch quit and moved to Oswego. I got a pair of apprentices who can't be trusted to do it right, so I end up doing it myself."

Most of the light came from the window, and the shadows the reflected snow cast on the composing room were long and deep. "How come you don't turn the lamps up?"

He looked up, as if he were only just then noticing that the room wasn't particularly well lighted. "Oh. Well, lamp fuel costs money and I'm used to doing it like this." He was growing annoyed, and I thought it best to keep my mouth shut until he finished the task at hand. I stood by the window reading the day's account of the Bender trial, and when he was ready he wiped his hands and sat at the desk opposite.

"You seem pretty sure those women aren't the Benders. Or is that just newspaper politics?"

"Have you had a look at those two? If that's what Katie Bender's sweet hindquarters have come to then it's a goddamned shame."

"I haven't seen them up close." I hadn't come to talk about the Benders, though, and I tried to remember that I had reasons to be mad at him. "What'd you write about me, Ed?"

"You didn't give me much to write. Just that you were back."

"I don't mean the other day, I mean when Maggie came back to town."

"Hell, you want to know what I wrote about Maggie?" He led me into the back of the printshop, into a room containing a multitude of newspapers hanging down from cylindrical racks. A bookcase held a large number of enormous volumes bound in light calfskin. "Help me with the date, here."

"Well, she left Greeley in September of seventy-five."

"Seventy-five . . . as I recall it was around the middle of October of that year that she came back . . . I was still a weekly, so that simplifies matters somewhat. Go on, sit down."

I sat at a large table, and shortly he produced a copy of the paper dated October 17th, 1875. The lead story was Maggie's:

VILLAINY UNPUNISHED

RETURN OF MRS. LEVAL TO THE SCENE
OF HER CRIMES—MR. NETTLE SAYS SHE WILL
NOT BE BROUGHT TO JUSTICE—OUTRAGE OF
THE CITIZENRY

The law-abiding citizens of Labette County are asking themselves why we now tolerate and even welcome the kinds of criminals we once set out after with torches ablaze. Mrs. Marguerite Leval has returned to Cottonwood to ask forgiveness of her husband, Marc Leval, who is in the frailest of health after being shot down by Mrs. Leval's own illicit paramour, the notorious Bill Ogden, who had treacherously played at being Mr. Leval's friend. That the two set off together immediately after the commission of the crimes does not move Mr. Nettle, the County Prosecutor, to file charges of attempted murder or accessory thereto.

"You've got some crust, you son-of-a-bitch," I said. "I ought to thrash you for that."

"Don't get too cross about it. Maggie didn't sue. Hell, Bill, I didn't think you were coming back, is the thing."

The next number in the volume, for October 24th, was even worse:

LOVE CONQUERS ALL

MR. MARC LEVAL'S MEMORY RETURNS
TO HIM—IT WAS THE BENDERS WHO SHOT
HIM AS THEY FLED—HIS WIFE NOT TO BLAME,
NOR HER FUGITIVE PARAMOUR

Mrs. Marguerite Leval, recently returned from an unknown location whence she and her notorious cohort, Bill Ogden, had fled after the failed assassination of Mrs. Leval's husband Marc, has effected a most remarkable recovery upon her husband, whose memory had been, it seems, damaged by the bullets that crippled him two and a half years ago. Previously, he had remained silent as to his assailant's identity, and most here assumed that the guilty party was his rival for his wife's affections, Bill Ogden. Now Mr. Leval has sworn, we are told, to the county attorney and others that it was the notorious Benders themselves that made him an invalid on the night they escaped into the ether. A lovelier testament to the healing powers of love would be difficult to imagine.

"Mr. Smight came over and punched me in the face over that one, and then Herbert told me to put a stop to it quick or he'd have me shut down."

"I don't guess you did."

"Story was losing steam by then anyway. What's more, people were starting to feel a lot of sympathy for her. Look at this here," he said, and he moved over to a separate set of volumes bound in the same light-colored calfskin. Selecting one he brought it over to the table. "I keep a separate morgue for the *Free Press*, but Cy's too cheap to keep the *Optic* on hand."

He flipped around until he found the issue of October 16, 1875. "Here's what Cy had to say about it." His index finger traced down the page to the pertinent article. Here, too, Maggie was the subject of the lead article, but she wasn't its villain.

MRS. LEVAL HAS RETURNED

IT IS HOPED THAT HER TESTIMONY WILL AID IN THE CAPTURE OF HER HUSBAND'S ATTACKER—SALOONKEEPER OGDEN SAID TO HAVE COMPELLED HER TO ACCOMPANY HIM ON HIS FLIGHT FROM JUSTICE.

To the great joy of all Cottonwoodians, Mrs. Marguerite Leval, the wife of our friend Marc Leval, has returned to Cottonwood after an absence of more than two years, during which, Mrs. Leval's intimates have informed the *Free Press*, she was held in the vilest of captivity by the outlaw Bill Ogden, who once operated a saloon here. Ogden's motive in shooting his friend and protector, Mr. Leval, seems to have been an unreciprocated love for Mrs. Leval.

Ed's arms were folded across his chest, and he looked down at me with great satisfaction. "So you see who your friends are and aren't in the press. Cy dropped all that about you when Leval came out and said it was the Benders who shot him."

Distracted as I was, I had nonetheless to admit that the *Optic*'s stories hit closer to the mark than the *Free Press*'s did. "Seems like old Cy thought even less of me than you."

"Nothing personal, on his part or mine. 'Course, like half the men in town, Cy was a little bit sweet on old Maggie. And he was doing what he did at least partly at Leval's behest."

"Leval was looking pretty poorly when I saw him yesterday."

"He has his good days, too. He was at the trial last week, looked pretty dapper there in his wheelchair. Speaking of which, you want to go see the ladies?"

"The Benders?" I said.

"I was thinking I might try and talk my way past that Mrs. Naylor, see if I couldn't get a few words with the ladies this afternoon after court lets out. Why don't you come along and see what you think. Court'll likely adjourn at three-thirty or four."

It was two-thirty now; in the interim I elected to stay and leaf through old volumes of the *Optic* and the *Free Press*, seated in a chair by the front window, catching up on any number of useless facts about Cottonwood's economy and society, and various aspects of local and state politics that had escaped me during my long exile. And then—in one paper, ten years old, in an article on a Christmas party at the Methodist Church, I was struck by the names of two of the students: Maria Canterwell, Ninna's girl, and Marc Leval, Jr. With strained voice I asked Ed about the latter child.

He peered at me over his spectacles, as though trying to decide if I was pulling his leg. "That'd be Maggie's boy. Born shortly after her arrival here."

I nodded. "Those articles from '75 didn't mention she was with child," I said.

"Hell, no," Ed said. "No need, for one thing. Still a small town then, everybody knew." He laughed under his breath. "Everybody except you, I guess."

When we left the offices of the *Optic* the snowy streets were hard to navigate, but they'd be worse in a day or two when the melting snow turned the frozen earth to mud and then to solid ice. We took Ed's buggy toward a neighborhood east of downtown, then turned onto a street of cozy little cottages and pulled quickly in front of one of them. If memory served, this was very close to where the whores' row of tent cribs had briefly stood during the boom. The Naylor residence looked quaint and comfortable beneath its white blanket, and gray smoke rose from its chimney. Before we had a chance to knock, a lady came to the door. She wore a plain brown dress covered by a heavily floured apron and looked none too happy to see Ed; I, on the other hand, might not have been there at all.

"Mrs. Naylor, allow me to present Mr. Ogden. Mr. Ogden, this is Mrs. Naylor, the wife of Deputy Naylor of the Labette County Sheriff's department. She's the de facto matron of women at the moment."

"Pleased to meet you, Mrs. Naylor," I said with a suave, continental bow that normally won me great favor with married ladies of a certain age. Mrs. Naylor was unimpressed.

"Here to see the ladies? I just got done feeding them."

"They ought to be pretty docile, then," Ed said.

"Docile? They're horrid, just horrid. The language they use!

And in front of the baby. It's just a shame." She led us through their small, warm parlor toward a back bedroom. "Don't misunderstand, I'm awfully grateful for the money, but I wonder if those two wouldn't be better off in the county jail."

"I thought it was decided there was no proper way to segregate them from the male prisoners?" Ed said.

"Hah!" It was an unladylike ejaculation that nonetheless underscored in her a certain attractiveness I'd missed theretofore. "Segregation from men is the last thing those two want," she said, and then she stopped and covered her mouth with her hands, grinning naughtily beneath them and flushing bright red. "Now the strict rule is a matron, that's to say me, shall at all times be present during any interviews with men. That's always the rule when we've got female prisoners, and apart from propriety's sake, it's to protect the women, of course. In this case, though, it's more to protect the honor of the men."

"I heard what you said, you mackerel twat," came the old woman's muffled voice through the door.

Mrs. Naylor took the compliment with greater equanimity than most of her peers would have, I think, turning to face Ed and me with a resigned look. "You hear what I have to put up with? This trial better not last much longer, is all I've got to say on the matter."

She unlocked the door and opened it, careful to remain outside the room, and Ed and I stepped in. Sitting in a rocking chair of hickory was a very careworn and haggard old woman, crabbed and bent over even seated as she was, and in a chair next to the window was a well-fed, idiotic-looking woman in her forties. A girl child two years old or thereabouts played at the latter's feet with the end of a shawl.

"Who the hell's this," the old woman snarled, with not a trace of Mrs. Bender's Alsatian sound in her voice; I would have guessed New York, upstate somewhere.

"You remember me, ladies. I'm with the *Optic*. Just came to ask a few more questions." Ed indicated me with his hand. "And this is Mr. Ogden. Mr. Ogden, this is Mrs. Eliza Davis"—indicating the younger woman—"and this is her mother, Mrs. Almira Griffith."

Mrs. Davis's leering smile made me cringe in much the same way Katie Bender's flirtations once had, and she laughed and held her baby's hand up in a wave. "You see there, Nattie? That there's Mr. Ogden." On her temple was a vivid scar partially covered by her coiffure. "Maybe he'll be your new daddy." She gave me a look of theatrically exaggerated sadness. "Her old daddy took off God knows where, and if he comes back to our house he'll find us gone and no way to find us."

The old woman glowered at the bunch of us; I'd scarcely known old Mrs. Bender and would be hard-pressed to say whether this woman was she or not. I was puzzled by her daughter, also. While it wasn't impossible to imagine that the lithe and vivacious Katie Bender had metamorphosed physically into this worn-out, obese creature, one thing that couldn't be said about Katie was that she was stupid, and the younger of the women in the room seemed eager to prove from the outset that she was a numbskull.

"Anything you want to ask the women, Mr. Ogden?"

I thought about it for a second. *"Habt ihr die Nacht vergessen, in der ich zu eurem Haus rausgeritten bin? Als eure Mannsleute mich umbringen wollten?"*

I discerned no trace of comprehension in their faces, nor of dissimulation. The younger woman cackled. "Damn if everybody down here in Kansas don't speak Dutch."

"You're not the first to try that, Mr. Ogden," Ed said.

They both looked pleased, as if they'd passed some sort of test.

I tried again in English. "Remember the night I rode out to your place and your menfolk wanted to kill me?"

"Our place in Michigan?" Mrs. Davis said.

"He means the Bender place, out this way," Ed said.

"We ain't the goddamn Benders," the old lady yelled, rising out of the chair and making a fist at Ed.

"I ain't a Bender, but she is," young Mrs. Davis said with the mischievous laugh of a naughty child, pointing at her mother. The old lady took several steps forward, claw extended at her daughter's face.

"That's a goddamn lie and you know it."

"No it ain't," the daughter yelled. "You're the Bender, Ma."

There was only one bed in the room for the three of them, covered with a patchwork quilt that didn't look any too warm. "Mind if I sit on the bed, Mrs. Naylor?" Ed asked.

"Go right ahead," Mrs. Naylor replied lackadaisically. "Just make sure those two don't climb on, too, out of habit."

"Cuntrag!" the old lady yelled, picking up a pincushion from a sewing basket to hurl at Mrs. Naylor, who ducked it as easily as if she had been expecting it.

She shook her head. "Assaulting the matron, and right in front of witnesses. You'll have no pecan pie this evening."

"I don't care a steamin' pile of shit about your fuckin' pie!"

I believe Ed was genuinely shocked at the language used, and even I was hard-pressed to recall when I'd last heard the mother tongue abused so colorfully by a member of the gentler sex. The daughter was laughing hard, full of joy at seeing Mrs. Naylor get the best of her mother.

"I hope you'll put that in your paper," Mrs. Naylor said. "Let people around here find out what they're like."

Ed looked at me, then at the old lady. "Tell Mr. Ogden how many husbands you've had."

The old woman looked as if she was trying to remember her multiplication tables, squinting at the ceiling and humming, before she finally spoke. "I ain't telling you anything without Mr. Lassiter here."

"She's been married six times," the daughter chimed in. "Widowed four times and then two of 'em up and run out on her, including my papa."

"Shut your hole, Eliza," the old woman yelled.

Eliza showed a certain amount of confusion, but her fear of her mother won out, and she kept still until the baby made a noise about something outside the window in the failing light of day. On a tree limb in the backyard was a squirrel, its long curved puff of a tail undulating jerkily, and Eliza Davis let out a squeal of excitement as happy as the baby's. "Looky there, it's ol' Handy."

"They have names?" I asked.

"That one does, we saw him yesterday. See? He's short a hand." On close examination the squirrel, barely six feet from the window, proved to be missing its left forepaw. She held her little girl up for a better look. "See how he's just got one hand, Nattie? Somebody must've cut it off with a knife." The child burbled with delight as Ed and I made our exit.

In the front room I was introduced to Mrs. Naylor's husband, who had just returned home. "Never had a lady prisoner like them. I don't know how we'll manage, I really don't. Becky's a woman of very delicate sensibilities and it isn't fair to expose her to that kind of language."

Mrs. Naylor stood beside him looking quite unconcerned, but she nodded her head. "That's right, and I'd be obliged if you'd put that in your newspaper."

"I certainly will, madame," Ed said, and we got our coats and hats and left. The snow was blowing still, and it was now dark. Ed didn't say much until we were nearing downtown.

"You remember a whore named Lottie, showed up around the time of the boom?"

"I do," I said. "Didn't she operate out of a big tent right around where the Naylors' house is now?"

"That's it, all right, she and a few others. Now Lottie, there was a woman who could cuss. One time I was down there with another one of the soiled doves, one by the name of Lulubelle, and a couple doors down we heard Lottie cry out 'Stop, thief.' I'd just finished up my business with Lulubelle, so I hiked up my drawers and took off after him, and pretty soon there was three or four of us chasing the poor fellow down. We caught him pretty quick and held him down, and old Lottie came over and kicked him right in the balls. She was barefoot, so it didn't hurt him as much as it might have, and so she grabbed 'em and squoze."

I winced at the thought. "What then?"

"She let out a string of violent obscenities the likes of which I'd never heard from the lips of a woman. Never have since, either, until this afternoon. Boy, she called him a cock-sucker and a fuckhead and a shit-heel and every other vulgar compound noun in the American vernacular. People were gathered around by then, and they started encouraging her to hurt him, and of course there were still men holding him down. I'd let go of the poor bastard by then. It got ugly after that."

We rode in silence again for a block or two; I watched the vapor blowing out the horse's flaring nostrils in long bursts and tried to connect the two women I'd just seen with Katie and Ma Bender. Finally Ed spoke again. "I miss those days, when the town was a little wilder."

"It's calmed down somewhat," I said.

"I suppose it could erupt again if those two are acquitted."

"You think they will be?"

He shrugged. "That depends. But if the public decides they're the Bender women and then the court finds otherwise, it'll be hard to get those two out of town with their necks intact."

"I don't see how anybody who knew the Benders could honestly say those two are they," I said, finally.

"Nope," he said. He stopped the buggy in front of the *Optic*'s offices. Inside a pair of young men worked at the press, and Ed shook his head at the sight of them. "Look at those two, like molasses. Well, I guess I'd better go show 'em how it's supposed to be done."

I could hear him yelling at the two apprentices, even once he'd shut the door and over the muffling effects of the snowfall. In a bleak mood I trudged through the snow to Herbert's, where the smell of Madame Renée's cooking was detectable even before I entered the front door. Herbert sat in the parlor reading the morning *Free Press*, and he waved me into the room.

"Say, Renée's cooking beef tonight. Bergy-own. You don't look too good, Bill."

"I just found out Maggie had a baby."

"She sure as hell did. Little Marc Leval. Not so little now."

"That's why she came back, isn't it?"

"You were gone and not answering her letters, is what I understand."

"And everybody knows he's my son?"

"A lot of people think so. Baby was born maybe five, six months after she got here, and she made sure people didn't get to see him right away, so she could say he'd come early. Well, hell, Renée was just about the only female in town who'd talk to her, so we saw him the day he was born. I'll bet the little fucker weighed ten pounds."

The clock on the mantle chimed six times. "I went to see the Benders today, at the deputy's house."

"That so?" He was momentarily apprehensive, as though expecting a pronouncement he didn't think he'd like. When I didn't express an opinion he relaxed. "Well, soon enough we'll see them two dangling."

"Where do you think the men are?"

"Dead, probably. And probably it was these two did it."

"You think it's really them?"

" 'Course I do."

"I'm not so sure, especially the young one. Give Katie her due, she was sharp as a tack; in fact if you ask me she was the ringleader. That woman over at the deputy's house is damn near a moron."

"Yeah, but she wasn't always. You see that scar on her head? One of her husbands did that with a brick, caught her fucking a railroad man. She's been half-idjit ever since, according to one of her sisters in Michigan."

"The young one's a lot heavier than Katie ever was."

"Since you saw her last she's had four husbands and six kids."

"Where are the other five?"

"Oldest two are already working, the other three had to go into the almshouse after they arrested her." That seemed to bother Herbert, and he shook his head. "Well, the tykes are probably better off away from the likes of that one."

A screech erupted from the kitchen. Hurrying there we found Madame Renée pounding with a tenderizing hammer at the wall where it met the floor and cursing in French at something with a vulgarity and vehemence that would have done Mrs. Griffith proud. Herbert bent down and pulled her away from the wall. The boards were visible where she'd hit, through the torn paper and broken plaster.

"Now goddamnit Renée, you're not going to get at it that way. You're just going to punch up the wall and make it easier for it to get up here."

She had calmed down a little, but the look of outrage persisted on her face. "Rats," she said. "Goddamn rats."

"I only ever seen one," Herbert said, "but it's a great big bastard." He patted her on the back. "Me and Bill, we'll go down and kill it."

"It's about goddamn time," she said. "Son of a beetch got into the flour."

She showed us a bag of flour in the pantry, the sack chewed through at the bottom and spilling a goodly amount. Dainty white rodentine footprints led from the sack to the spot where Madame Renée had gone after it with the hammer, with the larger floured impressions of her kitchen slippers blurring them at intervals.

"Supper about ready?" Herbert asked, sniffing.

She let loose another burst of Gallic obscenities, and Herbert discreetly backed out of the room. I followed him to his den, where he sat down at his writing desk.

"Jesus, that's some temper she's got. You'd think I'd bred the rat myself and trained it just to get that flour."

We could still hear her banging drawers and cabinets and yelling, and the younger servant girl appeared in the doorway. "It's that rat again, isn't it?" she asked.

"Mr. Ogden and me are going down there to kill it, Sally."

"Yes sir," she said, and curtsying, she left.

"The girls are all scared of the damned thing. He's a big old bastard, like I said." He opened a locked drawer and took from it a Colt Dragoon and handed it to me.

"Here you go," he said. "This used to be yours."

Loading it I indeed recognized it as the same iron I'd taken off Harticourt the drummer so many years previous. "Where'd you get this?" I asked him, rather pleased at the sight of that relic of my frontier days.

"Your saddle bag, the day you left," he said, loading an old Colt Peacemaker of his own. He lit two big lamps and, taking one each, our guns stuffed into our belts, we put on our overcoats and then proceeded to the kitchen, where Herbert loaded a plate with a small quantity of *bœuf bourguignon*. Madame Renée scowled but said nothing, and we exited the house via the side door.

The storm cellar was entered from the side of the house. I set down my lamp, since Herbert also carried the plate of stew, and dusted the snow off the heavy wooden trap doors before lifting them. I went down first, the stairs creaking so badly I was sure one of them would snap, but I reached the bottom safely and set the lamp down on the concrete floor. Behind me the stairs labored under Herbert's boots, and I took the plate from him, too. Herbert then returned to the top to close the trap doors. It wasn't as cold as I would have expected.

"Turn the lamps all the way up and set that stew on the floor," he said, and I did it. He got a couple of raggedy chairs from a corner of the room and we sat together near the west wall. In the poor light I could make out around the periphery pieces of derelict furniture, footlockers and valises, and what appeared to be a stack of paintings in gilded frames. Against the east wall was an enormous rack of wine bottles, numbering perhaps two hundred, with room for that many again.

"That's a lot of wine," I said.

"Well, Renée likes it with dinner, and it looks like it's going to be outlawed here pretty quick if we're not careful, so I bought a whole slew of it. I got more on the way."

"Outlawed?"

"Outlawed, all throughout the state."

"Not too cold down here."

"No, stays nice and fresh in the summer, too. Lots of days I'll sneak down here just to cool off."

"That rat won't come out if we're talking," I said; having killed several thousand rats in my day I considered myself an expert on the subject.

"Not this one, he's a bold son of a bitch. He steals food right out from under Renée's nose. This beef'll get him out in the open."

The smell of the beef and its thick, soupy gravy was making my mouth water, and I wanted that rat dead so I could eat. Herbert, however, persisted in his jawing.

"Last five years or so we've had two, three times as many rats as we used to. It's a hell of a problem at the mill, I got a man on it full-time. You ask me, they come in on the trains." He looked over at me, and in the harsh light of the lamp I noticed that his glass eye had gone considerably askew. Its pupil was oriented toward the floor, as if he were looking at me with the good one and watching for the rat with the bad.

We were quiet for a minute, and sure enough the rat, or a rat anyway, poked his head into the light of the lamps and gingerly approached the fragrant, steaming plate of *bœuf bourguignon*. It raised its head in our direction as Herbert raised his Colt, but I touched his arm to make him stop. He looked quizzically at me but held his fire.

As the rat began feeding a second rat of almost equal size cautiously made itself visible and crept up to the plate. Now I raised my weapon and Herbert his. The clicking back of the hammers merited only the slightest glances from the first rat, but the second turned tail and bolted for its hiding place. I fired and sent a bloody cascade of its various parts in all directions, and Herbert discharged his own a moment later, demolishing rat and plate both. The sound of gunfire in the cramped basement caused my ears to ring for some minutes afterward, and it took me a moment to realize that I was giggling ecstatically along with Herbert at the ghastly pile of fur, scales and entrails that confronted us.

"That'll show the sons of bitches," he said as we mounted the staircase, lamps in hand, leaving the gory remains for Beatrice and Sally to remove. "What do you know, there was two of 'em after all."

Madame Renée was in the kitchen, arms folded across her chest in a most forbidding manner. Herbert ignored this and embraced her, planting a kiss on her pursed lips and laughing again.

"Woman, we killed your rats. Let's eat."

She was still formal, if a little less angry. "They're in the parlor. Tell them time to eat."

In the parlor, to my surprise, I found my son, accompanied by a young woman I presumed to be his wife. He rose and, in a formal manner that reminded me again of my father, introduced me to her.

"Eva, may I present my father, William Ogden. Father, my wife Eva."

"Née Mickelwhite, if I recall correctly." She was small, with a long, equine face that was nonetheless pretty; when she smiled she showed a significant gap between her front teeth that did nothing to alter my previous impression. I took her hand and gently kissed the back of it, producing a small wave of giggling that underscored her childish quality. "I always knew you'd grow up to be a beauty," I added, though in fact I didn't remember her at all, except as an indistinct component of a gaggle of tots rampant on the Mickel-white farm.

"We're expecting a little Ogden," she said, and beside her Clyde reddened and nearly smiled.

"If it's a boy his name will be Flavius Josephus," he said, and though I thought that was a terrible name for a lad to grow up with I was glad that Clyde still gave some thought to his Latin.

Young Beatrice stepped past me. "Dinner's served," she announced, and then she slipped away again. I held out my elbow for Eva to slip her arm into and we moved along to the dining room, where Herbert stood behind his chair. Madame Renée sat at the head of the table.

Madame Renée turned to me as Beatrice began to pour the wine. Like Herbert's, her glass eye had a tendency to wander, and at that moment it was gazing placidly away from her nose and toward the door of the room. I wanted to ask what had become of the fleshly one, whether it had been plucked surgically or had just withered away. "You know for years Clyde used to come over and speak French," she said.

"Ninna left him and the girl here while she worked. He has an ear for languages."

"Oh, yes, that's so," his wife said, her voice still a girl's. "He's always got his nose in one of those old Greek books you left him."

I was inordinately, irrationally pleased to hear this additional evidence that Clyde's classical education hadn't ended with my going. "Is that so, Clyde?" I asked him over her shoulder. "You still looking at those Greek texts?"

"Yes, sir," he said. "The Levals have been generous enough to make their library available to me."

"They've been very kind to us," Eva said as Sally began serving a pâté of some sort.

"Best one-eyed French cook in southeast Kansas, male or female," Herbert said, and next to me I could sense Eva tensing up.

That tension carried through all of us until our hostess broke it by laughing, and by the time the main course arrived on the table the atmosphere at table was one of genial bonhomie, helped along by Sally's overattentive way with the wine bottle. I had counted three bottles opened so far for a table of five, and on the side table stood three more.

Herbert was a noisy eater, and his first bite of the beef, still giving off steam as he shoveled it past his lips, burned him so badly he had to swig down a whole glassful of burgundy. I, too, scorched my palate through impatience, but the succulence of the meat and the thick, blackish gravy wouldn't wait. The others sat there, blowing on forkfuls, mashing potatoes and carrots into the stew, taking tiny bites, but when the eating of the beef began in earnest not much was said for a good ten minutes, until we began to slow down.

"Your boy here's done a good job on the saloon," Herbert said, swabbing at his sauce with a crust of bread. "Gleason, too."

Madame Renée stood, with some expenditure of effort, and went into the kitchen to oversee the dishing out of the dessert, and Eva turned to me. "Maybe you could come over after supper and see our little house."

"I'd be delighted," I said, and we passed the time waiting for the pumpkin pie talking about the house and the improvements Clyde had made to it.

Dinner ended and I boarded Clyde's buggy, flanked by the happy couple. They lived a few blocks north of Deputy Naylor's, in a square little house much in the style of the others around it. There was a fence to mark the periphery of the lot, and Clyde gallantly carried his wife to the front door, since she wore no galoshes. His own he removed at the door, as I did mine, and we crossed the threshold into their parlor, already lit with a pair of small lamps that gave off an eerily warm glow. "Mama?" Eva called out.

"Coming," a female voice cried from the kitchen.

As I looked about the room I recognized several items that had once been part of Ninna's and my household: a small framed daguerreotype of my parents and me, taken when I was about three years of age, a miniature German Bible I'd carried to war at my mother's insistence and had held onto afterward for reasons still not entirely clear to me, that lithograph of the cathedral at Strasbourg.

Then from the kitchen came a woman I recognized as Agnes Mickelwhite, mother of Eva and various other little Micklewhites since grown to adulthood. She curtsied politely. "Mr. Ogden, so nice to see you."

I didn't think she meant it, though for all I knew the deep, corrosive scowl she showed me may have been permanently carved into her toothless jaw. Agnes was no more attractive than she'd been as a young woman, possessed as she was of her daughter's oblong face but lacking her softness of feature and sweetness of character. I smiled, though, and bowed and kissed her hand as I had her daughter's. "And how is Mr. Mickelwhite?" I asked her.

"I'm afraid he's passed on," she said. "I'm living with the children now, until the baby comes."

Eva then showed me some small things they'd received as wedding presents—including a large silver bowl from the Levals—and when she'd done Clyde showed me his bookcase. There were all the titles I'd left behind, in addition to those that had come from the Leval library. He'd added a few of his own, too, expensive-looking, leather-bound volumes of Marcus Aurelius and Herodotus.

"The saloon must be doing all right," I said, leafing through the commentary of the Herodotus and thumping its binding. "This is calfskin."

"The saloon does fine. I also do the bookkeeping for a dozen businesses in town, the flour mill and Braunschweig's brick factory among them."

"Is that so?" I said, and looking around the house I was pleased at how well my boy had done; a businessman and a scholar, he'd never spend another day of his life behind a plow. That I deserved no credit for his outcome didn't diminish my pride in him, nor my sudden enthusiasm for the grandchild Eva carried.

When we'd finished visiting Clyde offered to drive me home, but I assured him I was content to walk. He accompanied me to the door and stepped outside with me anyway, and I steered him away from the door.

"How well do you know the Leval boy?"

"Marc? Very well. He works for us sometimes at the studio, after school."

"Does he have any idea of his actual relation to you?"

"We don't ever discuss it," Clyde said, and I clapped his shoulder and bid him good night.

I elected to walk home through the snow, though Clyde had assured me he was happy to lend me the buggy. The snow had stopped, for a while at any rate, and I enjoyed the sight of the sleeping town, its sky a luminescent maroon. There were lights burning in various windows of the Naylor residence, and within I could hear Mrs. Davis's little girl crying. A block to the west I felt a blow struck at my shoulder, and I went down. It was too dark to see my attacker, but I thought he held a walking stick, and I concentrated my efforts upon wresting it from him. Once all four of our hands were clutching the thing I kicked him in the breadbasket, and all the air went out of him as he let go. I then swung the stick in an arc to my right, and its head hit his with a very pleasing crack. As he got up I saw that he was considerably bigger than I, and when he ran away it was with lowered head, bent halfway over to conceal his identity; nonetheless there was no disguising Mr. Smight's distinctly vertical silhouette as he stumbled off in the general direction of the Leval residence. I still held the walking stick, and adopted a boulevardier's jaunty stride as I resumed my walk home. It took me a minute or two to calm down and get my breath back, but once I had done so I felt invigorated and nearly happy; once I got downtown, where the streetlights were just being put out, I saw that I'd acquired rather a fine piece of woodwork, its head made of what appeared to me to be solid silver.

I stopped before the front window of Rector's Department Store, which was piled with goods of various kinds, their prices written next to them on small cards. A pair of dummies displayed the latest fashionable clothing from Chicago, and between them was a tabletop cunningly arranged with various kinds of feminine ornamentation, from combs to hatpins to costume jewelry. The interior of the store was as black as a cave, and though I tried to make out its secrets it held them there, inscrutable, in the dark. The young man extinguishing the streetlamps had placed his ladder on the lamp behind me, and when it went dark there wasn't anything to see in the storefront, either, so I moved along. Tiny crystals of snow spattered the exposed portion of my face, and the wind continued to blow the new snowfall in curvaceous patterns upon the old. I found myself before the Levals' house, staring up at what I thought might be her window, my grip tight on the walking stick; the windows were dark, and I didn't know if I was being watched or not. Starting on my way again I slowed at the sight of a lamp moving toward me, its carrier indistinct despite its light and that of the streetlamps. As we neared one another I made out the figure of a man with a spade in one hand. His clothes, too thin for the night's cold, were considerably soiled, and his face resembled that of a corpse several days in the ground, doughy and pale, framed by wild strands of white hair. He held the lamp in his other hand at the level of his face like Diogenes; so frightful was his appearance in the close light of the lamp that it took me several seconds rooted in place to apprehend that this was no revenant from Hades, but plain Michael Cornan.

"Who's there?" he yelled.

"Shh," I whispered, mindful of those sleeping nearby. "It's me, Ogden."

He looked at Maggie's house and nodded. "Sinner," he hissed. "Father of lies."

"What are you doing out in the middle of the night with the spade?"

He gestured with his grisly head toward the cemetery several blocks to our north. "My old dog Pal died."

"You buried him in the cemetery? Must be hard digging in this cold."

He stared me down, shaking his head. "Coming out of that whorehouse in the dead of night, and here I was ready to think you innocent."

"Good night, Cornan." I walked around him, careful to keep my eyes on the street. I didn't want to stay around and get mad enough to lose my temper.

"The wages of sin is death, Ogden," he yelled.

Without turning I waved at him, as if in agreement.

"Prince of Darkness. Lord of the Flies. Beelzebub."

I walked very slowly up Lincoln toward the Braunschweig home until I could hear him yell no more.

In the morning I showed the stick to Herbert, and told him I intended to have a word with Leval about Mr. Smight.

"No, don't, you'll make things worse. Tell you what, let me talk to him about it. Can't have murder in the streets."

"You tell him the next time Smight tries anything I'll cripple him, too."

Herbert thought that was funny. "There you go, a matched set."

I walked over to the courthouse after breakfast to attend the trial and managed to be at the courthouse for the beginning of the day's session, seated so close I could have jabbed a pencil into the defense attorney's ear if I'd been of a mind to do so. I was eager to hear the testimony of former Deputy Sheriff Gilbert Clevenger,

who'd tried to arrest me after I shot Marc Leval. He answered
Wembly's questions without emotion, and if I'd been a juror I'd have
thought his testimony credible. Clevenger had aged considerably
since our last meeting; in the seventeen years gone by he seemed to
have aged thirty, his long wrinkled neck flapping like a turkey's, his
mustache gone yellow-white with a fringe of tobacco brown at the
lip. After being awakened by the sound of gunfire he'd come upon
the injured Marc Leval—I figured in his story not at all—and soon
after encountered Braunschweig and Niedel. Shortly thereafter he
discovered that four of his horses were missing, stolen by the Benders to make their escape. He hadn't struck me as a man fresh out
of bed that night; he'd been fully dressed and seemed quite alert,
and I wondered how the Benders had managed to steal those
horses if he was indeed awake. I also chewed on the fact that he'd
mentioned the Bender killings that night, when there wasn't any
way I could imagine for him to have known about them then, as far
away as he was.

After a brief cross-examination of Clevenger by Mr. Lassiter,
Mr. Wembly called to the stand Mrs. McCann, Mrs. Davis's former
employer and the woman who'd brought the defendants to the attention of the Labette County authorities. Tiny-boned and fluttery
as a hummingbird, she barely came up to the middle of Wembly's
chest as she moved to the stand. She wore a set of apparently painful
false teeth that gave her a pronounced lisp, and produced a clicking sound with each movement of her delicate jaw; her voice was
extremely high in pitch and girlish, but her small face, round as a
pie-plate, was marked with the furrows of a lifetime of sour disappointment and disapproval.

After the usual preliminary questions Wembly asked her how
she'd come to know Mrs. Davis. Mrs. Davis had been her laundress, and had on several occasions told Mrs. McCann's fortune;
the two became close, and when Mrs. Davis became ill with a fever
Mrs. McCann had cared for her.

"When she became ill I considered it my Christian duty to care for her in her sickness, and for her babes. When feverish she confessed many, many awful things to me."

"What did she confess?"

"Terrible things both banal and extraordinary. That she and her mother had been prostitutes in a logging camp, for one. That she trafficked with spirits, for another. And then one evening she was raving, insensate, about her mother, that awful creature. She nearly died that night, might have anyway if I hadn't been there, swabbing her down with cool water."

Wembly nodded as if he'd been there himself. "Tell us what she said about the mother."

"That she'd killed three of her husbands."

Mr. Lassiter rose to object, but the judge sat him back down. Old Mrs. Griffith scowled and stared off at the window, and Mrs. Davis dandled the baby on her knee, to all appearances oblivious to her circumstances. Mr. Wembly then asked what had happened after Mrs. Davis's recuperation.

Mrs. McCann drew a deep breath, and I was reminded of a Chautauqua speaker about to deliver a monologue. "When Mrs. Davis recovered and realized what she'd told me, she knew I posed a threat to her and her mother. She tried to warn me off. 'Keep your mouth shut,' she said to me, 'my mother and I were the Bloody Benders and we know how to deal with the likes of you.' " It was a practiced speech, well-rehearsed and dramatically rendered; I guessed that Mrs. McCann had been through some elocution lessons. As she brought it to a close, her face became a mask of wounded goodness. "And after I'd employed her, nursed her back to health, cared for her little ones!"

Wembly shook his head, and I began to think he was a little smitten with Mrs. McCann who, though to my eye devoid of all erotic attraction, was possessed of the sort of overwhelming and slightly demented personality some men find irresistible. Mrs. Davis's baby chose that moment to squeal delightedly at Wembly, her tiny arms outstretched to him, and the entire gallery broke into laughter, as did the panel of judges.

The examination continued until lunchtime, after which I was intrigued enough to return, but I had lingered too long over my meal and would have had to settle for a much less desirable vantage point in the middle of the gallery. I elected to leave, and outside the courthouse I sat for a minute studying the comings and goings. It was easy to spot the country people in town for a glimpse of the notorious Benders, because they were the ones who stood and gawked at the rough limestone courthouse itself, four stories high. I began to stare at it myself, wondering at the cost of such an extravagant and massive structure. Constructed of rough-faced limestone, above each arched window on the ground floor was a gargoyle. I hadn't noticed these before, and I went from window to window noting their individual faces and expressions, which ranged from the genuinely horrific to the whimsical. I was delighted to discover, at the building's southeast corner, a gargoyle unmistakeably cut to resemble Herbert Braunschweig, with a horrific scowl on his mug, a tongue protruding grotesquely over his chin, and a disturbingly empty eye socket, hollowed from the limestone. I wondered what Herbert had done to provoke this sort of comment from the stone-cutter, and also why he hadn't ordered it hacked away. Maybe, I thought as I left, he thought it was amusing.

I felt rather good as I marched to the brick factory. The sky was clear by now, and nearing the plant the sun shone brightly on the snowy mantle, dirty gray with the falling soot from the enormous kiln chimneys. I hadn't visited yet and wasn't much interested in the brick business, but it was an impressively large industrial complex. A half dozen large kilns stood outside a warehouse, into whose open door I stepped. Inside it was hot and dry, with a great deal of loud noise. Over the clanking of some giant chain I could hear but not see, I asked a clay-smeared artisan where I could find Mr. Braunschweig's office. Wordlessly he gestured at the far end of the building, where some doors were set into the wall.

Inside one of the doors was an anteroom where a little lady in a starched white blouse sent me through to the interior office, where Herbert's desk faced the window. He sat reading the morning's *Optic*, none too happily.

"Goddamnit, Bill, did you see this here?" He read, haltingly: " 'It is clear to anyone who knew them even slightly that these women are not the feminine half of the Bender clan. The young woman is simple and dull, where Katie was sprightly and vivacious, and the old lady is a prime example of a New York Yankee, whereas Mrs. Bender was well known to be a Dutchwoman with no English. Mrs. Davis is considerably shorter than Katie was, and Mrs. Griffith a good deal taller than Mrs. Bender.' Hell's bells." He slapped the paper down onto his desk and folded his arms across his chest, pouting like a little boy.

"Pretty nice brick plant you got here, Herbert."

"Ain't it?"

"Went to the hearing this morning. That Mrs. McCann's crazy as a bedbug."

"What, all that spirit business? Don't pay that any mind, she caught those gals dead to rights."

"Those women just plain aren't the Benders, Herbert. Look at Mrs. Davis. She's an idiot."

He gestured with his chin at the anteroom. "Shut that, would you?"

I went over and pulled the door closed.

"That scar on Katie's forehead," he said, touching his own head above his glass eye. "The one that made her a simpleton. She says she got it from her husband. That's bunk." He swatted at the air before him as though at an invisible horsefly.

"How do you know it's bunk?"

He looked to his right and to his left, though we were alone in the office. "You gotta keep this quiet. I know because it's a bullet did that to her, and I'm the one that fired it."

That took me aback. "How's that?"

He drew in a deep breath. "I ain't told anybody but Renée in the last sixteen years. All right. That morning we come upon the Benders, maybe three miles from where we split up. Me and Tim. It wasn't like I told you, them firing on us. We got the drop on 'em, but young John fired and we fired back. Got John and the old man pretty quick, and Katie right after. The old lady was yelling her head off the whole time, but when Katie got hit she stopped and waved her arms to surrender."

"I heard some of those shots, after I'd shot Marc."

"So here we were, about to finish Katie off and the old woman, too—"

"Wait a second, there. Tim was going along with this?"

"Sure he was. Hell, he had a slug in his leg and it hurt like hell, he damn near bled to death. Anyhow, we were about to finish the both of 'em off, and old Ma said don't, and I'll show you where the money's at."

"She said that in English?"

"Sure did. So I thought, hell, let's see. And we left Katie bleeding on the ground next to her Pa and young John, and we rode back with the old woman to an old hollow tree. Had five thousand dollars in it."

"So you let the old lady go and split the money?"

He shrugged, wide-eyed. "A deal's a deal, Bill. I didn't think Katie'd live to tell about it for long, but sure looks like she did."

"What about the deputy?"

"We come across him tied to the tree where you left him, and he told us what you done to Marc. So we paid him two hundred dollars to lie about it."

"That's all?"

"He took a little convincing, but he took it. Anyway, part of your share went to your boy Clyde. I owe you, though, and if you're going to stay in town you'll need work. I'd set you up at the mill but I'm partners in it with Leval, you understand. I'll set you up with some equity in the company. Shit, I got more'n I can spend now anyway."

I thanked him and told him I'd give it its due consideration, and I left the office to wander back to the center of town. On the way I passed before the Naylor residence, from whose front window the lady of the house waved at me, holding Mrs. Davis's little girl who, home from the courthouse, laughed blithely.

4

LABETTE COUNTY, KANSAS
APRIL, 1890

In the Springtime

A lad of seven or eight years bounced lightly on the studio bench before a canvas backdrop, a seascape to match the sailor suit his parents had dressed him in. I tried to cajole a smile out of him, but he squinted at me in a suspicious way and held his poker face until finally his mother lost her temper and shouted, threatening him with a whipping if he didn't give the man a nice happy grin. To my surprise the smile involved was quite genuine-looking and suitable for the camera.

"Thank you kindly," the lady said when the sitting was finished. They left, pleased, and I had hopes that once they returned for their proofs she'd return again with the boy's father for a family portrait. I did the darkroom work myself, and while the plates dried I began browsing through the studio's backfiles. I was favorably impressed with the quality of the work, both technically and aesthetically, though in fact it was not much different from the output of any competent small-town photographer. Most of the negatives and prints were portraits, with a few street scenes and farm animals here and there, and very few of them were stereographic in format, which puzzled me, since the firm still owned the stereo camera I'd left behind in '73.

At this point I had been working for Gleason and Ogden, Photographers, for nearly two months as studio manager, which allowed them to attend to their other interests without leaving the studio idle. The reader will note that this made me a de facto employee of Marc Leval, who had a share in the business; this, however, did not bring us into any more direct contact than we'd had before. I had not spoken to him or Maggie since my first days back in Cottonwood, though I had seen them both several times, and had spoken to Marc Leval, Jr., twice. On neither of those occasions did he show any sign that he knew me to be his father, nor any awareness that his parents and I had a shared and eventful history.

I finally found the stereo views in one of two boxes resting on a high shelf in the storage closet, half forgotten, both of which I took to the front of the studio for perusal. The other box contained a bigger surprise: an 11-by-12-inch negative of myself, seated before a painted mountain backdrop I remembered owning some years before in Greeley. Maggie had taken it, and I thumbed through the rest of the negatives, fifty or so in number, pictures of herself and more of me, pictures of friends and neighbors and strangers, all dating to those unhappy months in '74 and '75 when I'd been chafing at the Colony's constraints and trying to get Maggie to leave with me. Some of the pictures of Maggie were of my own making, and some seemed to be self-portraits dating from after my departure for Golden; in those she looked so stoically bereft, even in the reversed tones of the glass negatives, that my eyes began to moisten and I put the crate aside.

I opened the other box and seated myself beneath the skylight with a Holmes Stereoscopic Viewer. The first card was a crudely mounted pair from which Paul Lowry's dead eyes, their vitreous darkened with blood, stared back at me from beyond the pale alongside his hapless, anonymous prisoner, both of them hanging from the rafter as pathetically as on the night they died; it was one of the most sublime images I had ever put to glass. There were a handful of others I'd taken myself, and a raft of the kinds of stereo views typically made to promote a growing town: the Leval/Rector and Braunschweig mansions, City Hall, the County Courthouse before and after completion, and a very attractive series of the downtown business district covered in snow.

At last there was a series in a box of its own, with the words THE BLOODY BENDERS OF KANSAS printed on a sheet of paper pasted to the lid above a list of the images contained therein:

1. *The Death House, as it Stood*
2. *Rear View, the Death House*
3. *The Cottonwood Hotel and Restaurant, Cottonwood Kans., Where Katie Bender Worked to Lure Unwary Travelers*
4. *Interior View of the Death House, Showing the Bloodied Canvas Dividing it, Behind which the Bender Men Hid with the Hammer*
5. *Satan's Own Hearth*
6. *The Bench on which the Victims Sat Before Death Struck*
7. *The Charnel Pit into which the Victims Were Bled After Death*
8. *Satan's Own Orchard, Looking North*
9. *A Row of Graves Amidst the Fruited Arbor*
10. *The Mayor of Cottonwood, Kans., the Hon. Henry Rector, Wielding the Death Hammer*
11. *The Bones of an Unknown Traveler, his Skull Staved in*
12. *A Box of Jewelry, Found on the Trail of the Killers' Escape*
13. *Members of the Posse that Failed to Overtake the Benders*
14. *The Crowd that Gathered Upon Discovery of the Crimes*
15. *Satan's Own Orchard: The Burning of the Blood-Fed Trees*
16. *The Tree that Awaits their Return*

The "members of the posse" were Tim and Herbert; Tim sat with his bandaged leg resting on a crude, handmade stool that may have come from the house, and Herbert's legs and arms were covered with dried mud from digging the graves of the men he'd supposedly failed to catch up with. Gleason was indisputably a skilled photographer, even at that early stage, and I took some pride in the professional quality of the images. Only the last two in the set had any element of *truquage*, and only the last, a cottonwood tree with a quartet of hangman's nooses hanging provocatively from its largest branch, was an out-and-out cheat.

The fruit trees of the orchard had been relatively young and healthy, and their burning probably required lamp oil as fuel, to judge from the inky blackness of the smoke roiling upward from the grove. I suspected that their incineration had been Gleason's own idea, for the sake of a dramatic picture. The only human figure in the tableau was Tiny Rector, and watching earnestly in the foreground right as the fire consumed the trees.

There was an admirable and unposed photograph of the swarm of curiosity-seekers at the scene, including a family unmistakably engaged in a picnic at the right-hand edge of the composition, not far from the remains of the house, whose dismantling had proceeded considerably since the taking of view number one, its roof gone altogether and its windows stripped of glass. I had been told that as of a week after the discovery of the graveyard not a trace remained of the house, the stable or the orchard, and that Tiny Rector had taken home the hammers for safekeeping against the possibility that one day the Benders would be captured; presumably they now rested in some drawer in the prosecutor's office.

At the back of the box Gleason had added a few extra views, well printed but crudely mounted. Of these the most interesting by far was the only photograph I knew to exist of Katie Bender, seated next to Marc and Maggie in their suite in the old Cottonwood Hotel. Her indeterminate face floated in a fog above her crisply defined body, a ghost in three dimensions, with just the suggestions of features. I was sure in retrospect that Katie's avoidance of the camera's prosecutorial gaze had been deliberate; a recognizable photograph would certainly have been a help in either condemning or exonerating the two ladies in Deputy Naylor's house, and I was willing to bet that wherever she'd lived before or after Kansas, no photograph existed of her there, either.

A while later a man and woman came in wanting a portrait, or at least the woman did. The man grumbled the whole time, and when I pressed him as to why, he explained that since November he'd been the proud owner of one of Mr. Eastman's box cameras, and couldn't understand why in God's name his wife wanted to pay someone to take their picture when he could do the same thing at home for the cost of the materials and processing. When I'd finished with them Gleason came in; his manner toward me was so deferential I had to remind him, not for the first time, who was the employer and who the employee.

Accompanying him was Marc Leval, Junior, who greeted me politely but showed no special interest in me. In Greek I asked him about his studies, and he responded in a bashful but perfectly correct manner, and in that awkward smile I saw traces of Maggie's own. When I complimented him on his Greek he gave the credit not to his schoolmaster but to his own mother and Clyde. He began straightening up the darkroom, choosing it instead of the studio in order to escape me, I thought, and my annoying questions.

"That was a good job you did on those Bender views," I said to Gleason when we were alone.

Gleason's tangled eyebrows shot upward and he nodded, his jowls aquiver. "Oh. Haven't looked at those in ten years, I bet. Sold quite a few through Haymeyer and Sons, out of Philadelphia. Never really sold many of the others, except for a few of that lynching down on Main Street."

"Who farms the Bender plot nowadays?" I asked him.

"I don't know if anyone does. I heard someone tried to plant vegetables where the orchard was but they all came up blood red."

I let that pass without comment. "I may just ride out there one day and see what's there."

"What for?" he asked. "Nothing left of the house or shed. I don't even know how you'd find it, any more."

"Still, I have the day after tomorrow free and nothing to occupy me. Maybe I'll hire a horse and ride on out there, take a picture or two." I put on my coat and hat and called out my good-byes to the pair of them.

"Wait a minute, Mr. Ogden . . ." Gleason took an envelope from his inside jacket pocket and handed it to me. "Somebody asked me to give this to you." He gave me a wink which would have been too broad onstage, and laughed out loud.

The envelope read "Mr. Bill Ogden" and nothing else, and it was written in Maggie's hand. I slipped the envelope into my own pocket, and again he laughed and winked so hard I thought he might hurt himself. Those flaccid jowls of his were apple-red when I took my leave, right up to his long ears.

Night hadn't fallen yet, and the day was still warm; walking east toward Kelley's rooming house, where I had a room but took no meals, I saw old people and children gathered on their porches already as though summer were on the horizon. At Kelley's I took the letter upstairs, avoiding the landlady, a handsome widow woman whose relation to me the reader will already have correctly surmised. I scrupulously paid my rent, however, and early, too; I had all the money from the sale of my studio in San Francisco, which I still intended to use to buy another once I decided where to settle, or to buy out Gleason and Clyde, if I stayed. In addition I had a not inconsiderable chunk of Adelle's farewell gift left over, and I was making a small amount every week working at the studio. My relations with Mrs. Kelley, then, were strictly carnal (though with a dollop of sentimentality on her part).

I opened the letter, seated on the thin mattress of my squeaky spring bed. It was written in very elegant Greek; translated, it read:

Bill,

I am sorry to have avoided you so studiously but propriety makes its demands. I have much to tell you about my life after your leaving.

Pray write back (in this dead tongue for the sake of discretion) and let me know if you are willing to meet me someplace.

M.

The letter left me stupefied after so many weeks of coldness, and when the rapping came at the door I opened without thinking. There stood Mrs. Kelley, whose first name I hadn't yet learned. She was a bit younger than I was, with auburn hair tending to blond, and a plump form that would soon, I feared, surrender to obesity; for the moment, however, her figure was pleasing, and her willingness to allow me access to it a welcome relief.

"It's four-thirty, Mr. Ogden," she said. "No one else is home 'til quarter past five at least. Will you join me?"

It would have been impolite to refuse, so I followed her down the hall to her room, where I enjoyed her charms under the watchful eye of her late husband Adolphus, who looked down from a portrait Gleason had done ten years earlier. He'd been a big mustachioed fellow, and his picture made him seem so goodnatured that I couldn't imagine him objecting to his wife's enjoying a quick lay in his absence. She was rather loud, though, and when the front door opened downstairs—well in advance of five-fifteen—she froze. I made haste to finish what I was up to, and we waited in silence, still conjoined at the hips, hoping that whoever it was would adjourn to his room so that I could dress and exit unseen. It was with some relief that I heard the door to our east open and close. I dressed and walked on tiptoe to my room, where I shut the door quietly and washed off my old fellow in the washbasin.

The next morning I wrote Maggie back, again in Greek:

> *M,*
>
> *I am contemplating a ride out to the Bender farm tomorrow. If you care to meet me there I will be there all afternoon with the camera.*
>
> *B.*

I took the letter to Gleason at the saloon and asked him to deliver it to Maggie. He accepted the assignment with another laugh, and in the light that shone through the entryway I saw him blush right down to his dangling earlobes. I wondered what it was that got him so flustered, since he was a married man now with children of his own and not unfamiliar with the ways of the world.

"I reckon I can get young Marc to deliver it to his Ma." He fanned himself with the letter, though the air in the saloon was cool. "Mr. Ogden, you just watch yourself."

"I'll watch myself."

He started getting red again. "I don't know what you got planned . . ." He touched the envelope in his pocket. "What you and Maggie . . . Mrs. Leval got planned . . . That Mr. Smight is a mean son of a bitch, and so's his boss. Sad old cripple or no, Marc Leval doesn't deserve her. No, sir."

That was when I understood what got him so flushed. After years of acquaintance, nearly fifteen of them as partners in business with her husband, Marguerite Leval still made him stammer and blush like a twelve-year-old with a crush on his schoolteacher. "I don't have anything planned, I was just replying to her letter."

"All right, well, you take care, though, 'cause that husband of hers is a goddamned snake." The way he yelled it after me I couldn't tell if it was me or Marc he was mad at.

The next morning I hired a horse and wagon from Thornton and Sons Livery at the western edge of Cottonwood and rode west in the direction of the old Bender claim. The day was magnificent, even warmer than its immediate predecessors, and the landscape I rode through was newly green, with some trees budding and a fair number showing leaves. Next to me was a basket containing a blanket, and a picnic lunch Renée Braunschweig had kindly packed for me consisting of cold chicken and fried potatoes, along with a bottle of burgundy from their cellar and a corkscrew; whether I would have them to myself or not was still in question. In the rear of the wagon was the stereo camera and its attendant equipment, including twenty dry plates, each in its separate holder. Crossing the Big Hill Creek ford I remembered the night I'd met young John Bender there, hiding in a clump of shrubbery to my right, and I wondered if Katie Bender hadn't saved my life that night; the number of travelers who left that shack alive was small.

Seventeen years on it seemed the Benders were about to claim two last victims. Mrs. Griffith and her daughter Mrs. Davis had been found guilty of the clan's crimes, despite the opinion of most of us who'd been acquainted with the female members of that family—and Labette County turned out to be full of men who'd known Katie quite well—that these were two other women entirely. When the trial was finally held in March, all of us old-timers who could have identified the real Bender women, down to a fellow who claimed only to have exchanged greetings once with Katie in front of the hotel, were excluded from the jury. The unfortunate pair now sat in the state prison at Larned awaiting an appeal that wasn't expected to save them from the gallows, and in Topeka they were gearing up for the state's first ever hanging of a woman; Mrs. Davis's little girl was in the care of Mrs. Naylor, who was expected to adopt the child upon the occasion of her orphaning.

When I reached the mound I found it remarkably familiar, despite the absence of the buildings and the orchard. It seemed absurd, even impossible that anything evil might have ever transpired in that bucolic, rolling vista, and the smell of the newly blooming wildflowers seemed to contradict my memory of the foul slaughterhouse stink that had clung to the farm the last time I'd seen it. I put the wagon underneath a budding cottonwood tree for the limited shade it offered, stepped down and walked to where I thought the house had stood, finding no trace of it, nor of the charnel pit. Where the orchard had been someone had laid down a large river stone, a little smaller than a man's head, where each of the bodies had lain. I noticed that by several of these stones a depression could be discerned, and taking a walk to the east of the orchard's former location, I noted a dozen or more such depressions in the grass; possibly they were naturally occurring, but I couldn't help thinking of all the men who'd gone missing in those days and hadn't ever been accounted for, and feeling that I was standing in a cemetery.

I set up the camera and began to photograph the property, using Gleason's stereographs as my reference, but before I was done I knew they were just pretty views of a hilly spring terrain; if Maggie didn't come the day would be lost. The Benders had left no photographable physical trace behind them. To the northwest a column of thunderheads rose like giant galleons, white as cotton at their fluffy tops and shaded gray below, moving too fast for me to capture their imperial beauty faithfully.

There were a few large trees left from the days of the Benders' custodianship, including the cottonwood under which I'd placed the wagon, which I thought I recognized as the one from which the nooses had dangled in Gleason's last stereo view. It must have been close to forty feet high by now; myriad red flowers drooped off of its branches in bunches close to a foot long. I sat under it and took from the buggy an edition of Ovid I'd borrowed from Clyde (its bookplate identified it as ex libris Marguerite Leval) and began reading.

After a while had passed I began to get hungry, and a glance at my watch (gold, made in Switzerland; a gift from Adelle worth half a year's rent on her studio) told me that the noon hour had come and gone. I rose, but before I could open the picnic basket I heard a voice command me not to move. Though I'm not particularly superstitious I couldn't help feeling a little frisson of panic at the speaker's German accent, and when I turned to face him, my hands in the air, I was greatly relieved to see that he wasn't the vengeful shade of John Bender, Sr. or Jr.

"This is private property," the man said. He had a shotgun trained on my head.

"Sorry," I said. "Just out taking pictures."

"You might have asked."

"Didn't know where to find you."

"You Ogden?" he asked. "You were out here that day."

"That's right. You're Linder."

He nodded and lowered the shotgun. "I guess I don't mind if you take a few pictures."

"You want some lunch?" I said. He shook his head no but invited me to go ahead and eat, and as I tore into the chicken he informed me that I was correct in assuming that there were more bodies buried on the farm.

"In '78 I bought this place from the fellow who had it after the Benders, and he told me he come across some bones down where the creek runs. Couple of years after that my old dog come running up to the back door with half a man's hipbone in his teeth, and one time I busted up a skull with my plow. Them damn lazy Benders didn't dig deep enough."

"Did you tell the sheriff?"

"What for?" he wanted to know.

Linder had known all four of the Benders well, as the farm was a mere quarter mile from his, and he sought them out on occasion for the purpose of speaking German. He told the story of the afternoon the Benders were discovered to have been gone, and then he told a story I hadn't heard, of an incident that had occurred after the posses had left the scene of the crimes.

"I went home that night, and went to sleep, and sometime in the night they broke through my front door and tried to hang me."

"Who did?"

"Some of the people that was over at the Bender place, twenty of them or so. They'd been drinking and they wanted to know was I in league with the Benders. I told 'em no, but they didn't care. They dragged me out of bed and tied a rope into a noose. Then they put that around my neck and threw the other end over the branch of a tree outside and then they took turns hoisting me up into the air."

"What the hell for?"

"To make me say I was with the Benders. I wasn't, though, and I wouldn't say it. After a while I passed out."

"And they left while you were unconscious?"

"Yes, sir. I woke up on the ground a while later, all alone. I guess they'd had all the fun they could get from me."

"You see those women they put on trial in Cottonwood?"

"Sure, I testified at the hearing. That old lady's American, and Mrs. Bender talked German like she was from Freiburg, or maybe Strasbourg."

"Didn't do any good, did it?"

"No, too many people wanted to see them two hang." From the northwest the thunderheads still approached, and he watched them carefully for a minute. "Well, Mr. Ogden, there's work to be done yet. Good day."

He left, and I finished up the chicken with a small amount of the wine. I had already packed away the camera and its accompanying paraphernalia when I caught sight of a two-seated black buggy headed towards me from the east. At its reins was Maggie Leval, and she betrayed no emotion whatsoever as she approached, not until she got within ten feet of me and slowed to a stop; then she gave me the shyest version I'd ever seen of that wicked secret smile of hers, the one I'd seen that first night in Cottonwood when she and Marc came. We'd crossed paths a dozen times since my arrival in Cottonwood without exchanging greetings, and I had come to believe that she hated me. The note she'd sent had offered some hope, but the real reprieve was in that look she gave me. That on my own face must have been one of great relief, for she brightened further and hopped from the buggy and strode toward me. We held one another for a moment—she smelled of lavender and soap—and then she pulled away.

"I brought a blanket, just in case you hadn't," she said.

We did not waste time, as I had feared we might, on the recriminations and tears that I knew would come eventually. Instead in rather short order we were pressed in an embrace on the blanket she'd brought. Our clothing was soon shucked, mine hastily tossed aside onto the grass, hers folded neatly upon the seat of her conveyance, and the only words she spoke came as I descended the length of her body to place my tongue upon her: "No one's done that to me in fifteen years," she murmured.

Naked, she revealed herself to have broadened since our last meeting, which pleased me more than it did her. As I exulted atop her, glorying in the nearness of her and intoxicated by her lovely face, timing the rhythm of my downstroke according to her least unspoken suggestion—an intake of breath, an arching backward of the throat or spine—I felt an abrupt, sharp jab on my right buttock. It burned, badly. My legs stiffened and I thrust myself forward rather faster and harder than I had been doing, resulting in an unintended ejaculation. This coincided with a delighted squeal of surprise from my paramour; looking upward, extracting myself from her, I saw a honeybee flying away to its doom, its rearmost part embedded in my ass.

When Maggie understood what had provoked my spasm she laughed, and after a minute to get used to the idea so did I. She plucked the offending stinger from my ham, and we sat down on the blanket, in my case very carefully putting the weight on the left cheek.

"What do you think of Marc," was the first thing she asked, and I suppose I looked confused when I responded.

"I suppose I was glad to learn I hadn't killed him," I said.

"Not that Marc." She stuck out her leg and playfully smacked my face with the sole of her delicate foot. "My son. He looks like you, don't you think? Even more than Clyde does."

"I suppose he does. He's a good boy. Doesn't seem to know I'm anything to him."

"I don't know. Now that you're in town people are talking again. I'm sure he's heard things." She slapped my ham where I'd been stung, causing me considerable pain, and I let out a cry. "That's for not answering my letters."

"I suppose I deserved that."

"You deserved worse. I don't suppose you even opened them?"

Those were, of course, the letters I'd burned, the still-sealed envelopes marked PLEASE READ! URGENT! "No, I didn't, or I would've gone straight back to Greeley."

She shrugged. "It occurred to me you might not have even read them, out of pigheadedness. After I'd been here a while, just before Marc was born, I tried to write you again, with Renée's return address, but they came back undeliverable. If Marc had found out he'd have thrown me out."

"I suppose Marc wishes me no good."

"He's not glad you're back. He wanted to keep Clyde and Gleason from hiring you on at the studio, but they overruled him. Now he doesn't want young Marc working there, but it turned into such a row he gave up and let him stay."

"I thought it was odd the boy was still working with me."

She blushed. "I threatened to tell him the truth and Marc backed down. He's afraid I've forgiven you, thinks I might fall back into my old bad habits now that you're in sight. That's one reason I didn't make any contact at first. It's taken me this long to get his guard down."

I stood, because my reclining pose was becoming untenable. "Are you going to stay with him?"

"It's a little quick to be talking like that, isn't it? After just one afternoon on the grass?"

"Maybe."

She lowered herself to her elbows, her breasts prominent and pale in the piebald sunlight splashing through the cottonwood's branches. The southeastern half of the sky was still clear, and the thunderheads were so close by in the other half that I thought I could hear the rain showering the trees in the near distance.

"The rain's going to reach us, isn't it?" Maggie said, the thought just then dawning on her. She stood and walked to her carriage, with the light from the southern sky fading to pale.

"Afraid so," I said.

"We'd better go, then." She began reapplying her corset, and before she had it halfway laced up she stopped. "Who knows how long 'til we get another chance to be alone like this?" she said, and loosened its laces again. The thing slipped to the ground, she stepped out of it and returned to the blanket.

I didn't want to get rained on, but with my prick stiffening in the wind I decided she was right. After a quick look around me to check for any further hostile *Apes melliferae*, I dropped to my knees and surrendered to instinct.

The blanket was growing damp by the time we were done, and we both hastily dressed as the more violent part of the storm neared.

"I'm going to have to be getting back soon, and we can't be seen coming from the same direction at the same time." Maggie's buggy had a canvas folding top to protect her from the storm, and I helped her attach the waterproof storm curtain to the sides of it. The wagon I'd hired had no such cover, but I agreed to wait an hour before following her back; in the meantime I went over to Linders' house seeking shelter but found no one there, and instead stood next to the wagon holding an umbrella, which offered little protection from the nearly horizontal wind-borne torrent. By the time I actually started back I was as drenched as if I had jumped into a pond.

I skirted the town limits to the north in case anyone had noticed Maggie's homeward route. The bouncing of the carriage on the slick, rocky terrain caused me considerable pain, and so I mostly rode tilted to my left, hanging awkwardly as though the buggy were about to overturn. My spirits were so high, though, that I found my own predicament amusing, and by the time I rode into town from the north I had formulated a plan to leave town with Maggie and our son. Tying the horse and carriage to the rail before the studio in the early evening, the rain still coming down hard, I laughed at the idea of sneaking out of Cottonwood with Maggie again.

There was a substantial leak in the northwest corner of the studio; I mopped up the collected liquid and placed a pair of buckets underneath it, and I moved the props and backdrops stored nearby. Since no one was about, I lit the stove and disrobed, hanging my clothing next to it, and, naked, set about preparing the stereo views.

When I had finished my work I left the darkroom and found Clyde in the office, working on the books.

"How was your visit to the killing ground?" he asked, with no comment offered as to my state of undress.

"Not much to see any more. Got stung by a bee, never mind where," I said. "How'd you know I was out there?"

"Gleason told me. He's a little sweet on old Maggie. Mrs. Leval. He's scared Marc'll kill you or her or both." He then turned back to his columns of figures and stopped speaking. My clothes were hot and dry in some parts, cold and moist in others, but I put them on anyway, wished Clyde a good evening and set out for dinner.

The rain had stopped. After returning the horse and wagon I stopped in at the White Horse Restaurant, as had become my habit in the evenings, and midway through my meal of ham and mashed potatoes Mr. Smight himself stepped through the front door and approached my table. He had on his fur coat, and he didn't remove his top hat; his eyes were bordered with red, and wet. A few diners, those who knew us both, stopped eating and stared as he stood there, fuming, his arms folded across his chest. I was at a disadvantage, since I didn't want a scene that would get me barred from the establishment, the only really good meal to be had in town outside of a private residence. I didn't want to start taking my meals at the rooming house, either, since that would mean more time with Mrs. Kelley, whom I planned to wean from my affections as quickly as possible. My weight was on my left haunch, as the right one was still considerably sore from the bee sting, and this made me feel somewhat ridiculous as I looked up at him.

"If I hear you've been seen at the Braunschweigs' I'll take you the hell apart," he said.

I had no idea what he meant, and I should have smiled and promised to stay away from there, but his stupid arrogance got my hackles up.

"I'll go wherever I damned please, you ignorant beanpole."

His big, knobby hands formed fists, and for a moment the

prospect of a real donnybrook made me regret my impulsive bravado as he clenched and unclenched them, angry beyond speech. I made a point of remaining outwardly calm and even continued to cut, chew and swallow my hamsteak, until finally he turned away and strode to the front door.

"You keep your distance from her, Ogden, or I'll kill you," he yelled, stepping out the front door. He slammed it shut so hard it blew back open, and the owner hastened to close it again. A few seconds of surprised silence followed before people started eating and talking again. I finished my meal quickly and left, knowing what they were mostly talking about. For the first time, it occurred to me that Mr. Smight might be more than simply Marc's *homme à tout faire*. If his outburst had been anything to go by, he at least aspired to be Maggie's as well.

My impulse, of course, was to hasten to the Braunschweig home, but instead I headed for Kelley's, where my landlady and several of the other tenants were gathered at the downstairs parlor piano singing "O Susanna." Upstairs in my room I put on a dry suit of clothes, then took the Dragoon out of my dresser drawer and loaded it. I was unnerved to realize as I descended the stairs that the group in the parlor was now singing "Johnny Get Your Gun," but in fact it was one they sang almost every evening, and I succeeded in slipping out the front door without them inviting me to join up for a chorus.

On the stoop I looked about for Smight but saw no one. Keeping to the sidewalk I walked north to Seventh Street, confident I had no one on my heels, and then west. The night was growing cool, and I decided to cross the cemetery. Though there was no pavement therein it was grassy throughout, with very little mud exposed, though with each step across the damp grass my fresh trouser cuffs got wetter. It was dark that night, with only a quarter moon for illumination, but having my eyes accustomed to the darkness might prove a tactical advantage. I stopped at Tiny Rector's lonesome grave and waited until I could easily make out the dates inscribed on the marker. I missed him at that moment more than I had at any moment since returning to Cottonwood, and wished he were there to offer some of his stern, commonsensical and useless advice.

Having quit the cemetery at its western end I spent a few more minutes skulking across dewy back lawns and through dampened shrubberies before finally reaching the Braunschweig home, very nearly as wet as I'd been that afternoon. My detour through the blackness of the bone orchard had been a profitable one; pressing myself flat against the side of the house, I spied Smight crouched in the shadows across the street with an eye on their front door. I slunk to the backyard and knocked on the kitchen door, and when Sally opened I raised my index finger to my lips.

She led me to Herbert, seated in his study cleaning his Colt. "What the hell happened? Old George Smight is out there camped in the goddamned bushes, and the girls won't tell me squat." He was in his shirtsleeves, and appeared quite relaxed.

"Where's Maggie? What'd he do?"

"Aw, she's upstairs with Renée." As I turned to leave he called out. "Hold on, she's fine, he just threatened her. Now how about you telling me what's going on? Why's George on the warpath?"

"I saw Maggie today, I don't know how he knows about it."

"You must have done more than seen her." He let loose with a caustic little snort. "Sit down, why don't you."

"I'll stand, thanks."

"Well, Marc's thrown her out, and he's sent Smight to watch her. I guess she's staying here for the time being."

"What are we going to do about Smight out there?"

His eyes crinkled, and the scarring around the glass one went white against the ruddy pink of the rest of his face. "I guess we could just shoot him." He started laughing pretty hard at that.

Beatrice cleared her throat at the door. "Mr. Braunschweig? Mrs. Braunschweig and Mrs. Leval want to know if he's gone."

"He'll be gone in a minute, soon's I'm done cleaning my Peacemaker."

He brandished it, pointing the barrel toward the front of the house; the girl's eyes got wide and she backed from the room. Herbert cackled and began loading the Colt. "You know I wouldn't mind shooting that useless son-of-a-bitch." He stood and I followed him to the front door. "You stay in here. He'll listen to me, but you're just going to make things worse."

"You think it might be better to send Beatrice or Sally to fetch a policeman?"

"Hell's bells," Herbert said. "Don't need any coppers to help me with this."

I sat back down in the study, and looked at a framed photograph of the façade of the brick plant. I heard a yelp of pain outside like that of a small dog being whipped. Barely two minutes passed before Herbert came back inside, with no shots fired. "He's gone now."

There was a vivid spray of fresh blood on his right shirtcuff, and I asked him about it.

"I pistolwhipped that sack of shit right across the face, cut his nose open with the sight." He started laughing, a nervous whooping that he had some difficulty in mastering long enough to speak again. "Got that pretty beaver coat of his bloodied up, too. Now tomorrow I'll go talk to Leval and tell him to call that son of a bitch off."

We went upstairs and knocked on the door of what had recently been my bedroom. Renée came to the door with much the same expression on her face that she'd worn ordering Herbert to destroy the kitchen rat. *"Alors?"*

"Goddamn it, woman, how many times I got to tell you to speak

English?" Her face didn't soften, in fact it hardened so thoroughly she managed to frighten him. "All right, all right, he's gone, and he won't be back. Not tonight, anyways, he's taking care of a bloody nose."

"Can I see her?" I asked.

Renée stepped back into the room and shut the door, which reopened half a minute later.

"Another night," she said.

Maggie didn't leave the Braunschweigs' house for the next seven days. Leval refused to allow young Marc to visit, and since by the next day most of the town knew the reason for her exile from her home (or some twisted version of it, altered in its details but accurate in its essence) no one came to call on her but me.

Herbert spoke to Leval as promised, and Smight stayed away from the house and from me, too. For the next few nights I surreptitiously visited the Braunschweigs' after dinner, where I joined Maggie in her room. The servant girls let me in, and Renée and Herbert pretended they didn't know I was there, though on one occasion Herbert and I bumped into one another in the hallway while I was on my way out. He punched me on the shoulder and snickered.

Maggie and I spoke as little as possible during those first midnight assignations, restricting ourselves, at her insistence, to the most practical kinds of speech: instructions to roll over, or move a leg, or help with a button. As the nights progressed, and the renewed novelty of one another's intimate company faded, we gingerly began bringing up subjects from our shared past, subjects that, had we not replenished our affection for one another in the physical manner, might have been cause for ill will on both our parts.

I told her where I'd lived and how, leaving out at first the women I'd known. Soon enough, though, she asked about them, showing little jealousy but great interest as I described them. When I first brought it up she claimed never to have noticed Smight's devotion to her, but the next night allowed as how she merely tolerated but never encouraged it. She nearly grew violent the next night when I mentioned it again, and though I felt sure there was more to be told I let it drop.

On the fourth night she began weeping uncontrollably as soon as I rolled off of her. Though I'd seen this behavior in half a dozen women over the years it was a first for her in my presence, and I placed a consoling hand on her shoulder. Perhaps I'd been too quick, or too rough; she shook her head no, it was nothing I'd done or failed to do.

She managed to regain her composure, but not her good spirits. "Everything's gone wrong again. It's punishment, Bill, just like last time. Chased from paradise, and after I managed to get back in, I spoil it by yielding again."

"That's goddamned foolishness," I said.

"It's not. Look at me. I can't even leave this house. I'm reviled. I can't see my boy. No one will speak to me when this is over."

"Let's leave. I can make a living anywhere."

"I'm a married woman, with property, and I stand to lose a good deal of it if I leave Marc. And I'm the mother of a minor child I won't leave behind."

"He can come along, too," I said.

"I don't think so, Bill. I don't think he'd leave his father, for one thing."

"I'm his father," I said.

"Things will go wrong again, Bill, I know it."

"I don't see how you and I can stay here, not together, anyway."

She lay back and let out a long, exasperated breath. "Well, I don't see how I can leave. Don't you want to see your grandchildren born and grow up? Our grandchildren?"

"That'd be nice, I suppose," I said with as much enthusiasm as

I could muster. I dressed and left shortly thereafter, feeling a bit of a chill at my back.

The next morning I got a surprise leaving Kelley's boarding house. Crossing the street ahead of me was none other than Gil Clevenger, former Wilson County deputy; he had on a hat just like the broad-brimmed white one he'd had on when I'd tied him to that tree in '73. I had a powerful urge to stop him and ask him if he remembered what had really happened. I thought of his testimony, and his claim that the sound of our gunfire had awakened him, though when he reached me he was fully dressed and showed no sign of having been freshly awakened from sleep. I thought again about him mentioning the Bender killings that morning, and then something really funny struck me. He'd asked me if I was part of the posse, a strange assumption for a peace officer to make about a man he's just seen shoot another, a man in the process of tying said peace officer to a tree. I watched him board a surrey and ride off, and thought that the subject would bear more thought.

Later I stopped in to Rector's Department Store for some tarpaper and nails to repair the roof of the studio and was waited upon by Michael Cornan, who seemed today to bear me no special ill will. As he wrote up my receipt I noted that his face was puffier than usual, with a red and swollen area on his left cheek.

"Did you hurt your face?" I asked him.

"Wasp stung me yesterday."

"I was stung by a bee last week," I said, omitting both the part of the body stung and the circumstance. "I suppose that's spring on the prairie for you."

"No, sir," he said with great solemnity. "There's nothing normal about it at all. I have never before been stung by wasp nor bee, nor bit by spider. Yesterday morning Mister Thorpe in Housewares came in with his hand all swole up, he'd been bit by a violin spider. Couldn't hardly use that hand at all, and today he was so poorly he had to miss his shift. And Mrs. Rector had a mad barn-swallow in the house, nearly took her eye out." He handed me my wrapped goods and the receipt, then leaned over the counter. *"Deus irae."*

Despite myself I had to swallow as I backed away from him. "Indeed," I said, and I hurried downstairs and out of the store into the now-sinister sunshine. Further evidence of Mother Nature's vernal malevolence came when I returned to the boarding house in the late afternoon to the sight of my landlady and one of my fellow tenants standing outside. Mr. Farraday, who worked for the city, bore several stings on his face and neck, and one on his hand. Unless I missed my guess he was next in line for Mrs. Kelley's favors, and while we were superficially friendly there was always a calculating quality to his dealings with me. I always allowed him the advantage in our small competitions, and he must have been puzzled as to his failure thus far to replace me in her arms. He swelled with pride and venom as Mrs. Kelley described to me how she'd opened my room with the intention of cleaning it and found the room aswarm with bees. She'd screamed and run downstairs and, uncertain where I might be found, hurried to City Hall where Mr. Farraday gallantly abandoned his post and returned to the house with her. Alone he entered the house and discovered that the swarm had distributed itself throughout the upper floors, and he was stung seven times before he managed to save himself. Farraday was of the opinion that a hive had been founded in the attic, and now they awaited the arrival of Mr. Lafflin, a farmer and apiarist who, it was thought, might buy the hive and transport it to his farm.

"Otherwise we'll have to smoke 'em out," Farraday said. Despite the enmity he showed toward me I liked him and, particularly now, wished him every success in his courting of Mrs. Kelley. I congratulated him on his bravery and resourcefulness, and told Mrs. Kelley that I would spend the night at my son's house. She seemed put out at my lack of faith in Mr. Lafflin's ability to rid us of the bees by nightfall; I was convinced, though, that the other tenants were fortunate that the evening promised to be a warm one without rain. I wished I might have a chance to take a change of clothes away first, and briefly considered braving a trip to my room, but looking into the parlor windows I saw them outlined with bees, clinging in their puzzled way to the interior panes like beseeching phantoms. I walked the few blocks to Clyde's house, where I asked Eva permission to stay the night.

"Will you stay for supper, too? You can go out for a ramble afterward," she added, making me wonder if the whole town knew about my nightly visits to Maggie's room.

"Supper would be delightful," I said. Though I saw Clyde frequently, we rarely socialized outside of the studio, and I was happy to have a home-cooked meal. Agnes Mickelwhite grumbled at the sight of me, and offered the opinion that there was something not right about me sleeping on the *canapé*—she, of course, had the spare room—but Eva ignored her, and I ascribed Agnes's hostility to circulating rumors.

To be polite, after dinner I inquired at the boarding house as to the disposition of the bees, and learned that Mr. Lafflin was still inside trying to manage the situation. Kindly neighbors had offered tents and blankets to the temporarily dispossessed, and the portly widow next door, she of the twinkling eyes and the permanently amused expression, informed me that every few minutes Mr. Lafflin, whose lantern could be seen intermittently in the upper story windows, let out a violent stream of blasphemies, which the widow repeated to me sotto voce. After paying my respects to the distraught Mrs. Kelley I made my nightly, laborious way to the Braunschweig home, taking as I did every night a different route. Tonight I circled to the south, along the railroad tracks, heading north at the city's westernmost limit and east past the cemetery, and then south and slightly west again to the back door of the former brothel my friends had made a home. As was the case with the previous few nights, I was certain I hadn't been followed, though I had certainly been seen and my destination surmised.

"I had a visit from Marc today," Maggie announced, before she allowed me to begin undressing her (for she was always fully dressed and coiffed when I arrived). "He pointed out that in divorce proceedings he'd have the advantage over me. Depending on the judge I might get nothing."

"I thought Herbert owned the judges around here."

"He doesn't own all of them, and there are plenty of them who remember me leaving with you." She took a deep breath. "Marc was fully contrite, though, and he didn't mention your nightly visits here."

"Maybe he doesn't know."

"Of course he does. He's willing to overlook a lot. He really does love me, you know."

"So he loves you. You don't owe him anything."

"He gave my child a name, and he took me in marriage when a lot of respectable men wouldn't have. And he stood by me even after seeing what people thought of me."

"Goddamnit, Maggie, you're not going back to Marc."

"I can't go with you again and have it go the way it did last time. I have a life here and I won't throw it away again."

"The hell you do. You think people will forget about this?"

"They won't forget me leaving with you again."

With that she began stroking my cock through my trousers. "Stop that until you can tell me. Are you with me or with him?"

"Tonight I'm with you," she said. "After I let him stew a few more nights I'll be with him."

"We don't have to go. I could stay here," I said. I grabbed her by the wrist, harder than I meant to, and she wrested herself away.

"You'd go again, Bill. Soon as you got bored, which wouldn't take long."

I went to the door, and though she called me back I kept going until I was out the Braunschweigs' back door. I took a circuitous route, first north, then west past the Leval mansion, and then up Main toward the boarding house. Passing the saloon I stopped in and spent a few minutes talking to Gleason. He was still concerned that Mr. Smight was going to try and kill me, and I tried to reassure him that there was no longer any need to worry about Smight and me. Just to change the subject I told him I'd seen Clevenger that morning.

"Old Clevenger comes in here once in a while," he said. "Doesn't drink all the time, but when he does he has to be picked up and carried home."

"I thought he lived up in Wilson County."

"Not for a long time. He lives out north of town, a ways north of where you used to farm."

"He farms?"

"His son does. He used to have something to do with the flour mill. I think he owns a piece of it."

When I got to Clyde's, the house was dark, and I was glad for that. I went to sleep, wherein I dreamt sad, horny dreams until the dawn.

5

LABETTE COUNTY, KANSAS
APRIL, 1890

Vortices

It was warm that morning, verging on hot, and it was muggy, too. I was to open the studio in the afternoon, but I went to the saloon and asked Clyde if I might switch days with him. He agreed with no evident curiosity as to my motive; doubtless he assumed that it was something to do with Maggie, and I didn't bother to enlighten him. I hired another horse, sans buggy, and rode in the direction of the brick factory. Since my first visit a new complex of a dozen circular kilns, each the size of a house, had been built, and the warehouse had been replaced with a three-story monstrosity. Herbert's office occupied essentially the same spot in the new building, and his secretary waved me on through.

"Just came by to tell you I'm going, probably in a day or two."

"Maggie going back with Marc?" He said it apologetically, and I was sure he'd known it before I had.

"Don't think there's much chance she'll soften on it," I said.

"Why don't you give it a day or two? Hell, she's not thinking straight. If it's money she's worried about, you're going to make plenty around here."

"I don't know what she's worried about, but I'm not staying to find out."

He tried some more to talk me out of it, and after a few minutes I left.

The horse I'd been assigned was a spotted gray gelding, and he moved with great reluctance, as if he resented being hired and ridden on an overly warm day when he might have been home inside his stable. I wasn't in any particular hurry, though, and I didn't rush the beast forward; instead I watched in a leisurely way the road I traveled every day back when I was running the saloon and trying to be a farmer at the same time, noting the myriad small changes to the route. When I passed a slight curve in the road I remembered that this passed close to a shallow creek where I used to take Clyde wading, and I found myself wondering about Clyde's coming son or daughter, and whether he'd take the child swimming there, too. Perhaps I'd return one day and see the child, even take him wading in the creek myself.

Not much farther up the road I passed my former homestead. I could see five children I assumed to be Haxley's playing in a puddle near the road, and I called out a greeting to them. The oldest ones waved back, laughing, just as the gelding reared back in a panic.

On the road ahead of me a snake had been crossing, and the horse had nearly stepped on it. The serpent was rearing back to strike, and this time my mount managed to throw me. I landed painfully on my back and scrambled to my feet; I had been thrown from a horse or two in my time, but never within striking distance of an agitated pit viper. I rolled away from the gelding and sat up. I withdrew the Dragoon—since my encounter with Smight I had been going out heeled—and fired a shot that tore a considerable hole into the rear of the snake, which I now judged to be a copperhead. The snake now ignored my mount and turned its primeval anger toward me. The horse had turned tail, but the eldest of Haxley's children, a boy of about ten or twelve, reached it in time to grab it by the reins and hold it for me.

The wounded copperhead struck at me then, and I stepped aside quickly enough to miss its lunge. I stamped my foot down and pinned its vile head to the dirt, then pressed the barrel of the Dragoon between its eyes and fired, making a mess of it all over my boots. By this time Haxley had come running, carrying a short-barreled shotgun, to see what the shooting was about.

His children gave him a quick accounting of what had happened as his son, who had managed to calm the horse considerably, led him back to me.

"Copperhead," Haxley said, looking down at it. "That'll kill you quick. I've heard it said a water moccasin's worse, but you'd be just as dead with a copperhead bite."

"Weren't too many snakes around here in my day. Never saw one crossing the road, anyway."

"They'll do that, when there's a rain coming." To the southeast the sky was heavy with distant storm clouds, yellow gray in color. We watched the clouds for a minute without speaking, until Haxley's son broke the silence.

"Remember that snake in the barn, Papa?"

Haxley nodded. "There was a big king snake in the barn when I bought the place, I kept it around for a while to get the rats, but my wife was so scared of it I finally cut off its head with a hoe."

His son seemed quite pleased with himself when I thanked him for his assistance, and he volunteered that he was eleven years old; I might have added that he handled the horse better at eleven than I did at the age of forty-four. I then bid them all farewell and continued on my way.

* * *

I was sweating by the time I got to the Clevenger farm, and the wind had picked up slightly, a warm, wet one from the southeast. It was likely already raining hard in the Indian Territory. The farm was four or five times the size of my old homestead, and I counted five men working, including one who stopped me before I got to the house. I told him I was looking for the elder Mr. Clevenger.

"That'd be my father," he said, and I explained that I was an old friend passing through. He walked me to the house, one of the biggest farmhouses I had ever seen, and we walked inside. He yelled for the old man, who came down the stairs slowly and with the aid of a hickory stick. The house was sparsely furnished for its size, and the dust that coated every exposed surface in the room seemed to suggest an absence of female habitation. Clevenger wore a frayed old shirt with a large brown stain over his heart, and his pants had holes worn through both knees; the day before in town he'd been dressed as nattily as anyone in those parts ever was.

"Hello, Mr. Clevenger," I said. "Bill Ogden."

He nodded, and when his son returned to his labors he indicated a chair in the parlor. "Sit down."

We both sat, and in the light from the parlor window he looked even older than he had the day before. He was a big man and his enormous paw gripped the walking stick as if he might hit me with it if he didn't like what I had to say. On his shirt was a tin badge, a circle with a star inside, reading LABETTE CO. DEPUTY SHERIFF, though he appeared too old to stop anyone from so much as spitting on the sidewalk or making fresh remarks to passersby.

"You're still deputized, Mr. Clevenger?"

"You're damned right I still am. Took a part-time job with the county when I moved here from Wilson County even though I didn't need the money. I just like sheriffing."

"How long since you left Wilson County, anyway?"

"Summer of '73. Right after I seen you last."

"That's what I wanted to talk to you about," I said.

He rapped his stick on the floor so hard I jumped, and then he yelled. "Mae!" Getting no answer he yelled again, louder, though the first try had surely been loud enough to hear outside the house. "Mae! Get in here!"

Disproving my earlier theory about the lack of a female presence in the home, a sturdy woman limped into the room, her hair and apron dusted with flour. "What is it, Papa?" Her tone suggested that it was not the first time that morning he'd hollered for her.

"I ain't your Papa. Now head on outside, this man and I have some things to discuss."

"But I'm doing the baking. I won't listen to what you're talking about, honest. It's about to rain, Papa."

"Get on outside, woman, before I use the stick." He made as if to rise, and she wiped her hands on the apron and went out the front door, rolling her eyes.

"You've done pretty well for yourself," I said, just to make conversation.

He snorted. "Not as well as some. Your friend Braunschweig, now, him and that Frenchie wife of his, they got a hell of a house." He turned his head and spat onto the floor, a large gob of mucous and saliva that sat there glistening against the wood floor, blanched in that area and several others near it by what must have amounted to years of such gobs being spat onto it.

"Still. Nice big house, nice big farm."

"Save your breath, Mr. Ogden. I don't know what sort of bargain you struck with that son of a bitch Braunschweig, but you won't get a shiny nickel out of Gil Clevenger."

"I didn't come looking for money, Mr. Clevenger."

"The hell you didn't, you're his ally. Money's all you and him and that Leval ever wanted, and Niedel. Shit, not an hour after you left that night they showed up with that old Bender bitch, all proud for having kilt the other three, and they were going to make her dig up the swag. Problem was she didn't know exactly where I'd buried most of it. I kept my share separate, see."

I stared at Clevenger, thinking that I was misinterpreting what he'd said. "Your share?"

"My share. I always kept fifty percent, for taking all the risk."

"And you just admitted to Herbert and Tim that you were the Benders' fencer."

"Shit, no use denying it. I was tied to a damn tree, and there was the old woman yelling 'There he is, there's our man, he'll show you where it is.' First thing I did when they cut me loose was go for an old shovel and smash the side of her head in. They damn near shot me, but I convinced 'em if they were to keep the money they couldn't bring her back anyway. So Braunschweig took his piece and finished her there on the ground." He snorted and spat again. "Shit, it should've all been mine. If those half-wits hadn'ta gone and kilt that banker none of it would have happened."

"Mr. Sheale, you mean?"

"That's the one. Shit, they shoulda known somebody'd be back looking for him. All they got offa him was five hundred, though, unless they was lying to me, which they was scared to."

I was amazed; I'd expected to have to drag the truth out of him, but here he offered it to me freely, on the assumption that I knew it already. I decided to ask my biggest question right up front: "Where'd you bury old Mrs. Bender and Katie, anyway?"

"With their men, down by the river." He chuckled, his eyes focused seventeen years back. "Katie was already dead. Died with the men, which is a damned shame. I would have let her live, if it'd been me. Me and Katie had kind of an understanding."

"You reckon those two women from Michigan are going to swing?"

He rapped the stick against the ground. "Now don't get all churchy on me about those two. Camp followers and baby farmers. The old one at least is a killer."

"The young one's got a baby."

"Hah!" He rapped the stick again twice. "Try and tell me that babe won't be better off by a damned sight raised by Mrs. Naylor. No, sir, this is the kind of business where you don't want to get religion all of a sudden. Your friend Niedel started feeling badly about what'd been done, and look what happened to him. Killed for the value of two weeks' payroll."

He narrowed his little blue eyes as if to let me know that such an unfortunate event could happen again at any time, and I understood that I was, in fact, sitting across from the last of the Bender gang. My hands began to grow numb and prickly, and I tried to remember whether the Dragoon had three or four shots left. I calmed myself, though, and continued speaking with Clevenger as though all our differences were philosophical. The more I talked without suggesting he give me money or suggesting that any of his actions or alliances had been blameworthy the more he warmed to me, and by the end of our interview he considered me his bosom friend and confidante. He told me how he met the Benders, how he moved what they brought him and converted it into cash, what he and Katie did when the others weren't present, and sometimes when they were. He regarded the whole affair with a sort of warm nostalgia, a happy, blameless enterprise that might have lasted forever if not for the Benders' rashness.

When he opened the door to let me out the sky to the southeast was dark as black tea, and before I got off the porch the cloud was briefly illuminated by a bolt of lightning, followed a couple of seconds later by a rolling clap of thunder, low and loud as artillery fire. The son invited me to wait the storm out when I reached the gate. "You might not beat it to town if you leave now."

I thanked him just the same and rode south. Passing the Haxley farm Mr. Haxley made the same offer, which I declined. "Might as well make use of the cellar," he said. "Only part of the house I didn't have to rebuild." I thanked him and rode on, my mind on confronting Herbert and Marc, storm or none. Before I cleared the property the first warm drops had begun spattering my face and coat, and by the halfway point I had to cinch my hat under my chin to keep it on my head.

By the northern limits of town I was drenched, the winds so wet and violent that even within the confines of my slicker I was sopping wet. The thunder sounded frequently, marking lightning strikes close enough to smell the sizzle in the air. Bells rang in the church towers, and a pair of mongrel dogs came tearing across the road to the west, yelping in terror, quick as greyhounds on a racing track. The larger of the two looked to be part sheepdog, his shaggy fur plastered to his sides; the smaller might have been some sort of terrier, and they were out of my sight through a hedge in a moment's time, where to judge by the frenzied yipping that followed, they joined others of their species in panicked flight.

The streets of Cottonwood were deserted; the only sign of human habitation was the ringing of the church bells, which continued unabated against the roaring of the winds. A siren blew thin and insignificant from the rooftop of the courthouse. Big trees whipped back and forth, elastic as saplings, and a fresh green leaf slapped me in the face as hard as a lady's palm as it careened unmoored through the warm air.

The sky was nearly as dark as night, except for a band of yellow gray at the western horizon. From the eastern distance came a sound like the roar of a waterfall, ranging in pitch from the depths of the bass clef to a screeching overtone extending past the human ear's ability to perceive. The sound drawing nearer and more cacaphonous, I rode for the Braunschweigs', where I tied the gelding's reins to a young sycamore and opened up the cellar door. I stomped down the rickety steps to the cellar, where Beatrice, Sally, and Madame Renée sat calmly in the light of the single lamp they'd brought down with them.

"Where's Maggie?" I asked.

"She went home to be with her boy," Renée said.

"When?"

"Just now," Sally said. "We tried to stop her."

At the top of the steps—opening the trap doors upward only with great difficulty—I found that the panicked gelding had managed to extricate his reins from the sycamore; I couldn't see in what direction he'd run, and so I started toward the Leval home on foot. The roar had become even louder and was now accompanied with that of large chunks of metal, stone, and wood being thrown together at random intervals. I could see the cloud now, a sinuous, massive black vortex perhaps an eighth of a mile in width, moving toward the center of town more or less parallel to the railroad. The percussive sound of an explosion augmented the general din for a few moments before dying away to leave only a shredding sound like the distant snapping of logs. The blast, I thought, had come from the new mill or the brick plant. I couldn't hear the bells ringing any more, nor the siren.

I stood in front of the Leval home and tried to gain entry, but its cellar appeared to be attainable only from the interior and the front and back doors had been barred shut. If Maggie had made it to the house before Marc and his Mr. Smight locked it she was fine; if not she was out in town somewhere. I hadn't seen her heading back toward the Braunschweig house, and so I headed south toward Main Street in search of her and of a safe place to hide myself when the funnel got too close. That time was now, I judged, when I was close enough to hear the piteous whinnying of a horse being lifted into the air. I could see the animal being folded into the mass of wind, its legs uselessly churning the air around it, but it was too dark to tell if the indistinct form vanishing into the dusty cloud was my rented gelding.

The tornado obscured both sides of Main Street to my east now, and the sound of crunching wood predominated, with a smattering of broken glass providing a delicate counterpoint. It had reached Rector's department store, whose façade seemed wrecked beyond repair; every few seconds I was hit with some tiny broken object, and I suspected that I'd become part of the vortex myself if I didn't find shelter in the next half minute or so.

The White Horse Restaurant had a cellar accessible from its rear, and I was gratified to see that its front doors were unlocked. The noise inside the building was, paradoxically, louder than it had been outside, and I took that for a bad sign, as I did the cracking that came from the walls, suggesting the block of buildings was being lifted from its foundations. I reached the cellar door and hastened down the steps to find the owner of the White Horse, his wife, several regular patrons I knew by sight, and several strangers I took to be neighbors or simply passersby. They welcomed me curtly and the owner's wife asked me, shouting at her lungs' full capacity, what it was like upstairs. I didn't have time to answer; if I had I wouldn't have been heard over the sound of the instantaneous destruction of the building above.

The cellar door blew off and brought with it a fair amount of dust and debris. The children screamed, and I was knocked to the floor, but I'd managed to stop the door, which rested now on my legs. My nose was pressed flat against the dirt floor, and judging from the pain I thought it was probably broken. My leg hurt, but seemed intact.

There was much screaming in the cellar, but it subsided as the worst of the upstairs din died away, and by the time I managed to get the door off of me daylight, or a pale gray copy of it, could be made out through the empty doorway at the top of the stairs. That was when I heard a woman's voice, ragged and strained, shouting.

"Marc," the voice said, and I rose from beneath the door, my nose pissing blood onto the dirt of the cellar floor. Ignoring the warnings of those behind me I mounted the debris-strewn steps and found myself standing out of doors in the ruins of the White Horse, only a few remnants of its frame and walls still standing. No one followed me as I limped over the shattered brick and glass, the splintered tables and chairs, and the piles of crumbled plaster, the rain still flying through the wind. On Main Street, bedraggled and as wet as if she'd just climbed fully clothed from a river, was Maggie, distraught and calling for Marc.

Stumbling through the wreckage I hurried as fast as my injured leg would allow to her side. "Get downstairs," I shouted, for out here the noise was still deafening.

"I can't find Marc," she said.

I tried to pull her with me back toward the cellar of the White Horse, but she wouldn't come. She wiggled free of my grasp and began running after the tornado; to the west it seemed to lift off the ground, and I hoped this meant the town might thus be spared further damage. It went fully aloft at the corner of Main and Seward, inflicting harm only to the shingles of the building on the corner. Then, the lower end of the funnel out of my sight, came another explosion, louder than anything I ever heard in the war.

"That's him, I know it," she shouted, and she took off running after the sound. I followed, but at a cripple's pace, loping with my injured leg held out straight, and she got away from me. The blast continued for several seconds before it subsided, and when I reached the corner the funnel and Maggie were both out of sight. What I did see was Maggie's former home, Lillian Rector's mansion, its southern half leveled, its northern half more or less intact, its rooms cut open. Pieces of timbers and floorboards and chunks of stone and plaster dangled and fell from the torn ceiling, and when one length of splintered plank broke loose and tumbled onto the floor with a crash I heard a squeal of fright I was certain came from Maggie.

When I reached the house I found her in Lillian's parlor. There was no more entryway, but the northern part of the parlor was strangely intact, and only slightly wet, since the storm had only reached the interior a moment before. She stamped through the wrecked house until she reached the back porch, where she opened the trap doors of the cellar with me close on her heels.

Inside it I could hear Lillian Rector sobbing.

"Marc?" Maggie yelled.

"Yes, he's here," Lillian answered, her voice thick and choking. "He's all right."

"What's he doing here?" I said, and before Maggie could answer I heard Marc Leval, Sr.'s voice coming from the cellar, thin and strained.

"I'm all right, Maggie," he said with some difficulty.

"I thought we were looking for young Marc," I said.

"No," Maggie said, her distress and panic having given way to anger. "He's at home in our cellar, with Mr. Smight." Her hair had come undone, and it cascaded down her back, plastered against her sopping dress.

"Come down, please, it can't be safe up there," Lillian said.

"We most certainly will not," Maggie said.

Still at a loss to understand what Marc Leval was doing in Lillian Rector's cellar, and with no special desire to spend any time in his company, I nonetheless took Maggie firmly by the elbow and directed her toward the steps.

"Stop it. I won't go down there with those two."

The wind and rain hadn't let up much, and visibility in all directions was very poor. I tested my knee, thought it would bear her weight, and I dipped down and picked her up across my shoulders. She pounded on my back and yelled, and my knee seemed suddenly not as dependable as I'd thought, but I managed to wrangle her down the steps, at the bottom of which she dropped to her feet and marched over to where Marc sat in a stiff-backed wooden chair. There she slapped him so hard he tumbled to his side, nearly overturning the lamp on the floor next to him. There were five other people in the basement. Four of them—two men and two women—were servants of Lillian's, and the fifth was Lillian herself; though Lillian rushed to Marc's side to comfort and set him right, no one objected to Maggie's attack on her shriveled, invalid husband. This struck me as odd, as did the fact that Lillian and Marc were only half-dressed.

Rain poured down the stairway, since I'd been unable to shut it with Maggie on my shoulders, and she seemed ready to haul off and hit him again. I thought I'd try and stop her if she did, but she held off, and then she scampered up the steps so quickly I was unable to follow. The damage to my knee was worse than I'd thought, and climbing out of the cellar was a painful and slow undertaking. When I finally reached her she was standing underneath what remained of the master bedroom.

"Look at that. He parked his goddamned wheelchair up there," she said with a little laugh, pointing at a wicker chair outfitted with wheels, lying on its side at the lip of the overhanging floor.

"How do you suppose he managed to get it up there?"

"She had a ramp built when Tiny was sick."

Over against the shattered staircase was an incline with a separate banister, and the whole picture began to solidify in my mind. "Why were you out looking for him?" I asked.

"I got home and found Smight and Marc Jr. in the cellar, and he wasn't there. Smight claimed he didn't know where he was, so I went out looking."

"How did you know where he'd be?"

"I didn't know for certain, I just knew he was crippled and there was a storm coming."

"But you knew he was laying down with old Lil Rector?"

"I knew he saw her from time to time. I didn't want to know any more than that. She was apparently very kind to him when he was first injured," she said. "During my absence. I've always been able to ignore it until now." She let out what might have been a sigh of relief. "Now that I've determined that he's all right I don't think I need to see him again anytime soon."

We were shielded there from the worst of the rain, and in the shadow of the room where she'd first accepted my attentions so long ago she once again took my hand.

"I suppose I'll go home and pack a couple of bags," she said.

I walked alone through the worst of the damage to the wreckage of the new mill, east of town. The silos were down, and the main building had collapsed, with only part of the north wall still standing. The railroad depot showed only damage to the loading platform, though, and the warehouse stood intact. Inside it I found Herbert, sitting on a stack of waterlogged flourbags.

"No dead," he said. His good eye was red and watery next to the pristine, healthy-looking artificial one. "Seven injured, one bad, hit by a flying brick."

"I talked to Clevenger this morning," I said.

He looked confused. "What's that got to do with anything?"

I kept my voice low, but not low enough for him. "We got to talking about where Katie and Ma Bender are buried."

"Well Jesus Christ on a pair of stilts," he said, louder than he probably wanted to. "This is a hell of a time to be bringing that up."

"You had better get ready to pull some goddamned strings and stop those two women from hanging. I don't care how you do it, but if you don't I'll make you damned sorry."

He stood up and pointed his finger out the door at the devastation without. "You see what I got to fix out there? You think I don't have other things to worry about?"

I turned to go. "I'm sure you have plenty to worry about, but you better keep this near the top of that list. I know where those two are buried," I said, even though I didn't.

I walked back to town along the tornado's path. People filled the muddy streets now, and the sun had started shining through holes in the cloud cover. The church bells were ringing again, and I turned toward the boardinghouse. Inside Mrs. Kelley was sitting in the parlor in the company of Mr. Farraday, who glared at me.

"Where were you, Mr. Ogden? We were terribly afraid for you," Mrs. Kelley said.

"Some of us were," Farraday said.

I assured her that I'd been perfectly safe, and I gave a week's notice; I was paid up through the end of the month and would require no refund.

"You're leaving Cottonwood, then?" she asked.

"That I am. How are your wounds, Mr. Farraday?"

"Bettter," he said. He folded his arms across his chest, as if to indicate that I wouldn't get another word out of him.

"It's Mr. Farraday's belief that the bees were trying to warn us." Mr. Farraday looked away, and I thought he resented Mrs. Kelley's sharing with me his grand theory.

"Bees gone, then?"

"Mr. Lafflin managed to get them out," Mrs. Kelley said. "With some difficulty and some injury."

"Good for Mr. Lafflin," I called out behind me, laboriously fighting my way up the staircase, and imagining the gladness my announcement must have kindled in Mr. Farraday's heart. There were a number of dead bees in my room, perhaps forty or fifty, and I hoped that not all of them had given their lives in stinging poor Mr. Lafflin. I put on some dry clothes, washed off my bloody face in the washbasin and left, my precious copy of *The Secret History* in hand.

* * *

Following the storm's path along the railroad tracks I found my hired gelding, broken and bloody on the rails near a lone box-car that had been knocked clean off of a sidetrack at just about the point where the funnel had veered northward into town. I hoped I wouldn't be held responsible for the animal's value, and felt sorry that I'd taken it out on such a day. The easternmost third of the block that had contained the White Horse Restaurant was flattened, and the people who lived and did business there wandered about in confusion and despair at the extent of the wreckage. The Cottonwood Hotel was undamaged except for broken glass, and the only building west of it to have sustained any serious damage was the Leval/Rector mansion. Floating on its back in a rain barrel on Seward was the largest opossum I had ever seen, its pointed snout bloodied and its surprisingly ferocious battery of teeth posthumously bared; its scaly tail was the thickness of my thumb. Nearby, in the First Episcopalian Church, a morgue had been set up, and I went inside out of morbid curiosity.

There were four dead lying in state, all pulled from the wreckage of a single house from which, according to witnesses, they had refused to adjourn to a neighbor's cellar. I heard the neighbor himself explaining it to the priest; they apparently believed that the power of their praying could avert the storm, that to repair to an underground shelter would have been tantamount to inviting God's wrath. The two of them debated the theological point for a while, and I couldn't help noting the expression of beatific calm on the face of one of the dead, a round little woman with brown hair going gray. The other three, two more women and a man, were so badly mangled their pre-mortem emotions couldn't be readily divined.

Outside the church I heard preaching of the damnation-and-hellfire variety, and around the corner of Second Street I saw Michael

Cornan, bloodied and dangling his left arm at a crooked angle at his side, haranguing passersby. He had drawn a small crowd of the curious and desperate, and when he saw me he pointed and shrieked at me, in much the same tones as he'd used the night he found me standing outside the Levals' window months before.

"There's the cause, friends. There's why God's grace has fled Cottonwood like Lot in the night; there's why misfortune has again visited our poor godfearing town."

I should have walked on, but something about his performance fascinated me. There was a gash in his forehead, just above his left eye, that had mostly stopped bleeding, and his beard was stained with caked blood.

"Fornicators! Faithless deniers of the commandments! There stands your ideal, your epitome, your king. Learn from the Pharaoh's mistakes! Repent now, and not after the next plague!"

His audience began looking at me instead of Cornan as he preached, and I moved on before he incited them to violence against me.

"You may walk away from me, sinner, but you can't walk away from the sins that fester here," he called to my back as I walked away.

That evening I called at Clyde's. Ninna was there with her husband and daughter, and when I announced my intention to go all but Eva's mother seemed genuinely sorry to hear it. Young Eva wondered if I wouldn't at least stay until the birth of the child, and I told her I might. I went out the front door with Clyde, where we surveyed the street in the failing light of day. Twigs and leaves and whole branches littered it, and puddles of dirty water pooled in the rutted sand, but here there was no real damage to any of the houses, and without knowing anything about the destruction a few short blocks away the scene would have had a serene, homespun charm. The air smelled of the rain still, and the few clouds that remained above us were fluffy and innocuous, floating slowly westward in the wake of the storm.

Clyde offered me a drink, which I declined. I told him he looked tired, and he told me he'd been sleeping poorly, out of worry about the baby and impending fatherhood.

"What are you reading these days?"

"Suetonius," he said. "Re-reading him. Maggie's library. You?"

"Nothing at the moment. My books stayed in San Francisco. For a long time I used to go to the Mechanic's Institute and read there in my free time."

"I do most of my reading at the saloon, in the slow hours." It was remarkable how he resembled my father, who'd died a much younger man than I was now, and not much older than Clyde. It was at that moment that I saw how much he resembled me as well, and I felt a sudden piercing sorrow and fervent hope that the resemblance was only physical.

I handed him the Procopius. "I found this in San Francisco before I left and read it on the trip east."

"I'm not familiar with this." He eyed it curiously, opened it, examined the title pages, and then began to read the first page. He was laughing before he could have been halfway down the page. "How salacious," he said. "May I borrow it?"

"Keep it," I said.

He nodded. "Do you think you'll come back sometime?"

"I only stayed away before for fear of being hanged."

"Not much chance of that," he said. "Unless you shoot Mr. Leval again." He snickered and looked out the side of his eye at me.

"I won't shoot him," I said. "He's not long for this world anyway." We watched a pack of dogs running east down the street, yelping and snapping at one another, and I wondered where they'd all come from, if they'd all got loose in the storm and banded together or if they ran together all the time. When they were gone I spoke again. "I might do something else before I leave, though, that I could swing for."

He looked sideways at me again, but this time there was no silent laugh implicit in his expression.

EPILOGUE

Ventura, Cal.
June the 10th, 1935

Dear Clyde,

Trust you and your young wife are well, and the boy. All here are healthy and as prosperous as can be hoped. Flavia is laid up with a cold and Jake is in a foul mood about dinner not being on the table when he comes home from work, but if the alternative is me cooking he's happy to do it himself.

We are in the midst of the "June Gloom" here, with fog lying heavy on the coast every morning, sometimes lasting all day. Today on my daily constitutional I witnessed an automobile accident at the intersection of Poli and Ann Streets, just a few blocks east of Flavia's house. A beer truck hit a Plymouth, both drivers blinded by the fog. No one was badly hurt, though the driver of the Plymouth—still drunk from the night before—cracked his head on his windshield and bled quite a bit. The yeasty smell of beer rising from the macadam was quite pleasant, to tell the truth.

Your brother Marc writes that his daughter is now out of nursing school, and plans to move to Wichita for hospital work. I trust you will keep abreast of her activities and watch over her in an avuncular manner; she isn't a city girl, though Marc says she likes to imagine that she will be one day merely by virtue of moving there.

Flavia has been mildly annoyed with me of late because I've been telling your grandchildren tales of the wild west, cowboys and Indians and outlaws, stories cribbed mostly from the moving pictures, since the real ones are mostly unsuitable for children. They don't know the difference, in fact I'm sure they prefer the made-up ones. Sometimes I take out my old Dragoon to show them; one day last week I even took out the LA-BETTE CO. SHERIFF'S DEPUTY badge—I long ago, you'll be glad to learn, got rid of the patch of blood-stiffened muslin it had been pinned to—and told them it had been my own. I imagine its original owner was gnashing his teeth in Hades at my lies, proud as he was of that hunk of tin.

The children lost interest in me and my stories quickly enough, though (as they tend to do), and went outside to play at gangsters, a far more salubrious and amusing game than cowboys and Indians in my view.

Write soon.
Affectionately yours,
Father

AUTHOR'S NOTE

The town of Cottonwood is a figment of my imagination, and I hope the real towns of Independence, Cherryvale, and Oswego, Kansas, will forgive my assigning bits and pieces of their histories to my fictional one. The characters herein are all fictional as well, with six notable exceptions: the Bender family, Mrs. Almira Griffith, and Mrs. Eliza Davis, whose actual lives were even more depraved and appalling than those presented here.

Readers interested in the true story of the Bender killings would do well to seek out *The Benders of Kansas* by John T. James (available from the publisher, Mostly Books, 111 East Sixth Street, Pittsburg, Kansas 66762). Written by the defense attorney who represented Mrs. Davis and Mrs. Griffith, this is by far the best account of the crimes I have found in print. I am grateful to Roger O'Connor, publisher of *The Benders of Kansas* and the man who knows more about the case than anyone else living, for his insights into the story. He is at work on a book about the case that promises to be the definitive account, and I anxiously await its release.

(Another noteworthy version of the story still available is Fern Morrow Wood's *The Benders: Keepers of the Devil's Inn*, which comes to a very different conclusion—an interesting one though I disagree with it—regarding the identities of the two women.)

I am also indebted to the staff of the W.A. Rankin Memorial Library in Neodesha, Kansas; to Sally Hocker and the staff of the Spencer Research Library; and to the staff of the Kansas State Historical Society.

For research into photographic technologies of the nineteenth century I owe thanks to Rob McHenry, and to David Starkman and Susan Pinsky of www.reel3d.com. Rick Lasarow, M.D., checked the manuscript for medical accuracy and patiently answered my foolish questions, and Tim Moore helped me understand elements of early Kansas law. Kerri Kowal answered my questions about human decomposition, and her husband, Erik Kowal, helped me with my queries into the Danish language. Though the central character in this book is a classics scholar, I am not, and so I am particularly grateful to Timothy Engels for his help in constructing Bill's Latin and Greek bibliographies. My brother-in-law Richard Monroe also helped out in the area of Latin grammar, and once again my friend and German translator Karl-Heinz Ebnet ensured that the German in the book was correct and appropriate to time and place.

Special thanks are also due to my editors, Dan Smetanka, Maria Rejt, and Joe Blades. Clair Lamb caught any number of inconsistencies and mistakes, and Charles Fischer, David Masiel, Terrill Lee Lankford, and Tod Goldberg all provided useful comments early on. Sylvie Rabineau, Abner Stein, Paul Marsh, and Dennis McMillan all have my gratitude, as of course does my friend and agent, the redoubtable Nicole Aragi, the best in the business. . . .